THIS TANGLED SKEIN

The Elizabethan Dilemma:
Catholic or Puritan

A Novel

by

Karen Rees

This Tangled Skein

"Yet through all, we know this tangled skein is in the hands of the One who sees the end from the beginning; he shall yet unravel all."
Alexander Smith (1830-67), Scottish poet

ENDORSEMENTS

THIS TANGLED SKEIN, the last installment of Karen Rees's trilogy about the Reformation era, explores the events of 1572 through the eyes of the book's central character, Anne Marie duChant. As a book of historical fiction, Rees combines the best of both historical and fictional writing.

For the readers of history, Rees delves deeply into the past and places her characters into an accurate historical context. Yet, for readers who prefer novels, Rees presents her story in a lively fast-paced style that matches what one would expect in a work of literary fiction.

From beginning to end, THIS TANGLED SKEIN so completely captivates the reader's interest that it seemingly carries the reader back to 1572 as though a first-hand witness to the unfolding events of that year.

> Richard J. Cherok, Ph. D.
> Professor of History
> Ozark Christian College

THIS TANGLED SKEIN is a wonderful trip back in time with a captivating story about the events during what has been known as the English Reformation. This work of historical fiction reads like a literary thriller with enough twists and turns to keep the reader engaged from start to finish.

I found Karen Rees's book to be both entertaining and historically accurate in the context of the time period. As a scholar of the time period myself, I have found a new author that I can highly recommend to all readers.

Rees's book gives any fan of this time period a way to immerse themselves in a story that resonates like true history. I cannot wait to begin to read her other works.

> Ted Booth, Ph. D. FRHistS
> Instructor of History and Religion
> Lincoln Memorial University

CONTENTS

CHAPTER 1 – MARCH 1572 – ROUEN, FRANCE

"I am alone. All alone."

The black words she'd just penned blurred. Anne Marie scrubbed her sleeve across her face, wiping her tears away. The time for weeping was past. She must look to her future or it would be taken out of her hands.

For a dozen heartbeats she sat staring out the glazed window that looked down from the Bossuets' great hall onto their little back courtyard. Somewhere below, a duck started squawking. The squawking stopped abruptly, a sign that the cook was starting preparations on the evening meal.

She took a deep, steadying breath then reached across the small writing table beside the window for a fresh sheet of white paper. After dipping sharp goose quill into bronze inkwell, she started the letter again.

"My right worshipful Cousin Jonathan Peterman. I commend myself to you and your good wife Lettice. I am writing to inform you that my dear parents, Paul and Margaret duChant, along with my brother Edmund and my little sisters were all taken in the pestilence that visited Strasbourg in the summer just past.

While sorting my parents' papers, I found the correspondence between you and my dear mother, your cousin. I feel it is only right that you should be told that she and the rest of my family are now with the angels. Only I remain.

I am currently living in Rouen with a kind family from this place, Monsieur Antoine and Madame Jeanne Bossuet, friends of my father's family. They fled France to escape the persecution and came to Strasbourg in 1568, some years after you left us to return to England.

Now that France is safer, they have returned to Rouen and brought me with them. Before I left Strasbourg, I sold my father's shop, our house, and other small properties so am not in immediate want. I also have learned the crafts of spinning and embroidery by which I can earn my way. My friends here have found a husband for me."

Anne Marie halted. She'd not meant to write that last sentence. Her hand and her heart had overtaken her caution. But a blank sheet of paper provided such freedom for words.

Rather than rewriting everything a second time, she'd have to make sure the letter was sealed before Madame Bossuet returned from the shoemakers.

What to say next?

She brushed the smooth goose feather against her chin for a moment thinking of Claude Goujon, the young wool merchant the Bossuets had picked for her, before re-inking the quill and continuing.

My opinion was not sought.

I have my father's lute and my grandmother's ruby ring you so kindly sent my mother after my Great Uncle Richard went to the stake. It is my wish to travel to England in order to renew your acquaintance and to visit Wynn-field Manor where I was born. I pray your family is well and prospering in the service of our blessed Lord Jesus.

From Rouen this 4th day of March 1572,

I bid you farewell.

Anne Marie duChant."

The odor of burning candle replaced that of acidic ink as Anne Marie sealed the folded letter with a blob of hot red wax. She'd scarcely finished when she heard quick footsteps approaching behind her. She straightened up at the writing table and looked over her shoulder, hopefully with a composed expression.

A thick waisted, gray-haired matron wearing a dark green gown and a self-satisfied look was bustling across the rush matting toward her.

"Is your letter finished, Anne Marie?"

"Yes, Madame Bossuet. It's ready for the courier."

Madame Bossuet stopped beside the writing table, a smile on her square face.

"Good. Good. Antoine is determined that the one he's penning to his business contact should leave on the next ship for London. I'm sure your mother's family will be glad to know you are well and soon to be wed."

Clamping her jaw against a useless protest, she handed over her letter. Madame Bossuet stepped past the glazed window to the warm fireplace and laid it on the mantel beside the lantern clock. She returned and settled on the padded chest near the pearl-gray plastered wall.

"I met young Claude when I was coming back along Big Clock Street. He plans to wait upon us this evening. You can play your father's lute for him."

"I still have embroidery to do," Anne Marie said. "I'm not sure I will be finished -"

"Nonsense. Work can wait when Claude comes."

The evening meal was over. The several candles on the linen draped dining table were burning low, the voiding dish was full of gnawed duck bones, and the last bite of sharp cheese had been eaten. The Bossuets' youthful shop assistant, having gained permission to spend half an hour with friends, dashed off before dusk faded. Monsieur Bossuet, in keeping with his age and paunch, left the dining parlor at a more leisurely pace.

Anne Marie began helping the kitchen maid clear the white tablecloth of dirty wooden trenchers and empty serving dishes.

"Let the servants finish," Madame Bossuet said, handing her a taper. "We should light the hall candles. Claude could arrive at any moment."

She reluctantly followed Madame Bossuet out of the dining parlor, past the stairs coming up from the ground floor, and into the great hall. While twilight still brightened the two tall windows at the far end and revealed Monsieur Bossuet by the fireplace feeding its amber coals, night was beginning to claim the rest of the room.

After lighting the wall candles on either side, she joined the Bossuets by the fireplace and set her taper on the mantel. Its bright yellow flame showed a second letter beside the lantern clock. She smiled with anticipation. By this time tomorrow her letter would be on its way to London.

The sound of footsteps coming up the stairs pulled her thoughts from the letters. Claude Goujon, garbed in fine but suitably somber Huguenot gar-

3

ments that set off his blond hair and short beard, stepped into the candlelit hall.

She watched him striding confidently toward her. Outwardly, he seemed a desirable match. He was the hardworking second son of a respected and wealthy merchant friend of the Bossuets who was as willing for his son to wed her as the Bossuets were. This was largely due to the money she would bring with her. That was only to be expected and troubled her little.

Rather it was Claude himself who made her hesitate.

It wasn't just his casual thoughtlessness or that her private religious views would be unacceptable to him and his strict Calvinist parents should they learn of them, and were she and Claude to marry, how could they not? But the way he sometimes ran his gaze over her when they happened to be alone made her uncomfortable. It was as if he were examining newly purchased property or, even worse, undressing her with his eyes. It was not something she could explain to Madame Bossuet.

Tonight, greeting her with a brief bow in the presence of the Bossuets, Claude kept his disconcerting gaze to himself. He straightened and looked down at her.

"What songs does my little red bird have for me this evening?"

Anne Marie, nettled by his patronizing tone, was saved a reply because Madame Bossuet spoke first.

"Claude, you shouldn't tease Anne Marie about her hair. Besides, it's more copper than red."

"What do men know of the subtlety between red and copper?" Claude said cheerfully. "We are all business and politics and war."

"Just business and politics now, thanks to God and Admiral Coligny," Monsieur Bossuet said. He waved Claude over to join him on the brown-padded settle near the fireplace. "With the wars over for more than a year, we have the best peace the Huguenots have ever had. Worshiping nearly anywhere we choose, being allowed to hold public office. Now that Coligny's become a favorite with the King...."

Claude folded himself down beside Monsieur Bossuet while Madame Bossuet chose a padded stool facing them.

"I have heard," Claude said, turning to Monsieur Bossuet, "that King Charles has put him in command of the fleet and also reimbursed him for his losses in the wars with the Catholics."

When Anne Marie was first getting to know Claude, his ability to easily forget her had proved annoying. She'd even lost her temper with him on one occasion. He'd merely laughed, pinched her cheek, and later teased her about the incident.

Now that she knew him better, she was glad to be forgotten.

She moved a stool off to one side between crackling fireplace and darkening window as far from Claude as she politely could. If she were fortunate, he would continue to forget her for the rest of the evening.

"Yes," Monsieur Bossuet said, "Coligny has also been appointed to the King's council. God is surely on our side. Today I even heard talk that the Queen Mother has offered her daughter Marguerite in marriage to King Henry of Navarre."

"Imagine," Madame Bossuet said, leaning forward, "the leader of the Huguenots marrying a Catholic princess. That is one wedding I would travel across France to witness."

The following day the letters beside the lantern clock began their journey to London. Late in the morning Anne Marie donned her dark brown cloak and slipped out of the Bossuets' half-timbered house with its cloth shop and kitchen on the ground floor and living area on the three floors above.

She hurried through the maze of narrow, dirty cobblestone streets with their overhanging upper stories, hastening past sellers crying their wares from shop doors, dodging ragged beggars, brown-robed priests, and marketgoers with laden baskets as she headed for Viscount Gate and the waterfront beyond.

Monsieur Bossuet had told her which ship was carrying her letter. It was to sail by noon.

Although Rouen lay some fifty miles inland by road from the port of Le Havre on the Normandy coast, the meandering River Seine would make the two-masted merchantman's journey much longer. Nevertheless, that same meandering river had allowed the walled city to become a booming port and outport for Paris farther to the east.

She passed out Viscount Gate and halted on the sloping river bank beyond the curtain wall encircling the city behind her. Faint odors of tar, sewage, and fish filled the air. Away on her left, jutting out from either riverbank, were the long ends of what had once been a wooden bridge stretching across the Seine. Off to her right, the Old Palace, a quadrangle-shaped castle with curtain walls and bastions, marked the southwest corner of the city.

Her gaze swept the river from broken bridge to Old Palace, searching for the two-masted merchantman carrying her letter. She passed over the small boats ferrying passengers across the river and the larger ones transporting cargo from ships to sloping river shore.

Vessels of every type were anchored in the Seine: weathered fishing trawlers from the Baltic loaded with herring, broad cog boats filled with Russian furs, graceful Venetian caravels carrying spices from Arabia or silks from China, three-masted carracks from Spain bringing exotic woods from the New World, sturdy merchantmen with pewter from England and hides from any place they could be found.

Rouen, made rich by its wool trade, had a thriving textile export business. Its blacksmiths also created and exported ironwork of all kinds – from church bells to scissors to lacy filigree. Cloth, ironwork, and French wines surely filled the holds of more than one of the merchant ships moored here. The merchantman she sought today was carrying, among other cargo, a shipment of diaper cloth to London for Monsieur Bossuet.

There it was, anchored across from the Old Palace.

She had arrived none too soon. Even as she watched, the ship began casting off. Within a minute the merchantman was drifting away in the slow current.

Hands clasped, eyes closed, she breathed a fervent prayer that her letter would receive a warm welcome at journey's end from the tall, resolute man and smiling, plain-faced woman who lived in her memory. Even more, she prayed that the letter would be the start of a new life for her far away from Claude Goujon.

She opened her eyes to see sailors clambering up the tall masts. Sails were unfurled and gradually swelled in the March breeze that brushed her cheek and filled her nostrils with the river's smell. The ship swung farther out into the slate gray river. Her letter was on its way.

6

Five days later the merchantman sailed up the dark blue Thames and docked at Wool Quay in London, a port even busier than the one it had left. The captain had the letters delivered to Monsieur Bossuet's business contact on Candlewick Street. The following afternoon the contact sent an apprentice with Anne Marie's letter to a half-timbered house on St. Mary Street off Aldgate.

There, the apprentice handed it to a kindly-faced matron in a dark gown and crisp white apron and cap. In turn, she laid the letter on the golden harpsichord sitting in a corner of their otherwise simply furnished great hall where it would remain until her husband finished the meeting with his fellow ministers.

From the intensity of the overheard voices coming from his study, it could be some time.

Jonathan Peterman breathed a quick prayer for patience as his gaze swept the five men sitting in a half circle of padded stools on the other side of his writing table.

They, like he, had fled to the Continent early in Queen Mary's reign. He'd spent the exiled years in Strasbourg. Two of those sitting here had gone directly to Geneva, one to Frankfurt, and one to Zurich. The fifth one, Clement Wood, had originally gone to Frankfurt. But due to disagreements over the use of the Second Prayer Book, he'd quit the English church there and gone to Geneva with John Knox. All had been active in the English congregations established in those cities. After Elizabeth was crowned, they'd all returned to England and, like himself, been hired by lay organizations to preach in London's parish churches.

"I know we had more freedom of worship on the Continent," Jonathan said, hands fisting on the oak table's hard surface. "Still, England's established worship is much closer to Scripture than before. No more idols or saints days, we have sermons, communion is given in both kinds -"

"But," the Frankfurt man interrupted, "people still have to kneel when taking it as if the bread and wine are something to be worshiped."

"The Prayer Book smacks too much of Popish teaching," Clement Wood said from his seat between the glazed windows. He fingered his dark chin beard. "We didn't even use it in Geneva."

7

"The required worship doesn't match what we find in Scriptures," the first Geneva man said. "What kind of respect are we showing to God if we don't worship as he prescribes? Look at the Israelites in the Old Testament. When they failed to worship correctly, God brought punishments on them."

The Zurich man, seated near one of the book cabinets, had his mouth open, trying to get a sentence in. He finally managed it.

"Yes, and what kind of church deposes ministers like John Field because they refuse to wear vestments when they officiate? Wearing clerical garb denies the priesthood of all believers."

Clement Wood spoke again.

"And what of Thomas Cartwright? When he pointed out how unscriptural the Church of England's structure is, he lost his Cambridge Professorship. But he spoke the truth. Elders should be appointed to carry out church discipline in the parish. Congregations should select their own pastors. Offices such as archbishops and archdeacons must be abolished."

"The French church here in London is ruled by ministers and elders," the second Geneva man said, "not by a religious hierarchy appointed by secular government. If they can do it, why can't we?"

"They aren't Englishmen," Jonathan said, shifting on his padded stool, "and don't owe allegiance to the Queen. But we are and we do. Especially now that she's been excommunicated, and the Queen's cousin Mary Stuart is in England."

He held up a hand to fend off interruptions.

"I know the English church isn't yet all it should be. But think of how many religious turnabouts we've witnessed. King Henry was loyal to the Pope and then broke with him. Under King Edward, England rid herself of much false Catholic teachings. Then Queen Mary brought it all back – or tried to – and lost the support of the citizenry because of it. Now we have Queen Elizabeth. I know she hasn't yet gone as far as she should in establishing the true religion. But I firmly believe that time and God are on our side. We just need to be patient."

"We might, instead, find ourselves facing more heresies," the Zurich man said with a frown. "We've already got the Anabaptists, Unitarians, and Family of Love. And what about the Catholics? Even as we talk, they're no doubt plotting to overthrow Elizabeth and put Mary Stuart in her place."

"All the more reason to stand with the Queen," Jonathan said. "I believe God's hand was at work when Mary Tudor's Catholic bishops refused to serve under Elizabeth. The Queen had to appoint Reformist ones. We also control the House of Commons. If we're willing to agitate and wait, we'll eventually see both church constitution and worship change into a more scriptural way of doing things."

The Frankfurt man spoke again.

"What if it doesn't happen? We tried to get reforms through the Convocation a few years ago. We lost."

"But only by one vote," Jonathan said, wagging a finger. "One vote. If we came that close to passing legislation binding on the Church of England, what might we accomplish in the future?"

"We could find ourselves at war with Spain at any moment," the Zurich man said. "Or, even worse, the Queen could take a Catholic husband. Then what would become of the true Church? Smithfield would see a whole new crop of martyrs."

"We certainly didn't get legislation through Parliament," Clement Wood said in a bitter tone, "despite controlling the House of Commons. Or have you forgotten that it just voted down the bill that would have replaced the old popish canon law with a new reformed system? Without such a system how can the Church have true discipline?"

"No, I haven't forgotten," Jonathan said. "I'm as disappointed as you. But, for good or ill, we must stand with the Church of England. We mustn't separate from it as the Plumber's Hall group and Fitz's congregation have done. If we do, we'll forfeit all opportunity of guiding the church toward purity."

Clement Wood frowned.

"How can we guide the church to purity if we compromise the truth?"

The discussion ended at last. Jonathan limped slowly across the paneled hall on a club foot inherited from his father to see his guests on their way. Having bade farewell to the last one, he stood in the entryway brooding on Clement Wood's challenge.

By standing with the Queen and the currently imperfect English Church, was he in reality forsaking the truth and allowing the devil a foothold? Or was it the devil himself causing him to doubt? He must search his soul and lay these issues before God.

When he returned to the hall, his wife Lettice was waiting for him with a letter in her hand and carefully controlled curiosity on her face.

"This came earlier … from France," she said, handing it to him. "At least that's what the delivery boy said."

"France?"

He was accustomed to receiving letters from their eldest son Thomas, a divinity student at Cambridge, and ones from his ministerial correspondents. But not from France. Momentarily setting his deeper concerns aside, he broke the red wax seal, unfolded the letter, and glanced at the signature.

"It's from Anne Marie," he said in surprise.

As he began to read, sadness crept over him like a shadow. So, Paul duChant was dead.

During their years together in Strasbourg, he'd spent many frustrating hours debating predestination, infant baptism, and the relationship between church and state with Paul. Unfortunately, he'd already been infected with Anabaptist heresies and couldn't see his error. Paul had allowed him to baptize Edmund and the little girls when they were born only because he himself had felt so strongly about it. Even then, Paul had made it clear that he saw no value in the ceremony since, as he said, babies can't have faith. Apart from his wrong ideas, Paul had been a good man and a very generous one to those in need. Pray God he'd repented of his heretical Anabaptist leanings in time.

He finished the letter and handed it to Lettice. Her expression softened and tears gathered in her faded blue eyes as she read. She handed the letter back and blotted her tears with her sleeve edge.

"Margaret and Paul gone. Poor little Anne Marie."

"How old would she be now?" he asked, picturing a talkative little girl with a head of curly copper hair, and brown eyes and brows.

Lettice's forehead creased in thought.

"Nineteen, I think," she said, looking up at him. "She was starting to talk when Thomas was born, and he's seventeen."

He glanced at the letter.

"It sounds as if these Bossuets have arranged a marriage for her."

"But apparently not one she wants."

"She's hardly old enough to know what's best for her."

"Her family should be picking her husband," Lettice said. "Not strangers." Then, "What are you going to answer?"

He suspected she wanted him to tell Anne Marie to come. Lettice had a tender heart, sometimes too tender. He'd not known that when, in taking a stand against the Catholic Church's requirement that priests remain celibate, he'd acquired a wife.

Still, he'd never regretted his decision to marry and then to keep his new wife when Queen Mary had ruled that priests who'd wed during Edward's reign must put their wives away and do penance for adultery. Instead, they'd fled to the Continent with the other exiles. Lettice had gone with him for love. He'd taken her for love but even more because of principle.

The answer to this letter as well would be a mixture of love and principle. Anne Marie was family. She also was the daughter of a man who'd been inclined toward heresy.

"What am I going to answer? I'll know after I've prayed about it."

CHAPTER 2 – LATE MARCH – ROUEN

Anne Marie sat on a padded chest near one of the windows in the Bossuets' hall, embroidery needle in one hand, fine woolen sleeve in the other. The lingering odor of wax filled the air around her, a result of work she'd done on a nearby cabinet the previous day. Today, she was embroidering blackwork flowers onto the sleeve of one of Madame Bossuet's gowns.

Sixteen days had passed since the ship carrying her letter had set sail for London. Over the last week, besides assisting with the housework as usual, she'd offered to embroider shirts, smocks, ruffs, and anything else wanted. The need to focus on the intricate designs helped combat her growing anxiety.

From comments Monsieur Bossuet had made regarding his cloth shipments, with favorable wind and tides, a merchant ship could reach London within four to five days. A return trip would take a similar amount of time. Why had she not already received a reply? Had her letter been lost? Was Cousin Jonathan no longer residing in London?

If he didn't receive her letter and provide her an escape, she was uncertain how much longer she could delay having to wed Claude.

When Madame Bossuet had suggested Claude as a suitable match for her several months ago, she'd mainly hesitated because of his strict Calvinist family, a reason she had no desire to disclose. Madame Bossuet had taken her silence as agreement. At that time, Madame Bossuet was still preoccupied with her husband's efforts to re-establish their business in Rouen.

With the business now doing well, Madame Bossuet would soon move from talk to action. When that time came, she must either wed Claude or risk losing the Bossuets' friendship. If she lost that, she'd be even more alone than she was now.

The sound of feet trotting up the stairs broke through her worrying thoughts. A moment later, the young shop assistant appeared with a letter in his hand. He crossed to where she sat.

"Monsieur Bossuet said to give you this," he said.

She shoved the embroidery aside and took the letter with an eager, trembling hand. Her name was written on the front.

As the young assistant started back down to the shop, she scooped up her stitching and hurried for the stairs leading to the second-floor bedchambers. She'd not wanted Madame Bossuet to see what she'd written to Cousin Jonathan. The same was true regarding his reply.

Reaching the stair top, she turned away from the Bossuets' bedchamber toward the small one she shared with Madame Bossuet's personal maid. Once inside and with the door firmly shut, she dumped the embroidery on the bed. She dropped onto the padded chest, broke the red wax seal, and unfolded the paper. Taking a deep breath, she turned the letter to catch the light from the single glazed window.

She began to read.

"My dear little cousin Anne Marie. Lettice and I commend ourselves to you. We grieve with you for your losses but trust that your family is even now in the heavenly abode. Praise be to God our good Queen Elizabeth is supporting the true faith. I am preaching regularly at various churches here in London. People need to hear the truth and be warned of the dangers of hell if they neglect so great a salvation.

Since you wish to visit England, now would be a suitable time. Twelve years have passed since we bade you farewell, so you are no longer the child we remember. We will be pleased to be acquainted with the maid you have become. You may know that my mother, Cecily Peterman Taylor, and my uncle Nicholas Denzil, brother of Richard, have both passed to their sure rewards.

I am confident that Uncle Nicholas's son Charles and his family will also wish to make you welcome. Cousin Charles and his second son, Roger, have the family goldsmith shop in London. His firstborn, Peter, owns Wynnfield Manor which once belonged to your grandmother. By God's grace Uncle Nicholas was able to purchase it from the Crown. Otherwise, it would have been lost to our family when your grandmother was condemned as a heretic and her manor confiscated.

Praise the Lord and our good Queen that those horrible days are past. No longer are men and women sent to the stake for following the true faith.

All Englishmen can live in peace if they are willing to conform to the religious practices laid down in the Thirty-nine Articles enacted by Parliament these few years past. Only such ones as Unitarians, Anabaptists, and those continuing to support the Romish pope against our good Queen and our English church have anything to fear.

From our time in Strasbourg, I know that your father had Anabaptist leanings. I trust he amended his position as he came to see the truth more clearly.

Now that the bishop of Rome has issued a bull excommunicating our good Queen and absolving her Catholic subjects from allegiance to her, we who love England must stand side by side against the papists who would overthrow her good governance and replace her with Mary, erstwhile Queen of Scotland, who fled that country and is now in confinement in England. Praise God that Brother John Knox and his Protestant government in Scotland would have none of her Catholic religion.

My dear wife and most faithful partner in serving the Lord, along with our four children, beg you to come.

Written in London this 14th day of March 1572,

Your elder cousin the Right Reverend Jonathan Peterman."

Relief flooded her; she breathed a fervent prayer of thanks. They had invited her to England. She could gracefully remove herself from Claude's attentions and Madame Bossuet's intentions. She reread the letter, savoring the relief.

Her gaze halted on a sentence near the end, a sentence that she'd failed to notice in the first reading.

She tensed, and the letter crinkled as her hand tightened on it. Cousin Jonathan remembered her father's Anabaptist leanings.

She read the letter again, measuring every sentence against that single one about her father. She studied the two sentences just before that one. Here were others she'd not fully grasped at the first reading. Was he sending a warning?

Her family had managed to live in Strasbourg because all faiths, to some extent, were represented and accepted there, and they'd had each other. Here in Rouen, and especially if she were to wed Claude as Madame Bossuet wished, life would not be so easy.

She read the letter a third time. It was unclear whether it carried a warning. But despite what he knew of her father, Cousin Jonathan's letter clearly carried a welcome. Whatever the risk to herself, she would travel to London.

While Anne Marie was reading his letter in Rouen, Jonathan Peterman was seated at the writing table in his quiet study, quill, ink, and white paper before him, preparing to compose another.

He paused for a moment to gaze out the window at the back courtyard where their older daughter was collecting dry laundry, considering.

With Charles living just across London, he could deliver the message in person. But from past experience, he knew his cousin would want to boast about how much better his goldsmith business was doing than others and how the guild relied on his advice.

Having taken on extra preaching during the week, he didn't have time to waste on someone so unconcerned with the state of his soul. No. Better to put his news in a letter and send it to Guthran Lane by one of the servants.

He dipped quill into black ink and, sharpened point scratching paper, began to write.

The servant duly delivered Jonathan's letter to the Denzil home above their goldsmith shop in the late afternoon and left it with Charles's long-jawed wife Ursula. Unlike Lettice, she'd been quite pretty in her younger years. Even now, though her waist had thickened with age and childbearing and her brown hair was graying, she was still a handsome woman. Few people, including her husband, noticed.

Ursula put the letter on the table in her husband's accounts room tucked between dining parlor and hall. She then went back down the stairs to the kitchen quarters to check on the roasting mutton and other dishes Cook was preparing.

Having fulfilled her wifely duty regarding the letter, she saw no need to mention its arrival when husband, son, daughter, and the two apprentices gathered with her in the dining parlor for the evening meal. As usual, she left the table conversation to others.

Charles found the letter later that evening after he'd lit the candles in the accounts room and had settled down at the table with the record books to list the day's income and expenses. He broke the red wax seal, unfolded the single sheet, and turned it to the candlelight. Impatient to get on with his bookkeeping, he started to skim it.

He halted abruptly, and his muscles tightened. He slowly read the letter in full, stared at it for a long moment, then dropped it on the table. It lay there like an ill omen. He stood, crossed to the open door, and peered out.

His anxious, impatient gaze swept the large candlelit hall with its paneled walls and numerous night-darkened, windows, sweeping past the blue livery cabinet and red brick fireplace with its bright crackling blaze, past the small table where his two adult children and the apprentices were engaged in a noisy game of cards.

He spotted her sitting, needle in hand, on a padded chest in a corner. She was stitching on a dark gray jerkin in the light of a nearby candle.

"Wife," he called, "I would have a word with you."

Ursula set her mending aside, crossed the hall, and joined him in the accounts room. Charles shut the door behind them and stepped to the table. He pointed a trembling finger at the letter.

"Did you put this here?"

Ursula nodded.

"It's from Jonathan. My cousin Margaret, her husband, and children are dead of the pestilence in Strasbourg. That is, all her children but one. Anne Marie still lives. Jonathan says she's coming to London. He's sure we'll want to welcome her. After all this time...." Tension began mounting within him like a clock spring being wound. "Why couldn't she have died with the rest? Had she, there'd be no one to raise questions."

"She doesn't know." Ursula's words came out in her usual harsh whisper.

Charles glanced at his wife. The clock spring began to loosen; a smile briefly lifted the corners of his mouth. He picked up the letter and began refolding it.

"You're right. She doesn't know. None of them knew. If they had, they would have returned long ago. No one knows. No one at all. And they never will." His confident tone sharpened. "Go back to your stitching. I've accounts to do."

Ursula turned and left the room, quietly pulling the door shut behind her.

CHAPTER 3 – TO LONDON

The sun was halfway up the morning sky when Anne Marie set off for the harbor with the Bossuets. Her two small chests, her father's lute, and the sack of food for her journey followed in a hired cart. In just over an hour the merchantman taking her to London would weigh anchor. She could scarcely contain her excitement.

Five hectic days had passed since the longed-for letter had arrived. Now, on the sixth day, her traveling documents were in order, her monies in safe keeping with a Rouen banker, and Monsieur Bossuet had found a respectable wine merchant and his wife with whom she could travel to London.

From the first, Madame Bossuet had been reluctant for her to go. Claude had been even more vocal; he would live with heartbreak till her return. She'd met his protestations with silence. No doubt he'd have forgotten her even before her ship sailed out of sight.

Given that he hadn't yet appeared to bid her a final farewell, he may already have done so.

They turned from the Street of Little Sheep onto the wider Big Bridge Street. A bread cart passed them. The fragrant aroma of freshly baked loaves momentarily replaced the sour odors from the filth dirtying the rough cobblestones underfoot.

When they neared Big Bridge Gate, Madame Bossuet tightened her hold on Anne Marie's arm.

They passed through the city gate. The Seine lay before them, its bluish gray ripples glinting silver in the sunlight.

"My friends are already aboard," Monsieur Bossuet said, nodding toward the couple at the rail of a two-masted caravel anchored nearby.

Moments later Anne Marie, her belongings, and the Bossuets were being rowed out to the ship. Once on board, Monsieur Bossuet and the wine merchant helped her carry her baggage below deck to the space allotted her.

Back on deck, they joined Madame Bossuet and the wine merchant's wife.

"After you return," Madame Bossuet said, "and you and Claude are wed, we can all travel to Paris for the royal wedding."

"He may grow tired of waiting for me," Anne Marie said.

"I'll see he waits."

She was relieved when Monsieur Bossuet interrupted the conversation.

"We should take our leave. The captain will soon be lifting anchor."

Madame Bossuet reluctantly clambered back down into the boat. Anne Marie remained by the rail to watch the boat head for shore.

She blinked tears away as she allowed herself to remember the Bossuets' kindness. Despite this, she could not stay and be the daughter Madame Bossuet had never had. She was someone else's daughter. Her family and her future lay elsewhere.

As the Bossuets stepped from boat to shore, the order to lift anchor rang out. She waved farewell to Madame Bossuet as sailors jumped to obey. Sails were hoisted, snapping and billowing in the strong breeze brushing her cheek. The caravel maneuvered carefully past the other water traffic and out into the sluggish gray current. Additional sail was added; the ship picked up speed.

The moment the Bossuets disappeared behind an anchored cog boat, she turned her back on the receding roofs and church spires of Rouen. She was finally on her way to a new life.

Anne Marie spent a good part of the first day hugging the rail and peering eagerly ahead as the Seine wound its tedious way through hills of new budding hazel, sweet chestnut, ash, and field maple. Now and again, the greening forests fell back to reveal a grand manor or monastery sitting among freshly plowed fields, water meadows, and grazing sheep. As they approached each new bend in the gray river, she hoped that this would be the last. She was keen to see the English Channel.

Night fell well before they reached Le Havre. They dropped anchor until dawn lightened the sky behind them. They set off again as sea gulls cried overhead. The sun was a hand's length above the horizon when they finally neared the river's mouth. The tide, previously roaring in to flood the low-lying salt marshes and mud flats that had replaced fields and forests, was turning in their favor.

With the tide now racing out to sea, their vessel flew through the estuary and past the port of Le Havre. Within minutes they were braving the strong fresh westerly winds and channel currents on their way north toward Dover.

She spent parts of a second day at the rail, this time retching over the side. By the time they sighted Dover's white cliffs early on the morning of the third day, her stomach had settled.

When the merchantman started up the Thames on the tail of an outgoing tide, Anne Marie was again at the rail. She wanted to see what Father had when, having been cast off by his staunch Calvinist family for his different understanding of Scripture, God led him to England and to her mother. But that was before Queen Mary came to the throne.

She'd been an infant when the Catholic queen ordered the expulsion of all foreigners. Rather than having her French husband sent alone into exile, Mother made the fateful decision that she and Anne Marie would go with him. They ended up in Strasbourg.

Once Mary was dead and England had a Protestant queen, Mother occasionally talked of returning. But nothing came of it. In truth, there was nothing to go back to. Wynnfield Manor was lost to them. Also, within two years of Queen Elizabeth coming to the throne, she'd ordered the expulsion of foreign Anabaptists. What if they'd returned only to have Father expelled again because he believed in adult baptism? Better to stay in Strasbourg where they had a good life.

Now that good life was gone. She was as alone as Father had been when his family cast him off. But God had not cast him off. God had given him a new life and another family in England.

She'd gone to Rouen hoping that God would do the same for her there. But for Madame Bossuet's determination to see her wedded to Claude, it might have happened. Instead, thanks to the kindness of her Peterman cousins, she could now seek that new life in England.

If only the tide, rather than hindering them, would turn and speed them on their way up to London.

Although her prayer was soon answered, they were still short of their destination when night fell and they dropped anchor. They weighed anchor early the fourth morning to cover the final miles as the sky was donning its light blue day dress.

Anne Marie gripped the rail in eager expectation as the merchantman made its slow way up the Thames. Compared to the Seine, this river followed a relatively straight course through the forest of leafless oak and chestnut that crowded its banks.

Soon they were passing Genoan carracks at anchor and lighters piled with cargo. A nobleman's gilded barge, bright with banners, liveried oarsmen, and richly clad passengers, swept past, leaving her agog. Water traffic increased as they neared their journey's end. Small boats darted about while barges, merchantmen, and fishing trawlers vied for passage in the bright waters. She peered eagerly ahead for her first sight of London.

Her first sight turned her stomach. As the forest ended and the city began, she spotted the bloated bodies of three pirates hanging at the water's edge, their fetid odor polluting the air.

She quickly looked away to the white pinnacles and curtain walls of a fortress coming up on the right bank. Farther ahead, a massive bridge spanned the river, its nineteen stone arches supporting a solid wall of houses.

She gazed at the bridge in wonder. What would it be like to live in one of those houses, to wake every morning to the sight of the shining blue river hurrying beneath?

She was still lost in her musing when, on the first day of April near the end of Lent, the little caravel nosed into a wooden wharf below the bridge and tied up. They had arrived.

Half an hour later she bade farewell to the wine merchant and his wife. With a hired porter and his cart as her guide, she set out across the unfamiliar city for the Peterman home on St. Mary Street. Lifting her dark skirts above the muddy filth, she followed the porter up busy narrow streets and across bustling wider ones filled with carts and hawkers shouting their wares. They passed housewives with loaded market baskets, blue-liveried servants hurrying along, and water carriers delivering door-to-door. In many ways this city was similar to Rouen – except the cries were in English rather than French.

They crossed one of the wide streets and turned down a narrower one running past a large church. On inquiry, a beggar pointed them to an open courtyard gate across the way. She followed the porter through the brown gate. The fellow unloaded her chests and the lute in the small cobblestone courtyard and departed, richer by a penny.

Standing in the courtyard, she studied the three-storied half-timbered dwelling. A multitude of glazed windows, clean lime-washed walls, and a row of potted plants gave off an air of respectable homeliness.

Dry-mouthed, she crossed to the entrance and banged the brass door knocker. A moment later she heard the door latch lift; the door opened. A little girl in a large white apron looked up at her.

"Is this the home of Jonathan Peterman?"

The child bobbed her capped head.

"Would you please tell him that Anne Marie duChant has arrived?"

"My father's at a meeting," the child piped, "but my mother's at home."

Leaving the door open, the child disappeared within. She reappeared a moment later with a middle-aged woman also garbed in dark gown and white apron and smelling of bread dough. The woman looked inquiringly at her and then past her to her belongings sitting in the courtyard. Anne Marie's memory stirred.

"Cousin Lettice, I am Anne Marie."

Lettice's plain face broke into a smile that wrinkled her eye corners.

"Anne Marie … it is you. You've grown." She laughed. "Of course, you've grown. Come in, come in. Jonathan and I prayed that you'd have a safe journey."

Anne Marie's vision blurred as she stepped into a small entry hall.

"Thank you for your prayers … and for letting me come."

"How could we not?" Lettice turned to her young daughter. "Prudence, this is your cousin, Anne Marie. She's come all the way from France to stay for a while."

Prudence gave Anne Marie a narrow-eyed stare. She moved close to her mother and whispered, "I told you she had a Catholic name."

Anne Marie's cheeks warmed.

"Hush, child," Lettice said. "Now run to the kitchen and find Henry. Tell him to fetch Anne Marie's belongings in and carry them up to the little south chamber."

Prudence cast another dubious look at Anne Marie then scampered away.

Anne Marie followed Lettice into a paneled hall furnished with several simple wall cabinets, a variety of colorful padded seating, and windows that offered a view of the courtyard. But it was the gilt harpsichord in the corner near the fireplace that caught her attention. She crossed to the lovely instrument and touched a key.

"It belonged to my mother-in-law," Lettice said. "She left it and the house to Jonathan when she died." Then, "Do you play?"

"A little. I am better on the lute."

"Our daughter Dorcas is taking lessons. She's at one now. Perhaps you and she can play duets. Jonathan quite likes music here at home provided there's nothing immoral about it. Of course, using musical instruments in church is a different matter. Especially organs. But the Queen allows it, so we have it for now. At least the whole congregation joins in the singing."

"In France we sing without the instruments." Then, lest her comment be taken as a criticism, "I've heard that, in Germany, they use the musical instruments."

Lettice glanced at the lantern clock on the fireplace mantel.

"Oh, dear. I'd not realized how late it was. Jonathan will soon be back from his meeting. Come, let me show you to your chamber. It's just off that of my daughters."

Anne Marie followed Lettice to a flight of stairs between the hall and dining parlor.

"Your English is very good," Lettice said as she huffed her way up the steps. "And your French as well, I'm sure."

"My mother spoke English with us," Anne Marie said, "just as my father spoke French. Father said that, as citizens of the world, we should also learn Latin, which I have."

They arrived at a small landing with three doors. Taking the door on their left, they passed through a bedchamber holding a double bed and into a smaller room with a single glazed window that overlooked the courtyard.

Anne Marie gazed around.

Her two chests waited in the middle of the wood floor. Her father's lute lay on the narrow bed against the pale blue plastered wall. A small table holding a pitcher and basin sat in the corner near a row of clothing pegs. A stool beside the window completed the room's furnishings. It was a delightful room. She would be happy here.

"Once we left Strasbourg," Lettice said, "Thomas and Lemuel forgot most of their French."

"I remember playing with them," she said, dragging her thoughts back to the conversation.

"Thomas is studying divinity at Cambridge so of course is learning Latin. Lemuel is apprenticed to a printer here in London."

Lettice stood for a moment frankly studying her.

"I don't know who you resemble most, your mother or your father." Then, "You made the right decision to come to us. Cousin Charles has also been concerned. In fact, he was quite insistent that we let him know when you arrived."

An hour later Anne Marie was sitting on a bench in the hall singing Huguenot Psalms to fourteen-year-old Dorcas Peterman, a younger version of her mother, when she heard a dragging footstep.

She looked up. A tall, black-garbed, balding man was approaching. Dorcas immediately came to her feet. Anne Marie hurriedly stood also.

"Good afternoon, Father."

Jonathan Peterman smiled down at Dorcas.

"Good afternoon, daughter." Then, turning to her, "Welcome to my home, Anne Marie. My wife said you'd arrived. I trust you had a safe journey."

"Yes, thank you. And, thank you for allowing me to come."

Further talk was cut short by the insistent banging of the brass door knocker followed by hurried footsteps coming from the entry.

Jonathan turned his head and stiffened into alertness. A moment later, a hawk-nosed man with a dark chin beard burst into the hall. He was waving a pamphlet.

"Jonathan, have you seen this?"

Jonathan moved to intercept his agitated guest.

"Seen what?"

"A proper answer to Parliament for voting down the bill that would have reformed the ecclesiastical law."

"No, Clement, I hadn't. I've been leading a scripture study most of the afternoon."

"I knew we had to do more than just sit on our hands when Parliament refused to provide the Church with true discipline," Clement said vehemently. "And now someone has. Here. Read this."

Jonathan scanned the first page of the pamphlet.

"Let's go to my study."

Passing her by without a glance, Jonathan and his guest headed for a door at the end of the long room.

"Mark my words," she heard Clement say as they disappeared through the door, "by this time tomorrow, this pamphlet will be found all over London."

With spring on the way, it was still bright outside when Anne Marie had her first meal as a member of the Peterman household. The platter of succulent roasted chicken sitting with other foods on the white tablecloth said that English Protestants had no more concern for Lenten food restrictions than French Huguenots had.

Discussion of the pamphlet dominated the conversation. Anne Marie, sharing a padded bench with Prudence, helped herself to the stewed chicken and parsnips as she listened carefully to the exchange between Jonathan and Lettice, seated at either end of the table.

If she hoped to make a new life in England, she needed to understand English concerns. She especially needed to understand her Peterman cousins.

"The pamphlet is ostensibly an admonition to Parliament," Jonathan told Lettice. "And that's the title. But it's more than that. It calls for the public to replace the current church hierarchy with a presbyterian style of governance like the churches on the Continent and in Scotland have."

"Aren't the authors and publishers taking a great risk," Lettice said, "to challenge the bishops in such a way?"

"The pamphlet was published anonymously. According to Clement, people already suspect that John Field may be involved. It would be quite like

25

him." Jonathan's expression grew pensive. "For some while I've felt that young Field is becoming too radical. Refusing to wear the surplice, collecting stories of the bishops' oppressions, and working to organize sympathizers across England in support of a presbyterian system...." His mouth firmed momentarily. "But there comes a point when, like the Apostle Peter, we must obey God rather than man."

"What do you mean?" Lettice said.

"Clement thinks we've not been doing enough to further church reform."

"You already preach three to four times a week all over London ... and hold scripture studies to train laymen in the Scriptures. I'd say you're doing a great deal."

Jonathan cast Lettice a brief appreciative smile.

"I'm not saying that Bro. Field is taking the right approach, especially given the current threat from Rome. We can't afford to see the Church divided. If the Catholics were to rebel again as the northern earls did a few years ago, we could well face not only a civil war but war with Spain and France. Still, are we to cower in fear?"

"Whatever do you mean?"

"This Saturday, I'm preaching about King Saul disobeying the prophet Samuel. By then, all of London will have heard about this pamphlet challenging the current church government. Whatever I say will be understood in the light of that. Also, it being Easter weekend, the attendance will probably be larger than usual. I may never have a better opportunity.... I must lay my sermon before God."

As if purposely ending the discussion, he turned to Anne Marie.

"I was sorry I couldn't remain to hear you sing this afternoon. Perhaps you'll sing for us later."

"It would be my honor, Cousin Jonathan." On impulse, she added, "And I would much like to hear you preach."

"You may accompany me to St. Mary Bow Saturday afternoon if you wish. Afterward, we might call on Charles Denzil. He lives nearby."

When the meal ended, Lettice sent Anne Marie to fetch her lute while she and her daughters helped a maidservant clear the table. By the time she returned, the tablecloth was bare, and the family were beginning to gather in the candlelit hall. Anne Marie settled on a bench near the harpsichord to tune her instrument.

She'd barely finished when a stocky, brown-headed young man wearing simple dark garb strode in. The small, sparse beard clinging to his cleft chin said he was scarcely older than herself. He crossed to Jonathan, seated near the fireplace, and doffed his black cap respectfully. He then bent onto a stool, pulled a paper from his sleeve, and began to talk with Jonathan.

Dorcas, seated on the bench with Anne Marie, leaned close.

"That's Simon Cole," she whispered, her round face turning pink. "He studies scripture with Father. He's very spiritual."

Simon stabbed a finger at the paper as he talked. His words were easily overheard.

"Reverend Peterman, the author of this pamphlet is right. Since Parliament won't act, we laymen must. We have to rid ourselves of bishops and archbishops and replace them with equality of ministers. The Antichrist must be totally removed, head, body, and branch!"

"I believe it will be … when the time is right."

"What does timing matter?" Simon said, pulling at his skimpy brown beard.

"We can only truly succeed in God's work when we do it in his timing," Jonathan said with calm firmness. "Just as your apprenticeship is preparing you to become a master glover, we Christians need to be trained in the art of spiritual warfare. That takes time." He smiled. "God's timing can also apply in small matters. You've been wanting to improve your French. God has sent you an opportunity.

"Come," he said, rising, "you haven't yet met my young cousin, Anne Marie." He began limping toward her, Simon at his elbow. "She's recently arrived from France. Her father was a French Protestant. Sadly, he's no longer with us."

She lay her lute aside and stood as they approached.

"Anne Marie," Jonathan said, "may I introduce Simon Glover. His father is a staunch supporter of our London lectureships. Simon is one of my most promising students."

"It's an honor to study with Reverend Peterman," Simon said. "To better learn how to win our battle against Satan." Then, "I admire you Huguenots. Fighting for the true religion. So brave."

"You're just as brave," Dorcas said at Anne Marie's elbow.

If Simon heard her, he gave no sign. His blue-eyed gaze remained fixed on Anne Marie.

"Is that how your father died?" he said. "Fighting in the French wars against the Catholic Antichrist?"

"My father was taken by the pestilence."

"Oh." He seemed disappointed.

"After he buried the rest of my family, he nursed our neighbors. He died with them." Her voice was all at once thick. She had to swallow before she could continue. "Is it more Christlike to die in the heat of battle than to die caring for the sick?"

Simon appeared more puzzled by her question than embarrassed.

"You'd not told us of your father's sacrifice," Jonathan said. "Having known him, I'm not surprised. He always was concerned for those less fortunate. But enough of sadness." He turned to Simon. "You've come at a good time. We're having a musical evening."

Lettice must have been listening. She immediately crossed to a chest and drew out a pile of music pages which she began passing around. Everyone started shuffling through them looking for their favorite songs. Soon the hall was filled with the sweet sound of melodious voices. At Jonathan's request, Anne Marie played her lute and sang. Then Dorcas played the harpsichord while Jonathan and Simon sang a duet.

Outside, the April evening slipped slowly into twilight. At evening's end, Jonathan requested that Anne Marie sing a Huguenot Psalm before the scripture reading.

Closing her eyes to better still herself for worship, she began to sing. When she opened them at the end of the song, Simon was watching her with rapt attention.

While Dorcas fetched the servants and Prudence brought the Bible, Lettice lit the wall candles beside Jonathan's chair. Once family and servants were all gathered in the hall, Jonathan opened the book. He turned it to the candlelight and began to read.

Anne Marie sat, hands still in her lap, listening to his sonorous voice and thinking longingly of her father who had spent his life caring for others. At the end of the reading, Jonathan prayed for his household then dismissed them all with his blessing.

The servants left to finish their work before retiring. Prudence was sent to bed. Anne Marie was collecting her lute when Simon approached, black cap in hand, to bid her goodnight.

"Mademoiselle duChant, your playing and singing. Truly superb. I hope to have the pleasure of hearing you again. The Psalm you sang was a real blessing."

Once he was gone, Anne Marie started for the stairs to go up to her chamber. She found Dorcas standing alone on the bottom step.

"He usually bids me good-night," Dorcas said. "But not tonight. He was talking with you."

Red-faced, she spun round and, feet pattering, rushed up the stairs.

Anne Marie followed more slowly and with a sudden understanding of another aspect of this household.

CHAPTER 4 – APRIL

Anne Marie, dressed in her dark blue gown, accompanied Jonathan to St. Mary Bow church on Saturday afternoon. They joined the flow of people crossing the porch and climbing the half dozen steps to the wide nave. Once there, Jonathan left her to make his way through the gathering crowd toward the chancel.

She paused at the back of the nave to glance around at the colorful stained-glass windows, carved hammer-beam ceiling, and large organ at the west end. Many in the assembly were dressed plainly or in somber colors like herself, but a good number were more ornately garbed. Seeing the variety, she decided it might be safe to wear her azure gown next time.

She moved up the nave and found a seat on one of the rough benches beside a tired-faced woman in a patched tawny gown who smelled of onions.

Jonathan mounted the pulpit beside a stone pillar at the front of the nave and launched into his sermon. She soon forgot how the rest of the crowd were dressed, her odorous neighbor, the hard bench, and the passing of time. She'd heard many preachers over the last years. Jonathan was one of the best.

She felt herself caught up in the vivid picture he painted of a king both proud and fearful, unwilling to be the true leader God wanted, too easily swayed by circumstances, too careless with his obedience, too ready with excuses when confronted.

"Despite King Saul's faults," Jonathan reminded his listeners, "he was God's anointed. Until God removed him, he was to be given the respect due a king. Nevertheless, Saul owed the same careful obedience to God, and to God's spokesman Samuel, as did the humblest citizen of his realm. God makes no distinction between men."

Jonathan's sharp look traveled over the audience.

"You there, in your jewels and velvets and silks, do you think yourself better than your neighbor in his plain woolen gown? Then the sin of pride has mastered you. The Catholic church would have one man better than another, pope better than bishop, priest better than layman.

"That is not God's way. The lowliest peasant is as valuable in his eyes as the highest nobleman in the land and has an equal opportunity of receiving his grace. God speaks equally to him through his conscience. God appointed Saul to a harder task than the worker who plowed his father's fields. For that, and that alone, he was owed more respect. God did not make Saul superior. Saul was to obey God's spokesman just as the plowman was to obey. And when he disobeyed, he had to face the same disapproving judge.

"Those who sit at Westminster making the laws of this great nation should heed the lesson of King Saul. If they fall short in carrying out the charge God has given them, they must be rebuked and called to a more careful obedience. But reproof should be done with the respect due their office."

Anne Marie glanced around. How many of the listeners had read the pamphlet reproving the Westminster lawmakers, and what were they now thinking?

"We all alike will be held accountable to God," Jonathan thundered in conclusion. "Whether we be high born or low, those of us who forget this, do so to our peril!"

The service ended. All around her, people began to depart. She remained seated, waiting while Jonathan spoke to a few who lingered.

"Mademoiselle duChant."

She looked up. Simon Cole was standing at the end of the bench, black wool cap in hand, blue-eyed gaze fixed on her.

"I thought I recognized you." He waved a hand at the empty seat beside her, "May I?" Without waiting for a reply, he settled onto the bench. "Wasn't Reverend Peterman's sermon inspiring? Listening to him is a real blessing."

"Do you come to hear him often?"

"At every opportunity. Will I be seeing you when he preaches next?"

"I don't know," she said cautiously, thinking of Dorcas. "I also wish to hear some of the other London preachers."

"Would you allow me to accompany you?"

"What about your work?"

"We could go after the shop closes. My father approves of my attending sermons. I'm sure he would also approve of you."

31

The compliment made her uneasy.

"I should ask Cousin Jonathan first."

"Of course, of course."

She glanced past Simon. Jonathan had finished his last conversation and was approaching. Relief washed over her.

Simon sprang up to greet him when he arrived.

"Thank you for remaining with Anne Marie," Jonathan said.

Simon glanced at her.

"My pleasure."

As they started toward the exit, Simon fell into step beside her. Once in the busy street, she expected him to take his leave. Instead, he detained them with praise for Jonathan's sermon.

"We can speak more when you come for our scripture study tomorrow evening," Jonathan said after a moment. "Now we must call on a relative."

"Of course," Simon said, bobbing his capped head. Then, "With your permission, I would like to come early and practice my French with Mademoiselle duChant." He turned a softer gaze on her. "Provided she is available."

Given Dorcas's feeling, that wouldn't be wise.

Jonathan spoke before she could answer.

"By all means, do."

She could think of no polite way to counter Jonathan's invitation. She shoved the problem aside, bade Simon farewell, and set off with Jonathan for the Denzil home on Guthran Lane.

They made their slow way along West Cheap, passing numerous locked and shuttered goldsmith shops, the gold plate and jewelry safely stored away in their cellars.

"Charles isn't the most talented goldsmith on the street," Jonathan said as he limped along, "but he's a shrewd businessman and has gained a position of influence in the guild. Besides his sons, Peter and Roger, he and Ursula have a daughter, Maud. I think she's slightly younger than you."

They stepped aside to avoid the muddy splatter from an approaching cart loaded with odorous raw hides.

"Roger is currently a journeyman goldsmith. He's already gaining a reputation as a gifted craftsman. If only he had as much concern for his soul...."

The cart passed, and they continued on their way.

"You'll soon notice Ursula seldom speaks," Jonathan said. "For some reason, her voice is little more than a rasping whisper."

They turned from West Cheap up Guthran Lane. Jonathan pointed to a sign jutting out from a shop ahead on the left, a prancing white unicorn on a blue background.

"That's Charles's shop. You should come sometime when it's open and the windows are filled with jewelry and plate. He's quite proud of it all. Not that gold plate can secure a place in heaven."

Jonathan passed the shuttered shop and stepped through a courtyard gate just beyond. She trailed him along a narrow, cobbled yard running beside a four-storied, half-timbered house. The end of an herb garden could be seen at the back of the yard. Jonathan halted before the main door and banged the brass knocker.

A blue-liveried maidservant let them in then disappeared through a door on the right. Judging from the savory odors wafting out, it must lead to the kitchen. Jonathan started up a flight of wide wooden stairs between the kitchen quarters and a narrow passage leading to the workshop's back entrance.

As she climbed the stairs, she heard a young woman's petulant voice.

"Roger, you cheated."

The accusation was met with male laughter.

"You're only saying that because I won. You owe me another halfpenny."

Anne Marie reached the landing and turned with Jonathan into a fine paneled hall. Its walls were bright with arras cloths, its benches and window seats padded with green velvet cushions.

Two stylishly garbed, dark-haired young people were playing cards at a small table in the near corner. They glanced up as she and Jonathan entered then turned back to their game.

Jonathan started toward the tall, heavyset man with the fringe of iron gray hair, short beard, and mulberry doublet seated in a carved chair near the fireplace. As they approached, he heaved himself up.

"Charles," Jonathan said, "This is Cousin Margaret's daughter, Anne Marie."

She smiled and dropped a curtsy.

Charles Denzil merely stared down at her with a cold look. His own smile, when it finally came, didn't reach his hazel eyes.

"Welcome to London." Shifting his attention from her, he waved Jonathan to the nearby settle. "I understand you're dining with us. If she speaks English, she can get acquainted with Roger and Maud."

Her face heated.

"Anne Marie's English is excellent," Jonathan said.

"Then she shouldn't have a problem." Charles turned toward the two at the gaming table and raised his voice. "Roger, Maud, this is your French cousin. She's in London for a short visit. Make her welcome."

The two looked up from their game in surprise.

"I didn't know we had a French cousin," Maud said. She beckoned to Anne Marie. "Come join us. But watch Roger. He cheats."

"She's merely a poor loser," Roger said with a grin as he fetched another stool.

Maud stuck out her tongue at him then turned to Anne Marie and began studying her unadorned dark gown.

"Is that the style in France now? I'm surprised it's not more fashionable. Unless your father is a Huguenot minister. I hear they wear nothing but black."

Disconcerted, Anne Marie settled onto the stool.

"My father was a maker of musical instruments."

"What is he now?"

"He and the rest of my family are in heaven."

"Oh, I didn't know. I'm sorry. Well, when you're ready to put off your mourning, I'll introduce you to my tailor. He makes the most elegant dresses." She touched the lace ruff on her peach velvet gown. "He made this one."

Anne Marie refrained from saying that she'd put off her mourning before she left France.

"It's beautiful."

"Forgive me for interrupting," Roger said, fingering his small pointed beard, "but how are we related?"

"My mother was Margaret Alton," Anne Marie said.

The looks Roger and Maud exchanged said the name meant nothing to them.

"Have you seen much of London?" Roger asked, apparently trying to be polite.

"I went to St. Mary Bow this afternoon to hear Cousin Jonathan preach."

"That's hardly entertainment," Maud said. "I know. You should join us the next time we attend a play or go to a bear baiting. Or we could take the barge up to Westminster. We might even catch a glimpse of the Queen."

Anne Marie, unsure how to answer, merely gave Maud a smile. She turned to Roger. "Do you go to hear Cousin Jonathan preach?"

"I hear enough sermons on Sunday. The remainder of the week, I'm fully occupied in the goldsmith shop."

"Except when he's off at the taverns," Maud said lightly, "or to dog fights with his friends."

Roger grinned and rolled his brown eyes.

"I doubt there'll be time for much of that for a while. Not with all the sketches Father wants done for the order of plate we received yesterday."

"I'm sure you'll make up for it later," Maud said. "Just be glad that you don't live in the country like Peter."

Roger straightened and peered at Anne Marie.

"Of course. That's who you are." He turned to his sister. "Peter's manor belonged to her grandmother."

"You mean…?" Maud said.

Roger nodded. They both turned and stared at her.

Anne Marie, feeling increasingly uncomfortable, lifted her chin and stared back.

Further conversation was cut short by the arrival of a handsome, long-jawed matron in a rich burgundy gown. The woman crossed to Charles and Jonathan by the fireplace and gave a silent nod.

"Come," Charles said to Jonathan. "Time to dine."

Charles immediately came to his feet and strode off toward the dining parlor. Maud and Roger quickly followed. Anne Marie hung back to wait for Jonathan, approaching more slowly with the matron.

"Anne Marie, let me introduce you to Cousin Charles's wife, Ursula."

This time her curtsy was greeted by silence and a distant smile.

Anne Marie took her seat beside Jonathan at a table spread with fine linen and set with pewter trenchers. She glanced across the room at the cabinet with its lavish display of silver plate. Even the mouthwatering fare on their sideboard spoke of material abundance. Although this was an unimportant evening meal at the end of Lent, it had three kinds of meat as well as fish, two vegetables, manchet bread, and a bottle of wine in a bucket of cold water.

The servants began bringing the platters, serving the mutton with gallandine sauce and cucumbers first to Ursula and then carrying the dish to Charles.

Once the meal was well underway, Jonathan looked across at Roger, carefully separating fish from bones.

"Your father tells me you've an order from the Earl of Chadwick that should bring in a handsome payment. As I told him, there's more to life than the pursuit of money."

"I certainly agree, Cousin Jonathan," Roger said.

"There's also more to life than the pursuit of sinful pleasure," Jonathan added.

"Or cheating at cards," Maud said, shaking her spoon at her brother.

Anne Marie, savoring a bite of white fish, saw Roger's eyes twinkle.

"Someday when I'm old," he said, "I'll give them all up and become a Puritan."

"Not everyone lives to old age," Jonathan said.

Roger reached for a roasted chicken leg.

"It's not in my stars to die young."

"God orders our years, not the stars. Who knows but you may meet with an accident and face our Maker much sooner and totally unprepared."

"Not, I hope, before I complete the sketches for Father."

"Accidents," Charles broke in unexpectedly. He fixed his gaze on her. "Have a care when you go about London. My brother Jerome was killed in the street. He fell under a wagon and was crushed. They said it was an accident."

Anne Marie shifted uneasily. It was as if a baleful presence had entered the dining parlor. Jonathan, seemingly unaware, switched his attention from Roger to Charles.

"I'd not thought of Jerome for years." He turned to her. "He was Charles's younger brother. Uncle Richard thought he had real talent and had planned to take Jerome on as an apprentice."

Charles's face darkened.

"Jerome had no talent. Uncle Richard would have found that out soon enough. No talent at all. Taking other peoples' designs and passing them off as his. Uncle Richard was a fool. They both were. And now they're both dead."

Uncomfortable silence followed Charles's outburst.

"He was no time-pleaser," Ursula said in a rasping voice, never lifting her gaze from her trencher.

"He certainly was not," Jonathan said. "Fool or no regarding Jerome, Uncle Richard stood firm to the death, a martyr for the faith which was delivered unto the saints. He is an example to us all."

"Given how insistent Charles was about meeting you," Jonathan said an hour later as he and Anne Marie were making their way home through the crowded streets, "I was surprised he didn't give you a better welcome."

"Roger and Maud talked of inviting me to see a play or going to Westminster," she said. "I didn't know how to answer. Their lives seem so different."

They halted briefly to let a handful of rowdy apprentices, out on their half-day holiday, dash past.

"Do you want to go?" Jonathan asked as they resumed walking.

"I want to get to know my cousins. But I'm not sure what's fitting here."

"You're wise to ask," he said. "Too often the plays glorify immorality. They're not suitable for building Christian character. You might enjoy seeing Whitehall Palace, though, and the other sights at Westminster. God may use you as a good influence on Maud and Roger. They certainly need one."

They continued on in silence for a time. Shortly before they reached St. Mary Street, Jonathan spoke again.

"Charles's mention of Jerome was odd. Uncle Richard once told me that Charles had stolen design ideas from another shop window. Apparently, Jerome did so as well. At least that's what Charles says." He gave a short sigh. "After all these years I don't suppose it matters what the truth is. Except the truth always matters to God."

As Jonathan and Anne Marie were arriving at St. Mary Street, Charles was venting his rage on his wife in their bedchamber.

"How dare you accuse me of being a time-pleaser in front of our guests. Especially her. I should have picked a wife with no voice at all."

Ursula stood unmoving. He lifted his hand to strike her but caught himself. He'd struck her once, a year ago. The next day, something he ate upset his bowels so badly that, rather than officiating at the guildhall meeting that evening, he spent his night running for the chamber pot.

Fortunately, no one else in the household was afflicted. A few days later, as he was self-complacently studying Ursula's bruise, he broke out in a cold sweat. He'd hit her, and the very next day his food was off. Had she put something in his meat?

Before that, he'd taken her any night he wanted and used her to his satisfaction. But not after. For whatever reason, since then, he could only satisfy his needs with whores. At least when he hit them, they couldn't tamper with his food. Here at home he had to be on constant guard lest she taint his food again.

He dropped his hand and contented himself with merely glaring at her. He'd been better able to deal with Jerome.

Of course, he'd not intended for his brother to die when he'd shoved him into the street. It was really Uncle Richard's fault. He'd had no right accepting Jerome as an apprentice after refusing to take him. How Jerome had gloated when telling him. No sensible person would blame him for becoming angry. Naturally he'd been sorry that Jerome had died. But the real responsibility for Jerome's death lay with Uncle Richard and that careless wagon driver.

Once Jerome was gone, though, he'd discovered life was much more pleasant without his rival. In just the same way, he'd discovered that he didn't need Ursula in bed any longer. But he still needed her to run his household, manage his apprentices, display his wealth on her person, and maintain his respectability with the guild and town.

"I'm going out."

Ursula remained impassive as he brushed past her. Even before he reached the door, a smile formed at the thought of the evening to come. The last time he'd paid a stealthy visit to the stews, he'd tried a new strumpet. She'd been quite satisfactory. He'd try her again tonight.

When Anne Marie arrived at the Peterman house with Jonathan, the rest of the family were in the hall. Prudence was stitching on a sampler by a window, and Dorcas was practicing the harpsichord. Lettice was seated on a padded bench in quiet conversation with a brown-haired, bony-faced youth.

As Anne Marie and Jonathan approached, the youth bounded up from the bench. Jonathan introduced him as their younger son Lemuel. Apprenticed to a London printer, he was home for the weekend.

Lemuel dropped back onto the bench beside his mother. Jonathan joined them. Anne Marie settled on a nearby stool.

"Husband," Lettice said, her brow furrowing, "Lemuel tells me that his master was the one to print John Field's tract."

"I didn't know at the time," Lemuel said, his voice cracking with adolescence and eagerness. "They did it secretly. But once the tract started circulating, I began hearing whispers in the shop."

"Well," Jonathan said, "have a caution who you mention it to. I doubt the Stationers Company approved the publication. They could penalize your master if they were to learn of it."

"Yes, Father. Now he's got a French tract from Geneva. But it's not a secret. He plans to print it as soon as he can find a suitable translator."

Jonathan threw Anne Marie a speculative look.

"I may know of one."

CHAPTER 5 – APRIL

The early morning sunlight was turning the chancel's stained-glass windows into a wall of glowing jewels when Anne Marie joined the Easter Sunday worshipers pouring into the parish church. Shoes whispering on the nave's cold stone floor, she followed Jonathan's family to a hard bench near the front. She took a seat between Lemuel and Prudence then glanced about at the empty saints' niches, the gilt organ, and the golden Holy Communion dishes on a lace-covered table.

Nostalgic memories of the previous year's Easter service flooded her.

She'd had her own family then, a younger sister sitting on either side, Mother just beyond with Father and her brother. They had sat thus at every service, week in, week out, for as long as she could remember, and they had belonged to one another. Now she belonged nowhere and to no one.

Blinking tears away, she forced her thoughts back to the present.

Accompanied by the organ, the congregation began their solemn singing. When they finished, the priest, in cope and white surplice, climbed the wooden steps to the carved pulpit. In a flat tone, he read out the Lessons and the Litany from the Second Prayer book. It contained much more of the abhorrent Catholic ritual than the simpler services she was accustomed to in Strasbourg, certainly more than the stark Huguenot services held in a barn outside Rouen that she'd attended these last months.

She glanced at Jonathan. Given his Puritan views, what was he thinking as he joined in a worship that could almost have passed for Catholic?

The time came for Holy Communion. The congregation began filing to the front to kneel and receive it from the priest's hand. It smacked so much of the mass that her knees nearly refused to bend when her turn came. Back in her seat and her mouth still tasting of wine, she tried to quiet herself and focus on the priest's homily.

When the service ended, she gladly returned home to spend the rest of the morning in quiet contemplation and Bible reading. Following their midday meal of onion pottage, stuffed quail, and bread, she walked back to the church with the family for the much simpler afternoon service. This time Jonathan delivered the sermon from the carved pulpit, and Simon Cole was in the audience.

As they returned home a second time through Sunday-quiet streets, Simon joined them, strolling at her elbow and chatting with her in halting French. She could feel Dorcas's glare boring into her back the whole way.

When they arrived, she would have escaped up the stairs and left Simon with Dorcas. Lettice made that impossible. She gathered everyone in the hall and handed around music sheets. To Anne Marie's relief, when the singing ended, Jonathan took Simon off to his study. Prudence and Dorcas disappeared. Lettice left to oversee final preparations for the evening meal. Anne Marie found herself alone with Lemuel.

"How about a game of chess?" he said.

He got out the board and pieces, and they settled down on either side of the table.

"My brother wants to be a preacher," Lemuel said after they'd played a few turns, "and help free England from Catholicism. But it'll never be done without the printers. Look at John Field's pamphlet. More people are talking of that than they are of any sermon. It will be the printers who'll have the greater impact for the faith."

They were still at their game when Simon emerged from the study. He strolled over to watch, pulling at his scanty beard and making sympathetic noises whenever she made a wrong move. As a result, she lost more quickly than she might have.

The moment the game ended, Simon launched into halting French. Aware that it was nearly time for the evening meal and Dorcas could appear any moment, she turned the conversation back to English.

"Lemuel thinks that the printers are invaluable in spreading the faith," she said to Simon. "What do you think?"

Simon's expression said he'd not considered the matter. He did his best to consider it now. To her relief, Simon was talking with Lemuel when Dorcas arrived.

She was not so successful at redirecting his attentions over the meal. Although she sat between Lemuel and Prudence while Simon sat across the table beside Dorcas, it was to herself that he addressed his conversation. And it was to her, rather than Dorcas, that he bade farewell before he departed.

Jonathan and Lettice were too occupied in a private exchange with Lemuel before he returned to his master's house to notice the glowering look Dorcas gave her. She could do nothing but go to bed and pray that Simon would lose interest in her.

Over the next days, Anne Marie set about making a place for herself in the household. Each morning after breakfast, she joined the family for devotions before they began their work and Prudence left for the dame school. Having overcome her suspicion of Anne Marie, Prudence became quite talkative. In contrast, Dorcas met all her attempts at friendship with a sullen look.

Lettice, busy ordering her household, and Jonathan, preparing sermons in his study, seemed unaware of their elder daughter's morose attitude. Anne Marie worked at whatever household task Lettice set her and prayed that, somehow, her relationship with Dorcas would improve.

It didn't help that Simon Cole, coming early on Wednesday to practice his French before his scripture study with Jonathan, again showered attention on her while ignoring Dorcas.

Anne Marie was on her way to the back courtyard Friday morning with a basket of wet laundry when she met Jonathan returning from a meeting.

"After you finish," he said, "come to my study. I've something for you."

She hung the washing to dry, returned the basket to the laundry room, then sought Jonathan out.

When she entered the study, Jonathan was seated at his writing table, Geneva Bible open before him, inkwell and paper within reach. Curious, she glanced around. Two shelves of books and a third holding pamphlets filled a cabinet on one wall while another equally full cabinet hung between the windows. The place smelled of ink, musty papers, and scholarship.

"Lemuel said the printers would have a great impact," she said.

"You may have a part in that." He picked up a paper from the table and held it out to her. "Here's that French tract Lemuel was talking about. Look it over and tell me if you can translate it."

Anne Marie sat by the glazed window in her small chamber and read the pamphlet with growing concern. She reread it as if somehow the second reading would be different. It wasn't.

She knew what she must do. Knowing wouldn't make the doing easier.

Tract in hand, she set off for the study. When she entered, Jonathan looked up from his scribbling. Her footsteps seemed unusually loud as she approached him. She braced herself.

"I've read the pamphlet."

"Good. How soon can you translate it?"

"I'm not the right choice for this," she said, laying the tract on the writing table. "I couldn't do it justice."

"Surely it's not that hard. Have more confidence in yourself."

"I can't." She swallowed. "I mean … I won't. I don't agree with what it says."

Jonathan's gray brows dipped.

"What does it say?"

"That God arbitrarily predestines who will be saved and who will be condemned. People can't even desire to believe unless they're among the elect."

"So…?"

"I don't believe God predestines people with no consideration for their actions."

He frowned.

"I had this same conversation with your father. Unfortunately, he held the letter of James in too high regard to see his error."

She knew she should hold her tongue. The words still came out.

"I mean no disrespect, Cousin Jonathan, but in your sermons you challenge people to live godly lives. Why tell them their behavior matters if it doesn't? Why tell that to Roger?"

His expression tightened.

"You've said enough … and are as mistaken as your father was. But I wouldn't have you go against your conscience. I'll return the tract to the printer and make your excuses." He paused. Then, "Speak of this to no one.

43

You're under my care and are still too young to fully understand these doctrinal matters."

She tucked her chin to hide her expression. She didn't remind him that Father, when three years younger, had stood firm in this same belief even to the point of imprisonment. And she was her father's daughter.

"Yes, Cousin Jonathan. Thank you."

"Well, Anne Marie," Lettice said over the evening meal, "have you started on the pamphlet?"

Anne Marie stiffened, a bite of juicy lamb halfway to her mouth. She glanced at Jonathan, sitting at the head of the table.

"She won't be translating," he said tersely. "She couldn't do it justice."

"That's a shame. Lemuel said the printers are getting a number of French writings."

"They'll find other translators. Anne Marie can continue helping Simon with his French. In fact, he's coming this evening for another lesson."

The following Wednesday Anne Marie, in her plain green gown and tan stockings, set out for the Denzil home. Given the tensions with Dorcas and the disagreement with Jonathan over the tract, Maud's invitation to accompany her to Westminster was a welcome escape.

When she reached the goldsmith shops on West Cheap, she slowed her pace. The dazzling shop windows she passed held more gold or silver plate and fine jewelry than she'd ever seen. She turned up Guthran Lane and paused outside the Denzil shop to admire the beautiful items in their window.

Someone called her name. She looked up. Roger, in a leather apron and with white sleeves rolled to his elbows, stood in the open shop door.

"Here to buy?"

"I'm meeting Maud. We're going to Westminster."

"Come in anyway. You might change your mind." He stepped back. "That gown could use a necklace."

Glad for a better look, she stepped through the door and into the faint odor of molten metal. She gazed around at the shelves laden with gold and silver serving dishes, salt cellars, goblets, and other plate.

A voice came from the workshop in the back.

"Roger, I'll see to our customer."

Charles Denzil appeared, heavy face red from the heat of the furnace. He stopped abruptly, and his welcoming smile evaporated.

"Oh, it's you. Here to buy?"

"I'm meeting Maud."

"She's not down here." Charles turned to Roger. "Get back to pickling that dish."

Roger winked at her and disappeared through the workshop door. She was left alone with his father.

Growing increasingly uncomfortable under Charles's silent stare, she excused herself and escaped back out into the street. She walked on to the courtyard gate and thence to the house. Before starting up the stairs to the hall, she looked down the narrow passage leading to the workshop.

Through the open door she saw Roger lift a silver goblet from one vat of liquid and plunge it into another. As if aware of her presence, he glanced up. When their gazes met, he winked again and then turned back to his work. Suddenly feeling foolish, she hurried up the stairs.

Maud, in a richly embroidered peach gown and elaborate white ruff, was impatiently pacing the hall.

"Let's go," she said. "We'll have little enough time at Westminster as it is."

She hurried Anne Marie back down the stairs and out the courtyard gate. Holding their skirts above the dirty cobblestones, they rushed down Friday Street and across Thames Street. Once at Queenhythe, they secured places on the next public barge bound for Westminster.

Anne Marie remained by the rail, fresh spring breeze stroking her face, as the barge made its slow way up the silver-gray river. Maud made no effort to identify the various grand houses and palaces dotting the north bank that they passed. Now and again Anne Marie spotted a herd of swans, white as snow, swimming on the river or along the green reedy banks. Gradually, the river's long curve fell behind, and Westminster came into sight. The city draped the right bank like a necklace of pearls adorning the throat of a beautiful woman.

Once past Whitehall Palace, the barge turned toward a wooden wharf jutting into the Thames. With practiced ease, the captain nosed his vessel against the wharf and tied up.

The boards gave off a hollow ring as the passengers, Anne Marie and Maud among them, made their way across the wharf and onto the dockside. Most scattered toward the various buildings ringing the courtyard. Anne Marie remained gazing around.

"Come on," Maud said. She caught Anne Marie's arm and drew her across the courtyard. "I want to go to Whitehall Palace. If we're fortunate, we can gain entrance to the Queen's garden. Who knows who we might meet there."

"What about Westminster Abbey?"

"We'll see it later."

Anne Marie followed her between two red brick structures to come out onto a busy cobblestone street lined with buildings that Maud identified as King Street.

"That's Westminster Abbey beyond the little gatehouse," Maud said, waving to the left.

Anne Marie paused to study the brilliant stained-glass windows and towering roof of the grandiose Abbey high above the surrounding structures.

With an air of intentionality, Maud set off in the opposite direction toward a tall, impressive gatehouse straddling King Street. Annoyed, Anne Marie hurried after. This was not the sightseeing trip she had envisioned.

"The Queen's gardens and Whitehall Palace are just beyond King's Gate," Maud said.

She continued at a brisk pace past black-and-white half-timbered houses, fine pale stone or rosy brick dwellings, and numerous taverns. As they neared the gatehouse, Maud slowed.

"If we meet anyone, pretend you're my maidservant."

Anne Marie stared at her in consternation.

"They'd never believe that."

"Of course, they will. Look at how you're dressed. Nobody of any consequence would appear at Westminster like that." Then, "Please? Just for today."

Anne Marie swallowed annoyance.

"Who are we meeting?"

"I don't know. It's merely in case we do. Come on."

With growing apprehension and noting anew how elaborately Maud was garbed, she followed her toward the gatehouse. Once through, Maud stopped. She took up a position as if she were waiting for someone.

They'd been there only a short time when two young men, sumptuously clothed in satins and velvets, came strolling by. Maud stepped forward.

"Forgive me," she said, "but have you seen...?" She bit her lower lip. "No, surely he would have sent word." She seemed to wilt like a flower exposed to too much sun.

The two courtiers had halted at her first word. Now the bolder faced one swept off his jeweled cap and bowed.

"May I be of assistance, Mistress?"

"A gentleman friend was to have met me here for a tour of the gardens. I fear he's been detained on Queen's business. I had so hoped...." She sighed and fluttered her dark lashes.

The other courtier ran his gaze over Anne Marie. She glared at him. He shrugged and returned his attention to Maud.

With growing alarm, Anne Marie listened to the easy banter between Maud and the two young men. The bolder of the two held out a hand.

"Would you allow me the honor?"

She spoke quickly before Maud could accept.

"But what of Westminster Abbey?"

Maud's eyes narrowed.

"You may go. Just see that you arrive back at the pier by four." She turned to the courtiers. "My maid is quite religious." Maud pulled a penny out of her purse. "Here. You'll need to pay the verger to gain entrance to the monuments. But forgo the guidebook. He overcharges."

Clamping her jaw against a sharp retort, Anne Marie stared at Maud. Was there a hint of pleading behind her haughty look?

She reluctantly took the coin and watched with misgivings as Maud strolled off with the men. Not knowing what else to do, she walked back along King Street toward Westminster Abbey.

When she entered the Abbey, sunbeams slanting through the stained-glass windows were filling the nave with rainbows. She paid her penny to the verger then wandered about the massive cathedral to view the gilt tombs of former royalty.

When she left the Abbey, a ribbon hawker gave her directions to the Old Palace. After admiring that, she continued on to Westminster Hall. The tall narrow brick building, home to the Star Chamber and other law courts, overlooked the Thames not far from the ferry pier.

She finished her tour and arrived at the pier just as a distant clock chimed the hour. Maud had said to be here by four. It was four by the clock, but Maud was not among the people coming and going across the courtyard.

As she paced the hard-packed earth, her misgivings over Maud's behavior grew. Only silly maids or strumpets willingly went off with two strange men.

To her intense relief, Maud at last emerged from between the buildings. She rushed across the courtyard and grabbed Anne Marie's arm.

"Come on or we'll miss our ferry."

Maud hurried her to the pier and got them both aboard moments before the barge started for London. Standing at the rail with Maud, Anne Marie vented her anger.

"You were a fool to go off with those men. Anything could have happened."

"In broad daylight in the Queen's garden? Besides, I can take care of myself. The only thing that ever happens is I enjoy myself."

"You've done this before?"

"It's not serious."

"It's a bad idea."

"Don't lecture me. I've got to have some pleasure while I can – before Father marries me off to someone I won't like. And if you tell, I'll say you knew from the beginning … that you helped me."

Charles Denzil adjusted his ruff, smoothed the black doublet over his paunch, and slipped on the velvet jerkin the manservant held out. It was his best, a rich dark red one that made him stand out among the other black-garbed guild members. At the same time, the garment's quiet elegance maintained his reputable image. He owed it to the guild to look his best at their meetings. After all, he was one of the more prestigious members, perhaps the most. Of course, it would be unseemly to voice the thought.

He added rings to his thick fingers.

At these gatherings he received the respect he deserved. He especially enjoyed those which included a dinner at the guildhall. There, he could eat whatever he fancied without fear. Already his mouth was watering in anticipation.

He dismissed the manservant. Peering into Ursula's bronze mirror, he ran a comb through his rim of hair and down either side of his short gray beard. Satisfied, he donned his hat and started down the stairs to the hall. Roger would be waiting.

He reached the hall as Maud came up the main stairs from the entry. Roger, also in his best garb, was lounging by the stair top.

"How was Westminster?" Roger asked.

"Anne Marie begged me to take her again."

At mention of the French girl, the clock spring within him began to tighten. How could they stand there idly talking about her? Didn't they realize the danger?

"We've a guild meeting to attend," he said gruffly.

He pushed his way past Maud to hurry down the stairs and out the door. Roger caught up with him in the courtyard. Together, they made their way up Guthran Lane toward the guildhall.

As Charles strode along the narrow busy street, his neck hairs began to rise.

Was someone following him?

He glanced back. He didn't see her, but suddenly he knew she was there. He glanced back a second time.

"Father, is something wrong?"

"It's that French girl. She's following us."

"Anne Marie?" Roger stopped and peered back through the passers-by. "I don't see her."

"She's there. She's just good at hiding."

Roger gave him a puzzled look.

"Probably you saw someone resembling her."

"It was her."

"Why would she follow us?"

He studied his son. Roger believed himself a good actor, pretending that he hadn't seen the French girl. But he must have because she was there. Was Roger also conspiring against him? The thought sent a chill through him. His own son.

He mustn't let Roger know of his suspicions. That would put him on his guard.

"Come on," he snapped. "We're going to be late."

He began striding rapidly along the street. He was nearly running by the time he reached the safety of the guildhall. Heart pounding, he burst through the door with Roger hard on his heels.

Once across the threshold, he halted. His terror began to fade. People here were fully aware of his importance and value. He mustn't fail them by showing fear.

Given how good the French girl was at hiding, Roger may not have seen her after all. He'd always been a loyal son. Why would he turn against him now? Still, he'd watch Roger. Sooner or later, if he had, he'd give himself away. Roger thought himself so cunning. But he, Charles, was more so.

As usual, when they arrived, he had a place at one of the main tables. Roger was seated with the other journeymen at a lower one. Spooning lamb stew onto his trencher, he began to enjoy himself. He took a sip of red wine, savoring its tangy flavor. It was excellent.

"It's humbling to have our sons show more skill than we possess," Master Nashe, the goldsmith seated on his left, said. "But it makes a father glad. You must be extremely proud of Roger."

Charles's fingers tightened on his wine goblet even as the clock spring tightened within him.

"What do you mean?"

"I hear he has a real talent for the craft, far beyond our ordinary skill."

Maud must have decided to forget the sharp words she and Anne Marie had exchanged earlier in the week because, on Saturday afternoon, she appeared at the Peterman home and invited Anne Marie to walk out to Moorfields.

Knowing her better now, Anne Marie would have declined except that Simon Cole was expected. Already Dorcas was sitting, stony-faced, in the hall. Given the choice of spending the afternoon with Maud or Simon, she decided Maud was the safer. It was unlikely she could repeat her Westminster behavior in the confines of Moorfields.

Leaving the city's fetid odors behind, they passed through Bishopsgate to join numerous other Londoners strolling across the fields and enjoying the fresher air. All around them, the new green of spring was brightening the faded tan of last year's marsh grasses. With skirts lifted, they carefully picked their way around patches of soggy ground as they ambled about. The young men of London, practicing at the butts or playing football in the more open areas, were not so fastidious.

They wandered for a time but were greeted by no one except the aggressive hawkers of hot chicken's feet or freshly baked tarts. If Maud had come with the hopes of meeting young men, the day appeared a failure.

As they were finishing their first circuit, Anne Marie spotted Roger taking his turn at the butts. Below his brown trunk hose, his stockings were well splattered with mud. She and Maud stopped to watch him. Roger must have also seen them because he said something to his companions and then trotted over.

"Have you come to congratulate the winner?" he said. "I bet Hal I could shoot better than he. Now I'm a penny richer."

"You probably cheated," Maud said.

Roger shook his head with a look of mock annoyance. He turned to Anne Marie.

"You see what a high opinion my sister has of me." Then, "Did you enjoy your trip to Westminster?"

Anne Marie saw Maud tense and give a warning shake of her head.

"I saw a lot of buildings."

"After you returned, did you happen to be on Guthran Lane?"

"No. Why?"

"I thought I saw you." He shrugged. "No matter. What are you two seeing today?"

"We've only been walking around Moorfields," Anne Marie said. "But I'd like to go to Smithfield."

"Why there?" Maud said.

"It's where our great uncle was martyred."

Maud shivered.

"Not me."

"Wait a moment and I'll take you," Roger said.

He loped off, exchanged a word with his friends, and came striding back.

"Sure you don't want to join us?" he said to Maud.

She shook her head, turned with a swish of skirts, and swept off.

"I hope I'm not causing you to miss something," Anne Marie said.

"The dog fights won't start for at least another hour. I should be back to make my bets well before then."

"You shouldn't waste your money gambling."

Roger chuckled.

"It's not a waste. I win more than I lose. Come along."

Roger led her at a brisk pace back into the city, along a street running between the high city wall and a close-packed row of houses, down Silver Street, and out again at Aldergate.

"We're almost there." He slowed as they made their way along Aldergate Street. "Smithfield isn't much to look at this time of year … or at any time. Mostly it's used as a cattle market. Not the sort of place I'd choose to die."

"What sort of place would you choose?"

Roger gave her a quizzical look.

"I thought we were here about Uncle Richard." He turned left onto a rutted street lined with cottages and their attendant gardens. "St. Bartholomew Hospital is ahead on the left. Smithfield is just beyond."

In a few more steps the street ended. There before her, partially surrounded by more of London's sprawl, stretched a large drab field of patchy winter-dead grass touched here and there by new spring green. A cool breeze carrying the faint odors of a barnyard tugged at her skirts and brushed her face. She gazed around. This was the last place Uncle Richard had seen before he went to heaven.

"What was he like?"

"Uncle Richard? I don't remember him that well. I was seven when he died." Roger cocked his head; his expression grew pensive. "I do remember his hands. They were long and narrow and covered with tiny burn scars." He held out his own hands. "Someday mine will be like his." He dropped them. "Peter might remember Uncle Richard better. He's older and was his godson."

"How was Uncle Richard found out?"

"He refused to make a saint's image for Queen Mary. Father has never forgiven him for the loss of custom we could have had. Like Father said, he was a fool." Then, more reflectively, "He's also remembered as the finest goldsmith on the Street."

"Would you make a saint's image if the Queen wanted it?"

Roger rolled his eyes.

"You do ask the oddest questions. If only her Grace would give me an order. Of course, if she did, it wouldn't be for saints' images. On the other hand, should she marry a Spaniard, we could find ourselves with a Catholic king. No doubt he'd want them."

"You talk as if orders are all that matters. Don't you care whether England is Catholic or Protestant?"

"Of course, I care. I want no pope in Rome telling us how to manage our affairs. The only advantage to being Catholic is they're easier on sin. Simply confess to the priest a few times a year and do your penance. There's none of this daily soul searching that Cousin Jonathan would have me do. That takes all the enjoyment out of life."

"I enjoy my life ... and I don't live with a guilty conscience."

"Who says I have a guilty conscience? Do you want to come with me to a dog fight?"

"No, thank you, and you shouldn't be going either."

Roger laughed.

"You're not going to reform me. I'm beyond it. Just ask Cousin Jonathan."

CHAPTER 6 – APRIL – WYNNFIELD MANOR

Peter Denzil, walking his mount across the meadow toward the west split field just outside Hensey village, noted that the bare brown furrows were touched with a faint green. The barley broadcast in March was starting to show itself and, with it, announcing the arrival of spring. The winter-bleached grass under his horse's hooves was already beginning to revive, holding out the promise of a good crop of hay later in June for both manor and village.

He saw a splash of rose at the edge of his vision and turned his eyes toward the track coming from Hensey. He smiled as he recognized the passing rider. Catherine Cox.

He kneed his horse into a trot and set off along the field edge heading for the road. By the time he arrived, she'd disappeared into the leafless forest. With luck, he would catch her before she passed the boundary line between his manor and her father's.

Urging his horse to a gallop, he splashed across the shining stream and up the slope into the gray woods. He reached the top and took the curve. Catherine was sitting her horse in the middle of the track looking his way. The pale April sun reaching down through the bare arching branches dappled her rose velvet overskirts and hanging sleeves. He caught the faint scent of lavender when he reined up beside her. Her voluptuous mouth curved in a smile.

"I thought I saw you when I left Hensey," she said. Then, with an arch look, "Of course, given how you're dressed, you could have been one of your field hands."

He laughed as he glanced down at his brown wool jerkin and cobbled boots.

"You'd have me mark trees and check sheep in a velvet doublet and satin trunk-hose? It's enough to be garbed in fancier wear for Sunday worship and visits to your parents."

She shook her blond head in mild disapproval. Then,

"Help me dismount."

He swung down from his horse, crossed to her and lifted her down from the sidesaddle. Even after her feet touched the ground, his hands lingered around her slender waist as hers did on his shoulders. He reluctantly released her. She moved away. He tied their horses to a sapling and followed her into the forest edge, their footfalls making little sound on last year's sodden leaves.

She stopped beside a massive oak to look up at him with a flirtatious smile.

"When will you be visiting next?"

"I'd rather meet you privately like this."

"Why? Are you afraid the neighbors will think you're turning Catholic if you're seen coming too often?"

His mouth firmed.

"That's something I'll never do."

"I know, I know," Catherine said, holding up a gloved hand. "Your Uncle Richard. But you yourself said he'd acted unwisely."

"He was still my uncle. Besides, have you forgotten that it's now high treason to convert to Catholicism? If I were hanged, drawn, and quartered, you wouldn't get to be the lady of Wynnfield Manor. But nothing would happen if you became an Anglican."

Her short laugh had an edge to it.

"Nothing? My parents would be furious, and I'd likely be disinherited. Then how would you get Cox Hall?"

"You know that's not the only reason for us to wed."

Catherine's blue eyes began to sparkle.

"You're right. Were I your wife, I might get you to go properly garbed."

"I doubt it."

He lunged for her. With a squeal of laughter, she darted behind the oak. When he finally caught her, she let him kiss her cheek.

After a moment she pushed him away and started back toward their horses.

"I must go. I just rode over to see if Master Weaver had our cloth finished."

He followed her, his breathing uneven. She was a minx. If he should take her to wife, he'd have a lively time in bed.

56

"Help me mount."

Once she was again in the saddle, she smiled down at him.

"Go back to your sheep and trees. I'll see you at Sir George's and, I hope, better garbed."

She slapped the reins and was on her way, jogging down the track. The sound of hooves thudding against hard ground faded. He watched until she disappeared. Only then did he swing into the saddle and trot back toward Hensey.

Hensey, straddling the road leading to Hensford town and watered by a meandering stream, consisted of two dozen cottages, mostly thatch-roofed wattle-and-daub, with their gardens, chicken coops, and pig pens; a black-smith's forge, a mill, and the small flint chapel of St. James the Less where Peter worshiped. With a few exceptions, its residents either scraped out a living as Wynnfield tenants or earned what they could as day laborers.

When he reached Hensey, rather than turning off to Wynnfield Hall a quarter of a mile down the side track, he reined up before one of the few black-and-white half-timbered village houses having a shingled roof and tied his horse to a post.

At his knock a stocky, black-haired young woman with cup-handle ears opened the door. Her face with its low forehead seemed almost too small for her generous nose and wide mouth. Seeing him, that mouth curved in a welcoming smile.

"Peter, come in," Gwen Weaver said. "But have a care for the baby. He just took his first steps yesterday."

Peter crossed the threshold into the main room that served as both hall and dining parlor. The steady thud of a weaver's loom coming from the adjoining room beyond the narrow stairs gave evidence that Will Weaver was at work.

As Peter started across the room, a sandy-haired toddler in a tan gown launched himself off the padded settle, took a few tentative steps, and grabbed his leg.

Gwen scooped up her offspring. He lay his head against her neck and stared at Peter.

"Little Rob looks more like you every day," he said, studying the toddler.

"Thankfully, he doesn't have my ears."

She turned her son loose again, aiming him at the dining table in the far end of the room.

Peter watched him totter off while Gwen stepped into the kitchen and exchanged a word with her young scullery maid. Judging from the sounds, the maid was chopping vegetables.

A moment later Gwen returned, bringing a whiff of pease pottage and a mug of apple cider with her. She handed him the cider, settled at her spinning wheel by the stairs, and set the wheel to turning.

"Catherine Cox was here earlier," she said. "She stopped by to see if Will had her cloth order finished."

He bent onto a stool and took a sip, savoring the sweet drink.

"I saw her pass on the road," he said casually.

She eyed him suspiciously across the spindle, and her dark brows bunched. She had her mother's frown.

"I hope you didn't go chasing after her."

"Now why would I do that?"

"Because you've no sense."

He didn't bother to reply. He and Gwen, sharing the same grandmother, had been a part of each others' lives from the time, as children, they'd fought over ponies at Wynnfield. Her father, Gilbert Harvey, had been Great Aunt Jane's bailiff and had had the pluck to wed his own father's outspoken half-sister Emma. In so doing, Gilbert Harvey had gained Charles Denzil's permanent ill-will.

"Are you going to Sir George's birthday celebration on Saturday?" he said, deliberately turning the conversation.

"Not with this one," she said, nodding toward Little Rob, banging a wooden spoon on a bench. "But if you can stop by on the way, I'd like to send him a gift."

"I'll do that." He drained his mug and came to his feet. "If you or Will should need anything from Hensford, let me know."

"How about thirty pounds and a journeyman weaver so we can expand the business?"

He grinned.

"In that case you'll need more spinsters."

"Bring me ten of those as well."

A short while later Peter rounded the curve of white-budded hawthorn bushes that marked the end of the track leading to Wynnfield Hall. He slowed his horse to a walk. Pride of ownership flooded him as he gazed at the manor house. The late afternoon sun was brightening the curling chimney stacks and shingled roof and turning its red brick walls to rose.

His mother had first sent him here as a two-year-old to escape the sweating sickness in London. That long summer sojourn had been followed by many other visits and had planted in him a love for Wynnfield and the country life that nothing had ever replaced ... not even Catherine Cox.

If he should wed her, no doubt she'd want to add to Wynnfield Hall just as her father had added to what once had been Stoke Hall. For himself, he didn't see the need. He liked the house as it was, a cluster of rooms at either end of the great hall, its numerous bright mullioned windows looking out on orchard, pleasance, and base-court.

He dismounted by the stable, handed his horse to the stable boy, then strode through the half-timber gatehouse and across the hard dirt base-court. He entered the house and, footsteps echoing beneath the rafters, walked the length of the brightly painted great hall, with its high narrow windows and hammer-beam ceiling, to the private chambers beyond.

The house steward caught him as he neared the dais.

"Master Peter, a letter came from London. I put it on the accounts room table. The courier said he'd stop on his return from Cambridge tomorrow should you have an answer."

He nodded absently and continued on past the dais, through the winter parlor, and into the accounts room. The afternoon sun slanting through the room's south-facing window fell on the waiting letter. He picked it up, broke the red wax seal, and unfolded it, expecting to see his mother's signature. Instead, it was signed by Jonathan Peterman.

Curious, he began to read.

"Cousin Peter Denzil, I and my good wife Lettice commend ourselves to you. I am writing to inform you of the arrival in London of Anne Marie duChant, the granddaughter of your great-aunt Jane Alton. Her parents, Paul and Margaret Alton duChant, along with Anne Marie's brother and sisters, died of the pestilence that hit Strasbourg nearly a year ago.

"She has come to England to make the acquaintance of her mother's relatives and to visit Wynnfield where she was born before her parents left for the Continent during Queen Mary's reign. I trust it will be convenient for you to offer her every hospitality. With your approval, I plan to ride up with her shortly after May Day.

Written in London this 14th day of April 1572.

Respectfully yours,

The Right Reverend Jonathan Peterman"

He stared at the letter with unfocused eyes as two long-forgotten images rose to mind. Great Aunt Jane, tall, gray-haired, with a lined and smiling face, bending down with a kiss to welcome him to Wynnfield. A Frenchman with a head of red-gold curls teaching him how to play a small pan pipe under an apple tree. Search his memory as he might, though he vaguely remembered their existence, he could find no picture of Aunt Jane's daughter or granddaughter.

He again focused on the letter's content.

Poor maid. To lose your whole family.

He settled at the table, penned an invitation, then folded and sealed it ready for the courier's return. That done, he turned his attention to more important matters.

After he'd recorded the plowing of the fallow south field, he must see the reeve about the final few trees to be felled before the frost was out of the ground and speak to the cattleman about the spring's calf crop.

The courier had collected the letter and had likely already delivered it before Peter, wearing a fine linen shirt to go with his tawny velvet jerkin and wool doublet, set out for Hensford Saturday morning with a brief stop at Hensey to collect Gwen's gift of quail for Sir George Terrell. Though gray cloud blanketed the sky and a damp breeze chilled his ears, the day currently was dry. He covered the three miles to Hensford in good time.

The guildhall clock across the busy square from St. Sebastian Church was striking ten as he turned south onto the familiar road leading to the Terrell manor. He'd lost count of how many different celebrations he'd attended there over the last eleven years since becoming a manor owner.

He'd just turned twelve when his grandfather died, and he inherited Wynnfield Manor. Soon after, his mother secured him a place in Sir George's Protestant household so he could begin making his way in the world of landed gentry. That Sir George was Great Aunt Jane's step-nephew had helped.

He'd spent six years in the Terrell household improving his Latin, learning manners and a smattering of French and, most importantly, learning how to run a manor. He then returned to London for a year to study law relating to land ownership at the Inns of Court. Finally, at age nineteen, he'd taken full possession of Wynnfield. Since that time Sir George had become his patron in the community.

When he arrived at the large, half-timbered manor house, he dismounted in the dirt courtyard and exchanged a friendly word with the stable hand who took his horse. Although servants frequently knew their master's business, he didn't ask about the rumor going around.

According to the rumor, Sir George, having served as Justice of the Peace from the reign of King Edward, would soon be retiring. Already there was much talk, and some rivalry, over who would next be appointed. Today's celebration with family and friends, including several possible candidates, would give opportunity for more of the same.

One hopeful contender for the appointment, a former Hensford town mayor, arrived right behind him. Together they entered the house and made their way to the large paneled hall where the celebration was being held. Stepping into the noisy hall, they met Dame Dorothy Terrell, Sir George's plump, industrious wife. After handing her the gifts they carried, the former mayor strode away to join the numerous, already assembled guests.

Peter set off to find Sir George. Spotting his stout, black velvet-clad back beyond the linen-covered tables set for the celebration meal, he approached him with birthday greetings.

"Thank you, lad," Sir George said, his heavy, pug-nosed face beaming. "Now I need to make an announcement." He crossed to the dais, looked out over the assembly, and raised his voice. "May I have your attention?"

Gradually the din subsided, and all eyes turned toward Sir George.

"Thank you for coming to help celebrate my sixtieth birthday. I also received a letter from her gracious majesty the Queen. She's accepting my resignation as Justice of the Peace on the appointment of a new Justice." His gaze traveled the room. "I wish my replacement well, whomever he may be."

As Sir George stepped off the dais, the hall began buzzing like a hive of bees about to swarm.

Peter glanced around for Catherine. There she was, standing with her father near the red brick fireplace. She looked fetching in a pale blue and silver gown. Her father, equally resplendently garbed in a burgundy velvet doublet and black satin trunk hose, looked like a brooding falcon. As usual, her mother was absent.

He wound his way casually toward Catherine, catching snatches of conversation as he went.

"Whoever it is, it won't be Eustace Cox."

"If he were Protestant, he'd likely be chosen. His father served the Crown."

"...what with Mary, Queen of Scots, here and that Catholic uprising in the north...."

"Catholics can't be trusted."

"...good that Parliament banned them from public office."

"He only attends St. Sebastian to avoid being fined. And he doesn't listen to the priest."

"You don't either, unless you do in your sleep."

Soft laughter.

"His homilies are so dull. We ought to get our own town preacher."

Catherine must have seen Peter working his way toward her through the assembled guests because, when he drew near, she intercepted him. This time she smelled of rosemary. She surveyed him and her lips curved.

"Well, you have come slightly better garbed. But you're still no match for my father."

He glanced at Eustace Cox, standing half a dozen arm lengths away.

"He doesn't look pleased that we're talking."

Catherine's face clouded.

"It's not you. It's the Justice of the Peace appointment. He should be getting it."

"He just might if he hurriedly became an Anglican," he joked.

Her blue eyes flashed with sudden fire, and her expression hardened.

"Sell our souls for a court appointment and betray my brother?"

"Betray your brother? How could becoming an Anglican betray Cyril?"

"I mean his memory," she hurriedly amended. "It would be a betrayal of his memory. With him dying of an illness in France, that's all we have. Besides," she continued in a rush, "being Justice of the Peace is an honor that comes with no salary and a great deal of work."

"So, if in some future year I should be offered the honor, you wouldn't want me to take it?"

Catherine's eyes were dancing again.

"I didn't say that. Someday, should you have the honor, I might well like being the wife of a Justice of the Peace."

"Wife!"

The sharp, angry voice made Peter jump. Feeling like a schoolboy who'd just spilled his ink, he turned to face Gwen's mother. Despite the special occasion, her stocky frame was garbed in a patched woolen gown, and wisps of gray hair escaped her hood. A frown further wrinkled the weathered face glaring up at him. As usual, she smelled of cows.

"Aunt Emma, when did you get here?"

"None too soon by the sound of it." She threw a hard look at Catherine. "You aren't planning to marry her, are you? She's Eustace Cox's daughter."

"With all due respect, Aunt, who I wed is my business."

"You needn't worry yet, Mistress Harvey," Catherine said, "I may decide I don't want him since he's not Catholic."

She spun with a swish of skirts and flounced back to her father, watching, hawk-eyed, beside the fireplace. Aunt Emma's sharp look followed her.

"Oh, she'll want you, all right. Or at least her father will. He's always coveted Wynnfield."

He had no wish to argue with her. From experience he knew that, even when proved wrong, she'd continue quarreling from sheer stubbornness.

"How's your calf crop this year?" he said. Talking cattle was the one topic Aunt Emma couldn't resist. She loved her cattle, especially the Galloways.

By the time he'd received a full account of the cattle situation on the farm north of Hensford where Aunt Emma lived with her son and his family, the guests were starting to find places at the long tables, and servants were appearing with platters of succulent roasted lamb and other foods. He quickly excused himself. He managed to gain a seat some distance from Aunt Emma between two Hensford merchants. He was nowhere near Catherine.

He sighed. This was going to be a long afternoon.

The Hensford merchants spent most of the leisurely meal talking business across Peter. Only as guests began rising from tables to take their leave was he able to again exchange a few private words with Catherine.

"I'll ride back with you," he said as they trailed her father out of the hall.

"We're staying in Hensford to attend services at St. Sebastian."

"You should attend worship in Hensey."

"You know Father can't abide Bro. Lawrence's services. Refusing to elevate the host and mumbling through the rituals. That misshapen little priest has robbed them of all their beauty."

"What you mean is," he said, frustration boiling over, "he doesn't follow Catholic ceremonies." Then, in a more conciliatory tone, "He still uses his organ."

Catherine's eyes flashed fire.

"There's more to a proper mass than organ music."

Jogging home by himself, rain dripping from his hat brim, he brooded over the day's disappointments. He suddenly realized he'd not told Aunt Emma the news from Jonathan Peterman. It didn't matter. Given how annoying she was, this Anne Marie would be fortunate not to meet her.

CHAPTER 7 – LONDON

After half a week of rain, the sun finally broke through to brighten the fields and forests of Wynnfield. In London the rain lasted longer. It filled the dark, littered streets with muddy puddles of floating trash and caused the town ditch running through Moorfields to overflow. Although the dreary weather created numerous other problems, it helped with one. Simon Cole only came once in midweek. When he arrived, his wool cap heavy with moisture and his dark hose spattered with muck, Jonathan immediately took him off to study the scriptures.

By the weekend the weather had improved remarkably, and people were venturing out again.

Saturday's noon meal was over. All that remained were the faint aromas of roasted pigeon and parsnips, and a dining table full of dirty tableware. While Dorcas carried a stack of trenchers to the kitchen, Anne Marie helped Lettice clear the white linen tablecloth of the remaining dishes.

"If I can be spared for an hour or so," Anne Marie said, adding a goblet to the tray, "I thought to walk out to Moorfields."

"Don't you want to wait a while in case Simon should come?" Lettice said. "He might enjoy accompanying you."

She shifted so Lettice couldn't see her face.

"I have no wish to interfere with his scripture studies."

"A commendable attitude." Lettice reached for a serving dish. "You'll make some young man a fine wife."

Anne Marie escaped to the kitchen with the last full tray before Lettice could carry the conversation further. She suspected that Simon was the young man Lettice had in mind. Lettice still seemed not to have noticed Dorcas's sullen stares whenever Simon paid Anne Marie special attention. She herself remained acutely aware of them.

Shortly afterward, she set out for Moorfields. She was relieved to have gotten away before Simon arrived and was happy to clear the disagreeable London odors from her head.

The recent rains had done much to turn the fields to green. Despite the boggy places, they were alive with London residents enjoying the day. As she was picking her way along, cool breeze tugging at her skirts, she heard a man call her name. She turned. Maud and Roger were approaching.

"We've not seen you recently," Roger said as, one on either side, they fell into step with her.

"I've been occupied."

A handful of happy screaming children dashed past.

"Still spending all your time going to sermons?" He tutted. "What a dreary life. At least May Day will soon be here. You'll have opportunity for some real enjoyment."

"Oh, yes," Maud said, her eyes lighting. "It's ever so pleasant frolicking all night in the woods. Then in the morning we'll decorate the maypole and dance around it. There'll also be games and Morris dances and a hobby horse...."

"Why don't you go a-maying with us?" Roger said as they skirted a brown puddle.

She glanced at Maud. Maud was wearing the same expression she'd had when she went off with the young noblemen at Westminster.

"I should ask Cousin Jonathan first. They may expect me to go with them."

He laughed.

"You'll never find the Peterman family indulging in such lighthearted behavior."

Unsure how best to respond, she held her tongue. They walked on in silence, enveloped in the odor of wet ground.

"Come to a play with us on Monday next," Roger said. "Cousin Jonathan needn't know everything you do."

His light mocking tone annoyed her. She was glad, this time, to have an excuse that even he couldn't fault.

"I'll be at Wynnfield. I'm riding up with Cousin Jonathan directly after the holiday."

Roger's dark brows lifted.

"To Wynnfield? Well, well. I wonder how Peter's going to take your arrival. Imagine playing host to the person who nearly owned his precious manor."

"I don't see how that should pose a problem."

Roger wagged his head as he looked down at her.

"You've a lot to learn about human nature."

Anne Marie arrived back at the Peterman house an hour later and went directly up to her small chamber. She dropped to her knees before her cedar clothing chest and pulled out the brief reply that Jonathan had received from Peter Denzil earlier in the week. She studied the unadorned writing as she tried to see the man who'd penned the invitation. Was his welcome as sincere as it appeared? Or was it a sham, and she'd find Wynnfield filled with as many disturbing undercurrents as she was finding here?

When she'd left Rouen to escape Claude Goujon, making a new life for herself in London had seemed simple. She'd not reckoned on Simon Cole and Dorcas. Now, judging from Roger's reaction, the visit to Wynnfield might not be simple either. Simple or no, at least with her there, Dorcas would have Simon all to herself again.

She refolded the letter and stuck it back in her chest.

Anne Marie had just returned to the hall when she heard a hinge squeak. She looked over and saw the study door opening. Jonathan stepped through with Simon close behind. When Simon saw her, his face lit. He hurried to intercept her.

"Mademoiselle, I had hoped to practice my French with you today. Imagine my disappointment to find that you'd gone out. Had you waited, I could have provided you with companionship."

"Thank you, but I wasn't alone. I was with my cousins." She looked up at Jonathan. "Roger and Maud were telling me how you celebrate May Day here. It all sounded so lively. Frolicking overnight in the woods, bringing in the maypole, the dancing-"

Simon snorted.

"The maypole. A stinking idol if you ask me. Decking it with flowers and prancing round it like heathen."

"There's more to May Day celebrations than the heathen activities," Jonathan said mildly. "It's a good day to be reminded of all the beauty God has given us and to thank him for it."

"Of course, of course," Simon said, bobbing his head. He turned back to her. "Sadly, I must take my leave. I've already stayed overlong studying the scriptures. Such a blessing. Perhaps I can call upon you another day."

"Perhaps."

To her relief Simon strode off toward the entryway and disappeared. The sound of his footfalls faded. She glanced at Jonathan.

Should she mention Roger and Maud's invitation to him or not?

"Why don't you join my lessons with Simon?" he said, smiling down at her. "You could increase your knowledge of scripture."

She tensed.

"I'd rather not."

"You have no interest in studying the scriptures?" His smile was gone. "Your father was willing to study with me. I believe if we'd not left Strasbourg when we did, he might even have come to a better understanding on the issue of grace and works. He allowed me to baptize your brother and little sisters."

She didn't tell him that her father had later taught them about adult baptism.

"It's not that," she said. "It's ... it's Simon."

"Simon? What's wrong with Simon? He's a fine young man, one of the best."

"Dorcas wouldn't approve."

"Dorcas?"

"She has feelings for him."

Jonathan's bewildered look suddenly changed to eye-widening comprehension.

"Ohhhh. I'd not been aware.... She still seems a child to me. Thank you for calling it to my attention."

Simon joined them for one of their singing evenings a few nights later. As usual, she was the reluctant recipient of his attention and, as usual, Dorcas's face clouded. But, this time, she noticed Jonathan watching his daughter with a thoughtful expression. As soon as Lettice brought the music to a close, he asked Simon to read the evening scripture. When devotions ended, she was able to escape up the stairs while Jonathan was complimenting Simon on his delivery.

The morning sun was chasing the darkness from St. Mary Street when Anne Marie, in her old russet kirtle, set out with the Peterman family to enjoy May Day with friends in the fields and woods beyond London. They had just left their courtyard when Simon appeared, hurrying toward them along the cobbled street.

Her mouth tightened in annoyance even as her hand tightened on the rough handle of the wicker food basket she carried. She hadn't seen him for several days. If only she'd accepted Maud's and Roger's invitation, she wouldn't be seeing him now.

Leaving Prudence and Dorcas to go ahead with their parents, she quickly stepped back to walk with Lemuel, home for the holiday.

"I've often wondered how a printing press works," she said, grabbing the first conversation topic that came to mind. "Perhaps you could tell me."

Lemuel, face lighting, began to comply. With ears tuned to his detailed explanations, she kept a watchful eye on fast-approaching Simon.

When he arrived, he exchanged greetings with Jonathan and Lettice, and nodded to Prudence and Dorcas. Then he was approaching her.

"Ah, Mademoiselle. What a pleasure to spend May Day in your company."

"Lemuel was telling me about the printing press," she said. "I find it fascinating, don't you?"

Before Simon could frame a reply, she returned to questioning Lemuel as they ambled up the street through the passersby. Although she kept her gaze fixed firmly on Lemuel, she was fully aware of Simon trailing at her skirt tails.

Lemuel was happily explaining how the metal type was inked with balls of soft leather when they joined other groups passing through London's high, encircling wall at Bishopsgate.

Leaving the city behind them, they strolled along Bishopsgate Street, with its collection of half-timber dwellings and inns for travelers, until they reached a lane running between St. Botolph Church and Bedlam Hospital. They turned down the lane, passed half a dozen wattle-and-daub houses, and soon came out on Moorfields. Already the weedy commons, both there and in Finsbury Field farther on, were filled with Londoners enjoying the bright, breezy morning or collecting greenery and flowers for the various parish celebrations.

Lemuel excused himself and trotted off to greet friends practicing archery. Simon quickly took his place at her side and insisted on carrying her basket. Seeing the dark looks Dorcas kept throwing in their direction as they ambled along, she prayed that Simon also would soon join one of the groups of young men engaged in wrestling or football.

He didn't.

They continued across reedy fields spangled with yellow cowslips and tender pink primroses. They were nearing the newly leafed forest of birch and elm, when Roger and Maud came out of the woods with a group of festive companions garbed in various shades of green. Many of the group were draped in colorful flower wreaths; nearly all were carrying armloads of leafy branches.

Maud and Roger must have seen them for they left their companions to come across the uneven ground and greet the Peterman family.

"You should have joined us last night in the woods, Anne Marie" Maud said. "We had such a pleasant time."

"Come with us now," Roger said. "We're off to decorate the maypole by St. Giles church."

She saw Simon stiffen and recalled his earlier words about the stinking idol. All at once she knew how to rid herself of his attention.

"I would like to." She turned from Roger to look up at Jonathan. "By your leave, I wish to see how they celebrate the day."

She saw him glance at a wide-eyed Dorcas and a clearly shocked Simon. He turned to her, his expression inscrutable.

"Go with your cousins if you so desire." His words came slowly, deliberately. "Only have a care not to involve yourself in anything unseemly. Or to stay overlong."

"But … but…," Simon stammered, "surely you're not going to join in their sinful frivolities!?"

She lifted her chin and met his look.

"I will behave myself properly."

"Have some flowers," Roger said.

He shifted his load of greenery, stripped the garland of sweet-scented bluebells from his head, and dropped it onto her hood.

"Come on," Maud said, throwing an impatient look at their departing friends. "If we don't hurry, we're going to be late and miss something."

Anne Marie reached up to adjust the wreath. As Roger set off, Simon turned to Jonathan.

"What if she doesn't? You must forbid it. She'd have to obey."

Maud started after Roger. Still clutching the garland, Anne Marie rushed after her.

"Obedience that is forced," Jonathan said, "is not -."

The rest of his reply was drowned out by Maud calling for their friends to wait.

Anne Marie quickened her pace across the green springing grass, hurrying to catch Roger, eager to be gone.

"Obedience that is forced," Jonathan said, "is not the obedience that pleases God."

"But why would she want to go with them?" Simon said, pulling at his scanty chin beard.

"Our decisions are like candle flames. They cast light on the true desires of our hearts."

"I'd never follow a stinking idol," Dorcas said in a resolute tone, stepping to Simon's side.

"I'm sure you wouldn't, daughter," Jonathan said. "Come, our friends are waiting."

Simon frowned at Anne Marie's dwindling figure then turned on his heel and stalked off toward the green forest. Dorcas hurried after him. Prudence, who had been gathering primroses, ran to catch up with her sister.

Jonathan limped across the rough meadow with Lettice at his side.

"Husband, why did you allow her to go? You know Simon disapproved."

"I'll not have his good qualities wasted on the wrong person."

"What do you mean?"

"Have you noticed that Dorcas favors him?" Jonathan said, glancing down at Lettice. "I really ought to speak to his father about a match. Simon will make an excellent son-in-law, one I can trust not to be misled by false teaching."

He looked back in time to see Anne Marie join the stream of people heading for St. Giles. As it swallowed her, doubts began to niggle.

Had he been right to let her go? What if she fell into sin? In carrying out a father's duty toward Dorcas, was he neglecting his duty to be a spiritual father to this child that God had placed in his care? Or was this uncertainty from the devil? Where did his greater duty lie? He must lay these questions before God.

Hiking her russet skirts above the tangle of winter-dead weeds, Anne Marie followed Maud, Roger, and their friends across the fields toward White Cross Street. As she drew closer, she realized that theirs wasn't the only group heading for St. Giles. A great crowd of noisy, happy Londoners, young and old alike, and many also garbed in green, were converging on the large stone church just outside Cripplegate. Maud, Roger, and their companions joined the parade, laughing and whistling and whirling their leafy branches in the fresh spring air.

Since the citizens of Strasbourg also celebrated May Day, she'd seen similar processions. But she'd never before been part of one. Her family, along with others in their small circle of Protestant friends, had celebrated the day more privately with music, games, and picnicking in the woods.

Anne Marie found herself swallowed up in the boisterous crowd. Roger and Maud were exchanging joking retorts with those around. To her horror she saw Maud also exchange lighthearted kisses with any number of young men. Anne Marie crossed her arms and clamped her lips. Already she was regretting her impulsive decision to accompany them.

She looked back to watch the distant figures of Jonathan's family disappear into the mottled green woods. She could hardly rejoin them now or her effort to rid herself of Simon would likely be undone. It would certainly open herself to his reproach. No! She'd just have to brazen it out and excuse herself as soon as she politely could.

They were nearing Cripplegate and the turn leading to St. Giles when Roger appeared at her elbow.

"Enjoy the festivities," he said. "I'll return later. I need to take this greenery to my parents and fetch my bow and arrows. I've some wagers to win."

"I'll come with you," she said, eagerly grabbing the unexpected reprieve.

Roger gave her an amused look as she fell into step beside him on the hard dirt street.

"Well, well. Picking my company over decorating the maypole. I do believe you're growing fond of me."

"Don't be ridiculous," she said, face heating. "I mean ... delivering greenery and paying my respects to your parents are of more value than decorating idols."

They passed through the arched gateway and started down Wood Street, weaving their way through the foot traffic.

"I suppose," Roger said, "you'd have all maypoles chopped up and burned like they did with the one at St. Andrew Undershaft."

"I wouldn't know."

"It happened under King Edward. Thankfully our current sovereign is more tolerant of the pleasures of life."

"Will your parents be joining us?" she asked, determined to direct the conversation to safer topics.

"It's unlikely. My father prefers walking out with the other master goldsmiths and later celebrating with them at the guild hall. It better suits his dignity. No doubt someday I'll be just like him, exchanging the joys of gadding about the fields for the dignity of the banqueting table."

A group of children dashed past, their joyful cries echoing between the overhanging buildings lining the street.

"And your mother? How does she celebrate the day?"

Roger shrugged.

"She decorates our hall with greenery. Other than that, I wouldn't know. I'm always off with friends."

73

They turned down a narrow alley and soon came out onto Guthran Lane. As they arrived at the Denzil courtyard gate, hinges squeaked. The gate opened. Charles Denzil, in a dark green doublet, strode out.

When he saw them, he jerked up short; his face paled. His cold hazel stare fixed on her.

"Why are you still here? Go back to France where you belong!"

His sharp words stopped her breath. Before her lungs could fill again, he shoved past her and, shoes slapping cobblestone, rushed away up the street.

Roger's brow puckered as he peered at his rapidly disappearing father.

"I don't know what's making him so out of temper recently." He shrugged and turned back to her. "No matter. Come on. Let's take these up to the hall."

Struggling to regain her composure, she followed Roger along the narrow courtyard and into the house. Apart from faint noises coming from the kitchen quarters, the house was silent. Apparently, most of the servants were out enjoying the holiday.

They climbed the main stairs to the hall where she thought they might find Ursula Denzil. The large room, with its bright arras cloths and green padded benches, was empty. Roger laid the birch branches on a nearby bench.

"I'll fetch my bow, and we'll be on our way."

Before she could reply, he was heading up the staircase leading to the second floor. He reappeared moments later, longbow in hand and quiver of arrows hanging from a green-clad shoulder.

"Come along," he said, waving her toward the main stairs, "or we'll miss something."

She hesitated.

"Shouldn't we see if your mother is here and greet her?"

"There's no need. She'll know we've come when she finds the greenery."

She reluctantly followed him out of the house, across the courtyard, and through the squeaking gate. They started back up Wood Street toward Cripplegate.

"Your father seems to dislike me," she said, thinking of the earlier encounter.

Roger glanced down at her.

"Don't take everything so seriously. Especially today with the maypole waiting and wagers to be won."

"It may be that you don't take life seriously enough," she said, annoyed by his flippant attitude.

"I do when the matter warrants it. Why, just last week I lost a wager at bowling that cost me a day's wage. That's serious coin."

She bit back a retort. For all his occasional considerate behavior, Roger was hopelessly irresponsible.

They were nearing Cripplegate. The same morning sun that was brightening the upper portion of the arching gatehouse and its tall flanking towers was casting dark shadows into the street.

"How are you at dancing?" he asked as they entered the shadows.

"We used to dance in our garden in Strasbourg," she said. "My father would play the pipe for us." She swallowed a sudden lump. "I've not danced since...."

"You'll have ample opportunity today," Roger said cheerfully.

"Perhaps another time. Today I prefer to watch."

He shrugged.

"As you choose."

They passed through the gateway and turned left. The round tower and dome of St. Giles could be seen in the distance. Her thoughts returned to the maypole. She could only hope that, by the time they reached the gray stone church, it would be decorated and already set in place.

"I suppose," Roger said, "you've no interest in attending a play with us this evening."

"I must return to Cousin Jonathan's house well before that. He and I are leaving for Wynnfield tomorrow."

"Oh, yes, I'd forgotten. I hope you're not traveling alone. I hear the forests these days are filled with footpads. In fact, just last week I heard...."

Roger was still recounting tales of footpads when they arrived at St. Giles. The church's spacious courtyard was swarming with activity. She was relieved to see that the maypole, draped in colorful ribbons, flowers, and herbs, had already been planted.

"Now where did my friends go?" Roger said, scanning the area. "Ah, there they are." Then, "When we compete at the butts later, you can watch me win."

He gave her a quick nod and strode off toward a group of young men doing battle with staves in a nearby field.

Loneliness enveloped her as she watched him go. Apart from Roger and Maud, she knew no one here, and no one knew her. Would she ever find a place for herself?

She glanced about, searching for Maud. At least she could join whatever she was doing.

She spotted her among the ones strewing branches around the maypole's base. A frown formed. Maud had earlier exchanged lighthearted kisses with this same group. No, joining her would be unwise.

She looked around for some activity that didn't involve the maypole or questionable conduct. A number of men and several women, many wearing various shades of green, were setting up summer bowers at the courtyard edge. A few shelters were already finished. Rough trestle tables waited before them, loaded with savory smelling venison haunches and jugs of fruity ale, and guarded by old grandmothers garbed in a variety of colors. Children happily chasing each other around the courtyard added to the festive atmosphere.

She knew it wouldn't be long now before the Lord and Lady of May were chosen and the dancing would start. Judging from the intemperate behavior she'd witnessed earlier, it wouldn't be the innocent dancing she was accustomed to. When it started, she must be busy elsewhere.

She noticed that several of the older women were carrying greenery and flowers across the church porch and into St. Giles. She'd be safer joining them than she would be spending the day with Maud and Roger. She turned and headed for the porch.

Anne Marie arrived back at the Peterman house in mid-afternoon to the sound of singing. Clearly the family was home again and, from the variety of voices, had guests.

Bracing herself, she stepped from entryway into a hall smelling of fresh greenery and fragrant flowers. She halted by the doorpost and glanced around. Bluebells, primroses, and birch branches now decorated the room's cabinets, window frames, and fireplace mantel.

The Peterman family, several of Jonathan's Bible students, and an assortment of family friends, many wreathed in flowers, were seated on benches or standing about the room, music sheets in hand. Dorcas was at the golden harpsichord. Simon stood at her elbow turning music pages for her.

When they finished the madrigal, Dorcas looked up and saw Anne Marie. She whispered something to Simon. He also looked her way. His expression hardened. He turned back to the music sheets and immediately began shuffling through them as if searching for the next piece.

Jonathan, seated with his back to the entryway, twisted round and saw her. He smiled.

"Anne Marie, come join us."

The next moment she was sharing a padded bench and music sheet with Lettice. Her tension gradually eased.

When the singing ended sometime later, Jonathan's students, along with Lemuel and Simon, departed to enjoy wrestling and foot races before the evening bonfires. Unlike previous occasions, Simon left with no word of farewell for her.

Their remaining guests took their leave soon afterward. While Lettice saw the last one to the door, Jonathan turned to Anne Marie.

"Would you join me in my study?"

As she followed Jonathan across the room, her tension returned.

Once in the study and with the door shut, she turned to look up at him.

"I behaved myself properly," she said, chin high. "I brought no dishonor on you."

"Had I thought you would, I'd not have allowed you to go." His serious expression relaxed. "Now you may tell me how you spent your day."

"Well, first Roger and I delivered greenery to his mother. After that, I helped the older women decorate St. Giles church. Later I joined some of the games and watched Roger win the archery competition. They wanted me to remain for the plays and bonfires, but you'd said I mustn't stay overlong. So, I came back."

Jonathan nodded, his expression thoughtful.

"I fear that your decision to join your cousins has cost you Simon's approval."

Her tension slipped away. A smile formed.

"Dorcas should be pleased."

Jonathan returned her smile.

"I believe that was your intent. Thank you." Then, "Go now and pack your traveling bag. We'll be leaving tomorrow at first light."

CHAPTER 8 – MAY – WYNNFIELD

The following day Anne Marie and Jonathan joined a small party of travelers setting out north for Cambridge. The anticipation she'd had upon docking in London a month ago resurrected as she rode out through Bishopsgate behind Jonathan, her father's lute and her bag of belongings tied securely to the saddle of her hired mount. Somewhere along the way they'd leave their traveling companions to turn east and, after a few more miles, arrive at Wynnfield Manor.

With spring well on its way, the dirt roads they took through the newly greening forests were beginning to fill. Carriers leading strings of loaded sumpter horses, peddlers with two-wheeled carts, sturdy vagabonds, and tinkers were all sharing the rutted thoroughfare with them. Recalling Roger's tales of footpads that preyed on lone travelers, she was glad to be part of a company.

Their party spent the night in a roadside inn. After breakfasting on day-old bread and ale, they continued on their way. A few hours later she and Jonathan bade farewell to their fellow travelers then turned onto a narrower forest track. But for the thud of their horses' hooves and the trill of a robin, quiet reigned. They were nearing their destination. She peered ahead along the sun-dappled trail, eager for her first glimpse of Wynnfield.

The track led them through leafy woods dotted with bluebells, past open fields, and back into more bluebell-scented forest. Coming out of the woods a second time, they jogged down a slope and splashed across a shimmering stream. More fields, some open, some hedged, and a long strip of freshly greening meadow watered by the stream, lay before them under a pale blue sky. A flock of drab white sheep nibbled its way along in an open field. A few thin brown cows accompanied by their calves grazed in the spring meadow.

Looking beyond, Anne Marie spotted the dark shingled roof and flint tower of a church. Clustered around it were the thatched roofs of a small village.

"That's Hensey," Jonathan said. "We're nearly there."

As she followed Jonathan down the track, her gaze remained fixed on the village that had been a part of her mother's life.

Riding into Hensey, she saw a man on a cottage roof beating back the thatch. Beside another cottage a woman in a patched tan kirtle was on her knees weeding a vegetable garden. Apart from a few half-timbered dwellings with shingled roofs, the rest were thatch-roofed wattle-and-daub.

As they drew near the little flint church, her ear caught the sweet, swelling sound of organ music. That such a poor place could boast of an organ and a master organist surprised her. Once past the church, Jonathan turned off the main track and took a trail through more fresh green forest. They left the organ music behind.

Her heart beat faster as they neared their journey's end. She had come a long way for this moment.

Ahead she saw a mass of white-flowered hawthorn bushes and, beyond them, gray shingled roofs and red curling chimney stacks. Rounding the hawthorn bushes, they were briefly enveloped in a pungent scent. She followed Jonathan as he rode through the half-timbered gatehouse and reined up in the base-court. She gazed in wonder at the outbuildings on the right, the corner of a walled enclosure on the left, and the imposing red brick manor house facing her.

Despite her mother's talk of Wynnfield Hall, she'd never imagined anything so grand.

By the time she'd scrambled down from her mount onto hard brown earth and Jonathan had retrieved their traveling bags and her lute, a stable hand and two blue-liveried servants had appeared.

Jonathan handed their horses to the stable hand while the servants took their belongings and started for the house.

She eagerly joined Jonathan to follow them across the base-court, through the entryway, and into the great hall. As the servants set the lute and traveling bags down, she gazed in awe at her surroundings. The morning light streaming through the great hall's high, narrow windows revealed cabinets and benches against paneled walls, trestle tables stacked in a corner, and a massive fireplace near the dais at the far end.

She was gazing up at the brightly painted hammer-beam ceiling when she heard brisk footsteps on the hall's stone flooring and a man's baritone voice.

"Cousin Jonathan, welcome to Wynnfield."

She turned. A tall, brown-haired, long-jawed man in a plain, dark blue doublet was approaching. While Peter Denzil was neither as handsome nor as fashionably garbed as Roger, he had a comfortable air about him which his brother lacked.

"And this must be Anne Marie," he said, stopping in front of her with a smile. "Welcome. I trust that your English is better than my French."

"Her English is excellent," Jonathan said.

"Good. My French is deplorable." He turned back to Jonathan. "I'll have your belongings taken up to your chambers."

His smile and relaxed greeting emboldened her.

"Could I have the one my mother had when she lived here?"

Peter's dark brows dipped over hazel eyes.

"I'm sorry. I don't know which that would be."

"No matter," she said quickly, remembering Roger's sardonic comment about Peter having to play host to her. "I will be pleased with any chamber."

He turned to the two servants.

"Take their belongings up to the passage room and then inform Bro. Lawrence that our guests have arrived. Ask him if he remembers which chamber Margaret Alton had." He turned back to her. "Bro. Lawrence has been our village priest for decades. If anyone knows, he will." His attention returned to Jonathan, "Come to the blue parlor. Did you have a good trip? And how is my mother?"

She trailed Jonathan and Peter through the hall, past the dais, and into a large parlor. As the two men stood talking, she glanced around the room. She noted its pale-yellow plastered walls, green-padded settle by the brick fireplace, red wall cabinet hanging beside the doorway to an adjacent dining parlor, two padded stools at a small oak table holding a chessboard and pieces, and a spiraling wooden staircase in one corner. She could see nothing blue about it.

"Why is it called the blue parlor?" she asked during a lull in the conversation.

Peter glanced at her and then around the room.

"I've never thought of it. That's just what it's always been called. Bro. Lawrence might know."

Feeling awkward, she bit back further questions and left the two men to their conversation. It appeared this Bro. Lawrence was the one she needed to talk with.

As she listened to Jonathan catching Peter up on family news, she wandered over to gaze out the mullioned windows. There, beside the house and enclosed by a high brick wall, was a large pleasance, its crisscross paths forming blocks of shaggy growth. Despite the somewhat unkempt appearance of the place, one nearby plot was bright with buttercups, primroses, and sweet William.

Would summer's arrival produce marigolds, snapdragons, periwinkles, and daisies in other plots?

Behind her, she heard hitching footsteps. She turned as a misshapen little man wearing a dark wool jerkin and black hosen hobbled in from the great hall. His large bald head sat between jutting shoulders while spindly arms and legs hung from his short barrel body.

He threw her a curious glance as he approached Peter and Jonathan, his irregular footsteps whispering on the floor's rush matting.

"I was told Margaret Alton's daughter has come," he said, looking up at Peter.

"Yes." Peter nodded in her direction. "This is Anne Marie duChant. I believe you met my father's cousin, the Right Reverend Jonathan Peterman, on a previous visit. Anne Marie, this is our village priest, Bro. Lawrence Hopwood." Then, "She'd like to have her mother's chamber. Do you know which that was?"

Bro. Lawrence's wrinkled brow knit momentarily.

"It was the front chamber looking out on the base-court."

"I thought he'd know. Come along."

Peter strode over to the staircase and started up to the floor above. She hurried after him. When she arrived at the landing, she reached for her traveling bag, sitting beside Jonathan's. With a smile, Peter took it from her. She picked up her father's lute and trailed him to a door at one end of the passage room.

"I don't know if the bed or dressing table it has now was your mother's," he said, pulling the latch string. He ushered her into the chamber and set the bag down on the four-poster bed. "The Crown may have taken some of the furnishings when they confiscated the manor."

She lay her lute beside the traveling bag and gazed around the room. Her mother had grown up within these pale plastered walls, had warmed herself at this corner fireplace, and had looked out of these two mullioned windows to watch activities in the base-court below. She blinked tears away.

"Just seeing the room itself is enough."

She heard uneven steps in the passage room. Bro. Lawrence came hobbling through the door. Jonathan limped in after him.

"Yes, this is the chamber," Bro. Lawrence said, nodding his large head. "I remember blessing it on your parents' wedding day." He crossed to the bed and peered at one of the carved bed posts. "This is the very bed ... and the one where you were born. See here, the nick in the carving. When your Uncle Edmund was young, he sometimes practiced throwing knives where he shouldn't."

"You officiated at my parents' wedding?" she asked in joyful astonishment.

"Then you must also have christened her," Peter said.

Even as she tensed, she saw Bro. Lawrence look away.

"No, I didn't."

The priest started hobbling toward the door.

She glanced at Jonathan. He, also, was looking sober.

Peter seemed not to notice the sudden tension.

"Come," he said, turning to Jonathan, "we've also prepared the staircase chamber."

With Jonathan's traveling bag transferred to the bedchamber just beyond the stairs, they returned to the blue parlor. She heard sounds in the adjacent dining parlor of a table being set.

"You're welcome to share our nooning," Peter said to Bro. Lawrence. "You might be able to explain to Anne Marie how the blue parlor came to be so named."

At that moment the house steward appeared and announced the meal.

"I think," Bro. Lawrence said, joining her in following Peter and Jonathan toward the dining parlor, "it was because of some blue arras cloths that hung on the walls during your grandmother's day. They disappeared after she was arrested."

She stepped through the dining parlor doorway after Bro. Lawrence. As the others took their seats at the linen-covered table, she glanced around the paneled room with its fireplace, two other doorways, mullioned windows, and sideboard.

"This has always been called the winter parlor," Bro. Lawrence said when she settled on the padded stool beside him at the table. "I don't know why."

Peter, at the table's head, had a prayer for the pottage, boiled pigeons, manchet bread, and new greens set before them.

Conversation resumed as they began filling their wooden trenchers.

During the simple, tasty meal she discovered two things about the misshapen little priest. He loved to eat, although where he managed to put so much in such a compressed body mystified her, and he had a wealth of information about Wynnfield Manor stored in his large head.

The Tudor clock on the fireplace mantel had marked a full hour before the table conversation slowed. The meal over, Bro. Lawrence took his leave. Jonathan excused himself to work on the sermon he'd promised to preach on the morrow.

Anne Marie saw Peter glance toward the windows looking out on the sunny base-court.

"I need to check some hedges," he said to her as a maidservant began clearing the table of dirty trenchers and cups. "Feel free to acquaint yourself with the house."

"May I do a little weeding in the pleasance?" she asked quickly. "I like working in a garden."

Peter's brow lifted in mild surprise.

"Of course." He turned to the maidservant. "Tell the house steward to see she's given whatever she needs." He turned back to her. "Now, if you'll excuse me."

With that final word, he strode off.

84

Anne Marie happily crossed the blue parlor and climbed the stairs to the chamber that had been Mother's and now was hers. Once there, she tried the view. She was in time to see Peter striding across the base-court. She watched until he disappeared through the gatehouse then busied herself with unpacking.

On impulse, she'd stuffed everything possible into her traveling bag before leaving London. She now dumped its contents onto the bed and began hanging her gowns on wall pegs. She placed other clothing items in an empty cedar chest and laid out her toiletries on the small dressing table. Finished, she changed into her old russet kirtle and covered her hair with a matching hood.

She caressed the rough nick in the carved bedpost, thinking of the uncle who'd made it, thinking with nostalgia of the brother who'd borne his name. After taking a final pleasurable look at the room, she set off to find the house steward.

A short while later, gloved and aproned and carrying a small rush mat, she ventured into the pleasance.

In Strasbourg, Mother had set aside a corner of their vegetable garden for flowers and had occasionally mentioned the enjoyable hours she'd spent working among the flowers and herbs in Wynnfield's pleasance. At the time with only their small garden as a frame of reference, she'd wondered how the work could have taken so long. Now, gazing around, she understood.

Humming to herself, she lay the mat beside a particularly weedy plot and dropped to her knees. Gripping the hard handle of the digging tool, she set to work.

As she labored, the spring breeze tickled her cheek, ruffled the lavender she was weeding, and filled the air around her with the sweet scent of flowers. In a nearby willow tree a song thrush started to trill. A bee landed on a blossom, clung for a moment, and then flew off again. For sheer joy she began singing one of the Huguenot psalms she'd learned while living with the Bossuets.

Cries of hungry young birds coming from the willow tree in the corner interrupted her. After the baby birds stilled, she began to sing again as she worked her way along.

The west wall's shadow had been almost nonexistent when she started. It had lengthened considerably by the time she began on her third plot. She was kneeling on the rush mat, digging tool in hand, weeding a bed of herbs and singing a song she'd learned from Father when Peter spoke at her elbow.

"I didn't expect to find you still here."

Shading her eyes with a gloved hand, she looked up at the man standing between herself and the sun.

"I told you I like to garden."

"You certainly must," he said, glancing back at the trail of weed piles that marked her progress. "The cows can use the extra feed. I'll send someone to gather it up."

He looked ready to leave.

"How were the hedges?" she asked quickly, wanting to continue the conversation.

"Good enough to keep the animals where they belong ... and out of where they don't."

She could think of no further question to detain him. This time he was the one with the question.

"Since Bro. Lawrence didn't christen you, who did?"

She stiffened. He had sensed the earlier tension. Laying her digging tool aside, she came to her feet and moved so she wasn't staring into the sun when she looked up at him.

"No one. My father didn't believe in infant baptism."

Peter's hazel eyes widened.

"He didn't?" Then, "Are you saying he was an Anabaptist heretic?"

Indignation surged.

"He was no heretic. He was a kind, humble man who happened to agree with some Anabaptist teachings."

"Perhaps if he'd studied with those more learned...."

"Which ones? Strasbourg was full of learned men. Yet even they couldn't agree. They each held that their understanding of scripture was right and all others wrong. My father believed that we should bear with each other's differences with love and tolerance."

"Is that what you believe?"

"I think it's better than killing each other in the name of Christ."

Peter's brow puckered.

"If you weren't baptized," he said slowly, thoughtfully, "you aren't a member of the Church."

"Of course I am," she said, lifting her chin. "I was baptized when I was old enough to decide for myself."

"But you can't do that."

"Why not? The early Christians did."

After Peter left, Anne Marie resumed weeding with angry vigor as she berated herself for her too-quick tongue. She had frankly told a virtual stranger information she'd carefully hidden from Claude Goujon and the Bossuets.

Her one consolation was that, because Bro. Lawrence and Jonathan already knew, Peter probably would have found out eventually.

She had finished another plot, and the shadows had lengthened still more when a servant appeared with a basket and gathered up the weed piles. With a sense of achievement, she wearily returned to the manor house and climbed the spiral stairs to her chamber. She arrived to find a wash basin and pitcher of water waiting on a stool.

As she pulled off her hood and dropped it on the dressing table, she happened to glance at herself in the bronze mirror. With chagrin, she looked more closely. Stretching nearly from eyebrow to chin was a brown dirt streak. Had it been there when she was talking with Peter?

In a clean tan kirtle and with a scrubbed face, she started along the passage room toward the stairs. On the way, she heard voices and the sound of wood scraping stone. She paused to look down through the lattice work at the great hall below where servants were setting up half a dozen trestle tables. She watched for a moment before continuing on her way.

When she reached the stair bottom, sunlight was slanting in through the windows of an empty blue parlor. The winter parlor was equally empty although the linen-draped dining table was set with trenchers, spoons and cups … but only for three. Evidently Bro. Lawrence wouldn't be joining them.

By the time Jonathan came limping in from the blue parlor a few minutes later, servants had added boiled capons, pease pottage, wheaten bread, and cheese to the table. Shortly after, Peter strode in from the accounts room.

He took his place at the table's head. She and Jonathan settled on either side. At Peter's request Jonathan prayed for the meal.

"How many people do you feed?" she asked Peter as she reached for a piece of boiled capon.

"Around twenty-five manor servants plus seasonal workers ... and any poor folk Bro. Lawrence sends me."

"How very kind to feed the poor."

"It's a manor lord's responsibility," he said, taking a bread piece. Then, studying her, "You've got your father's hair."

"You knew my father?"

"I remember him a bit from my childhood." His brow dipped. "But I wasn't aware he was an Anabaptist."

Jonathan set his cup of ale down and spoke before she could frame a reply.

"He was beginning to amend his position when I left Strasbourg." Then, "I would like to think that the scriptural studies I had with him were partly responsible." He turned to her. "Anyone who diligently reads the scriptures and prays earnestly for good understanding will find the truth."

She was sure that Jonathan's comment was aimed at her. She also re-called telling Peter earlier of the reformers' inability to agree on what the truth was.

She glanced at him. If he was remembering, she prayed he'd say nothing.

"They first have to be taught to read," Peter said. "The poor can't afford a tutor."

By meal's end, the sun was sinking behind the pleasance wall, and the light drifting in through the winter parlor's single west-facing window was beginning to fade. Leaving the servants to clear the table, they moved to the blue parlor. Its two west-facing windows made the room only marginally brighter. Peter lit the wall candles, then he and Jonathan fell to talking of family and village affairs. Wrapped in the faint scent of burning wax, she sat by the windows listening.

Sable night had slipped silently over the pleasance when Jonathan, at Peter's request, read a passage of scripture and had a prayer. Then, lighted candles in hand, they climbed the stairs and retired to their separate chambers.

In nightdress and with copper hair braided, Anne Marie blew out her candle and settled in the bed that had been Mother's. She lay back against the pillow with a sense of well-being as she reflected on the day.

She hadn't expected Peter to have known her father. He was so different from his brother ... steady, responsible. A person would be safe with him.

Sleep caught her before she could carry the thought further.

CHAPTER 9 – WYNNFIELD

Pearly dawn was beginning to outline the windows when Anne Marie awoke Sunday morning to the sound of a door opening. A maidservant entered with a bucket of water and a lighted candle. She set the candle on the mantel beside the enameled clock and departed. By the time Anne Marie had risen, washed, and pulled on her chemise, the maidservant was back with a breakfast of brown bread, cheese, and fresh cow's milk.

Darkness had fled when, wearing her azure gown and with an embroidered coif covering her hair, she went down to the blue parlor. Peter was already there seated by a window, head bent over an open Bible. Even garbed in his Sunday best of tawny velvet jerkin and black trunk hose, he still had the look of a countryman.

He didn't glance up when she entered. Not wishing to disturb him, she bent onto a nearby stool to wait. In the silence she found her gaze drawn to him, watching him as he read.

Only when Jonathan came limping down the stairs to join them did Peter look up. He closed the Bible and came to his feet.

"If you've no objection, we'll walk to St. James the Less. It's not far and the weather's good."

Three abreast, they passed through the gatehouse and rounded the flowering hawthorn bushes to make their way along the forest track in an early morning hush broken only by birdsong and the soft sound of footsteps.

A clanging bell calling worshipers to morning prayers welcomed them to Hensey. After passing the watermill and a handful of cottages, they turned onto the main street to join the village folk converging on St. James the Less.

They were nearing the little flint church when she heard a woman calling Peter's name. She looked across the green. A stocky young woman in a comely rose gown was hurrying toward them, a toddler on her arm. A lanky, tow-headed man in a neat brown jerkin trailed her.

"It's Gwen," Peter said to Jonathan. "She wants to meet Anne Marie."

Curious as to who Gwen might be, she watched them approach across the spring grass.

They arrived, exchanged familiar greetings with Jonathan, and were introduced to her. Unlike most of the other villagers, this Weaver family gave off an air of modest prosperity.

"Gwen is a cousin," Peter said. "Will is our local weaver."

"He'd be more than that," Gwen said, "if he had another weaver and more spinsters." She put her squirming toddler down; he headed for his father.

"I can spin," Anne Marie said.

Gwen cocked her black head.

"Peter said you were coming, but he didn't mention you were a spinster. I don't suppose you brought a dozen more with you."

"Unfortunately, I did not," she said, smiling.

"Well, one is better than none. You should come home with me later."

Anne Marie glanced questioningly up at Peter.

"Don't set her to spinning today, Gwen," he said lightly. "Bro. Lawrence overlooks Sunday field work when rain's threatening, but I doubt he'd be so lenient in this case."

When Anne Marie stepped onto the church porch with Peter and Jonathan, Bro. Lawrence, a white surplice over his dark robe, greeted them at the door. Once inside the unadorned house of worship, they joined Gwen's family on a hard bench at the front of the nave. The rest of the worshipers took their places, some on the remaining benches, others standing at the back or against the lime-washed walls.

Light from the clear glazed windows overlooking the chancel fell across a beautiful golden organ on a table at the front. This must be the one she'd heard earlier as they'd ridden through Hensey.

When Bro. Lawrence seated himself at the organ, a hush spread over the congregation. After the instrument's first rich notes, Bro. Lawrence began singing. The worshipers joined in. Not knowing the psalm, she listened instead to Peter's pleasant baritone.

The hymn ended. Peter stepped to the front and read the lesson from Old and New Testaments. Bro. Lawrence led in the Litany and a village man read the decalogue and Nicene creed. She was relieved that, although communion recipients knelt, it was offered using common loaf bread and not the Catholics' consecrated wafers. Finally, the little priest hobbled up to the pulpit. Although his message was somewhat rambling, the service was more to her liking than the ones in London.

After a closing hymn, Bro. Lawrence announced that Jonathan would preach for the afternoon service. He gave the benediction, and the villagers began heading for the door, taking the faint odors of soiled boots and musty clothing with them.

She crossed the chancel to admire the organ. A few moments later Bro. Lawrence was hovering at her elbow.

"It's a beautiful instrument," she said.

"Your father did excellent work."

"He made this?"

"Not the original organ. But he did extensive repairs on it after some de-spoilers came through the village. They smashed our stained-glass window and broke my organ." He reached out and caressed it. "Your father gave it back to me. He was a good man. But for his Anabaptist leanings, a fine Christian." He peered up at her. "Here in England, we follow the Thirty-nine Articles and the orders of the bishops. Those that comply have nothing to fear."

Was he cautioning her?

He nodded toward his organ. "Do you play?"

"Not nearly as well as you."

"You're welcome to play this one."

"Oh, could I?"

"Come tomorrow after sext."

By the time her conversation with Bro. Lawrence finished, the church had emptied. Only Jonathan remained at the back, waiting to depart with her. As they stepped off the church porch, her gaze swept the green, searching for Peter.

She passed over the children playing leapfrog in the morning sunshine, the young men kicking a pig's bladder about the grass, the women gathered by a huge oak tree in the middle of the green, the older men playing bowls off to one side.

She finally spotted him at the far end of the green by the bridge practicing archery with Will and several other men. As he lifted his bow to take aim, Jonathan spoke.

"I believe Gwen has seen us."

She reluctantly shifted her attention to the women by the tree. Jonathan was right. Gwen was approaching at a brisk pace, Little Rob riding her arm. She crossed the street with Jonathan and met Gwen at the edge of the green.

"Come meet Widow Miller," Gwen said to her, "and some of the other village women." Gwen turned to Jonathan. "If you've nothing against a game of bowls on a Sunday, I'm sure the men would welcome you."

"Thank you, but I must finish my afternoon message."

As Jonathan departed, limping off toward Wynnfield Hall, Anne Marie glanced again at the archery practice.

If only she could be there watching.

Gwen must have noticed, for she, too, looked toward the archers.

"Not all manor owners join in village activities," she said as they started across the uneven ground toward the huge oak. "Peter does and the villagers like it." Her tone sharpened. "At least he and Will have the sense to forgo the wrestling and football. It'd be no help to anyone if they came home with cracked heads or broken arms."

Having passed a handful of younger women starting a game of quoits, they reached the oak where three old grandmothers were sharing a rickety bench in the shade pool. Gwen set Little Rob down. He immediately toddled off toward the other children. She drew Anne Marie over to an old woman in a drab gray gown.

"Widow Miller, this is Anne Marie duChant, Jane Alton's granddaughter."

Ancient eyes in a wrinkled face peered up at her. Widow Miller broke into a toothless smile.

"Ye was hardly bigger than a new lamb when last I saw ye. Now ye's a woman grown. Tis time ye came home."

Anne Marie's vision blurred.

While Gwen joined the quoits game, Anne Marie perched on a second bench to talk with Widow Miller. Their conversation eventually began to lag, and Widow Miller started speculating on this year's honey output with her bench mates.

Anne Marie's thoughts returned to the widow's tales about her grandmother and her parents. They filled her with the same warm sense of connection that Bro. Lawrence's stories had.

When one of the quoits players dropped out to nurse her hungry infant, Gwen called Anne Marie to take her place. Tucking the tales safely away in her memory, she joined the younger women on the green.

The morning sun was well up the cloudless blue sky when the quoits game ended. The women began to scatter, drifting off in twos and threes toward the cottages that ringed the green. Some, like Gwen, headed for the huge oak to collect a small child from the older women watching over them.

Anne Marie looked across at the archery practice. The men had exchanged bows for broadswords, and Peter and Will were approaching.

They arrived as Gwen returned with Little Rob. Peter glanced about.

"Where's Cousin Jonathan?"

"At the manor house working on his sermon," Gwen said.

"We'd best be returning also." Peter turned to Anne Marie. "If you're ready -"

"I'm keeping her," Gwen said, "at least till the afternoon service. She can share our nooning and tell me about French cloth production."

Swallowing disappointment that she wouldn't be walking back with Peter, Anne Marie accompanied Gwen and Will home. The Weaver cottage, across from St. James the Less, was one of the village's few half-timber dwellings and boasted glazed windows in all three of its ground floor rooms.

Once there, seated on a padded stool in a main room which was both hall and dining parlor, she discovered that Gwen was serious in wanting to hear about European cloth production. She began asking questions even as she started for the kitchen to check on meal preparation. Following a short exchange with the young scullery maid, Gwen returned, bringing the odors of simmering pottage and boiled rabbit with her. Her questions continued.

Will, on the settle by the staircase, listened as he played with his young son. Anne Marie hadn't realized how much information about the cloth market she'd absorbed from the Bossuets until Gwen started questioning her.

"Monsieur Bossuet trades cloth through a merchant in London," she said. "The London merchant buys cloth produced in Rouen from Monsieur Bossuet and sells English cloth to him."

Gwen's black eyes brightened.

"Where does the London merchant get the cloth he sells?"

"I don't know. I could try to find out when I return to London."

"Would you? Will is an excellent weaver, but the Hensford guild refused to accept him as a master. They said Hensford already had enough." She sniffed. "They wanted him to remain a journeyman so they could pocket the profits."

Gwen fetched wooden trenchers and spoons from the corner cabinet.

"Renting this cottage from Peter allows Will to be his own master," she said as she began to set the table. "Peter's glad to have us since we provide another source of income for the village women." She added mugs and a jug of cider. "But the guild won't allow Will to sell his cloth in Hensford so we have to find other markets."

"We're not doing badly," Will said. "Several families in the area order cloth from us, and we sell at Stourbridge fair."

"But we'd do even better if we had more custom," Gwen said, planting hands on hips and staring across the table at her husband. "Why not sell to London merchants if we can?"

"We can't sell cloth we don't have. And before we hire more spinsters and another weaver to produce more cloth to fill more orders, we need money to buy the wool and pay the additional workers," Will said patiently.

"I know," Gwen said with a frown.

Evidently this was a well-worn argument. The seed of a thought stirred in Anne Marie's mind; she voiced a more full-grown one.

"While I'm here, I would be pleased to spin for you."

At meal's end Anne Marie helped Gwen and the scullery maid clear the table and wash the pots and tableware. The church bell began tolling as they finished. Leaving a sleepy Little Rob with the scullery maid, she walked across to St. James the Less with Will and Gwen for the afternoon service.

This time Jonathan was the one standing at the door to welcome attenders.

She entered and glanced around, searching for Peter. He was by the vestry talking with one of the village men. The tolling bell quieted. People began to find their places. Jonathan limped up to the front and took a seat beside Bro. Lawrence. She joined Will and Gwen on their bench. Warmth filled her as Peter settled next to her.

After the singing and reading of the lessons, Jonathan stepped to the pulpit. Always before, his messages had held her full attention. With Peter now at her side, she found herself distracted.

The service ended. She bade Widow Miller farewell, and Gwen and Will took their leave. Jonathan was in conversation with several of the village men by the pulpit when she rejoined Peter.

He glanced over at Jonathan then turned back to her.

"He'll likely be occupied for some time," he said. "If you're ready, we can return to the manor house."

In another minute she was happily walking at Peter's elbow on their way out of Hensey.

"Well, now you've met Gwen," he said as they passed the watermill.

"I like her," she said. "She was so full of questions about the French cloth trade."

They left the village, their footsteps making little sound as they ambled along a forest track dappled with afternoon sunlight and filled with the fresh scents of spring.

"I kept thinking she couldn't have more. Then she'd ask another."

"I'm not surprised," he said. "Gwen seems to love cloth production as much as her mother loves cows. By the way, they're joining us for the evening meal. Also Bro. Lawrence."

"He said I could play his organ." She cocked her head to look up at Peter. "Did you know that my father repaired it? Widow Miller also remembered that he'd mended the organ. She knew my grandmother ... and my parents. She even told me a few stories about them. Later, some of the women invited me to join their quoits game." She glanced up at Peter again. "They were all so kind and welcoming." Just like you.

She was recounting her conversation with Widow Miller when they rounded the hawthorn hedge with its pungent odor. As they neared the gatehouse, they met one of the outdoor servants. Peter stopped him.

"Have my horse saddled."

The man hurried off to the stable.

"I must call on some neighbors," Peter said. "I'll return before the evening meal. In the meantime, should you need anything, ask the steward. Oh, and tell him and Cook that we're having guests for the meal."

She tried to gather her thoughts at this unexpected turn of events.

"What should I instruct Cook to prepare?"

"Whatever he chooses ... or you could suggest something." He looked past her toward the stables. "Now, if you'll excuse me...."

He turned on his heel and strode off to his waiting mount.

Fighting disappointment, she remained by the gatehouse to watch until he swung into the saddle and trotted out of sight around the hawthorn hedge.

Uncertain what else to do, Anne Marie informed the steward and discussed the menu with Cook. That done, she climbed the stairs to her bedchamber and settled by a window to watch for Peter.

Jonathan arrived first, limping in through the gatehouse. She welcomed him, left him in his bedchamber to rest, and returned to her stool by the window. Peter could appear any time.

The shadows in the base-court had lengthened a hand's breadth when she saw him come striding through the gatehouse. She sprang up, took a critical look in her bronze mirror, then rushed out the door. As she crossed the

97

passage room, she glanced down at the great hall where servants were setting up trestle tables. Peter stepped from the entryway into the hall.

She hurried down the blue parlor stairs, ready to welcome him with a report on the evening meal preparations. When he came in from the great hall, he returned her greeting in an abstracted manner then headed for the stairs before she could say more.

She started to follow but halted. He'd probably prefer she give her attention to ensuring that everything was ready when Bro. Lawrence and the Weavers arrived.

"And so, our great God, we thank thee for this bodily nourishment just as we give thanks for thy word that nourishes our souls."

Jonathan concluded his prayer for the meal with a firm "Amen".

Anne Marie looked up from her place at the foot of the table. Bro. Lawrence, on a cushion beside Jonathan, was reaching for the bread. Will and Gwen, seated across from them, were surveying the several dishes laid out between herself and Peter, at the table's head.

She glanced around the winter parlor, checking the corners for shadows. There were none. With sunset still two hours away, it would likely be some time before candles were needed.

She relaxed, spooned pottage onto her wooden trencher, and added bread and leeks. With food now on her plate, she turned her attention to the table conversation.

"I was pleased at the response to my sermon," Jonathan said as he took a piece of boiled hen. "People in the countryside, especially in small places like Hensey, often cling to Catholic traditions."

Her gaze shifted to Peter, smiling as he helped himself to the fish and roasted onions. Did that mean he was satisfied with her choice of menu?

"You have Mistress Alton to thank," Bro. Lawrence said. He scooped up pottage with a bread piece and ate it. "When I was first given the living, I was instructed to set up a village school. She wanted everyone able to read the Bible for themselves. Also, the Lollards were strong in this area."

Jonathan turned to Will.

"Wasn't your grandfather a Lollard?"

Will swallowed the bite of hen he was chewing.

"Yes, he was. The Catholics burned him as a heretic. But that was long before good Queen Bess." He reached for the cheese. "Now it's the turn of the Catholics to live in fear."

"Better them than us," Gwen said as she took some leeks.

Jonathan nodded.

"Were they to have their way," he said, "we'd see a Catholic queen on the throne and persecutions of Protestants a daily occurrence."

"They'd have me conduct my services their way," Bro. Lawrence muttered.

Peter shook his head. His smile was gone.

"I doubt our Catholic neighbors want to overthrow the Queen."

"But they follow the Pope," Jonathan said. "He's excommunicated her and called on all Catholics to rise up against her. Of course they want her removed in favor of her cousin Mary."

"How can we be so sure of that? They're also Englishmen."

"Englishmen who put the authority of the Pope ahead of Scripture. Whether we like it or not, that makes them enemies of England."

Anne Marie saw Peter's jaw muscles twitch.

"Scripture teaches that we should love our enemies," she said.

Gwen laughed.

"That's it, Peter. You're loving your enemies."

Peter threw Gwen a dark look. Jonathan glanced around the table, his expression unusually sober.

"London rumor has it that young English Catholics are training for the priesthood on the Continent so they can return and lead England back into superstitious worship. We must prevent that at all costs. God commanded the Israelites to wipe out the idol-worshiping nations. We're facing a similar battle. If we lose, we'll see a persecution more severe than any we've seen before."

Silence fell over the table. Anne Marie broke it.

"But isn't dying for our faith better than killing for it?"

Jonathan's expression grew stern.

"There are times when the sword is the only option."

"If a man came at me with a sword," Peter said, "I'd kill him if need be. But we might be better able to live as neighbors if we allowed a little freedom of opinion."

"Not when the opinion supports overthrowing our Queen," Jonathan said.

They managed to finish the meal without further disagreement. While the servants began clearing the table, they moved to the blue parlor. Jonathan had her fetch her lute, and they ended the evening with song. Twilight had given way to moonlight before Will, Gwen, and Bro. Lawrence took their leave.

Lighted candles held darkness at bay in the blue parlor while Jonathan, again at Peter's request, read a scripture and led in prayers. Devotions over, they collected tapers and retired to their chambers.

As Anne Marie slipped on her nightdress, her thoughts returned to the disagreement over the meal. Apparently, Peter was more tolerant of religious differences than Cousin Jonathan. She donned her nightcap and settled into bed with a drowsy sigh of contentment.

Had she finally found a place to belong, a place where she could be herself?

On Monday, Anne Marie watched from the gatehouse as Jonathan rode off for Cambridge to visit his son Thomas. Once he disappeared around the hawthorn bushes, she skimmed back across the base-court to the house. She had four days till he returned and they'd leave for London. Already the list of things she wanted to do before then was growing long. She dared not waste a minute.

Soon she was on her knees in the pleasance weeding another patch and reviewing her list. After finishing here, she would gather flowers to decorate the table where she and Peter would be sharing meals. She must ask the steward if he could find an unused spinning wheel since Gwen still had wool from the previous year's shearing. She also wanted to play Bro. Lawrence's organ. But whatever other activities filled her days, she was determined to have every meal possible with Peter.

Happy at the thought of the days ahead, she began to sing.

Fields to be plowed and fodder needs dominated the noon meal conversation with Peter. After the meal, he rode off to check the drainage ditches. She walked to Hensey and found Bro. Lawrence in his cottage hard by St. James the Less. He accompanied her to the church and even pumped the bellows while she played. Her father's own hands had helped craft this instrument. The knowledge gave her the same sense of a connection to her parents that weeding in the pleasance and discussing manor affairs at dinner had given her. Here at Wynnfield she felt that, should she turn quickly enough, she might even catch a glimpse of them. With the anniversaries of their deaths approaching, it was a comfort.

When Bro. Lawrence began to flag, she thanked him and took her leave. Before departing the village, she stopped at the Weaver cottage to ask for wool and carding tools.

"You're serious about this," Gwen said as she waved her in. The steady thud of a weaver's beam could be heard in the adjoining room.

Anne Marie nodded. Even had she wanted to, how could she explain that, in doing what her mother must have done here, she was regaining something lost? Before tears could come, she changed the subject.

"Bro. Lawrence's service was much simpler than the ones in London."

"If you mean it doesn't have all that Catholic ritual," Gwen said, "it suits Hensey."

She started up the stairs. Anne Marie followed.

"We've enough villagers," Gwen said, "who still remember that two of their own were sent to the stake by Queen Mary. Widow Miller's husband was one. And, of course, your grandmother." She mounted the final step and turned toward the storeroom, her steps ringing hollow on the board floor. "Will would like to see better preaching though. Bro. Lawrence was monastery trained. That's not saying much. He does his best, but he's getting old. One of these days he won't be able to continue."

She trailed Gwen into a room piled with cloth bales. A large half-full sack of wool rested beside the door.

"Who will take his place?"

"That will be up to the bishop and Peter," Gwen said as she began transferring wool to a smaller sack. "They share the advowson. Will would like his brother to have the living. He's currently studying at Cambridge. But the living pays so little. Bro. Lawrence manages because Peter provides his food, and some of the village families pay him what they can to teach their children to read." Gwen added carding tools to the sack. "Hensey previously had a school. When my father was turned out as bailiff, the new one saw no need to use manor funds to help pay a schoolmaster. The villagers hadn't enough themselves, so he left."

Gwen tied the sack shut and handed it to her. "There you are."

She followed Gwen back down the stairs. Gwen was still talking.

"Peter supplies the villagers with what employment he can. It isn't enough. If Will could expand his business, Hensey would have more money. Then we could provide a decent living for both a teacher and a preacher."

When Anne Marie returned to Wynnfield with the wool, she found a spinning wheel waiting by the blue parlor windows. She was checking it when Peter strode in.

"First weeding," he said. "Now spinning. Tomorrow I'll probably find you making cheeses in the dairy house."

She laughed. "You just might."

"Have a care. If you become too useful, I might not let you return to London."

His unexpected words filled her with warmth. If the glow showed on her face, he didn't notice. He was already on his way to the winter parlor and the accounts room beyond.

"How were the ditches?" she asked Peter as they began their evening meal. She again had selected some of the dishes that sat before them.

Once Peter had reported on the drainage ditches, she voiced the question she'd been holding since her arrival.

"What kind of man was Uncle Richard? Roger showed me where he died. But he didn't remember him well. He said you were his godson; I should ask you."

Peter fingered his long jaw for a moment, his expression abstracted.

"He had candles in his eyes. At least that's how it seemed to me as a child. And my father had dead eyes." He gave a short, embarrassed laugh. "Not very complimentary of my father."

But true.

Peter dipped a bite of goose into sauce and ate it before continuing.

"Uncle Richard taught me my catechism and took me for strolls around Moorfields of a Saturday. He usually came to Wynnfield once or twice a year to see your grandmother. I still have memories of him sitting in the orchard carving molds. I always insisted on coming with him. And he'd bring me. I loved it here."

"Then you must remember my grandmother."

Peter's brow dipped.

"She was tall … and gray-haired … and kind. I was six when she died, and the Crown confiscated Wynnfield. I remember because, the following spring, Grandfather and Uncle Richard rode up to buy the manor. They wouldn't let me come. I was furious. Then Father told me Grandfather was buying it for me as a seventh birthday gift.

"When I came in the summer with Uncle Richard, I remember bragging to Gwen's father – he was bailiff – that now he worked for me." Peter's voice tightened. "Two years later, the Church sent Uncle Richard to the stake."

After a long moment he continued in a more matter-of-fact tone.

"Of course, with the Church condemning him of heresy, the Crown confiscated his half of the goldsmith shop. Father was furious with him for all the trouble he'd caused us. He thought him a fool to have refused the Queen's order."

She scooped up pottage with a bread scrap.

"Do you think he was a fool?"

Peter shrugged. "I don't know. Father said he told the Queen to her face that he wouldn't craft an idol."

She stiffened.

"Would you have had him craft it?"

"Of course not. Still, perhaps if he'd answered more carefully…." He tapered off, lost in his thoughts. After a moment he shook his head. "Uncle

Richard must have felt it was the right thing to do. If that makes him a fool, he died a brave one."

He took a bite of cheese.

"Later Father changed his mind," he said. "Now he's proud to have a martyr in the family. I was just glad to leave it all behind. My mother got me a place in Sir George's household the following year so I could learn how to run a manor. Roger can have the London house and goldsmith shop. I've never wanted anything other than Wynnfield."

"I'm so glad you have it."

Peter gave her a brief smile.

"It's been years since I've thought on some of this. Your being here is stirring up so much from the past."

Wednesday afternoon Anne Marie walked to Hensey to play the organ again. Gwen spotted her as she was starting back to Wynnfield and invited her in.

"If you were going to be here longer," Gwen said, "Sir George would probably like to meet you. He's a relative of yours."

"Another relative? I never knew I had so many."

"Having a lot of relatives can be a problem. They all have expectations."

"That's better than being alone."

"Well, if it matters, I think you should stay here in Hensey. Talk to Peter about it. We could always use another spinster."

After Anne Marie, seated on Peter's right, had heard about his day over their evening meal, she broached the subject uppermost in her mind.

"I saw Gwen today." She dipped bread into onion pottage. "She said I should meet Sir George."

"That's a good idea if you were going to be here longer."

"She also said I should stay here and spin for Will," she added casually.

Peter smiled and took a bite of stewed lamb. "She would."

She looked directly at him.

"She said I should talk to you about it."

"About what?"

"About staying longer." She hesitated momentarily. "Could I?"

He peered at her. "You're serious." Then, "Isn't Cousin Jonathan expecting you to return to London with him?"

"If he gave his approval...."

With pent breath she watched Peter rub his long jaw as he studied her.

"What of your Anabaptist ideas?"

"What of them?"

"If you stayed, you'd be under my care. I wouldn't want them to create problems."

"I see no reason why they should."

"In that case," he said slowly, "provided Cousin Jonathan approves, I suppose you can stay."

The following afternoon Anne Marie was working at the spinning wheel in the blue parlor when a house servant appeared and informed her that Jonathan had returned. She left off spinning to welcome him and see him settled in the staircase chamber. That evening he made a third person at the dining table.

As they began the meal, she left the two men to their conversation while she considered how best to present her request.

"How is Thomas?" Peter asked as he spooned bacon-flavored pottage onto his trencher.

"He's doing well. He should start on his master's degree in the fall."

"Did you see Will's brother, Ned?"

"Yes, I did." Jonathan took a sip of ale. "He has the same concern as Thomas – how to find a living after he has his degrees. The Church has never provided priests with a decent living in small places like Hensey. Now that it's been stripped of its wealth, even those in London struggle to survive. If it weren't for the financial support I receive from laymen...."

The conversation gradually turned to more immediate concerns.

"If we're to reach London Saturday morning," Jonathan said, looking across the table at her, "we should leave soon after we break our fast tomorrow."

She glanced at Peter then faced Jonathan again.

"With your permission, I thought to remain here for a while longer. Peter doesn't mind."

"Gwen has been wanting more spinsters," Peter said. "Now she's got one, she's determined to keep her, at least for the present."

Jonathan seemed to hesitate.

"I doubt Dorcas would mind," she said.

Jonathan's expression grew thoughtful.

"Yes, there is that." Then, "You have my permission."

Friday morning Anne Marie bade Jonathan farewell at the gatehouse and watched him ride off, taking the horse she'd arrived on with him. This time, he wouldn't be coming back in a matter of days.

After he disappeared behind the white-flowered hawthorn bushes, she walked back through the gatehouse. She stopped in the base-court to admire the red brick manor house. She had finally found a place for herself. More importantly, she'd at last found a man to love.

CHAPTER 10 – MAY to JUNE – WYNNFIELD

Sitting in St. James the Less for the second Sunday-afternoon service since Jonathan's departure, Anne Marie felt as if her every fiber was being drawn toward the man at her side. She had but to move her arm slightly for the edge of her azure sleeve to touch Peter's tawny velvet jerkin. Although only a portion of his face was visible from her eye corner, she could easily see his long-fingered hands resting on his black trunk hose.

They were brown and calloused, and work stains marked the ends of his nails. All in all, they were beautiful hands. What would they feel like wrapped around hers?

She was only aware that Bro. Lawrence had ended his short message when worshipers began singing the closing hymn. Service over, talk erupted across the nave. People began shuffling toward the door. Will and Gwen, seated on her other side, joined the departing worshipers. She trailed them out of St. James with Peter.

They all stepped off the church's stone porch into the thin May sunshine and paused beside the path for a final few words before going their different ways.

Peter looked down at Anne Marie.

"I should return by evening mealtime."

With that parting comment, he strode off across the grass toward his horse, tied in the shade of a nearby beech. He swung into the saddle and, hooves thumping dirt, rode away down the street past Bro. Lawrence's cottage.

"Where is Peter off to?" Gwen asked as they watched him trotting west out of Hensey.

"He has some business matter to attend to," Anne Marie said.

Gwen's black brows bunched in a frown.

"Any matter taking him in that direction has to do with the Coxes."

"Who are the Coxes? More relatives?"

"Pray God, no. They're our nearest Catholic neighbors. Peter goes to see their daughter, Catherine. He's got no sense when it comes to women."

Anne Marie stared at Peter's dwindling figure as shock and jealousy engulfed her. Just when she was beginning to feel she'd at last found a place for herself, the linchpin of that feeling was riding off to court another woman. And a Catholic at that!

"He isn't considering becoming a Catholic, is he?" she said, horrified.

Gwen snorted.

"And lose Wynnfield? I suspect he thinks he can turn Catherine into an Anglican. The more fool he. From what my mother told me about the Coxes, Peter may as well try converting the bishop of Rome."

Peter hummed to himself as he trotted through the forest of oak, beech, and silver birch, each its own shade of green, toward the turnoff to Cox Hall.

The Coxes customarily spent most of the weekend in Hensford, staying in the house which Master Cox had inherited from his father. Some weeks they stayed till Monday; other weeks they returned sometime on Sunday. According to the short message he'd received from Catherine the previous day, this time they were returning home after morning services. They would be available to callers in the afternoon.

He turned from the main track onto a narrower one running out of the forest, through a green meadow, and up a tree-speckled slope to a red brick manor house. Once across the meadow, he took the slope at a thudding gallop. He reined up by an oak tree near the courtyard, dismounted, and tied his horse to a low branch.

As he started across the base-court, he caught a glimpse of Catherine peering out one of the great-hall's mullioned windows. Was she watching for him?

When he reached the porch, the house door opened, and she stepped out bringing a scent of roses. Her full figure was garbed in a yellow satin gown, her expression somber.

"I shouldn't have suggested you come," she said. "It's not a good day."

"What's happened?"

"This morning we learned that the Queen appointed a new Justice of the Peace. It should have been Father. It would have been except we're Catholic."

"You don't know that. The Queen had any number of men to choose from."

Catherine's blue eyes flashed fire.

"You mean Father was passed over because he didn't meet the standard?"

"That's not what I meant."

"That's what you said."

"Look," he said, pleasant mood evaporating, "I'm sorry your father didn't get the position. Had he, I'm sure he'd have done a proper job."

"It's not fair."

He held his tongue. He had no wish to spend the whole afternoon arguing.

"Well," she said in a grudging tone, "since you're here, you may as well come in."

With a swish of satin skirts, she turned and reentered the house.

He followed her across the entryway, through the screen, and along the great hall toward the new wing, his boot heels tapping the stone floor. On the way to the Coxes' private parlor, they passed the family chapel. Usually when he visited, the chapel door was shut. This time it was open, and he caught the odor of scented candles.

Glancing in, he saw Catherine's black-gowned mother, rosary in hand, kneeling before a candlelit image of the Virgin Mary. She was counting her beads.

A frown formed.

They entered the parlor, richly furnished with red padded benches, oak cabinets, cushioned settles by the fireplace, and colorful arras cloth hanging on one paneled wall. Peter glanced to his left. Catherine's father was feeding bits of raw meat to his peregrine falcon, sitting on its perch in the near corner.

"Good day, Master Cox."

Normally his greeting would have brought forth a polite, if indifferent, welcome. This time, Catherine's father turned a hard, unsmiling face to him, gave him a short nod, and returned to his falcon.

Catherine was right. This wasn't a good day.

The next moment Catherine caught his hand. Pulling him along, she danced across the room. Having learned the rudiments of courtly dancing at Sir George's, he followed as best he could.

"You should have come with us to Hensford yesterday" she said. "It's so much more lively there than here. You could have danced the galliard with me. As it was, I had to spend my whole evening dancing with other men. Of course, they didn't mind. Not even the Protestant ones."

She dropped his hand and swept over to one of the mullioned windows looking out on their herb garden. If she was trying to stir him to jealousy, she was succeeding. He joined her at the window. Had her father not been present, he would have reached for her soft hand.

"If the Puritans get control," she said, "dancing and every other enjoyment will be banned. We'll be left to die of boredom."

"That's not likely to happen."

"It may in Hensford. Talk has it that some of the guilds want to get themselves a Calvinist preacher to go around preaching in all the churches." Her eyes narrowed. "They're going to teach the correct doctrine to us misguided Catholics."

"What arrogance," Master Cox said, breaking into their conversation, "to think that God has revealed the truth directly to them." He strode toward them, feet crunching the rush matting, brown eyes blazing. "Just look at the result. As many interpretations as you have men, and all fighting over which is correct." He halted an arm's length away, his blazing eyes level with Peter's. "They're as willing to kill those who disagree with them as you Anglicans say we are."

Peter searched desperately for a harmless response.

"You sound like Anne Marie."

"Anne Marie?" Catherine said. "Who's she?"

"A distant relative from France," Peter said, glad for the diversion. "She's currently staying at Wynnfield and spinning for Will."

Catherine threw a startled look at her father then turned back to him.

"I didn't know you had relatives on the Continent."

110

"She's Margaret Alton's daughter. Her parents lived in Strasbourg from her infanthood. They died of the pestilence last year."

"Margaret's daughter?" Master Cox's tone was ripe with scorn. "You mean that little Frenchman's daughter. I told Margaret she should never have wed that penniless foreigner."

"What's she like?" Catherine asked.

"I don't know," Peter said, distracted by her father's peculiar response. He pulled his thoughts back to her question. "I mean, she's small, with hair like burnished copper. She loves to garden. She's always busy at something. She plays the lute and sings … and she thinks a lot. She and Gwen seem to get along well."

"I wonder how she feels seeing some of what her grandmother lost." Catherine sounded more pleased than sympathetic. "To be reduced to having to spin for a living. She's welcome to come see Cox Hall if she wishes."

Anne Marie was watching the base-court from her bedchamber window when she saw Peter come trudging through the gatehouse. She grabbed up her Bible and hurried down the stairs to the blue parlor. Settling on a green-padded bench beside a window, she made a pretense of reading.

When she heard him walk in from the great hall, she looked up. His expression was glum.

"You're back early," she said, feigning cheerfulness. She closed her Bible. "Did your business go well?"

"It could have gone better."

Her spirits lifted slightly.

"Bro. Lawrence would likely say that's the result of doing business on the Sabbath."

Peter's long jaw twitched.

"It wasn't actually business," he said, bending onto a stool by the chess table. "I called on the Coxes. They're our near neighbors. They bought your grandmother's second manor. Master Cox was in a foul mood. The Queen has just appointed a new Justice of the Peace. Since they're Catholic, of course it wasn't him."

"Did he expect it would be?"

"No. But that didn't help his temper. He's never been an easy man to deal with."

"Then why go there?"

Discomfort flitted across his face. He looked away and began toying with the chess pieces.

"I get along better with others in the family. At least most of the time I do."

"But not this time?"

"I've known them from when Master Cox's son, Cyril, and I were part of Sir George's household," he said, rolling a king between fingers and thumb. "Cyril wasn't there long. He got into too many fights, even lost a piece of his ear in one. He disliked being part of a Protestant household."

"You were visiting Cyril?"

"No. He died on a visit to France a few years ago. But he has a sister … and of course his parents," he added with haste.

Her grip tightened on her Bible. She suddenly wanted to hear no more of the Coxes.

"Gwen said Sir George is a relative. Did you enjoy being in his household?"

Peter visibly relaxed. He returned the king to the chess board.

"Yes, I did."

Anne Marie met Catherine Cox at the very end of May. She was spinning wool in the blue parlor when a young maidservant appeared.

"Mistress Anne," she said, using the shortened form the house staff had taken to calling her, "you've a visitor. It's Mistress Catherine Cox."

The thread in her hand snapped.

Before she could find her voice, a full-bosomed young woman in a scarlet gown and elaborately embroidered hood sailed into the room. The maidservant slipped out.

Anne Marie stood and crossed to greet her unexpected guest, acutely aware that she was wearing her old russet kirtle, and the hood covering her hair lacked any kind of decoration.

"So, you're Peter's poor little French cousin," Catherine said, eyes sharp as she looked Anne Marie up and down.

Anne Marie stiffened. She lifted her chin defiantly.

"Welcome to Wynnfield, Mistress Cox," she said, determined to remain in control. "Would you care for some refreshment?"

Rather than answering, Catherine wandered over to the spinning wheel. She appeared to be examining Anne Marie's work.

"Your thread's broken." She turned to face Anne Marie again. "Peter said that you're helping Master Weaver in his business. Are you planning to stay indefinitely?"

"I might."

"Peter also said that you're living here at Wynnfield. He's always wanted to help those less fortunate. Of course, when he marries, should you still be here, you'll move to Hensey."

"That will be up to Peter."

"More likely it will be up to his wife."

"I doubt a Protestant wife would object to my presence."

Catherine's eyes narrowed.

"He might wed a Catholic."

"Peter would never do that."

"Who knows what a man in love will do. Well," Catherine said as she glanced toward the blue-parlor windows, "the shadows are getting long. I must be on my way. I merely wished to meet you and see if you fit Peter's description."

She fought the urge to ask how Peter had described her.

"Good day, Mistress Cox." She drew herself up as tall as possible. "I'll tell Peter you called. Perhaps when next you come, we can welcome you together."

Once Catherine was gone, Anne Marie returned to the spinning wheel. She stood glaring at the broken thread as wave upon wave of anger tore through her. It was useless to continue spinning at the moment. She was too furious. Better to vent her emotions on the weeds.

After half an hour's strenuous work in the pleasance, she felt calmer. Peter would also soon be returning for the evening meal. She carried her pile of weeds to the cow shed then returned to the house to remove any dirt stains and change her gown. Remembering how Catherine was garbed, she donned her azure gown and embroidered coif.

She was back at the spinning wheel when Peter walked into the blue parlor. She tensed at sight of him. Her afternoon's anger flooded back. Rather than risk another broken thread, she let the wheel slow to a stop.

His gaze swept over her.

"You're rather grandly made up," he said. "Are we expecting guests?"

"We've already had our visitor," she said, leaving the wheel. "Catherine Cox stopped by earlier."

"Catherine? Here?" Face lighting, he glanced around as if expecting her to suddenly appear. "Did you invite her to stay?"

His expression smote her heart. Why couldn't he look at her like that?

"She said she'd only stopped by to see if I fit your description." Anger roiled. "She thinks you'd wed a Catholic. Is she right?"

Peter's bright look disappeared, darkening into a frown.

"You're beginning to sound like Gwen and her mother. As I told them, who I wed is my business."

"But she's a Catholic."

"It's still my business. If you're so concerned about it, pray that she'll convert. Then I won't have the dilemma."

As Anne Marie knelt beside her bed that night, she asked God's forgiveness for her earlier angry outburst and her jealousy of Catherine Cox. She heard Peter's charge again, a charge her conscience demanded she accept even as her heart cried out against it. Heart and conscience reached an uneasy compromise. She would pray for Catherine's salvation. But she would pray even more fervently that Peter would not wed her.

June heralded in days of sunshine, yellow buttercups and daisies thick in green meadows, and bees busy in the pleasance. Except for Catherine Cox's existence, it would have been an idyllic month. After their one sharp exchange over Catherine, she made no further mention of the Coxes to Peter. On the days she suspected that he'd ridden over to call on them, she determinedly talked of other things.

To her relief, June was so filled with work for both manor lord and laborer, Peter had little time to visit neighbors. His flocks, nearly four hundred strong, were herded to streams to have their wool washed in preparation for shearing.

The day the washing began in the stream that flowed past the village, she left her spinning to walk down and watch. Peter was there overseeing the work and discussing with Will how much cloth the various types of wool would produce.

A week later the shearers arrived and set to work. Each day's sheared fleeces were carted to the wool house where she helped Gwen and the village women remove thorns and matted wool. That done, the ivory fleeces were rolled and tied into bundles to cool and later pack into sacks to await sale.

As she picked over the wool, the seed of an idea planted early in her visit began to germinate. But before she broached the idea with Gwen and Will, she wanted Peter's opinion.

A fortnight into the shearing, as the early evening sun was slanting in through the winter parlor windows and lighting their meal, she brought the subject up with Peter.

"You know Gwen wants to expand their cloth production," she said, "except they lack the necessary funds." She added cucumber salad to her trencher. "I thought to lend them some of the money left me by my parents. She once said thirty pounds would give them a good start. And I could rent a cottage in Hensey and spin for Will."

Peter's expression brightened as he helped himself to the lamb stew sitting between them on the white tablecloth.

"Why, this will give more employment for the villagers. But there's no need to move to Hensey. You can remain here if you wish."

He took a bite of stew.

"What would you like?" she said.

Fingers gripping hard spoon handle, she waited with pent breath to hear his reply.

"If Will expands his business," Peter said slowly, thoughtfully, "he'll need more workers in Hensey." His dipped brow lifted. "It makes more sense for you to stay here and leave the cottage for them."

She released her breath, both relieved and disappointed by his reply. A response based on logic was not what she wanted. At least he was willing for her to remain.

"Then I'll speak with Will and Gwen tomorrow after the worship service." She took a bite of pottage. "I've not said anything to them yet in case you didn't approve."

"Why wouldn't I?"

"I merely wanted to ask you first," she said, thinking of the exchange she'd had with Catherine Cox. "And I'll have to get the money. Most of it is still with a banker in Rouen. Monsieur Bossuet's London partner should be able to help me get it transferred. Once the shearing is over, I thought to go to London and make the arrangements."

After the Sunday morning service, Anne Marie was invited to join the village women's quoits game on the green. Telling Gwen and Will of her plan had to wait until she and Peter were seated side by side at the Weavers' dining table for the noon meal. Over the roasted pigeons, turnips, and onion pottage, she began explaining it to Gwen.

As Gwen listened, her eyes widened and her mouth formed an O. Almost before Anne Marie finished, her offer was accepted. Gwen turned to Will who, between his own bites, was spooning pottage into Little Rob's mouth.

"You'll have the money to buy more wool," she said in jubilation. "And to pay more spinsters and hire a journeyman weaver."

"I'd better get the empty cottages repaired," Peter said, "so you'll have housing for all these additional workers."

Little Rob sneezed. His mouthful of pottage went flying.

Gwen's shout sent the scullery maid, seated at the table's end, dashing to the kitchen. Gwen herself grabbed a napkin and started wiping pottage spatter.

The maid rushed back with a wet rag and began dabbing spots on the linen tablecloth.

Little Rob, pottage dribbling down his chin, grinned at Anne Marie.

She knew she should frown at him. Instead, she returned his smile.

Once Little Rob and the tablecloth were again relatively clean, the interrupted conversation resumed.

"In a year or so," Gwen said, looking across Little Rob at Will, "Hensey might even be prosperous enough to provide a decent income for a new vicar. Your brother would like that."

Will turned to Peter.

"Ned should finish at Cambridge in two more years. Of course, it will be your decision who replaces Bro. Lawrence."

"I don't see why Peter would object to him," Gwen said, her determined look swinging from Will to Peter. "Ned's family."

The shearing was finished shortly after St. John's eve. Peter turned his attention to the fields soon to be mowed, and Anne Marie walked into Hensey to deliver more skeins of yarn to Will. After a brief visit, she watched the Weaver family ride off toward Hensford. She returned to Wynnfield, checked on noon meal preparations, then picked herbs to dry for winter use.

Over their nooning of roasted duck, artichokes, and pease pottage, she listened to Peter talk of the preparations for haying. Once he'd finished, she shared what Will and Gwen had told her before they left.

"Will wants to find a journeyman weaver he can employ in the fall. That will give the summer to spin thread." She scooped up the last of her pottage with a bread piece. "Gwen and Little Rob are going on north to visit her mother while Will searches for the journeyman." Then, "Do you know if her mother knew mine?"

Peter tossed a duck bone into the voiding dish

"They had to have known each other. Aunt Emma lived here for a time. She wed your grandmother's bailiff, Gilbert Harvey."

"I'd like to meet them."

"That won't be possible. Master Harvey died some years ago." His tone grew wistful. "He was a good bailiff. For a time, he was my bailiff. At least that's how I saw it when Grandfather bought Wynnfield for me." He threw her a smile. "Master Harvey even promised to teach me how to run a manor." His smile faded. "When Uncle Richard was arrested, Father dismissed him and hired a new bailiff. Fortunately for me, Sir George hired Master Harvey, so he was able to keep his promise."

She dipped a dessert strawberry into cream and ate it.

"Once I return from London, I should like to at least meet your Aunt Emma."

"After you've met her," Peter said with a wry look, "you may wish you hadn't."

CHAPTER 11 – JUNE – WYNNFIELD

The trip to London was still a week away when Anne Marie, having played the organ for half an hour, stepped out of St. James the Less in time to see a lumpish, gray-haired woman in a plain yellow gown come riding into Hensey on an old bay nag. The woman reined up in front of the Weaver cottage.

"Will," the woman bawled. "Gwen!"

The woman was clambering down from her mount when the cottage door jerked open. Gwen came rushing out.

"Mother, what are you doing here?"

"Like I told you when you rode up last week, I want to meet Margaret's daughter. So here I am. I would've come sooner, but the cows needed me."

Anne Marie halted on the grassy verge. Could this be Emma Harvey?

She watched as the woman fetched a cane down from her mount and began hobbling toward the open cottage door. Gwen was left to deal with the horse. With an exasperated look, she threw her hands into the air, grabbed up the horse's dragging reins, and tied them to a nearby post. As she turned away from the horse, Gwen glanced across the street.

Relief flooded her face as her gaze met Anne Marie's. Gwen raised a beckoning hand.

Anne Marie crossed the street to join her.

"My mother's come," she said. "She wants to meet you."

A short time later Anne Marie was sitting on a stool in the Weaver's main room. Will, having halted his work to greet his mother-in-law, was again at his loom in the adjoining room. The steady thud of his weaving beam could be heard in the background as Anne Marie sat studying, and being studied by, Emma Harvey slouching on another stool.

Mistress Harvey's square face was scoured with lines, wisps of gray hair were escaping from her hood, and her mouth sagged in a perpetual frown. The hazel eyes peering at Anne Marie were surprisingly alert.

"You look like your father. But like your mother too. Why didn't Margaret come?"

Clearly Gwen had gotten her directness from her mother.

"My mother is in heaven."

Mistress Harvey's wrinkled lips screwed.

"I know that. I mean, why didn't she return years ago? Gilbert waited and waited. But she never came.

"There was nothing to come back for."

Mistress Harvey snorted.

"Nothing to come back for? There was her inheritance."

"Cousin Jonathan sent it to her."

"How could he send it to her?" Mistress Harvey peered at her. "What are you talking about?"

"The ring. My grandmother's ruby ring."

"The ring?" She snorted again. "That wasn't her inheritance. It was Wynnfield Manor."

"No, you're mistaken," Anne Marie said. She was having conversation with a simpleton. "It was the ring. Cousin Charles said so. He had it, and he gave it to Cousin Jonathan who sent it to Mother. I saw the letters myself."

"Charles. Of course." Mistress Harvey's eyes flashed. "Wynnfield Manor was your mother's inheritance. My husband told me so. Now it's yours."

Her jaw dropped; she gaped at Gwen's mother.

"No one told you?"

Mistress Harvey didn't wait for a reply. Gripping her cane, she pulled herself up and started hobbling for the door.

Gwen caught her mother's arm, tried to pull her back to the stool.

"Mother, sit down. You're just confused. Wynnfield belongs to Peter."

Mistress Harvey jerked her arm free and faced her daughter.

"I am not confused and I'm not sitting down. I'm going to see Peter and clear this matter up."

When it was obvious that nothing would stop Mistress Harvey, rather than see her mother hobble all the way to Wynnfield Hall, Gwen fetched Will. Together they helped her back onto the nag. She immediately set out for the manor house.

"We'd best go with her." Gwen threw the words at Anne Marie as she started down the street after her mother.

Anne Marie hurriedly fell into step beside Gwen. She hardly noticed her surroundings as they left the village, passed the mill, and entered the shady forest behind the plodding horse. Most of her mind was struggling with Mistress Harvey's revelation.

If it were true, it would topple Peter's world. But of course, it couldn't be true. If it had been, her mother would have known.

They rounded the green hawthorn bushes to the sound of chirping robins and followed Mistress Harvey through the gatehouse. A stable hand helped her dismount in the base-court. Once her feet touched hard dirt, Gwen's mother shrugged further assistance aside. Cane in hand, she hobbled off for the house.

Anne Marie, mouth dry, followed with Gwen. They quickly passed through the entryway, great hall, and winter parlor to arrive at the accounts room where Peter was working on the books.

He looked up in surprise when Mistress Harvey stumped through the door, Gwen at her skirt tails. Anne Marie halted just inside the door frame, reluctant to be part of whatever was coming, unable to stay away.

"Aunt Emma," Peter said, laying the goose quill aside, "what brings you here?"

Mistress Harvey stopped in the middle of the black and white tile floor. The afternoon sunlight drifting through the mullioned windows highlighted her shabby appearance.

"I'm here to set matters straight," she said firmly. "Wynnfield belongs to Margaret. Gilbert told me so. Since she's dead, it goes to her daughter."

Anne Marie held her breath as she watched consternation build on Peter's face.

He turned to Gwen.

"Do you know what she's talking of?"

Gwen shook her head.

"I told you," Mistress Harvey said. "Wynnfield Manor belongs to Anne Marie. It's what Uncle Richard wanted." She looked around. "I need to sit. Gwen, get me a stool!"

While Gwen fetched a stool, Peter appeared to be gathering his thoughts.

Mistress Harvey carefully lowered herself onto the seat then turned her attention back to Peter.

He was eyeing her with a determined look.

"My grandfather – your stepfather – bought Wynnfield."

Mistress Harvey replied with equal determination.

"But he did it with Uncle Richard's money. Gilbert said Uncle Richard told him he wanted the manor kept for Margaret till she came home. Only she didn't come."

"Uncle Richard couldn't have purchased Wynnfield," Peter said. "He didn't have the money. All he possessed was the cottage and a share in the goldsmith shop."

"Where did your grandfather get the money? He had a large family to support. Uncle Richard had his wife's money from her first husband. You wouldn't remember my sister Alyce. She died in childbirth before you were born. Bro. Lawrence knew her. Alyce bought him that organ."

Anne Marie saw a muscle twitch in Peter's jaw as he studied his aunt, a clear sign that he was fighting anger.

"If Uncle Richard bought Wynnfield for Margaret, why was my grand-father's name on the title deed?"

For the first time, confusion appeared on Mistress Harvey's weathered face.

"I don't know."

"And why didn't Master Harvey tell me all this himself?"

Mistress Harvey's look of confusion deepened. In the stretching silence, Peter's tense expression relaxed in vindication. He picked up his quill.

"Thank you for coming, Aunt Emma. Now, if you've nothing more, I've accounts to finish."

Gripping the cane with gnarled hands, Mistress Harvey struggled to her feet.

"You don't believe me. You think I'm a crazy old woman. Well, I'm not. I'm telling you what Gilbert told me." Her look sharpened again. "Why was Gilbert dismissed as bailiff only *after* Uncle Richard was arrested as a heretic? I'll tell you why. Because it was Uncle Richard's money bought this place, and he wanted Gilbert kept on just as he wanted Wynnfield to go to Margaret."

Gwen cast an embarrassed, apologetic look at Peter. Anne Marie crossed to Mistress Harvey and gently laid a hand on her arm.

"It's all right, Mistress Harvey. Peter can have Wynnfield. I don't know how to run it. Besides, Gwen and I are starting a business. We're going to set the Hensey villagers to spinning and weaving. I know about that."

Mistress Harvey looked down at her. The stubborn expression on her lined face softened.

"You're too generous. Just like your father. Giving all his coins away to the beggars." She turned back to Peter. Her look sharpened again. "I've said the truth. Your father knows it even if you don't."

"I'll ask him about it when I next go to London."

Mistress Harvey snorted.

"You do that. He'll lie."

She swung round and hobbled out the door.

"I'm sorry, Peter," Gwen said. "I don't know where she got such an idea. Her mind must be going."

She turned and hurried out the door after her mother.

In the silence they left behind, Anne Marie gazed across the room at Peter. She must say something, must somehow rectify the situation. The manor was Peter's first love. She winced at the thought. If ever he were to lose it, it must not be to her.

"It doesn't matter what Mistress Harvey says," she said. "Wynnfield belongs to you."

Peter's look was smoldering.

"Yes, it does."

He dipped quill into ink pot and, sharpened tip scratching paper, began recording an expense in the accounts book.

Anne Marie stared uncertainly at his bent head for a half dozen heart-beats before she, too, left the room.

Although Peter had his head bent over the accounts book, inhaling the odor of acidic ink, he was fully aware of Anne Marie's departure. Only after she quietly shut the door behind her did he throw the quill aside.

He banged his fist down on the table's hard surface. The ink pot jumped.

He's never in his life been so furious. How dare Aunt Emma come here claiming Wynnfield wasn't his? Gwen was right. She'd taken leave of her senses. If Wynnfield truly didn't belong to him, he'd know.

He came to his feet and headed for the door. The accounts would have to wait. He needed to be out with his fields and his forests, his flocks and his herds.

Soon he was galloping away from the house in the afternoon sunshine, past the orchard, across the water meadows, and then skirting a field of barley. Before he reached the rough ground bordering the forest, he reined up on a rise.

Taking a deep calming breath of the sweet country air, he sat and sur-veyed his domain.

Wynnfield manor was especially beautiful at this time of year. The rosy brick house in the distance with its curling chimney stacks was in good repair. The green meadows lying before him, watered by the wandering stream, would soon be ready for mowing. To his right, a flock of his sheep was nib-bling its way across the fallows, enriching the soil as they went, while their newly shorn wool sat sacked up in the wool house waiting for sale. In another month the green barley field to his left would whiten and be ready for har-vest.

Of course, the manor was his. His name was on the title deed. But even more than a name on a title deed, he'd stamped his ownership on Wynnfield by pouring himself into this land.

Grandfather must have gotten the money somehow because Father had said that Grandfather, not Uncle Richard, was buying Wynnfield for him. No doubt his father could easily clear up this whole misunderstanding. For that's what it was. Aunt Emma's memory was confused and, true to form, she was too stubborn to admit it.

When Anne Marie traveled to London, rather than sending a manservant to see her safely there, he'd ride down with her and talk with his father. That would require leaving the reeve totally in charge of the manor's outdoor work for a few days. But the man had grown up at Wynnfield, knew its running well, and was trustworthy.

He need only be gone three days. For Anne Marie's sake, he'd take a day and a bit riding to London. Once he left her at Cousin Jonathan's home, he'd have the rest of the day to talk with his father. Riding back alone, he could reach Wynnfield in one day. Three days, total. He should be back by the start of haying.

He nodded in satisfaction. Under him, his mount shifted uneasily. He leaned forward and patted its neck. The horse settled. As he straightened, a passing cloud's dark, ragged shadow swept the green meadow. Watching the shadow pass over his beloved acres, his earlier tensions began to abate.

Aunt Emma's claim had no more substance than that shadow. He'd been a fool to give heed to it. He also shouldn't be idling here while accounts waited to be finished.

He kneed his horse and set off at a gallop for his manor house.

Peter found the evening meal unusually quiet. Normally Anne Marie was quite talkative, asking about his day and telling him of hers. This time, studiously avoiding any mention of Aunt Emma's visit, she talked only briefly of her plans for the next few days.

"Tomorrow," she said, "I thought to do more work in the pleasance, provided that's agreeable to you."

He looked across the table at her. She'd not asked his permission to work in the pleasance since she'd first arrived.

"Go ahead. Do as you please."

He knew he'd sounded terse. It didn't matter. He was master here.

Two days before Peter was to leave for London with Anne Marie, he was riding through Hensey when he heard organ music. On impulse he reined up beside St. James the Less and tied his horse to the nearby beech tree. He crossed the chapel porch and stepped into the nave.

The morning light streaming through the chancel windows revealed Bro. Lawrence at his gilded organ. A village child, red-faced from exertion, manned the bellows. Peter bent onto a hard bench part way up the nave and let the rich, swelling music wash over him. When Bro. Lawrence finished the piece at last, the village child dashed off through the north door.

Peter came to his feet. He strode up the nave, took the chancel's three steps, and approached Bro. Lawrence, still sitting at the organ looking through music sheets.

"All these years listening to you play," Peter said, "I've never thought to ask how you came by such a fine instrument."

Bro. Lawrence shifted round on his stool to look up at him.

"It was a gift for performing a wedding." He laid a gentle hand on the organ. "Your Uncle Richard's wedding, in fact."

"He gave you this?"

"His wife did."

"It must have cost her a great deal."

"It did," Bro. Lawrence said, nodding his bald head. "She could afford it. Her first husband's death had left her extremely wealthy."

"I don't remember her at all."

"She died in childbirth a few years later. Probably before you were born."

Peter swung back in the saddle and morosely continued on toward the manor house. So Aunt Emma had been right about Uncle Richard's wealth. But it proved nothing. Even if his uncle's money had helped purchase Wynnfield, he was Uncle Richard's godson, and, as such, in line for the most favor. Not Anne Marie's mother.

He was glad he'd already arranged for the reeve to take charge in his absence. More than ever, he needed to talk with his father.

126

CHAPTER 12 – JULY – LONDON

Peter spotted the church spires of London on the cloudless blue horizon by mid-morning on Tuesday. Shortly after, he reined up on the grassy verge between beaten track and mottled green forest to look at the city before they passed through Bishopsgate into its confines. Anne Marie, following on her mount, pulled up beside him.

"So many spires," she said, gazing at their destination.

"I've been told there's nearly a hundred. I've never counted them."

She studied London a bit longer then looked across at him.

"It was kind of you to ride down with me. I know you don't like leaving your manor."

Her saying '*your*' manor was an unwanted reminder. He swallowed irritation and shrugged.

"It was nothing. Remember, once you've completed your affairs, write to me, and I'll send someone to fetch you."

"Thank you."

"You needn't thank me. Gwen will have my skin for leather if I don't get you and your coins back so she can have her business."

On that lighter note, they rejoined the travelers on the wide rutted road.

Following Bishopsgate Street, they trotted through the sprawling suburbs, passing Hog Lane, Bedlam Hospital, and the brick courtyard wall encircling St. Botolph's. Once through the city gate, the traffic increased along with the odors of rotting refuse. As they neared Leadenhall Street, industrious housewives, servants, and water carriers all heading for the pump on Cornhill added to the congestion.

They turned onto Leadenhall and made their way to St. Mary Avenue. Shortly afterward, they were reining up at the Peterman courtyard. He helped Anne Marie dismount, carried her traveling bag into the house – she'd left her lute at Wynnfield – and, after a brief friendly exchange with the Peterman family, took his leave.

After stabling their horses at a nearby hostelry, he set off across the city for Guthran Lane, his bag of necessities slung over his shoulder. When he arrived within sight of the goldsmith shop, they were closed for the midday meal. He passed under the shop's white-on-blue unicorn sign, stepped through the courtyard gate, and strode down the path running between house and boundary wall.

In the two years since he'd last come, he'd forgotten how crowded and odorous London was.

He entered the house as Roger stepped from the workshop into the narrow passageway. Roger halted at sight of him.

"Where'd you spring from?"

"Anne Marie had to come on business, so I rode down with her."

"Oh, yes, our little French cousin." Roger started up the stairs with Peter, the boards creaking underfoot. "How is she?"

"Fine, I suppose. I left her with Cousin Jonathan's family. Call on her if you wish. She'll be in London for a while."

They reached the landing and turned right toward the hall. Peter glanced around the long, comfortable room. Maud, in a Tudor green gown, was seated by a window adding embroidery to a coif. Father's two apprentices were lounging in a corner playing a noisy game of knucklebones while they waited for the meal. Father was in his carved chair near the cold fireplace at the far end.

The hoped-for talk that had brought him to London would have to wait till he could get Father alone. If the habit of the house hadn't changed, he should be able to do so after the meal.

Peter crossed the room to greet Father. Mother appeared a moment later to announce the meal with a nod of her head. Seeing him, her long-jawed face lit.

"I'm just here for the day," he said, answering her questioning look. "I've a matter to discuss with Father and you."

In the dining parlor, a servant hurriedly set a trencher, spoon, and goblet for him between Maud and one of the apprentices. During the meal of assorted meats and salads, he left the casual table conversation to others. Dominated by Roger and Maud, the topics included the latest styles in gowns, bets Roger had won at cock fights, and the most recent plays they'd seen.

His brother and sister lived in a different world.

Cherry tarts ended the meal. Maud disappeared up the stairs, and the two apprentices returned to their game of knucklebones. His parents remained seated at the table while Father finished off his goblet of wine. Roger helped himself to a second cup.

"What's this business you need to discuss?" Father said.

Peter glanced across the table at Roger, wishing he'd left with the others. But to ask to speak with his parents in private would be making too much of the matter. He shifted his gaze back to Father. His muscles tensed.

"Where did Grandfather get the money to purchase Wynnfield?"

Father's brow dipped as he peered at him.

"You rode all this way merely to ask that? Why does it matter where he got it?"

"Was it Uncle Richard's money? Was he the real purchaser?"

Father's expression tightened; his lips clamped. Peter turned to Mother. After a moment's hesitation she nodded.

"Then why was Grandfather's name on the title?"

Although he directed his question at Mother, Father answered.

"Uncle Richard didn't want it lost if he ended at the stake ... which he did."

Relief swept through him. Of course. Why had he not thought of that? As he'd hoped, Father did have the answer. But it didn't excuse his lie.

"You told me Grandfather was buying the manor for me."

"What does it matter?" Father's tone was gruff, almost angry. "You have it now."

"Aunt Emma claims that Uncle Richard bought Wynnfield for Margaret."

Panic swept Father's face; the goblet in his hand shook. He threw a frightened look at Mother.

"How'd she know?"

129

"Master Harvey told her," Peter said automatically. Then, feeling his once-solid world tremble, "What do you mean, 'how'd she know'?"

Father's heavy face reddened.

"Gilbert Harvey lied. He was always trying to stir up trouble for me."

Peter stiffened.

"Master Harvey was no liar."

"Everyone lies … especially when it's to their advantage."

"Father, what did you mean when you said 'how'd she know'?"

Father sat tight-lipped, glaring at him. Roger's eyes widened with interest. Peter turned to Mother.

"Mother?"

She opened her mouth.

"Hold your tongue, wife!"

Mother froze. Father swung his attention back to Peter.

"We hold the title deed. No one will believe Emma. They'll think she's gone crazy. They might even lock her up in Bedlam. This little French cousin should go back where she came from. She's a menace to us."

Listening to Father, the world on which he was building his life crumbled. He looked at Mother.

"Then it's true."

She nodded.

"Well, well," Roger said. "Sorry, brother. There goes your precious manor." His chuckle quickly changed into a polite cough.

Father was talking again.

"Margaret didn't return. Her daughter shouldn't have either. Had Uncle Richard lived, he'd soon have come to his senses and settled Wynnfield on you. You're his godson. Leave the past in the past. The girl need never know."

"But I know."

Taut silence filled the room as he struggled with this most unwanted revelation.

Mother broke it.

"Marry her."

"I don't want to marry her. I plan to wed Catherine Cox and get the other manor back." He glanced across the table. "Roger can wed her."

Roger straightened in astonishment.

"Why would I want to do that? What would I get out of it?"

"She has money."

"Given the way she dresses," Roger said, reaching for his goblet, "I doubt she has all that much." He took a sip of wine. "You'll have to sweeten the pot a great deal more before I'd consider that prudish little redhead."

"She's not so bad," Peter said, indignation momentarily overriding other emotions. "I doubt she'd have you anyway."

A bright, sharp look replaced the disdain on Roger's face. He set the goblet down on the white tablecloth.

"Want to bet?"

He'd forgotten Roger's love of a wager.

"Don't be ridiculous."

"I bet I can get her to agree to wed me."

"She's got more sense."

"A shilling says you're wrong."

Peter sat on a tree stump where London fields met forests, chewing the end of a tough grass stem. The robin trilling in a nearby ash tree did nothing to lighten his mood.

He should never have come to London. He'd been a fool to think that talking with Father would help. True, the manor was his by law. Nothing could change that. But it hadn't been meant for him. Never again could he gaze over its acres with the same pride of ownership.

If only Father hadn't lied to him when he was a child. He was Uncle Richard's godson. Why hadn't Uncle Richard given the manor to him? He felt betrayed by both father and uncle. Betrayed, and angry.

What to do now?

He tossed the chewed stem away and yanked another.

As wrong as Father had been about everything else, he'd been right about one thing. Anne Marie mustn't know. She'd already said that she didn't believe Aunt Emma. Quite the reverse. She seemed to be making every effort to stress his ownership. And, however it had come about, he was the legal owner. Telling her would only create trouble for everyone.

But he still had a moral obligation to her.

He came to his feet and started back along White Cross Street as he mulled over how to fulfill that responsibility.

Uncle Richard had intended the manor for her mother. He'd honor that intent by ensuring Anne Marie was well provided for. Since she wasn't a demanding person, that shouldn't be hard, especially if this cloth business succeeded. Later, he'd find her a good husband, someone certainly better than Roger.

When Peter had shared the noon meal with his family, he'd been too preoccupied with his own concerns to take much interest in those around him. Having had the afternoon to come to terms with his unwelcome discovery and knowing he was leaving on the morrow, he determined to give more attention to his family at the evening meal.

The long twilight was still brightening the dining parlor windows when he took his place at the table between Maud and an apprentice. As the servants began bringing the various dishes from sideboard to table, he looked at his brother and sister.

In the two years since he'd last visited, they'd changed little. Roger was as flippant and annoying as ever. Maud seemed only able to talk of the latest styles. She reminded him uncomfortably of Catherine Cox. His gaze softened as it shifted to his silent, richly garbed mother, waving aside a savory dish of lamb with sauce that a servant held out to her. She also never seemed to change from visit to visit.

His gaze moved to his father, staring at his mother.

"Take some," Father snapped, "and the sauce."

Puzzled, Peter studied his father. Had he seen a flash of fear in Father's eyes?

He watched as Mother took a small serving of the lamb, a favorite of Father's, and ate a bite. The servant then carried the dish to Father. He took a generous portion.

When other dishes were served, he noticed Father only took what Mother had taken.

As the meal progressed and the casual table talk carried on around him, he mulled over Father's odd behavior.

Why that flash of fear? Father had had a similar look on hearing Aunt Emma's charge regarding Wynnfield. What was causing his confident, shrewd father to show irrational fear?

He'd also earlier spoken of Master Harvey and Anne Marie as if they were enemies. Was something amiss with Father?

When the house began to settle for the night, Peter sought Roger out. He found him lolling in bed reading an astrology book by the light of a nearby wall candle.

"Is something wrong with Father?" he said, settling onto the edge of the feather mattress.

Roger looked up from his book.

"What do you mean?"

"The way he was with Mother, insisting that she take the lamb before he did."

Roger shrugged.

"Oh, he's been doing that for quite some time."

"It doesn't seem ... normal."

"You think not? Personally, I've not given it much thought. Mother chooses what foods are served. He may want her to eat whatever she's feeding others. It could be for any number of reasons." He gave a slight smile. "Perhaps, somehow, even a guilty conscience. Who knows?"

"A guilty conscience?"

"He's been visiting the stews," Roger said nonchalantly.

Stunned, he peered at Roger for a long moment before finding his voice again.

"He has? How do you know?"

"I saw him." He chuckled. "It's not every day a man picks the same brothel as his father. Fortunately, he didn't see me. He was too busy trying to shield his face so he'd not be recognized." Roger's expression grew speculative. "I have wondered if we shared the same strumpet. That would be embarrassing. Just in case, I'm now frequenting a different brothel."

"He's not the only one who should have a guilty conscience," Peter said, anger roiling.

Roger yawned.

"Don't lecture me, big brother. It's my life. I'll live it as I please."

Peter bit back a sharp retort. Tomorrow he was returning to Wynnfield. He needed Roger's cooperation so he could leave with an easier mind.

"Well," he said, coming to his feet, "I'd appreciate you keeping watch on the situation here. Let me know if I'm needed."

"You won't be," Roger said, his tone huffy. "I can take care of what's mine."

Peter was drifting off to sleep in the small chamber next to Roger's when he abruptly awakened. He'd forgotten to bid Anne Marie farewell.

He stared up at the night-black ceiling. On reflection, it was just as well he had. Given what his parents had told him, the idea of seeing her now made him uncomfortable. When she returned to Wynnfield in a few weeks, no doubt he'd feel more at ease.

On that thought, he rolled over and went back to sleep.

While Peter had been sharing the noon meal with his family in Guthran Lane, Anne Marie was dining with Jonathan's family. During the meal, she told Jonathan and Lettice of her plans to go into the cloth business with Gwen and Will. She purposely said nothing about Peter's reason for accompanying her to London.

Over the afternoon she helped with housework and waited for Peter to appear and bid her farewell. He still hadn't come by evening mealtime. Once family devotions finished and Lettice began snuffing candles, she was forced to accept that he wasn't coming. The fact left her feeling dejected.

Long after night descended on the city and Bow bell rang curfew, she was still awake. She lay staring into the dark in the small chamber she'd had previously. No doubt Dorcas and Prudence were already asleep in the next room.

At least she and Peter had parted on good terms. That brought some consolation. The sooner she could finish her business here in London, the sooner she could return to Wynnfield and Peter.

Shortly after shops opened the following day, Anne Marie set out for Guthran Lane. The littered cobblestone streets were filling with housewives setting off for market, porters staggering past under hefty loads, hawkers crying their wares, carts rattling along, and, here and there, a tardy schoolboy dashing by.

In all likelihood Peter was already gone. Still, she should pay a visit to his family and renew her friendship with Roger and Maud.

When she arrived at the goldsmith shop, she spotted Roger through the glazed window arranging gold dishes on a shelf. His father was nowhere in sight. The overhead bell tinkled as she pushed the shop door open and walked in. The faint familiar odors of melted metals, acid, and burning charcoal enveloped her.

Roger looked up and broke into a smile.

"Peter said you'd returned. You look even more fetching than I remembered. Country air must be healthy."

She glanced around on the slim chance that Peter might appear.

"I suppose Peter has left."

"He was up and gone at first light." Roger stepped closer. "What can I sell you today? A necklace for that pretty neck of yours ... or perhaps a ring?"

"Nothing, thank you. I just stopped to say I'll be in London for a few weeks."

"Perhaps I could come this evening, and you can tell me what country life is like."

"I'm going to hear Cousin Jonathan preach this evening."

"May I join you?"

She looked at Roger in surprise.

"Of course. I know Cousin Jonathan would be pleased."

"I hope you'll be pleased as well."

She peered up at him, expecting to see the familiar glint in his eye when he was making sport of someone. Instead, his expression remained serious.

Before she could think how to reply, she heard footsteps approaching from the workshop. She looked around as Charles Denzil stepped through from the back.

He halted and his hard stare locked on her.

"What's she doing here?"

Roger glanced at his father.

"She wanted us to know she's in London for a while." He turned back to her. "What time this evening?"

"He's preaching at St. Mary Bow at half past six." She glanced over at Roger's father, frowning at her from the doorway. Why must he always make her feel uncomfortable, unwelcome? She turned back to Roger. "I should be going."

As she started for the street door, Roger moved quickly to open it for her, setting the bell tinkling. Just before she stepped back into the street, he leaned down and murmured.

"I'll see you there."

Preoccupied by other matters, Anne Marie gave little thought to Roger's parting words as she set out along the narrow, crowded streets for the home of Master Browne, Monsieur Bossuet's London partner, on Candlewick Street. Having previously sent a letter to the Bossuets through him, she found her way to the four storied half-timber dwelling again with no trouble.

Sitting on a stool in Master Browne's accounts room, she told the rake-thin merchant of her plan to help expand Will's cloth business. He then explained how to transfer her monies from Rouen to London. She was relieved that it could be done without involving the Bossuets. They'd not be pleased to know she was remaining in England.

Returning to the Peterman home, she wrote the necessary letters and delivered them to Master Browne that afternoon. He added them to correspondence being sent to Rouen. He also gave her the names of several cloth merchants looking for new sources.

She returned to the Peterman home a second time in good spirits. If the winds were with them, the ship carrying her letters should reach Rouen within a week. By the end of July, she could have her money and be free to return to

Wynnfield. While she waited, she'd talk with the cloth buyers and continue praying that Peter wouldn't wed Catherine Cox.

Not until she set out for St. Mary Bow with Jonathan that evening did she recall Roger's parting words. Unsure whether he'd come, she said nothing to Jonathan as they made their way along through the foot traffic on Cornhill and Poultry to Bow Lane.

When they came within sight of the old stone church, crowded close with houses and shops, she saw Roger, dressed more somberly than usual, standing near the entry scanning the passersby in the street. He spotted them, waved, and came hurrying over.

"I thought I'd missed you," he said. He turned to Jonathan. "I've come to hear you preach."

"This is a surprise."

Roger smiled.

"A pleasant one, I hope."

"A very pleasant one. Come, let's go in."

With dusk over two hours away, daylight still reigned within St. Mary Bow as they joined other attenders flowing into the building. Judging by the variety of their dress and their odors, every level of society, from wealthy merchants and their richly garbed wives down to lowly serving men and women, had come to hear Jonathan.

Leaving Anne Marie and Roger to find their own seats, Jonathan made his way toward the front of the nave. When nearly there, she saw him pause to exchange a word with one young man who looked very much like Simon Cole. The young man took a seat near the front. She was relieved that Roger chose a bench only halfway up the nave. If it was Simon, she had no desire to encounter him.

A small sigh escaped her when Roger settled down beside her on the un-padded bench. If only Peter, rather than his brother, were at her side. She took herself in a firm grip and turned her attention to Jonathan as he limped up the steps to the carved pulpit.

He opened his Bible, read a passage from Romans, and launched into his sermon. Glancing around, Anne Marie saw that his listeners were hanging on his every sentence.

"Weakness, self-deception, overconfidence, the slackening of attention and will must first be faced and overcome if evil is to be deprived of its power. These are the consequence of Adam's fall, the abominations of man's sinful heart. They are the work of the devil," Jonathan cried, lifting his fist.

His words rebounded off the stone walls and echoed among the rafters. Dropping his arm, he gripped the pulpit with both hands and leaned toward his audience.

"But do not lose hope. God is a God of power over sin and the devil.

"Those the Lord predestines to salvation are called, are separated from this world, and are grafted into the body of Christ. We achieve this by diligent and attentive hearing of the word.

"Those he has called are justified and have attained a true and living faith. All those who are justified are also sanctified. They die to their sins and are raised again to newness of life.

"But those who are still living for the world are not truly called, justified, and sanctified."

His stare raked the audience.

"They make no effort to hear God's word diligently, reverently, and attentively. They do not treasure it up in their hearts. They remain unrepentant. They have no desire and make no effort to serve the Lord by living a holy and righteous life. They shall never be saved. Rather, they shall be cast into the eternal fires of hell."

Anne Marie watched Roger surreptitiously. He was sitting, sober faced, his attention locked on Jonathan. After giving him a final dubious glance, she turned her attention back to the sermon.

When the service ended, some of the attenders wished a word with Jonathan. Leaving her momentarily, Roger worked his way through the departing crowd, exchanged a quick word with Jonathan, and returned.

"I told him I'll accompany you home," he said.

They started back along Poultry and Cornhill through a gathering dusk made even darker by the overhanging buildings lining the streets. The shops they passed were closed and shuttered, and the street traffic was thin. Most of the horn lanterns hanging at house doors were not yet lit. Those that were gave off only a feeble light.

Roger was solicitous in guiding her around the refuse in the street and assisting her over rough spots in the paving. They turned onto St. Mary Avenue and came within sight of the Peterman home. He slowed.

"I'd like to hear more sermons."

"With preaching somewhere nearly every night," she said, "you can go any time."

"I'd prefer to go with you." He hesitated. Then, "When you were previously here, you asked me if I'd craft an idol. I gave you a flippant answer. But your question forced me to search my soul. I disliked what I found. I have you to thank for opening my eyes."

Anne Marie parted with Roger at the courtyard gate and pensively made her way toward the house. She was glad that he was showing an interest in sermons. Knowing that she'd been instrumental in his change was flattering. But was he, at the same time, also developing an interest in her? If so, that was a cause for concern since she had no interest in him.

She stepped from the entryway into the candlelit hall to the sound of Dorcas's voice. She was seated on a stool beside the cold fireplace reading a religious tract aloud. Lettice and Prudence were busy with needle and thread on a nearby bench.

As Anne Marie stepped farther in, Lettice looked up from her mending. She smiled and waved Anne Marie over. Anne Marie settled onto a nearby stool and watched Prudence practice setting a straight line of stitches into a red cloth scrap.

Dorcas had finished the tract and was beginning to reread it when Jonathan's voice was heard in the entryway. Dorcas paused in her reading. Lettice set her mending aside.

As Jonathan's limping step drew closer, Anne Marie heard Simon Cole's voice. She glanced at Dorcas. Her face was glowing.

"Thomas Cartwright should never have been expelled," Simon said as he followed Jonathan into the hall.

"A considerable number at Cambridge would agree," Jonathan said, pausing by the door. "Like you, they feel that the university was unfair to deprive him of his fellowship last year for criticizing the church hierarchy."

Jonathan started limping across the room toward them, Simon at his elbow.

"Now that he's back from his Geneva trip," Jonathan said, "I was able to talk with him when I visited Thomas at Cambridge. Of course, he's supporting the Admonition to Parliament. That pamphlet is as heated a topic there as it is here in London."

"And rightly so. Until Parliament implements measures to bring church governance more in line with the Biblical pattern...."

Anne Marie saw Simon's gaze fix on her. He halted abruptly, his comment unfinished. His expression stiffened. He hesitated for a moment then acknowledged her presence with a brief impersonal nod.

Even as she returned his nod, Dorcas tripped across to Simon, tract in hand.

"We've been reading this tract you gave me," she said, gazing up at him with admiration. "It's so spiritually encouraging."

Simon quickly turned to her. His expression relaxed.

"I've another you might find beneficial. I'll bring it when next I come."

Not long afterward, he bade a warm farewell to Dorcas and her parents, gave Anne Marie an impersonal nod, and departed. The echo of his footfalls faded.

She was relieved to see him go. After this first encounter, any future ones should be less uncomfortable.

Lettice soon sent Dorcas to fetch the household servants for the evening Bible reading. When they had gathered, Jonathan read a scripture passage and ended with prayer. The servants left to finish their work before retiring.

Lettice began snuffing wall candles. Dorcas and Prudence started up the stairs to their bedchamber. Anne Marie was set to follow when Jonathan stopped her.

"I was quite pleased that Roger joined us at St. Mary Bow," he said, smiling down at her. "I do believe you're a good influence on him."

His words filled her with warmth and helped quiet her earlier apprehensions regarding Roger's intentions toward her.

"He wants to hear more sermons."

"Then you must see that he does. You may have the opportunity to help bring an erring sinner into the fold."

The following day Anne Marie walked over to the goldsmith shop to deliver a message to Roger. When she glanced through the glazed window, she saw Charles Denzil waiting on a customer. Reluctant to encounter him, she went on past to the courtyard gate. She had yet to call on Maud. There should be time enough to see Roger later.

The maid who answered the door directed her up to the hall then disappeared back to the kitchen quarters. She looked along the narrow passageway leading to the workshop. If Charles Denzil was still in the front, she might be able to catch Roger now.

Slipping quietly down the passageway, she peeked through the half-open workshop door. Immediately, odors of molten metal and acid filled her nostrils. The younger apprentice was stoking the furnace; the older one was sitting at the far end of the workbench carving a mold. Roger, in leather apron, was seated at the near end engraving a goblet.

She spoke his name softly. He looked up, saw her and broke into a smile. Laying his engraving tool aside, he rose and crossed to her.

"Jonathan thought you might like to hear the preacher at Paul's Cross Saturday afternoon."

"Will you be there?"

When she nodded, he smiled.

"Afterward," he said, "we could walk out to Moorfields. I've still not heard about your visit to the country."

"All right. Now I want to see Maud. And I've interrupted your work long enough."

"Not long enough for me."

His tone, even more than his words, heated her cheeks and sent her emotions into confusion.

"I don't think your father would feel the same," she said, trying to regain control.

She glanced at the door connecting workshop to the front. Now she wished that Charles Denzil would appear.

"I really must go. I'll see you Saturday."

Saturday afternoon Roger, again in more sober garb, accompanied her to St. Paul's Cathedral. There, they joined the listeners seated on the rough benches filling the towering Cathedral's northeast courtyard. When the preacher climbed the steps to take his place in the elaborate roofed pulpit, Roger turned a serious face to him.

Afterward, the day being bright and breezy, they joined others escaping the city odors and strolled out to Moorfields. Roger listened attentively as she told him about the plan to build up Will's cloth business.

"Master Browne has given me names of several cloth merchants," Anne Marie said as they ambled across the rough grass, spangled here and there with colorful wildflowers. "Maud says she knows most of them and has promised to take me there on Monday."

Cries of an approaching hawker selling roasted chicken's feet momentarily interrupted their conversation. They passed him by; the cries and the aroma faded.

"Leave it to Maud to know every cloth merchant in London," Roger said.

"She will be a help."

He stopped near a blue clump of cornflowers and caught her hand. His palm was hard against hers.

"Truth be told, I'm jealous. She's free to go all over London with you while I'm slaving away in the shop."

She tried to hide her discomfort as she slipped her hand free.

"But you've got an occupation. From what I hear, you're becoming an excellent goldsmith. Besides, we're seeing each other often. Just this week we've attended two sermons. And now we're walking in Moorfields."

"Don't think I don't appreciate what time you've given me. I just find it easier in my battle against the devil and all my old sinful habits when I'm with you. I need your prayers."

Touched by his admission, she laid her hand on his black-clad arm.
"Of course, I'll pray for you."
This time, when Roger covered her hand with his, she didn't pull free.

CHAPTER 13 – WYNNFIELD

Peter reached Wynnfield on the second evening in July as the sun was slipping behind the pleasance wall. From the moment he reined up in the basecourt, he purposely turned his full attention to overseeing the work of the manor. Hay to be cut, dried, and stacked, flax and hemp to be harvested and dressed, and honey to collect from the hives in orchard and pleasance helped block unwelcome thoughts about the intended ownership of the land on which he labored.

Such thoughts were most likely to come when he sat alone at meals. Ironically, that also was the time he found himself missing Anne Marie. In the nearly two months she'd shared meals with him, he'd grown accustomed to having someone to talk with about his day. Now all he had was her lute, leaning against the paneled wall in a corner of the winter parlor.

Of course, should he wed Catherine Cox, he could talk with her at mealtime. Unfortunately, he doubted she'd have as much interest either in manor affairs or its residents as Anne Marie had shown.

The Sunday following his return, he walked into Hensey to attend services at St. James the Less. There, he joined Gwen and Will on the bench near the front of the nave. The seat beside him that Anne Marie had occupied was empty. He found her absence distracting.

When the singing ended, he stepped to the front to read the Psalm. He opened his Bible to the assigned passage.

"The earth is the Lord's...." His tongue stumbled unexpectedly. He started the passage again. "The earth is the Lord's, and the fullness thereof...."

Having completed the reading, he resumed his seat.

At odd moments during Bro. Lawrence's homily and other parts of the service, that opening phrase repeated itself in his mind.

The earth is the Lord's.

Having no one with whom to share his nooning, after the service he accepted Gwen's invitation to join them once the village games ended. Over the fish pottage, bread, and cucumbers, Gwen talked of little else but the plans she and Anne Marie had for expanding Will's business.

If Gwen had guessed his reason for accompanying Anne Marie to London, he was thankful she made no mention of it.

When the afternoon service finished, Peter set out alone along the shady forest track back to Wynnfield. He came out of the woods and started around the hawthorn hedge toward the gatehouse. He heard the disquieting phrase again.

The earth is the Lord's. The very earth you tread is the Lord's.

Peter was working on manor accounts two weeks after his return when Gwen appeared in the accounts room door. Feet tapping the tile floor, she came hurrying toward him, a letter tight in her hand.

"A courier passing through Hensey left this with Bro. Lawrence not half an hour ago," she said, her expression a mixture of eagerness and apprehension as she handed him the message. "It's for you from Anne Marie. What does she say?"

She hovered at his elbow as he broke the red wax seal and unfolded the letter. He skimmed the neatly written contents.

"She hopes to have her monies by month's end," he said, looking up with a smile. "And she's sent the name of a London cloth dealer who showed interest in finding new cloth sources."

"Good." Gwen's apprehensive expression evaporated to be replaced by a radiant smile. "We need to find additional spinsters...."

A short time later Gwen left with the London cloth dealer's name scribbled on a paper scrap. No doubt as soon as she reached home and had given the name to Will, she'd start scouring Hensey for undiscovered spinsters.

With Gwen gone, quiet returned to the accounts room. Peter read Anne Marie's message a second time, this time more slowly, as he pictured the writer. In closing, she promised to write again when she had the money and was ready to return.

After reading her letter a final time, he carefully refolded it then tucked it safely away in the accounts cabinet.

Since the money for Will's business would be arriving soon, he really should pay Master Cox a visit to ask if he knew of additional spinsters. With so much else occupying his mind since his return, he'd given little thought to seeing Catherine. He could call on her at the same time.

Peter rode over to Cox Hall the following Saturday morning garbed in his Sunday best. The servant who answered his knock sent him off to the family's private parlor. Putting the great hall behind him, he passed the closed chapel door and stepped into the long, paneled room. His gaze swept the parlor. Master Cox and his black-gowned wife were seated by a window playing chess. As usual he was wearing what, for Peter, amounted to Sunday garb. Catherine was absent.

Master Cox must have heard his footsteps because he looked up. When their gazes met, Master Cox gave him a welcoming nod. He came to his feet and crossed the room to greet him. Master Cox seemed in a much better mood than he had on Peter's last visit.

"Catherine's off riding somewhere," he said. "Stay for a while. She should be back soon."

"Actually, I came to talk with you."

Master Cox threw a speculative glance at his wife then shifted his gaze back to Peter.

"Regarding...?"

"Will Weaver. He's expanding his cloth production. He's found a journeyman weaver to join him in the fall. In the meantime, he'd like to have additional spinsters working over the summer. If you should know of any, would you inform him?"

Master Cox fingered his wine velvet doublet as he eyed him.

"I thought you'd come about another matter."

"What other matter?"

"My daughter. It hasn't escaped my notice that you and she get along well. I rather expected that you were here to suggest a match between the two of you. After all, that could be a possibility."

Master Cox's comment caught Peter by surprise. Despite the half-serious talk of marriage that he and Catherine had indulged in, neither believed her father would ever consider the idea. Yet, Master Cox himself was bringing it up.

He unexpectedly found himself hesitating.

"I'm Anglican."

Master Cox pulled up what for him was a jovial smile.

"The Queen hasn't forbidden marriages between Anglicans and Catholics. Catherine would bring Cox Manor as her dowry, and she's heir to my other properties. We're already neighbors. If you two were to wed, the tie would be even closer. We also could get a proper priest for Hensey."

"Bro. Lawrence has been there a long time."

"Precisely. He's getting old. It's time he retired and was replaced by someone who can hold a proper service."

Before Peter could think of a safe reply, a blue-clad manservant appeared with a letter in his hand. He approached them.

"Master, a courier arrived with a message for you."

He passed it to Master Cox and departed. Master Cox glanced at the back. His look sharpened with pleasure. Just as quickly, his expression closed. Still holding the letter, he turned to Peter.

"Well, think on my suggestion."

Sensing this was a dismissal and glad to escape, Peter bowed himself out. As he stepped back through the parlor door, he heard Mistress Cox ask eagerly.

"From Douay? What does he say?"

He was crossing the great hall toward the entryway when he met Catherine coming through the screen. This time she was garbed in a crimson gown and smelled like a gillyflower.

"So, you're back from London," she said. "Had I known you planned to call, I'd have returned sooner."

"I had some business regarding Will Weaver to discuss with your father." Then, "Have you said anything to him about a match between us?"

Catherine's blond brow dipped.

"Of course not. Why do you ask?"

"He broached the subject. And also said that I should appoint a new priest at Hensey."

Her blue eyes widened with surprise.

"He did?" She gave him a coy smile. "What did you answer?"

"I didn't. We were interrupted."

"Well, what would you have said?"

"I doubt the Hensey villagers are ready to give up Bro. Lawrence and his organ."

"I don't mean about that." She didn't wait for a reply. "Even if we couldn't rid ourselves of Bro. Lawrence right away, were we to wed, we could have a family chaplain who could provide more correct worship. After all, you do have a chapel at Wynnfield."

Peter hesitated momentarily. Then,

"Suppose I didn't have Wynnfield Manor. Would you still want to wed me?"

"That's a silly question since you have it."

"But what if I didn't? What would you do?"

"Of course, I'd want to wed you," Catherine said lightly, "but Father wouldn't allow it. You'd be penniless so couldn't care for a wife."

"We'd have Cox Manor. And you'd inherit your father's acreages and the Hensford house."

"But it wouldn't be you providing for me" she said, with a slight pout. "It'd be me providing for you. Father wouldn't allow it."

As Peter trotted home along the shady forest track, he pondered on Master Cox's offer. Had it been made two months ago, he'd likely have immediately accepted it. But it hadn't, and too much had happened in the interim that now made him hesitate.

True, the thought of Catherine in his bed was appealing. And once she was his wife, he'd be in a better position to win her to the Anglican church. Also, marrying her would unite their two manors and later bring ownership of other properties.

Except, in the truest sense, Wynnfield wasn't his. But did he dare share that fact with Catherine?

148

Leaving the forest behind, he jogged down the slope, splashed across the stream and, to the soft clip-clop of hooves on soil, started past the meadows toward Hensey village.

Then, too, there was Catherine's response to his question about Wynnfield. It wasn't only what she'd said. It was what she hadn't. Though he couldn't name exactly what was lacking in her response, that missing something bothered him.

And what of Bro. Lawrence? Master Cox had made replacing him sound like a condition for the match. Of course, should Master Cox have his way, that replacement would conduct the service as close to the old Catholic mass as possible.

But Will and Gwen wanted the living to go to Will's brother, Ned. Given the family's Lollard background, Ned would likely follow Bro. Lawrence in altering, when possible, any part of the proscribed Anglican service smacking of Catholic ritual.

That wouldn't please Master Cox ... or Catherine.

Peter rounded the hawthorn hedge, filling now with green, unripened berries, and reined up at the stable. Leaving his horse with the stable boy, he strode through the gatehouse and across the base-court. Once in the house, he made for a little-used ground floor room at the far end of the family wing.

There, he stepped through the door and gazed around at what had once been the family chapel. Except for an unpadded bench against the pale, plastered, west wall and a small table beneath one of the east-wall's mullioned windows, the room was bare of furnishings. But it wasn't empty. Bro. Lawrence's stories about this room filled it.

When old King Henry had ordered all public Bibles removed from the churches, Anne Marie's grandmother had transferred here the one she'd previously purchased for St. James the Less. Despite the risk to herself, she'd made it available for all to read.

Later, when Queen Mary restored Catholic services, her grandmother had instructed Bro. Lawrence to hold private services here following the Reformed style. She'd taken a risk in doing so. Had they been discovered and reported to the authorities, she would have been arrested much earlier than she had.

Suppose he married Catherine and she refused to convert. Would this place once more be used for worship, but this time for Catholic mass?

He pictured again the idolatrous statue of the Virgin Mary in the Coxes' private chapel. Would a similar statue end up here?

That question troubled him through the following week. At the end of it, on the last Saturday in July, he received a short message from Catherine. She and her father would be returning home immediately after Sunday morning service. He knew what that meant. He sent his apologies, pleading the need to finish the haying and prepare for the August harvest.

On the Monday after, he was riding through Hensey to check on the hay making in the nearby fields when he met Catherine by the green. She reined up to sit looking at him, a slight frown marking her face. She was the first to speak.

"I expected you to call on us yesterday. After all, we did return from Hensford right after the service."

His muscles tightened.

"Didn't you get my message? As I said, with all the hay making, I'm extra busy."

"Too busy to give my father an answer about a match between us?"

"You said your father wouldn't allow us to wed if I didn't have Wynnfield."

"Of what concern is that? You have Wynnfield."

"I have it," he said, the words coming slowly, thoughtfully, "but is it mine?"

"What does that mean? It's simple. Are you or are you not going to speak to Father about a match between us?"

He shook himself, trying to throw off the questions that had been plaguing him since his return from London. He forced his attention back to Catherine's question.

"Of course, I am. But you know this is a busy time of year – what with the haying and now the harvests. I'm sure your father's equally busy."

"No, he's not. He has the bailiff do what you're doing. You should also."
She peered at him. "Have you changed your mind? That you don't want to
wed me?"

"Of course, I still want us to wed. But with the haying and harvests needing my attention...." He swallowed. "I'll call on your father as soon as the
workload eases."

Somewhat mollified, Catherine rode off. He watched her leave.

Had he just lied to her?

He didn't know.

CHAPTER 14 – JULY to EARLY AUGUST – LONDON

The pattern set during the first week of Anne Marie's return to London continued through the rest of July. Once or twice a week, Roger accompanied her to hear preaching at one of London's many churches. Several times Jonathan was the preacher manning the pulpit. When the weather was good, they attended Saturday afternoon preaching at Paul's Cross and later walked out to Moorfields.

On the one Saturday it rained, Roger invited her to the Denzil home. Fearing an encounter with his father, she demurred. Instead, he joined her at the Peterman home for an hour of singing in the hall. His baritone voice was superior to Peter's, something she would never admit to either brother.

During the first two weeks, she revisited the cloth stores that Master Browne had recommended and talked with the owners about purchasing cloth from Will. By mid-July she found one merchant who seemed interested. That provided the excuse she needed to write to Peter. Although her message was short, she spent some time composing it. For now, it was the only contact she had with him. She wanted it to be exactly right.

An acquaintance of Jonathan's, traveling to Cambridge, agreed to deliver it. Knowing her message was on its way, she returned to cleaning the Peterman-house windows, a smile curving her lips. Hopefully, in a fortnight she'd be sending another letter saying that she and her money were ready to return to Wynnfield.

Throughout July, Simon Cole remained cool toward her on their few chance encounters. In contrast, she seemed to meet with more approval from Jonathan now that he saw her as a positive influence on Roger. Dorcas's attitude toward her also improved. She assumed it was due to her no longer being seen as a rival for Simon's attentions. Then Prudence let slip an even stronger reason. Dorcas believed that she would soon wed Roger.

On hearing that, she would have immediately distanced herself from him. Jonathan's expectations and her own sense of responsibility for his soul made that impossible. She could only escape when her money arrived and she could leave for Wynnfield.

As July drew to a close, she waited eagerly to hear that it had.

On the last Saturday afternoon of July, having just come from preaching at St. Giles, she and Roger were taking a short stroll around Moorfields. As they made their way across the coarse grass, a fitful breeze tickled her cheek and filled her nostrils with the scent of boggy soil.

Roger, strolling at her side, was quieter than usual. She glanced up at him. He was staring across the fields toward the distant elm woods, his expression troubled.

"Are you thinking about the sermon, Roger?"

He threw her a brief smile.

"Actually, I was thinking of Father." His brow furrowed. "He's been acting peculiar of late. He claims someone's trying to steal our designs. He's even gone up and down West Cheap looking in shop windows for proof. Of course, it's ridiculous. But he seems to believe it." He shrugged. "No doubt he'll soon come to his senses." He glanced at the sun hanging in a white sky above the green forest. "Come along. It's getting late. I should accompany you back to Cousin Jonathan's."

The following Tuesday morning Anne Marie had finished hanging out the laundry in the back garden and was passing through the kitchen when Lettice, working on meal preparations, stopped her.

"You've a message from Master Browne."

Lettice pulled a folded paper from her apron pocket and handed it to her.

Anne Marie opened the paper with eager fingers. Relief flooded over her as she read the short message. She looked up with a smile.

"The bill of exchange has arrived. I can collect my monies any time."

She'd already attended a sermon with Roger the previous evening. Hopefully, it would be the last. If a message were sent to Peter tomorrow, she might even be back at Wynnfield by Sunday.

"With your permission," she said, "I'd like to tell Roger and Maud I'll soon be departing."

Permission given, she removed her work apron and hurried off.

After Guthran Lane, she'd visit Master Browne to collect the portion she was loaning to Will and Gwen, return, and write her letter to Peter.

Reaching Guthran Lane, Anne Marie glanced through the goldsmith-shop window as she went past toward the courtyard gate. Charles Denzil was showing wares to a customer. If she hurried, she could catch Roger in the workshop while his father was absent.

A maidservant answered her knock then returned to the kitchen quarters. She slipped down the short passageway and looked through the workshop door. Her gaze swept past the two apprentices in their leather aprons to fix on Roger. Shirt sleeves rolled to his elbows, he was sitting on a stool wearing a look of deep concentration as he planished a bowl.

She called his name softly. He seemed not to hear. She called again.

He looked up, concentration broken. He set hammer and bowl aside and came out to her with a smile.

"This is a pleasant interruption. But what brings you?"

"I've come to bid you and Maud farewell."

Roger's brown eyes widened.

"Farewell?"

"Yes, my money's arrived. I'll be returning to Wynnfield shortly. Now I must go up and say farewell to Maud."

"This is all rather sudden." He yanked apron strings loose, slipped his leather apron off, and tossed it onto a workbench. "I'll go up with you."

Maud was in the hall embroidering flowers onto a blue sleeve when she arrived with Roger. After she again explained why she'd come, Maud threw Roger a speculative look. She turned back to Anne Marie.

"Well, have a good journey."

Anne Marie started for the stairs, Roger trailing at her elbow.

"Before you leave, could I have a private word?" he asked, waving toward the open accounts-room door.

Uncertain what he wanted, she stepped into the room and wandered over to the accounts table.

Behind her, Roger cleared his throat.

She turned to him.

"I'd hoped to have more time," he said. "But now, with you leaving ... I have to speak, to ask the question I've been carrying in my heart for weeks."

She tensed. He continued, his expression hopeful.

"Do you think a fine woman like you could ever consider marrying a sinner like me?"

She swallowed, fighting panic.

"We're all sinners."

He stepped close, bringing with him faint odors of the workshop, and caught her hand.

"That's not the answer I'd hoped to hear."

She wanted to pull free, but that would be too unfeeling.

"I'm honored to be asked ... but I can't."

He gazed down at her with a mournful look.

"I've no chance with you? None at all?"

"I'm sorry," she said, shaking her head.

She heard a giggle.

Roger released her hand, crossed to the partially opened door, and jerked it wide. Maud was standing there, neck craned, ear bent close to the door frame. She straightened, unabashed, and wagged her dark head at him.

"Well, brother, it sounds as if you've lost the wager."

Roger glared at her.

"What do you mean?" Anne Marie looked in bewilderment from brother to sister. "What wager?"

Maud's eyes were dancing.

"He had a wager with Peter as to whether he could get you to accept a proposal of marriage."

Her jaw dropped as she stared at Roger. He gave her a shamefaced grin.

"It's not as bad as it seems," he said, spreading his palms. "After all, you turned me down."

Rage enveloped her, momentarily robbing her of speech. She found her voice.

"You're despicable!"

She jerked up her skirt hem, stepped forward, and kicked him on the shin.

He yelped and fell backward onto a stool. It promptly toppled over, sending him sprawling. She glared at Roger, lying red-faced on his back on the hard wood floor, and at Maud, bent double with laughter by the door.

The next moment the tears came.

She rushed from the room, down the stairs, and out of the house.

Once in the street among the passersby, she stifled her tears as she fled along Guthran Lane to Wood Street and through Cripplegate.

After passing out the gate, she headed for Moorfields. There, in the privacy of the empty, open field, she released her pent emotions, weeping in fury and anguish.

All these last weeks, Roger's reformed behavior and honeyed words had been nothing more than a sham. As childish as her response had been, she was glad she'd kicked him. He deserved it.

But Peter! Discovering that he valued her so little as to make her the focus of a wager with his brother broke her heart.

He was as despicable as Roger. She could never go back to Wynnfield now. She couldn't even remain in London. She'd have to return to Rouen.

A light breeze carrying the sweet dusty scent of harvest brushed Peter's jaw as he reined up at the edge of the barley field. His glance swept the field. The heads were beginning to hang, a sign that the barley would be ready to harvest before the week was out. The wheat, standing stiff and open in the first field he'd checked, was ready now. The oats, not yet shedding, would need at least another week. So would the rye, beans, and peas.

The crew of hired harvesters should arrive in the next day or two. He'd talk with the reeve to ensure that the workers' gloves, food, and sleeping arrangements were all in place.

This looked to be a good harvest – and an extra busy August.

Satisfied, he turned his horse and headed back toward Hensey, and Wynnfield Hall beyond. As he was walking his horse along the main road through the village, Gwen appeared in her doorway. She called to him.

"Peter, another message from Anne Marie just arrived."

He swung down from his mount and met Gwen in front of her half-timber cottage. She handed him the message. He broke the seal and unfolded the letter. A second one, tucked inside, was addressed to Gwen. He passed that one to her.

He smiled. It would be good to have Anne Marie back weeding in the pleasance and at the spinning wheel. Her cheery conversation would also once again brighten his meals.

He turned his attention to her short letter.

Her message killed his smile.

"Cousin Peter, I commend myself to you. You did not need to make a wager with your brother to rid yourself of me. You merely had to inform me that my presence was no longer welcome. I shall not be returning to Wynnfield. Written from London this 30th day of July 1572. Anne Marie duChant."

He stared at the letter in consternation.

"What's happened?" Gwen's sharp, questioning tone broke through his daze. "Anne Marie says that Jonathan has our money and will see we receive it. Except she's not returning."

"I don't know." He crumpled her note in his fist. "But I'm going to find out."

Peter galloped down the forest track to Wynnfield Hall. When he arrived, he swung out of the saddle and hurried toward the house. He sent the first servant he met running for the reeve then bounded up the stairs to his chamber. There, he collected his sword and began throwing garments into a traveling bag. When he came back down with the bag and sword, the house steward was in the blue parlor. He sent him off to have Cook pack some food.

He was in the accounts room scribing furiously when the reeve arrived minutes later. He finished his scribing and flung the quill aside.

"I'm leaving for London within the hour." He waved at the note he'd just finished. The drying ink was already losing its sheen. "This authorizes you to be in charge of all harvest matters until my return."

"How long will you be gone, Master?"

Peter tensed.

"I don't know. A few days. Work with Cook and the house steward over the harvest meals."

Peter had put a good number of miles behind him by the time darkness fell, and he was forced to find lodging in a wayside inn. He spent most of his short night tossing restlessly in the bug-infested bed. He was up and on his way again at first light.

He spotted the spires of London against the blue-gray horizon shortly before midday. Just a month ago he'd paused somewhere along here with Anne Marie to admire the scene. He had no intention of pausing today.

He galloped along Bishopsgate Street till he neared the city gate. He reined up in the next inn yard he came to and arranged boarding for his tired mount. That done, he slung his traveling bag over his shoulder and set out, fast-paced, for the Peterman house. Soon he was turning onto St. Mary Avenue. Cousin Jonathan's courtyard gate was just ahead. He entered the courtyard and made for the house. Once on the porch, fist gripping door knocker, he halted, stomach knotting.

In his rush to reach London, he'd not given thought regarding what he would say to Anne Marie. Now that he was here, he only knew he had to convince her to return to Wynnfield. Will and Gwen were depending on her.

He banged the metal knocker. The sharp sound reverberated within. He was preparing to bang the knocker a second time when the door opened. Lettice, in a dark gown and white cap, stood looking up at him. A smile broke across her lined face.

"Peter, what a pleasant surprise." She stepped aside. "Come in." Then, "We've just finished our meal, but if you're hungry...."

He crossed the threshold into the entryway. He was vaguely aware of voices coming from the dining parlor.

"I'd like a word with Anne Marie."

Lettice peered at him, a puzzled look in her faded blue eyes.

"She's not here."

"Not here? What do you mean? Where is she?"

"Didn't you know? She sailed for Rouen two days ago. I thought she wrote and told you."

His stomach knotted even more tightly.

"She didn't say that," he said. "How could she just leave? She has responsibilities. You don't simply walk out on your responsibilities."

Lettice gave him a brief uncertain look. Her expression firmed.

"I think it was because of Roger. This last month he's been a different person. Attending sermons with Anne Marie, showing real concern for the state of his soul. Jonathan was so pleased at the change. She was such a good influence on him.

"Then, something happened a few days ago. She wouldn't tell us what. But it must have been serious. She came home after seeing him to say she was returning to Rouen. There was no dissuading her. The following day she found a place on a ship. And on Thursday she left."

By the time Peter reached Guthran Lane, the knot in his stomach had spread to the rest of his muscles. It being Saturday afternoon, the shop was closed for the weekend. He strode across the courtyard to the house, jerked the door open, and bounded up the stairs to the main floor. He reached the landing to find the hall empty.

Judging from the voices coming from the dining parlor, the family were still idling over their midday meal. He flung his traveling bag down on a nearby bench and headed for the dining parlor.

As he stepped in, he was vaguely aware of his parents at either end of the linen-draped table, cluttered now with dirty trenchers and empty serving dishes, and Maud seated on the far side. Roger was on the near side, back to the door ... and to him. His fists clenched.

"Roger, get up."

Roger twisted round on his stool to look at him in surprise.

"Peter, what are you doing here?"

"I said, get up."

Roger shrugged, came slowly to his feet, and turned toward him.

He punched Roger in the face.

159

He heard his mother gasp as his brother staggered backwards, blood pouring from his nose.

"You broke my nose!"

"I'll do worse than that before I'm finished." He advanced on Roger. His brother retreated along the table, hand pressed to nose, fingers turning red.

"Stop it." Father banged his goblet down on the tabletop. "What's this about?"

He glanced at Father then turned back to glare at Roger.

"You told Anne Marie I'd made a wager about her."

"No, I didn't." Roger grabbed a napkin and pressed it against his nose, trying to staunch the red flow. "It was Maud," he said in a now-muffled tone. "And if you come at me again, I'll-"

"If you wish to break each other's heads," Father said, "do it in the court-yard. Not here."

"I made no such wager," Peter said, swinging his glare from Roger to Maud.

"I doubt she was that upset," Maud said hurriedly, rising and backing away, keeping the table between them. "She'd already rejected his offer of marriage before I said a word."

"She was mad enough to kick me," Roger said. "I still have the bruise. What brought you here anyway?"

The details were none of their concern.

"I had a message from her. She's returned to Rouen."

Roger's eyes widened.

"You mean she's gone?"

He nodded.

"Well," Roger said, drawing the word out. "At least that solves your ownership problem."

Father stood, crossed to him, and caught his arm in a tight grip.

"She's gone? She's really gone?" A slow smile broke over his heavy face. His grip loosened. He stepped back. "If we're lucky, she'll get herself killed in France's religious wars. Good riddance."

Father's malevolent tone sent a chill through him. He'd forgotten how cold Father's eyes could be.

He stepped back, trying to distance himself.

Anne Marie was gone, and he had to do something. But what? Standing here with Roger, Maud, and Father, he was too furious to think clearly.

He turned on his heel and strode out of the parlor, back down the stairs, and out of the house.

CHAPTER 15 – LONDON

Peter strode through the courtyard gate onto Guthran Lane and impatiently wove his way through the heavy Saturday foot traffic to Wood Street. There the traffic grew even heavier. Rage threatened to erupt when he was forced into a shop doorway by a rapidly approaching nobleman's carriage. The carriage passed, the horses leaving a string of turds on the dirty cobblestones. Dodging the turds, he followed a group of rowdy apprentices up the street and out of the city at Cripplegate.

He started up Fore Street toward Moorfields, fist gripping sword hilt, trying to walk off his anger, as he grappled with the situation.

When he arrived, the reedy unkempt field was filled with Londoners: young men practicing at the butts, children playing leapfrog in grassy portions, families strolling about, hawkers selling hot chicken's feet, all enjoying the bright breezy afternoon.

He was halfway across, heading for Finsbury Field, when the hard truth hit. He had to bring Anne Marie back. Only then could he see that she was properly provided for. And if he didn't provide for her, how could his conscience rest easy as the owner of Wynnfield?

Then, too, she'd left believing the worst about him. He had no option. He'd have to travel to Rouen.

He groaned at the thought. With the harvest just starting, it was absolutely the worst time to be gone. He'd simply have to make the fastest trip possible. Hopefully, Jonathan could help.

Jaw twitching in frustration, he set off across Moorfields toward Bishopsgate and St. Mary Avenue.

Peter arrived at Jonathan's home to the sound of harpsichord music. Stepping from the entryway into the hall, his gaze swept the long room searching for Jonathan. On the far side, Lettice was sharing a bench with Prudence, instructing her in stitchery. On the near side of the room, Dorcas was seated at the harpsichord. Jonathan was missing.

When Lettice saw him, she left the stitching lesson and approached, concern etching her face.

"Were you able to speak with Roger?" she said. "I'm sure it was a misunderstanding."

"You could say that," he said brusquely. He was in no mood to share details. "I must speak with Cousin Jonathan. Is he here?"

"He's finishing his sermon. Normally I wouldn't interrupt him, but…. Let me see."

She crossed to the study door, knocked, then disappeared within. A moment later she reappeared and beckoned to Peter.

"Jonathan wishes to speak with you," she said. "He's as concerned about Anne Marie and Roger as I am."

When he entered, Jonathan was seated behind his writing table, goose quill in hand. Two open Bibles and numerous sheets of paper, some blank but most filled with writing, were spread out before him while an ink pot and several more quills sat within easy reach.

Jonathan lifted a somber face to him as he approached, boot heels clacking on the wood floor.

"Lettice tells me that you've spoken with Roger about Anne Marie."

Having no more desire to share the details with Jonathan than he'd had to share them with Lettice, he came straight to the point.

"I have to go to Rouen. Do you know how I can find Anne Marie when I reach there?"

Jonathan's eyes narrowed; he studied him with a questioning look. For a moment, Peter feared he'd press for an explanation. Apparently, Jonathan decided not to ask.

"I don't, but Master Browne, the Bossuets' London agent, would."

"How do I find him?"

"I've met him once. He lives on Bow Lane." Then, "Anne Marie left a sum of money with me for the Weavers. I'd thought you could carry it back. But if you're traveling to Rouen…. I'll find someone else."

"When you do, I'll have a message to send with it."

With no time to dawdle, Peter strode down St. Mary Avenue to Leadenhall Street, sidestepped the water hawkers and housewives gathered at the conduit on Cornhill, and hastened past the currently empty stocks and drunkards' cages where Cornhill Street met Poultry. Soon after, he arrived at Bow Lane in the shadow of St. Mary Bow church.

Following Jonathan's directions, he found the four-story, half-timber dwelling with little difficulty. He breathed a prayer of thanks when the servant who answered his knock said Master Browne was at home. He was led up to the first-floor hall where the servant announced his arrival to a rake-thin man with a receding chin, large ears, and kindly amber eyes.

After introducing himself to Master Browne, Peter gave a purposely vague explanation for his trip to Rouen and the need to know how to find the Bossuets and Anne Marie once he arrived.

"Unless you plan to sail immediately," Master Browne said, pulling on his chin, "you may still miss them. In recent correspondence Monsieur Bossuet mentioned they plan to travel to Paris for the royal wedding. Hopefully, this union between Huguenot and Catholic will bring an end to the fighting in France." He shook his head and again pulled on his chin. "War is never good for commerce."

"I'd sail today if I had the queen's permission and could find a ship."

Master Browne's expression grew thoughtful.

"I might know of one sailing on Monday. If you wish, I can inquire."

"Please."

"Come tomorrow afternoon."

In no mood to join his family for the evening meal, Peter stopped at a busy tavern for its shilling dinner and a mug of cider. He arrived back at his parents' home as his father and Roger stepped from the house into the courtyard. They were both garbed in their best starched collars, velvet jerkins, and trunk hose. The bright bruise staining the side of his brother's nose was a vivid reminder of their earlier encounter.

Roger halted to glare at him. Peter tensed, his earlier anger reviving.

"I'm ready for you this time, big brother," Roger said, hands fisting.

"Leave it," Father said as he grabbed Roger's arm. "We'll be late for the guild meeting."

Dragging Roger with him, Father headed for the courtyard gate. With a squeak of hinges, they passed through the gate and disappeared. He continued on to the house.

He climbed the stairs to the hall. Mother was sitting at the card table reading Foxe's Book of Martyrs; Maud was on a padded bench adding embroidery to another sleeve.

Maud, pausing in her stitching, threw him a nervous look.

Although in no mood for conversation, he felt he must say something.

"I met Father and Roger in the courtyard."

"They're attending a guild meeting," Maud said, obviously glad to focus on an innocuous topic. "Father expects to be selected as the next guild president. He's already preparing his acceptance speech."

"Hungry?" Mother asked in her husky voice.

"I've already eaten." Then, "I've letters to pen."

Leaving Mother to return to her reading, he stepped into the accounts room and shut the door behind him. With dusk still an hour away, the light slipping in through the room's two windows provided enough for his needs. He bent onto a seat at the accounts table and reached for paper, quill, and ink.

The reeve and Gwen must be told of the change to his plans. Given Father's attitude toward Anne Marie, it was probably best if, for the moment, he didn't tell his family.

The window light was fading by the time he finished the second letter and sealed it will a blob of red wax. He collected the letters then returned to the hall to bid his mother goodnight. Carrying the letters and a lighted candle, he climbed the stairs to the small chamber adjoining Roger's where a bed had been made up for him.

He was pulling on his nightshirt when he heard his father and brother arrive home. Having no wish for further exchange with Roger, he quickly snuffed the candle and settled into bed.

Well before sleep finally caught him, he heard Roger snoring in the next chamber.

Roger was breathing more quietly when Peter awakened Sunday morning. He dressed, breakfasted on food laid out on the dining parlor's sideboard, and left without seeing family apart from his mother.

165

If the rest of the family planned to attend worship services, they were going to be late.

He made his way across London to join the Peterman family for worship at St. Andrew Undershaft. Afterward, he accompanied them home and shared their noon meal. In mid-afternoon he called on Master Browne. He came away with the name of a captain whose ship was leaving for Rouen late Monday morning. A note from Master Browne helped him secure passage on it.

If he got around quickly on the morrow, he should be able to obtain the queen's permission well before the ship was due to lift anchor.

After satisfying his hunger at a tavern, he returned to Guthran Lane in the long twilight. When he walked into the candlelit hall, Roger and Maud were playing cards, and Mother was mending a shirt. Father was absent.

Roger, the bruise on his nose now black, looked up. His expression tightened.

"Why are you still here?"

It was time to tell his family what he intended.

"Thanks to you two," he said, his gaze swinging between Roger and Maud, "I can't return to Wynnfield yet. Not until I've fetched Anne Marie from Rouen."

Roger's eyes widened as surprise overrode residual anger.

"You're going to Rouen?"

"I've been given little choice." Then, wanting to change the subject, "Where's Father?"

Roger shrugged and turned back to his hand of cards.

"He's probably out with friends. He'll be home later."

His father still hadn't returned by the time the rest of the household began to retire. As Peter settled down in bed, his ear caught the distant sound of the night watch calling the hour. He'd not yet heard Father arrive.

He abruptly recalled Roger's admission that Father visited the stews. Was he even now with a prostitute? Or had Father already returned home, and he'd failed to notice? For Mother's sake, he hoped that was the case.

The night watch was calling the hour when Charles Denzil finally left the Southwark stews. He knew he'd stayed overlong and had drunk more wine than usual. But it was a night to celebrate. As if by magic that girl had gone back to France where she belonged. She was no longer a threat to him.

Also, within a week he could well be the head of the goldsmith guild. As such, it would be unseemly to visit the brothels. This might be his last night to do so for some time. At least, if he came after he was elected, he'd have to take even greater care than he did now. But he could do it.

He'd never yet been caught. Of course, there was the night when he'd walked into a bawdy house and seen Roger. But Roger hadn't seen him. He was sure of it.

He swore as he stumbled over the unexpectedly rough cobblestones underfoot. He stumbled again and nearly fell as he made his way down the dark street toward the Thames to find a waterman to row him across. Once he secured a boat, he clambered aboard. The unsteady boat rocked wildly, and he lost his cap overboard. The waterman left him to retrieve it. He wetted his sleeve while doing so.

When the boat reached the London side of the river, he crawled out and began climbing the steps to Dowgate Street. These steps were as uneven as the earlier cobblestones. They almost sent him pitching backwards into the dark Thames.

Reaching the top at last, he started up Dowgate Street. The steep black street was lit here and there by horn lanterns while a smiling quarter moon floated overhead. He knew the night watch would be out patrolling the city.

He giggled, then clapped hand over mouth to still the noise.

Roger thought himself such a clever fellow in avoiding the night watch. But he could take a lesson or two from his father.

He opened his eyes wide to take in every scrap of light from lanterns and white moon. Several times he nearly tripped into the odorous gutter running down the middle of the street.

As he neared Candlewick Street, he heard the heavy footfalls of the night watch. He hugged the shadowed doorway of the nearest overhanging half-timber dwelling until the sounds faded. Then he continued on his way toward Budge Row.

Abruptly the street dropped. He staggered and fell. He lay in the street swearing.

Hands suddenly grabbed his arms and yanked him to his feet.

"Le' go o' me," he said, struggling to break free.

The hands tightened. He found himself staring into the faces of two night watchmen.

"What's your business out so late?"

"Not yur affair."

"He smells of drink and the gutter," one night watchman said.

"It's Cornhill for him till he sobers," the other said.

"No!"

Desperate to escape, he threw his whole weight against the gripping hands. His head exploded in a blinding flash. The dark swallowed him.

Peter rose early Monday morning, dressed, and packed his traveling bag. When he went down to the dining parlor to break his fast, Roger and the apprentices were already helping themselves to the bread, cheese, and ale.

Mother greeted him, worry marking her lined face.

"Your father hasn't returned."

He glanced at Roger. Judging from his brother's indifferent expression, he didn't share Mother's concern.

"Most likely it's nothing," Roger said, throwing him a warning look.

He turned back to Mother.

"Is he often absent like this?"

Mother shook her head. Then, "He's becoming like your grandmother."

"Grandmother?" he repeated in bewilderment.

She spread her hands in a helpless gesture.

I have a ship to catch.

"There's probably nothing to fret over," he said, trying to sound convincing. "Whatever it is, I'm sure Roger can deal with it."

After gobbling his breakfast, he bade his mother farewell, belted on his sword, collected his bag, and left the house. An hour later he had the necessary queen's permission. Not long after that, he was boarding the two-masted merchantman that would take him to Rouen.

His mouth thinned. He should be on his way to Wynnfield.

He was at the rail when the vessel weighed anchor below the bridge. Sails raised to catch the fitful breeze, it swung out into the dark blue current. Jaw twitching in frustration, he watched London Bridge grow ever smaller as the ship began making its slow way toward the Thames estuary and the English Channel beyond.

CHAPTER 16 – LONDON

When Charles was again aware of his surroundings, night had faded, and he was lying on a hard floor with only his cloak as bedding. He struggled to sit up, leaning for support against the uneven wall. He squinted against the early morning light as an anvil pounded in his head. Abruptly he vomited down the front of his doublet. Acrid odor filled his nostrils. He groaned and squeezed his eyes shut, willing the pounding to stop.

He heard Ursula snoring. Angered, he swung his leg and kicked her.

The snoring changed to a deep growl. Charles's eyes flew open. He was staring into a dirty unshaven face.

He jerked back in shock.

"What are you doing in my bedchamber?"

"This ain't your bedchamber."

He looked around, taking in the surly stranger, the bars of a cage, the stocks and pillory on a wooden platform to his left, and the early morning traffic of Cornhill Street. He shrank back in horror as the clock spring within began to tighten.

He was in the drunkard's cage!

This had to be a nightmare. Surely in a moment he would awaken.

Instead, he sat frozen with terror as London housewives, servants, and water hawkers came to fetch water from the Tun just a few steps away. Customers flocking to the long bread carts from beyond London with their fragrant, tuppence, wheat loaves added to the early morning bustle.

All who passed by threw curious, contemptuous glances at him and his surly cage mate. He pulled his now stinking cloak close about his head and prayed he wouldn't be recognized.

After an eternity in purgatory, the city watch arrived and unlocked the cage. They dragged him and his companion out and marched them off through the now crowded streets toward the Magistrate's office. All around him, the shops of London were open for business.

He should be in his own shop. Instead, he was being herded like a common criminal through a throng of gaping Londoners, cringing at the shocked looks of those who knew him, until he at last arrived at the city magistracy. Upon paying a fine, he was released.

Agonizingly aware of his disreputable appearance, he slunk home through the back alleys. He was forced to take to the main street when he reached Guthran Lane. He fled down the street and burst through the courtyard gate, heart pounding in terror.

Once inside his own home, the door slammed against the degradation he'd experienced, his knees gave way. He collapsed onto the staircase leading up to the hall. Curling over, he began to shake so violently that his teeth chattered.

He heard footsteps approaching. He looked up.

Terror engulfed him again as he faced his betrayer.

"Father, where have you been?" Roger said. "Mother's been worried about you."

"You know where I've been!" He lunged to his feet, the clock spring tightening near to breaking, as he spat the words out. "You're the one who reported me. But don't think you'll take my place with the guild."

He spun round and rushed up the stairs.

Bewildered, Roger watched him go.

Earlier that morning he'd set the apprentices to opening the shop, expecting Father to appear at any moment. But as the hours passed, he'd grown increasingly annoyed, then puzzled, and even somewhat worried by Father's continued absence. When one of the apprentices informed him Father had returned, relief washed over him.

Setting his work aside, he'd hurried out to the staircase. He was shocked at the foul-smelling, unkempt, wild-eyed man he'd found. He was even more shocked by Father's preposterous accusations.

Now, watching Father flee, he was uncertain what to do other than to follow. He reached the landing in time to see Father disappear up the stairs leading to the bedchambers.

At least he could end Mother's worries.

He went back down the main stairs and found her in the larder counting bags of lentils.

"Father's come," he said, speaking softly so the servants wouldn't overhear. "He didn't look well." That was an understatement. "I believe he went up to your chamber."

Mother immediately left the larder and started climbing the two flights of stairs to the bedchambers. On impulse, he accompanied her. They arrived at his parents' chamber door to find the latch string pulled inside.

He knocked.

"Father, are you all right? Open the door."

Rather than lifting the latch, Father shouted back.

"Bring water so I can wash."

Reluctant to involve the servants, he left Mother by the door, and he himself fetched half a bucket of tepid water. When he returned, he rapped again.

"Here's the water, Father."

He heard the latch lift; the door opened partway.

Father, fleshy torso bare, peered out at them, spittle dribbling down into his short gray beard. He flung his stinking garments at their feet, grabbed the bucket, and pulled it inside.

The door slammed shut. Roger heard the latch drop.

There was silence for two heartbeats.

Without warning, Mother gave a guttural cry and lunged at the door. She pushed against it with both hands, trying to force it open. Her usual calm composure was gone, replaced by building anger and alarm.

He must do something.

"Come, Mother," he said, catching her arms and pulling her from the door. "He'll likely come out once he's cleaned himself." He bent down, retrieved Father's soiled garments, and pressed them into her hands. "You'll want to see the laundress about these."

He managed to draw her away and down the stairs with him. Leaving her by the doorway to the kitchen quarters, he returned to the workshop.

He should be relieved that Father was back. Instead, he found himself unable to concentrate on the goblet he was decorating. He had little doubt that

Father had visited the brothels the previous evening. Had something happened there? If so, what? And what had Father meant by those preposterous accusations?

When Roger and the two apprentices gathered in the dining parlor for the midday meal, he expected to see Father at the head of the table. His seat was empty.

"Where's Father?" Maud asked as they started on the boiled hen, artichokes, and manchet bread.

"He's feeling unwell," he said, studiously avoiding glancing at Mother, sitting at the table's foot.

After a meal eaten mostly in silence, Roger and the apprentices returned to the workshop. The afternoon dragged on. Between pickling a goblet and waiting on a customer in Father's place, he hurried up to his parents' bedchamber. When he reached the door, the latch string was still missing. Father again refused to lift the latch.

On his way back down to the shop, he saw his normally industrious mother sitting on a bench in the hall, hands idle in her lap, desolation marking her lined face.

In the late afternoon he was planishing a bowl when the bell over the street door rang. He stepped from workshop into shop expecting to greet a customer. Instead, he found himself greeting Master Nashe, the tall, narrow-faced master goldsmith whose shop was close by on West Cheap and who was Father's occasional table companion at guild meetings.

"I've come to see your father," Master Nashe said, glancing about.

"My father's feeling unwell today."

Master Nashe nodded his grizzled head with a knowing look.

"'Tis no surprise after a night spent in the drunkard's cage."

Roger's jaw dropped. Master Nashe peered at him from under gray, shaggy eyebrows.

"You didn't know? Half the guild members are talking of it. With disapproval, I might add."

"But ... but that can't be true."

"He was seen," Master Nashe said in a firm tone. "I doubt he's any hope of being selected guild captain after this." He brushed an unseen speck from his dark jerkin sleeve. His tone softened, grew cautionary. "His actions shouldn't affect your being accepted as a master goldsmith ... provided it's not 'like father, like son'." Then, "I must be going. Greet your father for me."

The bell clanged as he passed out the street door.

Confounded, Roger remained staring at the closed door.

It couldn't be true.

But instinctively he knew it was. He'd seen men leave the stews so filled with wine they staggered. Even he'd departed in that condition on one occasion and had barely evaded the night watch. This time it had been his own father; he'd not been so fortunate.

A noise from the workshop broke into his thoughts. He frowned.

If the apprentices hadn't already overheard Master Nashe, they'd soon hear it from others in the guild. It wouldn't be long before all London knew. Mother also would learn of it. As much as he resented having the responsibility thrust on him, he'd have to tell her. It was either that or let her hear it from talebearers.

He swung round and headed for the back.

Best to tell her now and have it done.

When he passed through the workshop, the apprentices had their heads together, whispering. Seeing him, they straightened and hurriedly returned to grinding enamel slabs into powder.

His mouth tightened. They'd overheard.

With evening meal preparations well underway, he expected to find Mother either in the kitchen working on the meal with Cook or in the dining parlor overseeing the table setting. She was in neither place. Rather, he found her in the hall staring out a glazed window overlooking their narrow courtyard.

He halted behind her and cleared his throat.

"Mother, Master Nashe was just here. He told me why Father didn't return home last night." He cleared his throat again. It was as if he were confessing his own misdeeds. "He was in the drunkard's cage."

Mother remained silent, her back to him.

174

"Mother, did you hear what I said?"

She turned slowly, her expression unreadable. She finally spoke.

"He's like his mother." Her shoulders slumped. Then, "I must see to the meal."

She brushed past him and plodded toward the main stairs.

He stared after her, mystified by her response. Had both his parents taken leave of their senses?

When Roger took his place at the dining table for an evening meal of lamb and parsnips, Father was again absent.

If he wishes to go hungry, let him.

For the first part of the meal, he was forced to listen to Maud blather on about her need for new gloves and her detailed description of the type she desired. She eventually paused and glanced at Father's empty seat.

"Is Father still feeling unwell?"

Roger, sopping up lamb gravy with a bread piece, halted to glare at her.

Why avoid the truth? The rest of the table already knew.

"Yes," he snapped, "he's still feeling unwell. You'd also be if you'd spent the night in the drunkard's cage."

Maud's eyes widened in shock.

"Oh."

They ate the remainder of the meal in uncomfortable silence. As soon as it finished, the apprentices excused themselves and disappeared up the stairs to their bedchamber.

While Mother and Maud helped a maidservant clear the table, Roger strode off to the accounts room to record the day's sales before the light faded. He fetched the record book and metal money box from the locked wall cabinet in the corner, then settled down at the accounts table with quill and ink pot.

Father should be doing this, not hiding away in his chamber.

Opening the book at random, he gazed at entries from a previous year. They were in Mother's hand. He'd forgotten that she'd once kept the accounts. For some reason Father had taken to doing them in the last year or so. Apart from the few entries he himself had penned, they were now all in Father's handwriting.

He entered the sales, added two coins to those already in the box, then returned account book and money box to the cabinet, locked it, and hid the key in the usual place.

When he stepped out of the accounts room, Maud was sitting on a nearby bench in the otherwise empty hall, obviously waiting for him. She jumped to her feet. Her expression still tinged with astonishment, she intercepted him.

Her voice dropped to a conspiratorial whisper.

"Did Father truly spend the night in the drunkard's cage?"

Before he could answer, Mother appeared, coming up the stairs from the ground floor. Rather than turning into the hall to join them, she continued on past and started climbing the first-floor staircase.

"I've no time now, Maud."

He headed for the stairs after Mother, steps creaking underfoot, only vaguely aware that Maud was trailing him. He reached the top step.

Mother was crossing the passageway toward his parents' bedchamber. She stopped outside the door. The latch string was still missing.

She began pounding on the door with both fists.

"Open the door! Let me in."

Her harsh cry was like the growl of an animal in pain.

He hurried to her, caught her arm, and pulled her away from the door. She was trembling, whether from anger or anguish he didn't know.

"Mother, calm yourself," he said. "Let me talk with him." He stepped to the door, "Father, aren't you hungry? Mother can fetch you some food."

Apparently, Father was standing close on the other side, for his frenzied reply was clearly heard.

"And have her poison me? No! I'll not have your mother in this room. She'd kill me in my sleep."

"Why would she do that?"

I'm having a conversation with a lunatic.

"Jerome told her to. You all want me dead. Well, you won't succeed. I'll see you dead first."

Mother sucked in her breath at Father's chilling, maniacal words.

When he looked across at her, her face was the color of bleached linen, and her eyes were filled with despair.

"He's much worse than his mother," she said, head drooping.

"What do you mean 'worse'? What was wrong with her?"

Mother remained silent for so long he wasn't sure she'd answer.

She lifted her head and her gaze met his.

"She was deranged." Her words came slowly, hesitantly, as if she were inching her way along the edge of a precipice. "Your father wanted to send her to Bedlam. Your grandfather wouldn't allow it. Then the sweating sickness took her. You weren't born yet. He's become like her ... but much worse. She never had a devil." Then, with a ragged cry, "What will become of me?"

If only I could walk away. This is not my responsibility.

Hearing a sound behind him, he glanced over his shoulder and saw Maud. She was standing, mouth agape, eyes bulging.

In desperation, he grabbed the first thought that came to mind.

"Mother, you can share a bed with Maud tonight. Father will surely be more himself in the morning."

As night descended on the house, Father was still locked in his chamber, and Mother was settled with Maud in hers.

Roger tossed restlessly on his bed, unable to sleep. Thin light from the quarter moon drifting in his chamber window touched his clothing chest and outlined the door. Father's words kept repeating in his head. And Mother's claim.

Surely, she was mistaken in thinking Father had a devil. Hopefully, he was sleeping off whatever had so disturbed him. At least all had been quiet when he'd earlier tiptoed out to put an ear to Father's chamber door.

He eventually drifted into oblivion.

He woke suddenly. Had he heard a noise?

He listened intently but heard nothing. He turned his face toward the window hoping to determine the time. The first rays of dawn were brushing the sky. The day would soon arrive.

There it was again ... a noise. This time, it was of a door opening and then stealthy footsteps in the passage room.

177

He slipped quietly out of bed. Barefooted, he crossed to the door and noiselessly lifted the latch. He looked out into darkness. Dawn's faint light coming from his parents' chamber said the door was ajar.

He heard a stair step creak. Someone was descending the stairs.

He hurried across the passage room to the open chamber door and peered in. The half-light showed an empty room in disarray ... bed covers thrown aside, wardrobe open, Mother's gowns littering the floor. The clothing chest was on its side, its contents spilling out.

Convinced that Father had been the one on the stairs, Roger made his way as quietly as possible down the staircase after him. When he reached the hall, dawn was outlining its windows. He noticed candlelight coming from the open accounts-room door and caught the faint odor of burning wax.

His bare feet made no sound as he crossed through the dark to the accounts room. He stopped in the doorway.

The lighted candle on the accounts table revealed Father, garbed in the wine doublet he always wore to guild meetings, lifting the money box down from the wall cabinet in the corner.

"Father, what are you doing?"

Father spun round. The box lid flew open; coins scattered across the floor.

Father slammed the lid shut and rushed to the accounts table. He jammed the box into a half-full sack sitting there, then jerked a dagger from his belt.

He waved the knife at Roger.

"Keep away from me, Jerome, or I'll kill you again."

"Father, it's me, Roger."

Father grabbed the sack in one hand. Waving the dagger with his other, he started for the doorway. As Father neared, he jabbed the weapon at him.

Heart pounding, Roger leaped back out of the doorway barely in time to avoid the blade.

"You know I'm the better goldsmith." Father's tongue flicked out like that of a snake's. "I've always been. I always will be. Now keep away."

As Father rushed past him toward the dark ground-floor stairs, he swung the dagger again. Sharp pain shot down Roger's arm as the blade sliced through his nightshirt sleeve and nicked flesh.

He stared in horrified disbelief as Father bolted down the steps. He heard the house door latch lift. For three heartbeats, Father was a black silhouette in the open doorway. Then he was gone.

Clutching his arm to staunch the trickle of warm blood, Roger cautiously descended the stairs. He reached the open door and looked out into the dim courtyard.

Father was lifting the bar from the courtyard gate. Hinges squeaked. A moment later the gate was open.

Father disappeared.

Breath quickening, Roger paused on the doorstep to stare uneasily at the open gate.

Mother was right. Father was possessed by the devil.

The knowledge left him shaken.

He was only vaguely aware of the rough cobblestones beneath his bare feet as he cautiously made his way to the courtyard gate to close it and replace the bar.

Before pulling the gate shut, he peered up and down Guthran Lane, short hairs rising, muscles taut. At any moment Father could lunge at him out of the darkness.

Apart from the occasional horn lantern glowing dimly over a doorway, the street was black ... and empty.

Where had Father gone?

As he stood staring into the street, Master Nashe's words sounded in his head. "Like father, like son."

Words from a sermon he'd attended with Anne Marie to which he'd briefly listened rang even louder.

"The sins of the fathers are visited on the children to the third and fourth generation."

An icy chill swept over him. He began to tremble.

Copying his father, he'd dismissed his Maker as he'd dismissed so much else that promised to interfere with the pleasures he'd chosen. And these last few weeks, pretending to be the penitent sinner to win a bet with his too-perfect older brother.... Was this where those decisions led?

His grandmother had been demented. His father had become a raving lunatic. Would he be next?

His legs gave way; he fell to his knees in the open gateway.

Oh, God, help me. Tell me what to do. Don't let the devil have me.

As if in response to his frantic prayer, he suddenly thought of Cousin Jonathan. He grabbed the thought like a lifeline thrown to a drowning man.

Yes, Cousin Jonathan would have the answer. He can tell me what to do.

CHAPTER 17 – MID AUGUST – ROUEN, FRANCE

Boot heels tapping wood, Peter restlessly paced the deck as the two-masted merchantman made its slow way up the Seine against the sluggish current. Every time they rounded another curve in the blue-gray river, he prayed that Rouen would come into view.

When they'd laid up at Honfleur across the estuary from Le Havre two nights ago, the captain said they'd made an unusually speedy crossing from Dover. Peter, resentful of having to make the trip at all, was not mollified. The tides being in their favor as they started up the Seine, they'd soon exchanged the estuary's salt marshes for endless hills covered with the various greens of oak, ash, and field maple.

Whenever the forests gave way to the freshly harvested fields of some manor or monastery, he was reminded of his own fields needing his attention.

The only distraction from the seemingly endless, upriver trip was meeting other water traffic. Yesterday they'd passed both a fishing trawler and a cog boat heading downriver. Earlier today a three-masted Spanish carrack had glided by.

The sun was just starting down the afternoon sky when they passed a barge loaded with barrels and crates. Soon after, they rounded another curve.

Far ahead on the left, in a natural amphitheater of hills, a church spire stretched into the azure sky. Other spires and towers floated into view, reaching above the city's curtain wall. Rouen. At last they were nearly there.

Furling most of the sails, the merchantman slowed and began making its careful way through the increasing water traffic. Boats of all sizes and types vied for passage in the busy river.

They took the final curve. There, ahead, jutting into the Seine from either bank, were the two long ends of what had been a wooden bridge.

Numerous vessels were anchored off the sloping grassy shore between broken bridge and the near corner of the city's curtain wall. They passed two anchored cog boats, a Venetian caravel, a carrack, and another English merchantman before the captain gave the order to drop anchor.

Peter was one of the first off the ship.

Once ashore and not trusting his limited French, he searched till he found someone who could speak Latin. With the man's help he secured a guide. For a coin, the guide led him through a city gate, along streets smelling faintly of sewage, filled with carts and passersby, and lined with numerous top-heavy half-timber houses, until they arrived at the cloth merchants' street.

His guide pointed at the sign of The Ram hanging over one of the shop doors. Master Browne had told him that the Bossuets lived in a three-storied half-timbered house above. He'd know soon enough if he'd been brought to the right one.

He stepped through the courtyard gate, crossed to the house door, and banged the metal knocker.

Anne Marie gazed glumly out her bedchamber window and watched a robin flit among the branches of the pear tree in the Bossuets' back garden. The garden was small compared to the pleasance at Wynnfield. There were fewer birds here and hardly any bees. She'd been gazing out this window for a week now, ever since she'd arrived, and wishing for what could not be.

Perhaps she'd acted unwisely, rushing back to Rouen without thought. But where else could she have gone? Roger had made a fool of her, and Peter had broken her heart. Between them, they'd made it impossible for her to stay happily either in Hensey or London.

Now that she was here, Madame Bossuet was again talking of her wedding Claude. He still seemed willing to have her. He didn't yet know that most of her money was currently sitting in London and, thanks to what she'd given Gwen, there was less than before. Despite all the pain her time in England had brought, knowing that Gwen could now expand the business was something worth remembering.

It was fortunate that Madame Bossuet was preoccupied with preparations to travel to Paris for the royal wedding. Once they'd made the trip and were safely back at Rouen, Anne Marie would have to tell them all that she had no intention of wedding Claude.

She shook herself, trying to shed her despondency. Her father had always said that work was a good remedy for sorrow. Before Madame Bossuet had gone out earlier, she'd mentioned that the large chest in the parlor needed a good polishing before they departed for Paris. Why leave it to one of the maids when she could do it?

A servant's white apron over her kirtle, Anne Marie knelt on the reed matting by the chest. Fumes filled her nostrils as she began applying wax to the smooth lid.

She heard footsteps approaching behind her. A maidservant spoke.

"Mistress, there's a man here asking for you."

Anne Marie looked around as Peter walked through the door. His garments were travel-stained, his long jaw unshaven.

Her treacherous heart began to pound.

As the servant departed, she came to her feet to stare at him in disbelief.

Peter stopped two arm lengths away, his expression tense.

She broke the silence.

"What are you doing here?"

"I came to fetch you home. You have responsibilities. You can't just walk out on Gwen like that."

Anger flooded her.

Responsibilities!

"You came all this way simply to tell me that?"

"She was relying on you." A jaw muscle twitched. "And what of the villagers' need for employment?"

"I kept my word to Gwen. I sent her the money."

"But she needs spinsters."

"Then find her some." She flung the rag down. "Use the money you won in your wager with Roger."

"I made no wager."

She stared at him, confusion overriding anger.

"You mean it was all a lie?" Her voice trembled. "That Roger and Maud made the whole story up?"

"Well, not exactly," he said, looking uncomfortable. Then, hurriedly, "But I never agreed. You know how Roger is. When I told him I planned to wed Catherine Cox, he said he bet he could get you to agree to wed him."

His mention of Catherine Cox was gall. Her anger returned.

So, he was marrying that Catholic. I mustn't let him see how much the knowledge hurts.

She lifted her chin.

"I'll soon be marrying also ... probably once we return from Paris."

Peter's dumbfounded look was pleasing to see.

Before he found his tongue, she heard Madame Bossuet's voice. She drew in her breath and prayed for a calm, pleasant expression.

Madame Bossuet stepped into the parlor with Claude Goujon. As usual he was dressed in somber elegance. Seeing Peter, they halted momentarily.

"Madame Bossuet," Anne Marie said, forcing a smile and switching to French as they approached, "let me introduce my cousin, Peter Denzil, from England."

"Your cousin? You never mentioned that he was coming for a visit."

Peter bowed.

"I wished to surprise Anne," he said in halting French.

Anne Marie moved to stand beside Claude.

"And this is Claude Goujon, a friend of mine."

Claude slipped an arm around her shoulders. She forced herself to lean against him.

"Soon I shall be much more than that, my little red bird." He released her and turned his attention to Peter. "What reason brings you to Rouen?"

Peter mustn't be allowed to answer that.

"I was just telling him," she said quickly, "that we must leave shortly if we are to reach Paris before the royal wedding."

"You want to travel to the wedding?" Madame Bossuet said to Peter.

"I've never been to Paris," he said.

"Then you should ride with our company. My husband, Antoine, can secure a mount for you. And allow us to offer you the hospitality of our home until we leave."

184

Anne Marie opened her mouth to protest, to say that Peter had no interest in attending the royal wedding. She quickly shut it again. This matter was between herself and him alone. Besides, she wasn't sure his French was good enough to have understood the invitation.

"Go with you to Paris?" Peter said.

He'd understood enough.

Peter turned to Anne Marie and changed to English.

"Are you going?"

She nodded.

"All France is preparing to see King Henry of Navarre wed Princess Marguerite. Madame Bossuet wishes that we also go. We could be gone almost a fortnight."

He'd never stay away from Wynnfield and Catherine Cox that long.

"Will he be accompanying you?" Peter asked, casting a narrow look at Claude.

"Of course."

He turned back to Madame Bossuet and switched to French.

"I would like to go."

"It will be an event not to be missed, this union of Valois and Bourbon," Claude said.

"The union of a Protestant with a Catholic," Anne Marie added, feeling perverse. "But how long will he stay Protestant? King Solomon was led into idol worship by his wives."

"No true man is swayed by his wife," Claude said.

"He is Protestant to his very heart," Madame Bossuet said, "and the heart does not change."

Anne Marie glanced at Peter, thinking with bitterness of Catherine Cox.

"You're right. Hearts don't change."

Claude surveyed her more closely.

"My little red bird, why are you wearing the apron of a servant?"

How like him to only now really notice me.

"How else can I keep my kirtle clean while I'm polishing the chest?"

185

"Let the servants polish it," he said, catching up her hand and kissing it. His nose wrinkled and he dropped it. "You should spend your days sitting on a perch singing happy songs."

Acutely aware of Peter watching, Anne Marie smiled up at Claude. She was relieved when he turned to Peter. He was beginning to forget her again.

"Tell me, Monsieur Denzil, what is it like living under a Protestant queen?"

Peter must have understood something of the question because he first tried to answer in French. With a look of frustration, he switched to Latin. As Claude also spoke Latin, they soon were discussing rulers and religions.

Madame Bossuet pulled Anne Marie to one side.

"Since your cousin is to travel with us, I must inform Antoine immediately. And your cousin can have the little chamber for the night."

When Madame Bossuet left, Anne Marie turned her attention back to the conversation. She wasn't surprised that Claude, standing by a window with Peter, was already doing more talking than listening. She retrieved her rag, reached for the wax, and returned to work on the chest.

"We French should do what your old king did," Claude said, banging fist into palm. "Strip the Catholic Church of its wealth. With tithes, tolls, and depreciated currency, it is nearly impossible for a businessman to make a decent living. Two-thirds of our country's riches are in the hands of greedy, immoral churchmen who are under the influence of Spain. I say, strip the Church. End Spain's influence, and put the wealth in the hands of better men. There is nothing we could not do then."

Peter shook his head.

"Merely stripping the Church won't solve all your financial problems. It didn't for us. If anything, we have even more poverty than before."

"Ah, but we have Admiral Coligny," Claude said with a confident smile. "And he has the King's ear. Spain is not an ally, it is our rival. It would control France and see your Protestant queen overthrown. Now that the Pope has excommunicated her, you English should join us in supporting William of Orange. Ending Spanish domination of the Netherlands will benefit both our countries."

"Perhaps. But, right now, peace is what will most benefit England."

The lantern clock on the shelf struck the hour.

"I had not realized the time," Claude said. "We shall continue our discussion on our way to Paris. I have much to do before we leave on the morrow."

Anne Marie saw Claude give Peter a quick bow and stride out the door. He'd forgotten to bid her farewell. She continued waxing in the silence that he left behind.

Peter broke it.

"You're not actually going to wed that man?"

She lay her rag down and stood to face him. His mouth was a thin line.

"Why not? His family is well-to-do and Protestant."

"He's not a suitable choice."

"How would you know? You've only just met him."

"I know his type."

And I know Catherine's.

"As you once said to me, who I wed is my business. Come, I'll show you to your chamber."

Swallowing anger, Peter followed Anne Marie out of the parlor, up a set of stairs, and across a second room to a small chamber off the one where the two menservants slept. He dropped his traveling bag on the trundle bed and glanced out of the single glazed window to the street below. He turned back to her.

"I'll send a servant with water so you can wash," Anne Marie said. "And if you'll give him your laundry, I'll see it's done before we leave."

Then she was gone. He stood staring at the empty doorway.

He was a fool. He'd been away from Wynnfield and the harvests far too long already. This trip to Paris would mean at least another fortnight wasted before he could start back for England. But for Anne Marie's stubbornness, they could be on their way home tomorrow. If only his conscience would let him return without her. But it wouldn't. Especially now that he'd met Claude Goujon.

A manservant soon appeared with the promised water and took Peter's travel-stained garments away. Half an hour later, his jaw newly shaved and wearing his least soiled clothing, Peter found his way back to the parlor. Anne Marie was there polishing the chest. She looked up when he entered, then returned to her work in uncharacteristic silence.

Peter wandered over to the parlor windows and tried the view. He saw a linen shirt and stockings hanging out in the small garden below. A moment later a maid appeared and added another shirt and pair of stockings. His shirts and stockings. He'd originally expected to be away from Wynnfield for a few days only and had packed accordingly. It would be good to have clean linens again. Besides, remaining angry at Anne Marie wouldn't help matters. He turned away from the window.

"Thank you for having my laundry done."

Anne Marie looked up.

"You're welcome."

She returned to her silent waxing. He tried again.

"How far is Paris?"

"Monsieur Bossuet says it's some eighty miles by road."

"You've never been there?"

Anne Marie shook her head.

"Then we can see it together."

"Monsieur Bossuet has gone several times on business. Madame Bossuet doesn't like him going." She was becoming more talkative as she worked. "She worries that something will happen while he's away. They were here ten years ago when the Duke of Guise and his Catholic forces sacked Rouen. But the religious wars ended three years ago and, this time, we'll all be going together. Still, it's good you brought your sword. We could meet robbers along the way."

"How many are going?"

"The Bossuets, you, me, a couple of the servants, some friends of theirs and their servants. And, Claude, of course. I doubt he'd mind meeting robbers. He fought under Admiral Coligny in the last war."

Peter said nothing. Anne Marie continued.

"We'll be staying with Monsieur Bossuet's Huguenot business connections. Probably the others will stay in an inn or with acquaintances. Madame Bossuet says it's not easy being Huguenot in Paris. The city is strongly Catholic." Anne Marie gave the chest one final hard wipe then stepped back and examined it. She nodded with a look of satisfaction. "There, that's done."

"It looks good."

She glanced at the clock.

"Monsieur Bossuet should be arriving home any moment."

Her words were followed almost immediately by the sound of voices. Madame Bossuet entered with a portly, balding man in a black doublet.

"My husband, Antoine Bossuet."

"We are pleased that you are joining us," Monsieur Bossuet said to Peter. He turned to his wife. "All arrangements have been made. We leave at first light."

Peter smiled politely, resignedly. There was no turning back now. This trip was going to happen. Pray God that, during the trip, Anne Marie could be made to see sense.

CHAPTER 18 – TO PARIS

Since the weather was dry, the roads passably good, and they met no robbers along the way, they made the journey in two and a half days. Peter shared a mount with the Bossuets' several traveling bags. With twelve in their party and Anne Marie riding beside either Claude or Madame Bossuet most of the trip, Peter had little opportunity to do more than exchange a word with her now and again.

A Huguenot manor owner gave them housing the first night. The second night, fifteen miles short of Paris, they found beds in a village inn within sight of the meandering Seine. Monsieur Bossuet jogged along with Peter for the final few miles. They reined up on top of a steep chalky rise to survey the enormous walled city and overflowing suburbs spread out below.

"That is Paris," Monsieur Bossuet said, motioning with a gloved hand, "the largest and most beautiful city in Europe."

Sitting his mount under a warm sun, Peter studied the multitude of tiled roofs, numerous church spires, and the roofs and towers of impressive stone mansions. Unlike London where the Thames marked the city's southern boundary, the Seine flowed through Paris, dividing it into two walled, half-circles.

He preferred London.

"Do you see the island?" Monsieur Bossuet said, pointing at an area of close-packed buildings rising up from the center of the dark blue river. "That is the Island of the City, the oldest section of Paris. Notre Dame Cathedral is there, at the far end. The fortified complex at this end with the towers is the Conciergerie. Our friends, the Derbords, live between, on the Street of Old Drapers.

"The Conciergerie was once a part of the royal palace. Our kings now live on this side of the river in the palaces of the Louvre while the Conciergerie is used for administrative purposes. The complex also contains a prison, the Palace of Justice, and the Holy Chapel. The Holy Chapel houses sacred

Catholic relics that supposedly include the Crown of Thorns and two pieces of the true cross." Monsieur Bossuet spat in contempt. "Pure idolatry. Be thankful that your kings have rid England of such things."

Monsieur Bossuet kneed his horse and started down the slope after the rest of their company. Peter followed.

A short while later they were trotting by hedged fields, two-storied half-timber cottages, and vegetable gardens. Shortly before they reached the city gate, they passed one end of a long, pale-stone palace stretching nearly to the Seine, its many glazed windows looking out across a large walled enclosure.

They entered the city gate behind a herd of grunting, odorous swine.

Peter found himself on a cobblestone street coated with fetid mud, made dark by tall overhanging buildings, crowded with both foot and animal traffic, and filled with the velvety sound of French.

It would be easy to become separated from fellow travelers in this congestion. At least Anne Marie was riding ahead of him where he could keep watch over her.

They passed several narrow side streets. Monsieur Bossuet fell back to ride with him again. Monsieur Bossuet waved a hand at the row of crowded buildings to the right.

"The Louvre, where King Charles lives, is beyond, by the Seine," he said, raising his voice over the raucous cries of street hawkers. "The Queen Mother makes her home in the Tuileries Palace, that which we passed as we entered the city. Admiral Coligny has his lodgings on the Rue de Bethisy not far from the Louvre. The King greatly values the Admiral. Naturally he wishes him to remain close."

A vegetable seller shoved his cart in from a side street, rudely cutting Peter off. By the time he'd freed himself, swallowed his anger, and rejoined Monsieur Bossuet, they were nearing an intersection. Anne Marie was still ahead riding behind Claude.

Monsieur Bossuet pointed to the right as they crossed the intersection.

"There at the street end, across from the Louvre and the palace of the Bourbons, is St. Germain l'Auxerrois, the church of the royal family. Admiral Coligny lodges nearby. He is a great man, a great leader."

The intersection now behind them, the street began to narrow, and the congestion increased. Peter was forced to fall behind Monsieur Bossuet. Once past an enormous stone cross in the center of the street, the swine herd turned left. Their party took a right turn.

They wound their way along more dim, dirty streets until they passed out another city gate. Peter found himself on a stone quay running along the Seine's right bank.

They clattered across a wooden bridge, tall thin houses riding its back, to come out on what Monsieur Bossuet said was Palace Street. There they parted with the other Huguenot family who rode off up a side street. Monsieur Bossuet now took the lead. Peter was left to bring up the rear with the two servants on their shared horse. The stench here on the Island of the City was even worse than on the Right Bank and the streets even more constricted.

They continued along Palace Street past the high outer walls of the Conciergerie and the two lofty stone towers guarding an entrance. Soon, they turned up another street. It, too, was lined with four-storied, half-timber buildings. Judging from the merchandise in the shop windows, they'd reached Old Drapers Street, the cloth merchants' district.

They made their way along, passing a church, and weaving around creaking carts loaded with cloth bundles. Just before they reached a side alley, Monsieur Bossuet reined up in front of a shop window filled with colorful ribbons.

He dismounted and disappeared through the shop door. He quickly reappeared with a thin middle-aged man in a drab brown jerkin and an equally thin but younger one whom he introduced as Monsieur Derbord and his son Rennie.

Monsieur Derbord welcomed them with a smile and a flood of French. Seeing everyone else dismounting, Peter also stepped down. The Bossuet servants collected the traveling bags. Madame Bossuet and Anne Marie followed Monsieur Derbord along the alley to the house entrance a few steps away.

Peter started after them. Monsieur Bossuet caught his sleeve.

"The Derbord home is somewhat small for so many. We will secure beds for you and Claude at The Rose. It is an inn not far from here."

"I can make my own arrangements."

"No, no. You are our guests. Monsieur Derbord says the innkeeper, one Emile Tricost, is Catholic, something that must be forgiven. His son, Rennie, will take you there."

With limited coins in his purse, Peter accepted the offer.

Leading his mount, Peter fell in behind Claude and his horse. They clip-clopped after Rennie Derbord along Old Drapers Street and onto Lantern Street. Some distance ahead was a second bridge, this time of stone and also rimmed with houses, leading back to the Right Bank. Well before they reached it, they left Lantern Street for a narrower one. They soon made a final turn onto a short street running behind a stone church. This street ended at the Seine.

There, at the end, edging the quay, was a three-story half-timber inn. A sign with a large red rose against a white background hung over its doorway.

Rennie left them at the inn's open stable yard gate. After tying their horses to a post in the small yard, Peter trailed Claude back to The Rose's street entrance. Following Claude, he stepped through the wide doorway into a dimly lit common room. The place smelled of pottage, ale, and sour mud. Light from the single large unglazed window showed customers dotted about the long tables that filled the room.

Claude's brief exchange with a patron identified the innkeeper. He was the smiling, gray-haired man with a large nose, apron around his thick waist, standing on the far side talking with a diner.

Street filth from his boot soles joined other filth on the rush matting as he and Claude approached the innkeeper.

While Claude secured housing for them, Peter glanced around. Several men at one of the rough wooden tables were carrying on a lively exchange over their food. Shelves filled with pewter dishes, earthenware mugs, and pitchers hung on the back wall between hearth and kitchen door.

As he watched, a tall square-faced young woman, stained white apron covering her green gown, entered from the kitchen. She made her way briskly across the common room and plunked a mug down before a customer. Then, with a swish of skirts, she returned the way she'd come.

Peter turned his attention back to Claude and the innkeeper, Monsieur Tricost. As he tried to follow the rapid exchange between the two men, he wondered. Had he been wise to accept Monsieur Bossuet's offer?

Once accommodations were secured, Monsieur Tricost stepped to the kitchen door and gave a call. The husky young man who responded had to duck to clear the door frame.

"My son, Demont," Monsieur Tricost said. "He will see to your mounts."

Peter looked up at Demont. For someone who appeared capable of also lifting the horses he'd be caring for, his brown eyes were surprisingly gentle.

The square-faced young woman bustled past with a bowl of pottage. On her return Monsieur Tricost stopped her.

"My daughter, Joliette, will show you to your sleeping places."

Joliette led them out of the common room and up two flights of stairs. She halted before a door and lifted the latch. She waved them inside, turned, and headed for the stairs.

Only then did Peter discover he'd be sharing a small second-floor chamber, and its only bed, with Claude. His mouth tightened. He should have made his own arrangements.

He dropped his traveling bag onto a stool by the unglazed window overlooking the Seine then followed Claude back down to the common room, expecting that they'd return to the Derbord home.

"Go if you wish," Claude said in Latin. "I am calling on Admiral Coligny."

With that, Claude headed for the street door. Peter was left standing in the common room. A frown formed. As Claude disappeared out the door, Monsieur Tricost·approached.

"Your friend seems eager to be on his way," the innkeeper said in reasonably good Latin.

"He's not my friend," he snapped. "We merely happened to travel here in the same company."

Monsieur Tricost pressed his thick lips together, his brown eyes studying Peter for a moment. Then he smiled.

"You have come for the royal wedding?"

Peter nodded.

"It is unusual for English to come to a French wedding," he said, "even such a momentous one. You pay France a great honor. Of course, some in Paris disapprove of the wedding. And with His Holiness the Pope withholding his blessing...." His expression sobered. He gave a short sigh, pulled up a new professional smile, and continued. "While you are here, you must see our fair city. There is none like it in all the world. You must visit Notre Dame Cathedral and our new City Hall and of course Les Halles … the best meat, vegetable, and fruit market in the country. After that.…"

Before Peter could escape, Monsieur Tricost had listed half a dozen other Paris sights that required a visit. He also let slip that the powerful and staunchly Catholic House of Guise opposed the wedding.

Once in the street, Peter walked over to the quay running behind The Rose to try the view. Directly across, a cluster of half-timber dwellings lined the Right Bank. Farther along to the right, beyond a long wooden pier, cargo from several large boats was being unloaded onto a sloping shore. Off to the left towered the huge stone bridge he'd glimpsed on their way to the inn, its six massive arches supporting the wall of houses. Below him, the Seine flowed slowly past, the blue-brown water dotted with refuse.

The river itself was busy with water traffic, mostly small boats ferrying passengers. Even as he watched, a lone boatman came rowing through one of the bridge's high stone arches. A few moments later he pulled up at river steps behind the inn, chained up his boat, and climbed the stairs to the quay.

The boatman strode past him, hurrying on his way.

He, also, needed to be on his way. He threw a final glance at bridge and river then set out for the Derbord home to see Anne Marie. It was good, after all, that Claude wasn't with going him.

When he arrived at the ground floor entry, a servant took him up the stairs to the hall. The narrow room filled the whole of the first floor and boasted as many colors as the ribbons in the shop below. Of the several padded benches and stools, the high-backed settle at the rear end near the fireplace, and the cabinet on the pale plastered wall, no two were the same hue.

Monsieur Derbord was sharing a bright green bench and mugs of ale with Monsieur Bossuet near two large glazed windows overlooking the street. Shoes whispering on rush matting, Peter crossed the room to greet them.

"Madame Derbord has taken my wife and Anne Marie to call on friends," Monsieur Bossuet said. "Won't you join us?"

Curbing his disappointment, he bent onto a blue padded stool across from the two men and accepted ale from Monsieur Derbord.

Monsieur Bossuet nodded toward his bench mate.

"Monsieur Derbord has been telling me of the attitude of Paris toward this royal wedding. The parish priests are denouncing it, and Parliament is refusing to attend. It seems that most of Paris is against their Catholic princess marrying our Huguenot king."

"It is good," Monsieur Derbord said, "that so many Huguenots have traveled here to show their support for the wedding."

Peter had no desire to spend the remainder of his afternoon hearing about the religious tensions in Paris. As soon as he politely could, and after accepting an invitation to dine with them in the evening, he bowed himself out.

With nothing to occupy the next few hours, he decided to follow the innkeeper's suggestion and visit Notre Dame.

He wove his way through the crowded streets and soon came out onto a large cobblestone square partly filled with hawker carts selling cabbages, turnips, leeks, dried fish, and cheeses. There, on the far side, beyond the market, stood the massive limestone cathedral with its three tall intricately carved main entrances, elaborate rose window, and strong twin towers reaching heavenward.

According to Monsieur Tricost, the bishops and other members of Notre Dame's clerical community lived in what amounted to a small city to the north of the Cathedral.

He joined the square's foot traffic to make his way across, passing an onion hawker, numerous women with market baskets on their arms, two brightly garbed gallants, a small group of monks, and a one-legged beggar. As he reached the cathedral, four black-robed nuns came out of the open middle doors and passed him by.

Leaving the busy square, he stepped through the open doors into dim quietness. Immediately the scent of lighted candles and the faint odor of incense enveloped him. He instinctively hesitated, cautious, as if stepping into the temple of a foreign god.

To redirect his thoughts, he began studying the cathedral and the nave stretching out before him. A long row of huge columns and arches ran down either side of the nave, separating it from side aisles and ambulatories, and supporting an upper story of columns and arches. At the far end, beyond the choir, three large, brilliantly colored, clerestory windows looked down from the apse.

Stepping farther in, he came upon a colossal, brightly painted statue of St. Christopher beside one of the columns. He deliberately turned his back to it.

A hundred feet above, well beyond the rows of jeweled clerestory windows illuminating the cathedral, the vaulted ceiling was cloaked in sable.

He wandered down the nave toward the crossing where transepts, nave, and choir met, admiring the architecture as he went. On the way, he did his best to ignore the various chapels in the side aisles with their colorful saints' images and gold crosses.

He was standing in the crossing gazing up at the glowing lavender, blue, and primrose of the south transept's stained-glass window when he heard men's voices coming from a nearby side chapel. His ears pricked. They weren't speaking French. They were speaking the welcome sound of English.

"We also must say prayers at the shrine of Ste. Geneviève."

"Seeing Paris's sacred relics has made our journey here worth the effort."

One voice sounded vaguely familiar.

A moment later three brown-robed priests stepped from behind a column and started in his direction. His breath caught.

As they neared, he moved to block their way. He focused on the tall one in the middle whose bony face glowed with religious fervor.

"Cyril. Cyril Cox. They said you were dead. And … you're a priest."

Alarm swept fervor away; the priest's mouth set. His two shorter companions halted; uncertainty marked their faces as they eyed Peter. The priest shook his head and muttered something.

Brushing past Peter, he and his companions continued on toward the north transept.

Peter followed them. He caught the priest's brown-clad arm.

"Cyril … it's me … Peter Denzil."

The priest halted, and his blue eyes narrowed.

"You've mistaken me for someone else," he said in Latin.

He jerked his arm free and strode down the north transept with his friends.

Peter stood staring after them.

Could he be mistaken? Cyril was dead.

No, he wasn't!

He rushed after him and pulled Cyril around. He touched his left ear with its missing piece. Eyes blazing, Cyril knocked his hand away and hurried out the north transept door with his fellow priests.

He watched Cyril leave. But for the ear, Cyril might well have convinced him that he was mistaken. But for the ear....

Peter wandered back out the Cathedral's west entrance into the noisy square, puzzling over his encounter with Cyril.

That Cyril had entered the priesthood was no surprise. He'd always been passionately loyal to the Catholic Church.

But why allow his family to think him dead?

He halted abruptly as a bit of remembered conversation leapt to mind. Cousin Jonathan had mentioned hearing rumors of young English Catholics being trained for the priesthood on the Continent with the intention of restoring England to the Catholic Church.

Could Cyril be one of those? If so, how much did the Coxes know? Did they truly believe him dead? Or was it mere pretense?

CHAPTER 19 – PARIS

Anne Marie gazed out the rear window of the Derbords' colorful hall watching a maidservant collect dry laundry from their little back courtyard. Nearby, on the settle beyond the cold fireplace, Madame Bossuet was giving her husband an account of their afternoon while they waited for the evening meal.

Madame Derbord's lame, bright-eyed daughter-in-law, Lucet, was setting the tables in the second-floor dining parlor. Madame Derbord herself was in the ground-floor kitchen with the cook and second maidservant finishing the food preparation.

She would have offered to help Lucet had not Monsieur Bossuet informed her that Peter had come earlier seeking her and that he'd be returning for the evening meal. She wanted to be here to greet him. Although, what she could say to him...?

If only she could calm herself and think clearly.

Her emotions had been in turmoil from the moment Peter, standing in the Bossuets' hall, had denied making the wager with Roger and in the next breath repeated his intention to wed Catherine Cox. She'd remained conflicted on the ride to Paris, wishing one moment that she was riding at his side, the next moment determined that somebody should always be at her elbow when he approached.

Hearing boots coming up the stairs, she turned away from the window. She held her breath, watching the stair landing, praying it was Peter. He stepped into the great hall. Heart quivering, she released her breath.

He glanced around. When their gazes met, his sober expression lightened, and he started toward her. She met him halfway. Determined to maintain a cool exterior, she greeted him with formal politeness. Then,

"I understand you came earlier. I'm sorry you found us absent. We were calling on one of Madame Derbord's friends on the Left Bank. Tomorrow she's taking us to see Les Halles and to call on a friend on the Right Bank."

Her next words came out before she could stop them. "You're welcome to join us."

His response was instantaneous.

"I would like that."

Anne Marie heard more feet on the stairs. A moment later Monsieur Derbord and his sons arrived. Claude was close behind.

He strode across the room toward her.

When he joined them and knowing Peter was watching, she forced herself to smile up at him.

"Ah, my little red bird, I trust you had a good afternoon." His hand went to his sword hilt. "I have just come from Admiral Coligny and have much to tell."

His gaze shifted from her to the Bossuets. He clearly was more eager to share his news with others than with her.

She was saved a reply when a maidservant appeared with a platter of roast duck bound for the dining parlor. Other dishes were quickly carried up, and the meal was announced.

Claude accompanied Monsieur Bossuet up the stairs. Anne Marie followed with Peter and Madame Bossuet. Already Claude was giving Monsieur Bossuet an account of his day.

The dining parlor, although smaller than the great hall, was as colorful. The plaster walls were the color of cream, the sideboard a dark blue, the wall cabinet red, and the short benches a variety of colors. With so many guests, Madame Derbord had ordered a second linen-covered table set up.

Rennie Derbord, his wife Lucet, and his two younger brothers were already in their places at one. Anne Marie was given a seat at the other between Peter and Claude with the Bossuets across the table and the senior Derbords at either end.

The moment Monsieur Derbord finished the meal prayer, and while everyone began spooning food onto their wooden trenchers, Claude resumed talking.

"The King's council was wrong to reject Admiral Coligny's proposal," he said as he reached for a piece of roasted duck. "Of course, France should help the Netherlands free itself from Spanish domination."

"It would already be free," Monsieur Derbord said, "but for the traitor."

Anne Marie wondered how much Peter understood of the French flowing around him. After helping herself to the mutton stew, she leaned closer to him and spoke softly in English.

"Do you wish to know what they are saying?"

He looked up from the parsnips he was eating and nodded.

As she quietly began giving Peter a summary of the exchanges, Monsieur Bossuet interrupted the meal conversation.

"I fear our English guest may not be aware of recent happenings here." He turned to Peter and switched from French to Latin. "Perhaps you have not heard of the disaster that befell our troops in July."

"I must confess I've not."

"Earlier in the summer King Charles allowed Admiral Coligny to send Huguenot troops to the Netherlands to join Louis of Nassau in his fight against the Spanish." Monsieur Bossuet's grave expression hardened. "A traitor at the French court warned the Duke of Alva. As a result, his Spanish troops overwhelmed our forces. That traitor cost the lives of many of our soldiers."

"The Admiral refuses to give up," Claude said to the table in general. "He is still pressing the King to send troops to assist the Netherlands. He does not want to see France bowing to Spain. But for the need to attend the wedding, he would have already set out with his own troops to help drive Alva out."

Claude looked past her to focus on Peter, dipping a bit of goose into sauce.

"Your Queen stands with us," he said. "That is why she sent Ambassador Walsingham here to help us negotiate peace with King Charles and why she is supporting William of Orange in his revolt against the Spanish. She knows that Spain must not be allowed to rule either here or in the Low Countries."

"I understand that you've fought under Admiral Coligny," Peter said. "Will you be accompanying him into battle this time?"

"Unfortunately, no. My father insists that I wed and produce an heir before engaging in more battles. Once I have met his demands, I shall be free to rejoin Admiral Coligny."

Indignation swept through Anne Marie. She was nothing more to Claude than the means by which he could satisfy his father. She quickly tucked her chin lest her indignation show.

Thankfully, the conversation soon returned to more mundane subjects and the language reverted to French. Between bites she translated for Peter. As the meal neared its end, the Mesdames Derbord and Bossuet fell to discussing the visit to Les Halles the following day. Having already invited Peter, Anne Marie reluctantly turned to Claude.

"Will you be joining us tomorrow to see the Paris market?"

"I shall be with Admiral Coligny, my little red bird." He swallowed the last of his dessert tart. "Perhaps I can join you another day."

With the meal finished, most returned to the great hall. Anne Marie remained to help Lucet and a maidservant clear the tables. She gathered up a load of dirty tableware and started down to the ground-floor kitchen. As she passed through the great hall, her gaze swept the candlelit room searching for Peter.

The three Derbord brothers were playing a board game near the fireplace. The older Derbords and the Bossuets were sitting chatting at the street end. Peter was not with either group. He and Claude must have left immediately after the meal. Disappointment weighing heavier than the tableware in her hands, she continued down the stairs to the kitchen.

At least she'd see him on the morrow.

As Anne Marie was delivering the dirty tableware, Peter was accompanying Claude and his lighted torch through the maze of dark streets back to the inn before the church bells rang curfew. The last faint glow of twilight and the three-quarters moon were of little help in illuminating their way. The overhanging upper stories of shops and dwellings blocked most natural light, and the windows they passed were shuttered.

When they arrived at The Rose, Claude immediately retired to their bedchamber. Peter chose to have a mug of ale in the common room before following. Light from the odorous tallow candles revealed a few other customers scattered about the tables.

Monsieur Tricost himself brought the ale. He settled down on a stool across the table from Peter.

"I hope you have seen some of our fine city," Monsieur Tricost said.

"Yes, I did," he said, deciding to try his French. "I saw Notre Dame." Then, thinking of Cyril, "Do many Englishmen visit Paris?"

"I would not know. You are the first to lodge with me. And what did you think of our grand cathedral?"

"It was magnificent." *And filled with idols.*

One of the two shabbily garbed customers at a nearby table pushed into the conversation.

"But for those foul Huguenots, it would be even more so."

Monsieur Tricost glanced at the customer then turned back to Peter.

"A Huguenot mob broke into the cathedral some years ago," he said gravely. "They damaged the saints and other holy items."

"And now they're here again," the customer said, his voice hard with anger. "They should be banned from Paris – from all of France – and their heretical ideas with them."

"Our priests are right," the second customer said with an anxious look. "This marriage will bring the wrath of God down on France."

"It is a surrender of the government to Protestants." The first customer banged his fist on the table; the mugs jumped. "France must remain Catholic!"

"Of course, it must," Monsieur Tricost said, his tone soothing, "but not as a servant to Spain. Spain is our rival, not our ally. We do not need its king dictating to us."

Some while later Peter bade Monsieur Tricost good night and climbed the stairs to his bedchamber. When he arrived, the small room was dark. Claude was already abed and snoring lightly. Peter's mouth tightened. Claude hadn't bothered to leave a candle burning. Fortunately, he'd left the shutters open allowing pale moonlight to drift in through the window overlooking the Seine.

In that thin light, Peter pulled off his boots and began preparing for bed. After donning his night shirt, he closed the shutter and settled down on his side of the straw mattress. Gradually, as he lay staring at the night-dark plaster ceiling, his thoughts shifted from the heated conversations in the common room to brooding over Claude and Anne Marie.

When he'd earlier suggested to Claude that they bid her farewell before leaving the Derbord home, he'd declared it unnecessary. The man clearly had no manners. Also, Claude's habit of addressing Anne Marie as 'little red bird' grated like sand between his teeth. And this evening to discover that Claude saw her as nothing more than a brood mare.... She was of so much more worth than that. He must somehow find a way to stop her wedding this man.

At least he'd have Anne Marie to himself on the morrow. He'd continue to keep her close over the next days by having her translate for him. While he understood more French than he could speak, she needn't know that.

On that vague plan, he finally drifted off to sleep.

Faint light from the three-quarters moon slanting through the gable window fell across Anne Marie's straw pallet in the bedchamber she was sharing with the Derbord's two maidservants. Judging by their breathing, they were already asleep. If only she could quiet her thoughts and join them.

She rolled onto her side hoping a change of position would help.

She heard a dog barking in the distance. According to the Derbords, the unlit Paris streets were dangerous at night. After a moment the barking ceased.

How she wished she'd not acted on impulse in returning to Rouen. At the same time, she was glad she had because, regardless of his reason, Peter had followed her. And every minute he was here was another minute he was not with that woman.

She rolled back to her previous position on the straw pallet.

She should never have told him that she planned to wed Claude. Now she had to pretend it was true.

Her impetuous actions had trapped her. She couldn't return to England with Peter because of Catherine Cox. But if she stayed in Rouen, she'd face pressure to marry Claude, something she would never do. She had only one option left ... return to Strasbourg where her family were buried and support herself as a spinster. She would grow old there, all alone, not belonging anywhere or to anyone.

A tear trickled. She dabbed it with her finger. She mustn't dwell on the dreary future. For this short, precious time Peter was here with her. She must enjoy it to the fullest for it would be her last.

The sound of a shutter being thrown back wakened Peter on Saturday. He briefly lifted an eyelid. Early morning light drifting in through the window revealed that Claude was up and dressing himself. He seemed unconcerned at the noise he was making. He soon departed, snapping the door shut behind him.

Eyelids closed, Peter relaxed the best he could on the hard pillow. If he delayed a bit, Claude could well have eaten and left for Admiral Coligny's lodgings before he himself went down to break his fast.

When he entered the common room some time later, Claude was nowhere to be seen. He smiled. After exchanging friendly greetings with Monsieur Tricost, he settled at a table for a breakfast of bread, sharp cheese, and cider. The Admiral was welcome to Claude for the day. He'd enjoy his day seeing the Right Bank with Anne Marie.

Peter had expected to have Anne Marie by his side for the day. Instead, to his frustration, when they left the Derbord home, Monsieur Bossuet took up residence at his elbow. As Monsieur Bossuet had done on their arrival in Paris, he commented on places they passed. Peter only half-heard the comments. His attention was on Anne Marie, walking ahead with the Mesdames Derbord and Bossuet. Now and again she glanced back as if to see that they had not become separated in the heavy foot traffic.

They trailed the women onto Palace Street, past the Conciergerie's square clock tower, and across Pont au Change with its row of goldsmith shops and money changers, their footsteps ringing hollow on the wooden bridge.

Once on the Right Bank, they passed between the Grand Châtelet's prison and administrative offices. Peter didn't need Monsieur Bossuet to tell him the large stone edifice shared the locality with slaughterhouses. The acrid scent of dried blood was proof enough.

As they made their way along Saddler Street with its leather workers' shops, the smell gradually changed to something more putrid. He began drawing shallow breaths.

They were nearly to Iron Workers Street when the women stopped. When he and Monsieur Bossuet joined them, Anne Marie had covered her nose with her sleeve.

Madame Bossuet's face wrinkled in disgust.

"What is that foul odor?"

"It is the cemetery of the Church of the Holy Innocents," Madame Derbord said, "or rather the mass graves there. It is the city's largest and most occupied cemetery. Les Halles is just beyond."

When they entered the first of the large stone halls that made up Les Halles, the odor of putrefying corpses lessened. Monsieur Bossuet excused himself to visit the cloth hall. The Mesdames Derbord and Bossuet began surveying the pork, butter, and lamb being sold at nearby stalls.

At last he was walking with Anne Marie. Following the two older women, they rambled along the aisles, weaving their way among marketgoers, and stopping now and again to take a look at stalls displaying cooking pots, brooms, and several varieties of cheese.

"Lucet wished to come with us," Anne Marie said as they strolled past a stall selling ropes. "But she is merely the daughter-in-law. Madame Derbord assigned her other tasks."

"If you wed Claude, you'll also be merely the daughter-in-law."

She cocked her head to look up at him.

"That would be true whomever I wed … something I will decide for myself." Her chin lifted. "And I do not wish to discuss Claude."

Biting back a response, he continued on with her past stalls selling wheat, barley, and rye. The stacks of bagged grains were frustrating reminders of his own harvests that he'd been forced to leave in the hands of another because of her stubbornness.

They followed the Mesdames Derbord and Bossuet through a hall selling wines and one selling assorted fruits, vegetables, herbs, and flowers. They arrived at the cloth hall as a nearby church chimed the noontide bell.

"My husband will be here somewhere," Madame Bossuet said as they made their way along the busy aisles.

The stalls they passed were overflowing with bolts of cloth in a rainbow of colors and in a variety of materials from wool to linen to velvet and satin.

"Gwen would love this," Anne Marie said wistfully. She glanced up at him. "Please tell her I pray daily that her venture will succeed."

"You'd do better being there to help."

Anne Marie's chin lifted. Any reply she might have made was cut short by Madame Bossuet.

"There he is."

Madame Bossuet quickly set off through the foot traffic toward the end stalls. Madame Derbord was left to follow with Peter and Anne Marie. They arrived as Monsieur Bossuet concluded his conversation with the cloth seller.

The next moment Madame Derbord was hurrying them out of Les Halles, along the cobbled street past the odorous Cemetery of the Innocents, to Saint Merri Street, and the home of the Huguenot friend with whom they were to dine.

Despite their earlier tense exchanges, he was relieved that, on their arrival, Anne Marie seated herself beside him at the table.

After a meal of boiled pigeon, bread, and cabbage, and a great deal of conversation that she quietly translated for him, they took their leave to return to the Derbord home.

His hope of walking with Anne Marie was again overridden by Monsieur Bossuet.

"We should return by way of Place de Grève," he said, claiming Peter. "You must see Paris's new City Hall."

This time he and Monsieur Bossuet took the lead. As they made their way along the streets, it was his turn to glance back. They soon came out onto a huge, open rectangle filled with life. The gallows and pillory in the center said this also was a place of death.

He gazed around. Four-story half-timber buildings framed much of three of its sides. The open fourth side sloped gently down to the Seine where several large cargo boats were being unloaded at the river's edge.

Monsieur Bossuet waved a hand at the huge rectangle.

"Place de Grêve." Then, pointing to a building of elegant simplicity on the east side, "And our new City Hall."

Unlike the other structures facing Place de Grêve, the several-storied City Hall was built of pale stone. Its main tower reached high above its neighbors, and numerous glazed windows looked out across the square and shingle beach.

Three mounted riders, nobility by their garb, were ambling across the top of the square. On the still-firm ground farther down from where he stood with Monsieur Bossuet, hawkers were crying their produce to numerous marketgoers. Near the gallows a small gathering of citizens was listening to a priest.

The square and its occupants were forgotten when Anne Marie arrived with the Mesdames Bossuet and Derbord. His attention shifted to her.

The women had only just joined them when a scabby tan cur, tail between its legs, erupted from between the hawker carts. Two small boys chased close behind.

The cur fled up the square toward them, the boys in quick pursuit.

For a heart's beat, the cur looked ready to dive under Madame Bossuet's skirt.

She screamed and grabbed her husband.

At the last moment the cur altered course, flashing past her.

The little boys sprinted around them, one on either side.

A moment later the cur disappeared down a side street. The boys followed.

Although cur and boys were gone, Madame Bossuet continued to cling to her husband's arm as they set out down Place de Grêve toward the Seine. Peter breathed a silent prayer of thanks for the dog as he fell in behind the Bossuets.

He finally had Anne Marie at his side.

They were nearing the gallows and the citizenry assembled there when Madame Derbord, walking at Anne Marie's other side, began talking.

"This is the gathering place for Parisians," Anne Marie said, translating for him, "especially for public executions of important criminals. She says that some Huguenots were martyred here. Many more have died at Place Maubert. Thanks to Admiral Coligny, those horrible times have ended."

They were passing the group listening to the priest. While he understood little of the priest's rapid speech, the volume and furious tone carried their own message.

Madame Derbord's expression hardened; her face flushed with anger.

"He is denouncing the marriage of Princess Marguerite," Anne Marie said softly, "to the son of an excommunicated Huguenot. And warning that they will all be sent to hell if they bow to heretics."

They were nearly to the sandy shore before Madame Derbord's color returned to normal. They paused to watch wood being unloaded from a large boat anchored along the river's edge. Farther up the quay, other boats carrying hay or sacks of wheat were being emptied of their cargo.

He glanced around. This was the sloping sandy quay he'd seen from The Rose.

His gaze shifted to two smaller grassy islands a little farther up the Seine, reeds and the occasional willow tree marking their edges. Ducks swam among the reeds, and at least one white heron stood beside the shore. The sight of so much greenery in this crowded city was a feast to his eyes.

"Do people live there?" he asked.

Anne Marie had an exchange with Madame Derbord.

"She says the islets are mostly used for dueling. The militia also practice there with sword and musket."

"Militia?"

Anne Marie had another exchange.

"They are tradesmen who are used in time of trouble," she said. "Monsieur Tricost's son is a member. But then he is Catholic. Huguenot tradesmen are not accepted."

Sunday morning Claude joined Peter for breakfast in a nearly empty common room as church bells throughout Paris rang for early mass. Monsieur Tricost's tall, big-boned wife brought their bread and ale before disappearing out the street door. Her clean gown, lace cap, and rosary dangling from her girdle said she was on her way to hear mass at the nearby Church of St. Denis of the Cross.

209

A short while later, their mugs empty and breadcrumbs dotting the table's rough surface, Peter headed for the door after Claude. As they neared it, Madame Tricost stepped in from the street. Demont, also wearing Sunday garb and a small crucifix hanging from his neck, was with her.

Claude passed them without a word. Peter gave them a polite nod before following Claude out the door. Once in the street, Claude threw a contemptuous look across at the Church of St. Denis.

"They think salvation can be earned by attending a quarter-hour mass and wearing a crucifix. No. Salvation is a matter of predestination." Then, "Come. The Bossuets are waiting."

With that, he set off along the street leaving Peter to come after.

When they arrived at the Derbord home, Claude took possession of Anne Marie for the walk to the Left Bank where they were to attend a Calvinist worship service in the home of a wealthy Huguenot. Peter was left to walk with the Derbords' downy-whiskered second son, Edouard.

During the austere service, he watched Anne Marie sitting quietly beside Madame Bossuet. Given what he knew of her Anabaptist background and her own beliefs, how could she wed a Calvinist, especially one like Claude? It was simply wrong.

Both on the way to the service and on the return, Anne Marie pretended that Peter, not Claude, was walking at her side. At least she'd be sitting with Peter at mealtime.

Back at the Derbord home, the noontime conversation in their colorful dining parlor soon turned to the royal wedding to be held the following day. From her place between Peter and Claude at the table, she gave Peter a summary of the comments flying back and forth.

"With the Pope refusing to grant a papal dispensation," Monsieur Derbord said, "Queen Catherine had great difficulty finding a French prelate to officiate. Praise God the Cardinal du Bourbon finally agreed to perform the ceremony."

"I doubt the Guises were pleased," Monsieur Bossuet said as he reached for a roasted chicken leg.

Madame Derbord turned to Madame Bossuet.

"The ceremony will be held just outside Notre Dame."

Madame Bossuet sighed as she mopped up gravy with a bread scrap.

"Having traveled all this way for the royal wedding, I wish we could at least witness the exchange of vows." Her look brightened. "The square outside the Cathedral is quite large. Might we not find a place from which to watch?"

"With so many nobility attending...." Madame Derbord said. Then, "We could try."

"After this royal wedding," Claude said, "the ban on Huguenot services in central Paris most certainly will be lifted. Admiral Coligny will insist on it."

"Yes," Monsieur Derbord said, "We should be free to worship wherever we wish."

"I believe," Madame Derbord said, "that the newlyweds will lodge at the Louvre until they travel to Navarre."

"Speaking of newlyweds." Madame Bossuet turned to Peter. "Upon our return to Rouen, we shall be celebrating Anne Marie's marriage to Claude. I hope you will stay for it."

Anne Marie spoke quickly, fearful that Peter might have understood and would accept the invitation.

"Oh, no, Madame. Peter will not be able to stay. He is needed on his manor."

CHAPTER 20 – THE ROYAL WEDDING

When Peter awoke Monday, he again waited until Claude left before rising and going down to the inn's common room to break his fast with bread and ale. After another lengthy conversation with Monsieur Tricost, he strolled over to the Derbord home, a bundle of dirty linens dangling from his hand.

Normally at this time of morning, the shops he passed would have had their shutters thrown back and their doors open. The royal wedding had changed that. With all of Paris focused on today's momentous event, most shops were closed. This was especially true for shopkeepers like Monsieur Derbord with businesses on the route the royal procession was taking to Notre Dame Cathedral.

As he made his way along the dim, odorous streets, he noticed that most passersby wore disgruntled looks. He'd seen similar looks earlier among the inn's breakfast diners. From what Monsieur Tricost had quietly shared, it wasn't only the wedding that many opposed. It was the four days of lavish celebration to follow.

According to Monsieur Tricost, the damage done to the French economy in recent years by gold and silver flooding in from Spain's American colonies had caused prices to increase much faster than wages. That fact, combined with recent poor harvests and rising taxes, had pushed many citizens deep into poverty. For people already incensed by a highly unpopular wedding, having so much spent on tournaments, banquets, and grand balls afterward only added to the feeling of outrage.

Listening to Monsieur Tricost, he'd thought of the poverty in Hensey village. Thankfully, Hensey showed little of the tensions that were rife here. But England hadn't been caught up in religious wars for much of the last ten years.

When he arrived at the Derbord home, he climbed the stairs to the great hall. Anne Marie greeted him with a happy smile as he stepped into the long, colorful room.

"The Bossuets left for the Cathedral with the elder Derbords some time ago," she said. "They hope to find a place from which to watch the ceremony." She glanced toward the three Derbord sons and Lucet standing by the two large windows overlooking the street. "The others plan to watch the royal procession from here."

Peter, following her glance, noticed an unexpected and unwelcome addition to the group.

"Why is Claude here?"

Her expression stilled.

"Since Admiral Coligny is attending the royal wedding," she said, not meeting his gaze, "Claude has decided to join us." Then, "Is that your laundry?"

He nodded and handed her the bundle. Clutching it close, she started down to the ground floor. His gaze followed her until she disappeared through the door to the kitchen quarters.

Only then did he cross the room to join the others. Rennie's youngest brother, Gaston, a thin fifteen-year-old with a freckled face, was leaning out one of the windows, obviously eager to see the procession. After acknowledging Peter's arrival with distracted nods, the others turned back toward the windows.

With Claude and the younger Derbords standing near Gaston, Peter took up a place at the outer edge of the second window. He made no effort to follow the occasional exchanges as everyone waited for the procession to appear.

Gaston abruptly pulled back from the window, his face aglow with excitement.

"They are coming. I can see the Royal Guards."

He leaned out again. Claude and the other Derbords crowded up beside him at the windows.

Peter moved so he could look along the street in the direction of the Conciergerie. There, marching at the head of the procession, were the King's Swiss Guard, garbed in brown and amber, swords on their hips and muskets against their shoulders.

He heard footsteps tripping rapidly across the room behind him. He glanced around. Anne Marie was hurrying toward him, her expression bright with anticipation. When she arrived, he stepped aside to let her take his place while he watched across her shoulder.

Standing so close to her, inhaling her lavender scent, his gaze shifted from the approaching procession to her. He noticed, as if for the first time, the tender curve of her cheek, the escaping copper curl at the nape of her slender neck, and the corner of her delicate mouth. A completely unexpected desire to enfold her in his arms and taste that mouth seized him, heating his loins and setting his heart racing.

As the Guard drew closer, boots tramping the cobblestones, he struggled to regain control of his emotions. Tearing his gaze from her, he forced his attention back to the procession that was beginning to pass in the street below.

The Swiss Guard led the way. A golden carriage with Queen Catherine, dressed in her usual black, and her sumptuously garbed son King Charles IX came next. They were followed by King Henry of Navarre on horseback, resplendent in a cream satin cloak. Admiral Coligny, in dark wine jerkin, rode at his elbow. Princess Marguerite was carried past in an ornate chair, the dim light in the street muting the beauty of her rose gown and jewel encrusted cap resting on her brown hair. A string of richly garbed nobility came after, the clip-clop of iron horseshoes echoing about the street. Finally, a long tail of well-dressed citizens brought up the rear.

He glanced over at Claude and the Derbords. Were they noticing, as he was, the other watchers at windows across the way? Rather than the high spirits exhibited here, many of their faces were dark with anger.

When the procession passed out of sight, he stepped away from the window ... and from Anne Marie.

She excused herself to deal with his laundry. Lucet limped off to the kitchen. The Derbord brothers and Claude made themselves comfortable on the colorful padded benches and began a lively conversation in French. Before long, Edouard was asking Claude about his experiences fighting under Admiral Coligny.

Peter settled on a stool by a window. At first, he attempted to follow the conversation. But soon his thoughts turned to Anne Marie. With newly awakened passion, he saw again the copper curl, her delicate mouth, the curve of her soft cheek.

He set his jaw. He must not let such thoughts take hold. To do so was to betray Catherine. Had he not come to France, they'd likely be betrothed by now. He had a responsibility to her, one he could not, would not, take lightly.

Restless and having no part in the conversation, he began to stroll about the hall. As he neared the fireplace for the third time, he glanced out the rear window and saw Anne Marie. She was draping his wet laundry over ropes in the back courtyard. His mouth softened into a smile as he watched her.

Had she done his laundry herself? If so, it would be like her.

The Bossuets and elder Derbords returned sometime later, exhilarated at having seen the royal couple arrive and, after the wedding ceremony and the Mass, take their departure. Talk of the royal wedding dominated the noon meal conversation and carried on into the afternoon.

While Anne Marie helped Lucet and Madame Derbord with housework, he listened to Claude, the Bossuets, and Monsieur Derbord. Apparently, Admiral Coligny and the leading Huguenots were staying not just for the four days of celebrations. They had some outstanding grievances to discuss with the King afterward.

When he returned to the inn with Claude after the evening meal, he carried a bundle of freshly laundered linens tucked tenderly in the bend of his elbow.

The day following the wedding, shopkeepers all over Paris reopened their doors. After another long conversation with Monsieur Tricost, Peter set out for the Derbord home.

The royal wedding being over, he should have opportunity to talk with Anne Marie privately and somehow change her mind about wedding Claude. She must return to England with him so he could hold Wynnfield with a clear conscience.

He arrived at the Derbord's great hall to find the Mesdames Derbord and Bossuet gossiping on the settle and Claude sharing a red padded bench with Monsieur Bossuet. Since Admiral Coligny was attending the first day of wedding celebrations, Claude had decided to pass the time here.

His hopes of talking with Anne Marie were dashed when he learned she was assisting Lucet with housework. Although she was at his side during the noon meal, when they finished the sweet dessert tarts, she began gathering up dirty tableware.

His mouth set.

No doubt Madame Derbord would keep her similarly occupied for the rest of the day. He'd spent a weary morning listening to Claude and Monsieur Bossuet. He had no desire to spend his afternoon the same way.

Promising to return before the evening meal, he left for Notre Dame Cathedral.

The square, cleared for the previous day's ceremony, had returned to its normal state. Already malodorous refuse was beginning to appear on the rough cobblestones, and the singsong cries of hawkers filled the air.

Weaving his way through the maze of hawkers' carts, marketgoers, beggars, and dark-robed clerics, he crossed the square to Notre Dame. He stepped through the Cathedral's central portal into the quiet, dim, incense-scented interior.

Would he again encounter Cyril Cox?

On the previous occasion, he'd overheard Cyril and his companions talking of having traveled to Paris. But from where?

The sound of his boots on the pale-stone floor seemed unusually loud as he passed the colossal colorful statue of St. Christopher.

Douay.

The unfamiliar name floated up from the dregs of his memory.

When he'd last visited the Coxes, they'd received a letter from Douay. Immediately after, they'd bade him farewell. Wanting, himself, to escape, he'd not given thought to the letter until this moment.

Had Cyril come from Douay? Where was he now? Was he boarding in one of the city's religious houses? Was he with the clerical community living in the walled cloister north of Notre Dame? Or had he and his companions already left Paris?

What were his intentions? Did they include returning to England with the plan of restoring it to Catholicism?

He wandered around the Cathedral for some time, ignoring as best he could the candlelit shrines with their jewel-encrusted saints, but caught no glimpse of Cyril.

Leaving Notre Dame, he ambled about the narrow streets and along the muddy, foul-smelling quays lining the Seine until nearly time for shops to close.

When he returned to the Derbord home, Monsieur Bossuet was absent, Claude was seated at the street end of the great hall sharpening his knife with a whetstone, and Lucet was carrying a stack of wooden trenchers up to the dining parlor.

Having no wish to join Claude, he settled on a stool by the cold fireplace. A short while later Monsieur Bossuet returned and took a seat near Claude. Monsieur Derbord and his sons arrived soon after.

Anne Marie came up from the kitchen with a platter of succulent roasted pork ribs for the dining table, tossed him a quick smile, then continued on up the first-floor stairs. Madame Bossuet and the maid servants followed with other dishes. Madame Derbord, appearing with the final dish, announced the evening meal.

He trailed the rest up to the dining parlor and took his seat beside Anne Marie at the linen-draped table. The delicious aromas of the various dishes spread before him set his stomach to growling.

Once the meal was underway, Madame Bossuet turned to her husband.

"Tomorrow afternoon," she said, motioning with a pork rib, "we must visit Place Maubert to pay homage to the many Huguenots who have died there."

Monsieur Bossuet looked up from his pottage.

"Perhaps Claude can accompany you. I am meeting with business contacts."

Claude shook his head. "I shall be with members of the Admiral's household."

As Peter began spooning chard onto his trencher, he saw Madame Derbord glance at him.

"At least Peter can accompany us," she said.

He began to eat with new relish. Tomorrow he'd have Anne Marie to himself. If only he could find a way to change her thinking about Claude....

"Place Maubert is on the Left Bank in the Latin Quarter," Anne Marie said, smiling up at Peter as they trailed the Mesdames Derbord and Bossuet up Old Draper's Street. "Madame Derbord says it has a fruit and vegetable market. That's why she brought her basket."

They turned onto Jewry Street and soon reached Petite Pont. Once across the stone bridge to the Left Bank and through the massive fortified gate that guarded it, the older women led the way along a wide, busy street littered with horse turds and the occasional dead rat. Not long afterward, they turned up an equally busy and odorous narrower one. The overhanging upper floors of the half-timber dwellings lining the way draped the street in shadows.

Anne Marie fell to commenting on the variety of shops they passed.

The street gradually widened. They came out onto a long sunlit triangle, its edges marked with buildings. A heavy stake, taller than a man, sprouted from the middle of the open area. An even taller gallows and a wheel of torture stood nearby.

Madame Derbord halted partway across.

"This is Place Maubert," she said in a muted tone.

They stood in silence, looking at the instruments of death.

It was not silent around them. Hawkers cried their wares, marketgoers called to each other, and horseshoes clanged on cobblestone as riders passed by from other streets feeding into it.

After a time, Madame Derbord stirred.

"We should also visit the market," she said softly. "It has excellent bread."

She and Madame Bossuet set off for the market hall on one side of the triangle. Anne Marie continued to stand gazing at the stake with a pensive expression. Peter remained with her.

"So many Huguenots died here," she said, "just as Great Uncle Richard died at Smithfield." She fell silent for a dozen heartbeats. Then, "When my father was small and his family was living in Rouen, someone plastered posters here and in other cities denouncing the Mass. A great many people were arrested. My father's family escaped to Antwerp. Other Huguenots were not so fortunate. A number of those arrested likely died right here."

She turned away from the stake to look up at him.

"Why must people be killed merely because their beliefs are different?"

"It's always been so. The government sets the religion and those that don't comply-"

"What gives the government," she said, chin lifting, "gives anyone, the right to dictate the religious beliefs of others? And to kill those who refuse to comply? What if our conscience objects? Are we to disobey God in order to obey the government?"

"It's not that simple."

"Of course it is."

He must change the subject or soon they could be arguing.

"What opinion does Claude hold on this?"

Anne Marie looked away.

"I've never asked him."

He studied her, only vaguely aware of cartwheels grating on cobblestone as a hawker passed.

"Does he know of your Anabaptist leanings?"

She threw him a sideways glance then looked away again.

"I'll tell him when the time is right."

"And when will that be?"

She refused to meet his gaze.

"When I decide. We'd best rejoin Madame Bossuet."

She swung round with a swish of skirt tails. Dodging the hawker's cartload of dried fish, she set off toward the market. Jaw twitching, he could do nothing but follow.

Thursday morning Peter remained abed as Claude dressed and departed. This time, rather than joining Admiral Coligny's household, Claude would be meeting with his father's Paris trading partner. After he snapped the door shut behind him, Peter rose from the straw mattress and readied himself for the day. When he went down to the common room to break his fast, Claude was gone.

Monsieur Tricost's daughter, Joliette, brought his bread and cider.

He was halfway through the meal when Monsieur Tricost settled across the table. Before the innkeeper could ask his usual question about the places Peter had seen the previous day, he asked one.

"Do you know of a place called Douay?"

"Ah, Douay," Monsieur Tricost said with a nod. "It is a city in the Spanish Netherlands on the Scarpe River. The city is rich from the wool trade. A Flemish textile merchant from Douay boarded here for a short while last spring. He told me much ... including that Phillip II established a university there some few years ago. Of course, it will never equal our Sorbonne. He said the many English Catholics residing in Douay were greatly pleased as it is allowing them to continue their religious studies."

"They would be," Peter said, thinking of Cyril.

"Have you friends there?"

"Not that I'm aware of. I'm Anglican. But the woman I plan to wed is Catholic."

Monsieur Tricost's eyes widened; he gave an approving nod.

"Like the royal wedding – the joining of a Huguenot and a Catholic. Interesting. And the one sharing your chamber ... Monsieur Goujon. He, too, is Huguenot?"

"Yes."

"From the way his eyes travel over Joliette as she serves the food, I think he also is not opposed to Catholic maids."

It took a moment for the implication to register. When it did, Peter stiffened.

Did Anne Marie know this about Claude?

"I was unaware."

"It need not concern you," Monsieur Tricost said, with a shrug. "This is Paris. Joliette is accustomed to the way some men look at her. Should any customer try to do more, Demont will reprove him."

Peter's mouth twisted in a wry smile. Demont's size was warning enough.

Peter arrived at the Derbord home in time to accompany Anne Marie and Lucet to the market at Notre Dame. Hopefully, he'd finally have opportunity to talk privately with her.

Lucet made that impossible. Her shorter leg slowed her pace; nothing slowed her lively tongue.

On their way to the market, she hardly paused in her conversation with Anne Marie. At the market, Lucet turned to bartering with the hawkers filling the square that fronted the towering Cathedral. Even then she threw an occasional comment to Anne Marie.

He stood nearby listening in frustrated silence while odors of dried fish, onions, and raw meats floated past on the light breeze.

They left the market with a basket full of purple cabbages, parsnips, two freshly slaughtered chickens, and a small amount of figs. Fist tight on the basket's handle, he trailed Lucet and Anne Marie, again engaged in conversation, back to the Derbord home.

Once there, Lucet retrieved the basket and limped into the house. Before Anne Marie could follow, he caught her arm.

She looked up at him with a questioning look.

Best to confront it directly.

"Why are you planning to wed Claude? You don't even like him."

Even in the alley's dim light, he saw her color heighten.

"You don't know that."

"I don't? You've told him nothing about your religious beliefs. You hardly even exchange a word with him."

She lifted her chin defiantly.

"At least he'd never wed a Catholic."

She jerked her arm free and disappeared into the house.

He remained standing in the alleyway, anger roiling. He could follow her but to what purpose?

He turned on his heel and started down the side street running past the Derbord home and back courtyard. The rambling lane was so narrow he could have stretched out his arms and hit the buildings on both sides.

He must escape this close-packed city with its filthy streets and fetid odors so he could think clearly.

Following the lane, he soon came out onto Lantern Street. Pont Notre Dame was to his left. Directly across, behind a row of half-timber dwellings, the church of Saint Denis of the Cross looked down at him. Another minute saw him through the gap between the dwellings, across the churchyard, up the path beside the church, and back to The Rose.

After a quick word with Demont Tricost, he saddled the horse he'd arrived on. Soon he was trotting out the same Paris gate he'd entered the previous week.

Fresh breeze brushing his face, he jogged past Tuileries Palace, past the fields and cottages outside the walls, and up the long hill. When he topped the limestone ridge ringing Paris, he reined up, closed his eyes, and took a deep breath. The air here smelt of clean soil, of grass and dusty leaves, of the welcome scent of the countryside.

He opened his eyes and looked down across the walled city. His gaze fixed on the portion where Anne Marie was. Frustration returned.

He'd wasted all this time traveling to France and then to Paris because of his sense of responsibility for her. What had he accomplished? Nothing! She seemed determined to wed Claude.

As much as he disliked the man, perhaps he should accept her decision. What else could he do? Responsibility had to end at some point.

But he still had responsibilities at Wynnfield. It was time to return home.

CHAPTER 21 – ASSASSINATION ATTEMPT

"Isn't Peter sharing our nooning?" Madame Bossuet asked as they took their places at the dining table.

Anne Marie glanced at the trencher beside her for the man who hadn't arrived. She wasn't about to admit to Madame Bossuet that they'd parted in anger. Was his absence her fault? Or had something happened to him?

"He didn't say," she said, hiding her worries behind a weak smile.

Peter still hadn't appeared when she left for the Right Bank with the Mesdames Derbord and Bossuet. There, they strolled about in Le Marais's fresher air to see the dozen or so stone palaces of the nobility. Increasingly anxious over Peter's absence, she had little interest in the tall, sumptuous dwellings with their walled courtyards and gardens.

She followed the two older women back to Pont Notre Dame, fervently thankful that, soon after their arrival, she'd had Lucet show her where The Rose was located. Lucet thought it was because of Claude. She'd not corrected her. Now, as she crossed the stone bridge, she frowned at the houses lining it. But for them she'd see The Rose.

Once on Lantern Street, they passed the alleyway, tucked between two half-timber dwellings, that led to St. Denis church and the inn behind it. They soon turned onto Old Draper Street and arrived at the Derbord home. She quickly slipped out again and hurried to The Rose.

She entered the inn's dimly-lit common room and glanced about for someone to speak with. A tall, aproned young woman bustled past with a customer's order of pottage. On her return, Anne Marie plucked at her sleeve.

"I'm seeking Peter Denzil. Is he here?"

"He rode out this morning."

Her throat tightened.

"He left?"

The young woman nodded then hurried on her way.

Vision blurring, Anne Marie fled out to the street.

Had he departed without a word?

Not wanting passersby to see her crying, she started for the path running beside St. Denis. As she reached it, she heard the clip-clop of horse hooves on dirty cobblestone. She glanced back. A long-jawed man in a brown jerkin, black hat brim shading his hazel eyes, was riding up the street.

Peter! He hadn't left.

This time the tears blurring her vision were tears of relief.

Half hidden by the church corner, she watched him ride through the stable yard gate. Once he disappeared, she scurried back past St. Denis, across the courtyard, and out to Lantern Street. Taking the winding alley, she was soon again at the Derbord house. Thankfully, her brief absence had passed unnoticed.

Now if only Peter would arrive for the evening meal.

Peter handed his horse to Demont Tricost then went up to his bedchamber. He threw himself down on the straw mattress to lie staring up at the plaster ceiling.

On the bluff overlooking Paris he'd decided to leave. Had he done so, by now he'd be well on his way to England and home. Instead, he'd sat with his back against a tree as the sun arched across the sky, scowling at the horse and struggling with the thought of Anne Marie wedding Claude.

He'd stay until they returned to Rouen. But he had no intention of attending the wedding. Judging from Anne Marie's Sunday response to Madame Bossuet, she didn't want him to.

No, the moment they reached Rouen, he'd leave.

He arrived at the Derbord home shortly before the evening meal, an explanation for his earlier absence ready on his lips. He'd gone riding and had failed to notice the time. Fortunately, Claude arrived moments later, and the meal was announced. By the time everyone settled at table, the conversation had moved on.

Peter, thinking of Wynnfield as he ate, only half heard Anne Marie's quiet summaries of the exchanges.

Partway through the meal, Anne Marie abruptly stopped translating. He glanced at her. She was staring at Madame Bossuet, talking to Claude.

He hurriedly focused on the conversation.

"Claude, you have yet to take Anne Marie to see Paris. And we leave for Rouen immediately after St. Bartholomew's Day."

"He need not waste his time on me," Anne Marie said quickly.

"Nonsense," Madame Bossuet said. "Soon you will be man and wife. Giving time to you is exactly what he should do."

Claude turned to Anne Marie.

"I would be most pleased, my little red bird." His blond brows dipped. "Admiral Coligny is meeting with the King tomorrow morning. Perhaps we could go while he is occupied."

Irritation gripped Peter at the thought of Claude having Anne Marie to himself.

"Could Peter join us?" Anne Marie said. "He may never again visit Paris."

"I'd like that," he said before Claude could answer.

"He is most welcome," Claude said.

If Claude was dissatisfied that Peter would be joining them, he hid it well.

Peter frowned when, with a deliberate air, Anne Marie stepped to Claude's side as they set out from the Derbord home Friday morning. He was left to come after. She didn't glance back as they wound their way through the foot traffic.

Claude led them along Old Drapers Street, past the Conciergerie, and over Pont au Change to the Right Bank. There they turned left onto a wide stone quay running between the dirty blue Seine and the buildings on the Right Bank. A light breeze shared the river's odor; herring gulls wheeled and cried overhead.

Once on the quay, Peter stepped up to walk beside Anne Marie, their three shadows stretching before them.

"Isn't the day lovely?" Anne Marie said, glancing up at Claude. "Perfect for drying laundry."

Claude nodded.

"And the Seine has so many boats," she said, "like those loaded with hay. Where do you think they're going?"

"I wouldn't know, my little red bird."

Peter glanced down at Anne Marie. Her smile seemed fastened in place.

"This is a pleasant walk," she said as they passed two roughly clad laborers.

Claude looked over at Peter.

"That," he said, pointing ahead at the gray slate roof, tall spire, and apse of a large Gothic church overshadowing the surrounding buildings, "is St. Germain l'Auxerrois ... the parish church of the royal family."

"On a sunny day like this," Anne Marie said, "their stained-glass windows would be beautiful seen from within."

"We are not entering a place with idols," Claude said. "Besides, we have no time."

"Of course," she said. "I didn't mean –"

"The slate roof and tower beyond St. Germain," Claude said, focusing on Peter, "is the Bourbon palace, Petite-Bourbon. The Louvre is on the street behind. A number of Huguenot nobility, here for the wedding, are lodging there with the King."

They turned from the quay onto the Street of the Pulleys. Pedestrian numbers increased. Hawker carts appeared, the owners crying their wares and adding to the noise and congestion.

They started along the street with its malodorous center gutter. Trim brick dwellings shared the left side with Petite-Bourbon. On the right, St. Germain towered over the wall of five-story buildings separating street and churchyard. Knowing Monsieur Tricost would ask, Peter took note of the exquisite rose window high above the church's west entrance and the prominent bell tower on its north side.

They'd gone only a short distance when Claude halted abruptly. He peered ahead through the passersby and hawker carts.

"There is Admiral Coligny," he said, pointing. "The one holding the paper."

226

Following Claude's finger, Peter spotted a handful of richly and soberly garbed men emerging from a side street beyond the Bourbon palace. The gray-bearded nobleman leading the way, reading as he walked, must be Admiral Gaspard de Coligny.

"Apparently he has completed his business with the King," Claude said to Peter. "Come, you must meet him."

Before Peter could reply, Claude rushed off through the heavy foot traffic. He was left to follow with Anne Marie. Having little interest in meeting the Admiral, he set a slower pace.

Claude was nearly to Admiral Coligny when, ahead on the right, Peter noticed a man at an upper-story window pointing a stick at the street.

Puzzled, he stopped. His muscles tensed.

It wasn't a stick. It was an arquebus!

Suddenly, with a loud pop and puff of black smoke, a shot rang out.

As its echo ricocheted off the surrounding buildings, Peter's gaze dropped to the passersby ahead.

A second shot rang out.

Admiral Coligny jerked round, stumbled to his knees. The paper fluttered out of his grasp.

At the first shot, passersby and hawkers started, heads swiveling. The second sent them fleeing in all directions.

One hawker drove his cart into the gutter. Onions went rolling.

Peter quickly stepped in front of Anne Marie, shielding her. Stomach clenching, he looked ahead again.

Two of the Admiral's men were helping Admiral Coligny to his feet. He was clutching his left arm, fingers red with blood.

As Claude pointed at the man in the window, he disappeared.

Leaving one of the Admiral's companions with him, Claude and the others rushed to the building's entrance. The wooden door was locked. They began throwing their weight against it.

Passersby who, a moment earlier, had been fleeing, now began to gather in the street. They gaped and whispered and pointed as Admiral Coligny's men tried to force the door.

The door crashed open. Drawing their swords, the men dashed inside.

An eternity passed.

They appeared again, swords sheathed, expressions furious, and rejoined the Admiral.

Peter was vaguely aware that Anne Marie had moved to stand beside him.

Then Claude was shoving his way through the curious milling crowd, coming toward them.

He arrived, face ablaze with indignation.

"The assassin has escaped," he said. "I am accompanying the Admiral back to his lodgings. And the King most certainly will be told." He turned to Anne Marie. "Your cousin can see you safely to the Derbord home."

He hurried back to rejoin the others departing with Admiral Coligny.

The crowd began to break up, their faces ablaze with jubilation. Their expressions filled Peter with unease. News of the assassination attempt would spread like fire in dry grass.

He turned to Anne Marie.

"I'll accompany you back to the Derbords."

She looked up at him. Her face was pale, her expression determined.

"I don't wish to return yet."

He glanced at the passersby.

"Given what's just happened, I'm not sure how safe it is to go about Paris."

"Can we not go to The Rose and get a mug of cider?"

When they arrived at The Rose, Peter claimed a table for them in a corner of the half-full common room. He felt safer with the wall at his back. Although it was time for their nooning, neither he nor Anne Marie had much appetite.

Monsieur Tricost himself brought their cider and plate of coarse bread. He settled onto a stool and turned his friendly gaze to Anne Marie.

"Ah, Monsieur Denzil, whom have I the pleasure of welcoming to my inn?"

"This is my cousin, Anne Marie duChant. Anne Marie, this is Monsieur Tricost."

"You are French?" Monsieur Tricost said, thick lips curving in a smile as he turned to Anne Marie.

"My father was," she said. "My mother was English."

Their conversation was abruptly interrupted when two men burst through the street door.

"It has finally happened! Someone shot that Huguenot heretic, Admiral Coligny."

Startled, Monsieur Tricost twisted round to stare at the men. Peter exchanged guarded looks with Anne Marie as heads turned and customers cried out.

"When?"

"Where?"

"Is the heretic dead?"

"Unfortunately, he was only wounded," the first man said.

Food and drink were left forgotten on tables as the diners began gathering around the two men.

Peter glanced at Monsieur Tricost, sagging on his stool. His cheerful look was gone. He shook his head, his expression weary, somber.

"This is not good for France," he said softly, "not good at all."

"He was shot on the Street of the Pulleys," the first man said, speaking over his listeners' excited comments. "From the window of a house owned by the Guises."

The second man chimed in.

"The man escaped out the rear into the courtyard of Saint Germain. He had a horse waiting so was not apprehended."

"Thank the blessed Virgin."

"May the saints reward him."

"We should follow his example and rid ourselves of them all."

Monsieur Tricost stepped to the middle of the common room, his professional smile on his face.

"My friends," he said, raising his voice above the clamor, "this is news of great importance. Nevertheless, you may wish to finish your victuals before my daughter clears the tables."

The gathering began to break up. Customers returned to their food and drink. The two news bearers pulled stools up to a table and ordered ale. Excited exchanges continued to fly about the common room.

As he and Anne Marie ate their meal in wary silence, Peter listened to the exchanges. While he only partially understood what was being said, what he did increased his unease.

When they returned to the Derbord home, Anne Marie hesitated in the open doorway. He remained standing in the alley gazing down at her.

In a matter of days, he'd no longer be here to protect her. She'd only have Claude ... who'd gone with Coligny.

His jaw set. Better to think on matters under his control.

"You left your father's lute at Wynnfield. If you wish, I'll send it once I've returned home."

A shadow drifted across her face. Then the corners of her mouth lifted.

"Oh, yes. Please."

He turned to leave. She caught his sleeve.

"Aren't you coming in?"

He looked at her slender hand. He could so easily cover it with his. But she was wedding Claude; he was all but pledged to Catherine.

He slipped his arm free.

"I'll return later."

He swung round and strode off.

Anne Marie watched Peter disappear among the passersby on Old Drapers Street. Her feeling of safety, even during the dangerous situation they'd earlier found themselves in, disappeared with him. Now his kind offer to send the lute was another painful reminder that soon he'd be gone from her life forever. Her vision blurred.

She entered the house and closed the door. Dabbing tears with her sleeve edge, she started up to the great hall. At the stair top she nearly collided with Madame Bossuet.

"Anne Marie, you're crying. Is something wrong? Where's Claude?"

She gave the first safe answer that came to mind.

"Admiral Coligny has been shot."

Determinedly blocking thoughts of Anne Marie, Peter strode along Old Drapers Street. As he turned onto Jewry Street, he gradually became aware of the tensions around him. He slowed.

He began to notice passersby stopping in the street to talk, their faces alive with agitation and ferocious joy. Now and again he passed small gatherings whispering at street corners, their expressions fearful, angry.

He eventually arrived at the square fronting Notre Dame. The usual filth and collection of hawkers' carts, marketgoers, and occasional beggars gave the place a look of normalcy. But even here he saw jubilation, anger, exuberance, apprehension.

Peter returned to the Derbord home in the late afternoon. A worried and indignant Monsieur Bossuet greeted him in the great hall.

"Anne Marie told us of the assassination attempt and that Claude is with Admiral Coligny."

"I hope he comes soon with news of the Admiral," Madame Bossuet said.

Peter glanced around the great hall with sudden apprehension.

"Where is Anne Marie?"

"Helping Lucet prepare the dinner tables," Madame Bossuet said.

Peter released his breath. Monsieur Derbord and his sons appeared.

"I felt it wise to close the shop early," Monsieur Derbord said.

"Yes," Edouard said. "Several Catholics shouted insults at us as they passed by."

Claude arrived as Monsieur Derbord was concluding his prayer for the meal.

"What news of Admiral Coligny?" Monsieur Bossuet asked. "How serious are his wounds?"

"One bullet broke a finger," Claude said, settling at the table on Anne Marie's other side. "The other struck his arm. The King has sent his personal physician to tend the wounds. Thank God the physician is Huguenot."

"Catholics can no more be trusted than Judas," Madame Bossuet said.

"The King and the Queen Mother visited Admiral Coligny while I was there. The King has vowed to avenge the attack."

"And well he should," Monsieur Derbord said.

"The Council is to meet tomorrow to conduct an inquiry into the crime," Claude said as he scooped fish pottage onto his trencher.

"They will discover the Guises were behind it," Madame Derbord said.

"Some of the Admiral's retinue wished to go immediately and kill the Guise leaders. The Admiral stopped them. When I left, Henry of Navarre was meeting with Admiral Coligny to discuss defense measures."

"What is King Charles doing to protect the Admiral?" Rennie asked from the other table.

Claude turned to him.

"Fifty of his own Swiss Guard are stationed around the Admiral's lodgings. He also has ordered all Catholics removed from nearby dwellings."

"Good, good." This from Monsieur Bossuet.

"The King has instructed our Huguenot leaders to move nearby," Claude added. "They, too, will be protected. He has stationed guards in the neighborhood and has chained off the street." Then, "I am moving to the Admiral's lodgings to provide additional protection."

"You must come tomorrow evening," Monsieur Derbord said, "and bring us the latest news."

Peter left with Claude immediately after the meal. Two men with swords would be safer than one in the dark streets. They arrived at The Rose without incident, and Claude disappeared up the stairs. Peter settled in a corner of the common room with a mug of ale. Claude appeared a few minutes later, his bag of belongings slung over his shoulder. He strode out the street door without a glance in Peter's direction.

At least he'd no longer have Claude as a bed companion.

As he sipped his ale, he listened to talk at nearby tables.

"Bands of armed heretics gathered outside the palace where the Guises are lodging. They were shouting death threats."

"The King has closed all but two of the city gates."

"With the heretic's brother and his army sitting just a few leagues away, that's wise."

"Thankfully, we have our own Catholic troops already within Paris to protect us."

"And our militia."

"Yes. If only they all were as husky as Demont Tricost."

Peter remained where he was long after he'd finished his ale. Given the tension pulsating about the common room, he couldn't bring himself to leave. Better to stay here till closing time and know what was happening than to sit in ignorance in his chamber, fearing the worst.

By the time curfew rang, the customer numbers had dwindled to three. Monsieur Tricost, expression sharp with anxiety, bent onto a stool beside Peter. He spoke in an undertone.

"Listen to them. You would think they are talking of war. We French have spent enough years in warfare. And to whose benefit? King Philip of Spain. If it should start again...."

Despite having the bed to himself, Peter slept fitfully. Several times during the night he rose, opened the shutter, and peered at the dwellings on the Right Bank. He neither heard nor saw anything to rouse concern. The city seemed to be sleeping peacefully under an almost full moon.

When he breakfasted in the common room Saturday, the overheard conversations of other lodgers and customers from off the street were as filled with apprehensions as they'd been the previous day. Even Monsieur Tricost appeared as worried.

He made his way to the Derbord home in mid-morning. As requested, he took his dirty linens to be laundered before they departed on Monday. When he arrived, Anne Marie took his laundry and disappeared.

With nothing else to do, he wandered about Paris again, senses alert. Of the several city gates he visited, all but one were shut and barred. Everywhere he went, he heard the rasp of swords being sharpened.

He rested his hand on the hilt of his sword. This city was a pile of tinder ready to burst into flame.

He returned to the Derbord home as shops were closing for Saturday's half-day holiday. Over the noon meal the Derbords and Bossuets began discussing the Bossuets' departure on Monday.

Peter turned to Monsieur Bossuet.

"Given the tensions here, have you considered leaving sooner? Perhaps even today?"

Monsieur Bossuet shook his head.

"That would require traveling on the Sabbath. Monday is but two days away. By then Admiral Coligny should be much improved, and we can depart with easier minds."

Although still apprehensive, Peter didn't press the issue. He was a foreigner here and unfamiliar with the city's normal mood. Also Monday was only two days away. And they'd be departing for Rouen at daybreak.

He longed to be back to London. This being St. Bartholomew's Day eve, in Smithfield, Londoners would be preparing for the Bartholomew's Day trade fair. As a young child, he'd eagerly anticipated seeing its puppet shows, wire-walkers, and acrobats. Later, the memory of Uncle Richard going to the stake there had sullied his enjoyment. Nevertheless, it was a grand fair.

He didn't know how Paris would celebrate the day. But however they did, it could never equal London's Bartholomew Fair.

When the meal ended, Anne Marie began helping Lucet and a maidservant clear the linen-draped table. No doubt Lucet would keep her occupied till evening.

As Peter slowly followed the others down to the great hall, he considered how to fill his afternoon. He certainly had no desire to sit here watching the hours pass.

Cyril Cox had mentioned visiting Ste. Genevieve's relics. He could go to the church housing the idolatrous items. While it was highly unlikely, he might see Cyril.

He glanced around the great hall. The Derbord sons were gone. Monsieur Derbord and Monsieur Bossuet were already in conversation on the green bench. Their wives were on the settle by the fireplace.

It would be unwise to ask them which church housed the relics. Monsieur Tricost was the one to ask.

Once down to the ground-floor and out the door, he set off along the winding alley. Soon he was crossing Lantern Street, passing St. Denis, and entering The Rose. He settled at a table and ordered a mug of ale. The atmosphere in the half-filled common room seemed less tense than it had at breakfast.

Monsieur Tricost was chatting with a customer. When he finished, he crossed the room to greet Peter. He also seemed more relaxed. Even as he was lowering himself onto a stool, he began talking.

"The King has been seen riding about Paris. And I've heard that the Queen Mother appeared at court as usual."

"Is that good?"

"Most assuredly. Seeing His Majesty going about and with the Queen Mother following her ordinary routine.... The Council must have matters under control."

Peter let out his held breath. Monday suddenly seemed nearer than it had just an hour ago.

"I thought to visit the church housing Ste. Genevieve's relics," he said. "But I'm uncertain which that would be."

Monsieur Tricost's eyes widened; he broke into a broad smile.

"Ste. Genevieve is our city's patron saint. Pilgrims come from all over France to worship at her shrine. And the miracles that have occurred at her tomb.... You must see it."

For some minutes Monsieur Tricost enthused about Ste. Genevieve and her shrine. Peter grew increasingly uncomfortable as he listened. He'd expected to be given directions. Instead he was being told about miracles.

Apparently, Monsieur Tricost was more staunchly Catholic than he'd assumed. Did he, like Demont, have a small silver crucifix hanging around his neck?

Monsieur Tricost eventually paused. Peter quickly inserted his question.

"Which church should I visit?"

"The Church of Ste. Genevieve. It is on the Left Bank … and is a part of the Abbey of Ste. Genevieve."

Once on the Left Bank and following Monsieur Tricost's directions, he started along Garland Street with its Saturday-shuttered shops and overhanging upper stories. Only a few days ago, he'd walked this street with Anne Marie. He paused at Place Maubert, recalling her protest over people being killed for holding a different belief.

Leaving Place Maubert, he began following the Street of Ste. Genevieve up the hill. Monsieur Tricost had said he'd find the abbey at the top. This cobblestone street, lined on either side by half-timber dwellings, was just wide enough for carriages and was littered with horse turds.

He crested the hill. A short distance ahead, the street ended at another gatehouse in the Left Bank's protective wall. This gate also was shut and barred.

He looked down a side street. There, behind a high wall running along the street edge, were the clerestory windows, steep slate roof, and tall bell tower of a church. The cluster of nearby buildings would be other parts of the abbey.

He followed the wall to the entrance and stepped through into the small cobblestone square fronting the church. Apart from the high, round, stained-glass window, Ste. Genevieve's pale limestone facade was simple to the point of plainness.

A crippled beggar, begging bowl in hand, sat beside the church porch.

Five black-robed Canons Regular emerged from an adjacent building. They strolled past him toward the street.

The only other foot traffic crossing the square were people coming or going from the church. How many of these were pilgrims who'd come expecting a miracle?

An old woman, cane in hand, hobbled past him to disappear through the church door.

He remained standing in the square.

Monsieur Tricost's stories made him want to flee. But the innkeeper would certainly inquire as to his opinion of this place. Also, if he didn't enter, he'd always wonder whether he'd have seen Cyril.

He crossed the square and stepped through the entrance. The nave stretched before him, the double row of heavy pillars separating it from the side aisles. The light slipping through the clerestory windows brightened the pillars and cast their shadows in the aisles.

He again considered leaving.

Drawing a steadying breath, he began making his way up the nave toward the chancel. Had this been morning, the stained-glass windows in the apse would be glowing like jewels. With the sun now in the west, the colors were dull.

Intricately carved parcloses marked off a section of side aisle near the chancel. He reached an opening between the screens. There, behind them, was a fragrantly scented, ornate chapel. A brightly decorated wall niche held the figurine of a woman. Lighted candles sat on a lace-covered table before it. This had to be Ste. Genevieve's shrine.

The old woman he'd seen earlier was kneeling before the image, a rosary in her gnarled hand, her lips moving in silent prayer. Cyril wasn't here. But had Mistress Cox been, she'd certainly be kneeling like this old woman, praying to this useless idol.

He swung round and strode quickly out of this place of superstitious idolatry.

Peter returned to the Derbord home in the late afternoon. He was climbing the stairs to the great hall when Madame Bossuet called out in an anxious voice.

"Claude? Is that you? What news of Admiral Coligny?"

A moment later he reached the top. The Bossuets and Monsieur Derbord were seated at the street end looking his way.

"It's only Peter," she said in disappointment, turning back to the others. "I do hope Claude arrives soon."

Before Peter could join them, Anne Marie came up the stairs with his dry laundry. He took the bundle and followed her over to the settle by the cold fireplace.

"The Derbords have rats in their larder," Anne Marie said. "When Lucet and I saw them earlier...." Her eyes began to twinkle with suppressed laughter. "I've never heard anyone scream so loudly." Then, more soberly. "Lucet wants to get a cat, but Rennie doesn't like them. He's gone to arrange for a rat catcher to come next week."

All too soon Lucet called her away to help with the final evening meal preparations.

He remained on the settle until Rennie arrived, Eduard and Gaston close behind. When the meal was announced, he climbed the stairs with Monsieur Bossuet. He was carefully vague when Monsieur Bossuet casually inquired about his afternoon.

Although Anne Marie had laid a place at the table for Claude, he failed to arrive.

"The rat catcher will come on Monday," Rennie said from the other table.

"If only we had news of Admiral Coligny," Madame Bossuet said.

"Had there been anything of concern," her husband said, "Claude would have sent word."

The conversation presently turned to talk of the morrow's Huguenot worship service. If Claude again failed to appear Sunday morning, he could claim Anne Marie for the walk there.

At meal's end he bade her farewell, collected his laundered linens, and left for The Rose.

Torch in one hand, laundry in the other, Peter made his way along the black, winding alley, across Lantern Street, and past St. Denis. Before entering The Rose, he walked over to the river edge to admire the full moon. It hung above the Right Bank's black roofs, a pale gold plate in the quickly darkening sky. Before long he'd be gazing at the moon from Wynnfield.

But Anne Marie wouldn't be there with him.

On that gloomy thought, he headed for the inn.

In the common room, he settled at a table near the entrance and ordered mead. Monsieur Tricost was moving from table to table, conversing with the few customers still there as curfew drew near.

The curfew bell had just rung when a man in a dark jerkin stepped through the door. He halted near the table where Peter sat and called Monsieur Tricost over.

"Tell your son," the man said, voice low. "The militia have orders to report to the City Hall at midnight."

Monsieur Tricost's smile abruptly disappeared.

"For what reason?"

"That is for the King to announce. Until then, say nothing. If your son fails to appear, he'll be hanged."

The man swung round and strode out. Monsieur Tricost remained staring at the closed door, his expression apprehensive.

"Monsieur Tricost," Peter said quietly, "is there a problem?"

Even in the dim candlelight, he could see the innkeeper throw him a startled look.

"Oh, no," Monsieur Tricost said, glancing away. "Not at all. It is merely a small matter regarding the militia. A message I must relay to my son. You have nothing to fear."

Monsieur Tricost hurried away across the common room and disappeared through the kitchen door.

Peter's fingers tightened on his mug.

Nothing to fear?

Monsieur Tricost's assurance only increased his concern.

He remained at the table with his empty mug until the last customer had departed, the other three lodgers had retired, and a sober-looking Monsieur Tricost locked the outer door.

After bidding Monsieur Tricost goodnight, he collected his laundry and a candle, and retired to his chamber. Once there, he threw the shutter open to peer across at the Right Bank. He looked up the Seine toward the City Hall. All seemed to be quiet.

He pulled off his boots, pulled on his night shirt, and settled down on the straw mattress. With Monsieur Tricost's words replaying in his mind, it was some time before sleep caught him. Even then he slept restlessly, waking now and again to peer out the window at the silent city.

Sometime during the night, he heard men's voices coming from the river. He scrambled out of bed, hurried to the window, and opened the shutter. The full moon high overhead cast light on four boats, filled with the dark shapes of men, being rowed up the Seine.

He watched until the boats pulled up at the sloping shingle beach beside Place de Grêve. The men began climbing out and making their way up the beach. They soon disappeared from his view.

Demont Tricost had been ordered to go to the City Hall by midnight. But the militia were used only in emergencies. Was Demont among the men in the boats? If so, what emergency had caused him and the other militia to be called out?

Although he remained at the window for some time, he saw nothing more.

He eventually returned to bed to doze fitfully.

CHAPTER 22 – ST. BARTHOLOMEW'S DAY

A bell clanged!

Peter woke abruptly.

Another nearer bell rang. Then another … and another.

It was as if all the bells of Paris were clanging.

He scrambled out of bed, banged open the shutter, and peered across at the buildings on the Right Bank.

Candlelight flickered in a window.

Terrified screams and the sharp sound of musket fire joined the clanging.

Heart racing beneath his nightshirt, he jerked on trunk hose, rammed feet into boots, grabbed his sword, and dashed for the stairs.

He reached the common room as Monsieur Tricost, also in nightshirt, entered with a lighted tallow candle. Demont, fully dressed and with sword on hip, was close behind. He wore a white arm band, a white cross marked his black hat, and he was carrying an unlighted torch.

They were making for the street door.

"Monsieur Tricost," Peter said, following on their heels, "what is happening?"

They reached the entry, lifted the wooden bar, and pulled the door open.

Demont touched candle flame to torch. As it caught fire, the odor of pitch joined that of tallow.

Blazing torch in hand, Demont stepped into the street and pulled the door shut behind him.

Monsieur Tricost turned to Peter. The candle trembled in his fingers even as his voice trembled when he spoke over the clanging.

"You have nothing to fear. It is only Huguenots who are being sought."

241

"Sought for what?"

Monsieur Tricost threw a quick glance at the street door.

"The bells are ringing now. It can no longer be a secret." He pressed his thick lips together momentarily. When he opened them, words began gushing. "The Huguenots were plotting to kidnap the King and the royal family. When the militia reported to the City Hall, they were told about the plot. The Huguenots tried before, some years ago. The King has ordered that they all be killed. The bells are the signal. The Guises and their followers are dispatching the leaders. Our soldiers and the militia have been given free rein to rid us of the rest."

"They are attacking Huguenots?"

"You will be safe here. This is not a Huguenot home."

Anne Marie!

His muscles clenched.

"I must get Anne Marie."

"No," Monsieur Tricost said, shaking his head emphatically. "It is too dangerous to venture out. Even now the militia are setting up torches to light the streets and stretching chains across them."

"I'm going."

He pushed past Monsieur Tricost and jerked the door open. He paused in the entrance, fist gripping sword hilt, his gaze darting up and down the moonlit street. For this moment it was empty. A torch, its flames doing a grotesque dance, was jutting out a window farther along the way.

He heard more screams and then shots coming from the Right Bank.

He sped across the street and into the dark passageway beside St. Denis. Another moment saw him through the churchyard and to Lantern Street. He again paused.

Torches jutting out unshuttered upper windows lit the street in both directions. Partially dressed people were standing in their doorways or gathering in confusion in the road.

Farther along to the left, men were stretching a chain across a main intersection.

To the right, on Pont Notre Dame, men wielding swords were trying to break into one of the houses that lined the bridge.

He could hear their furious cries.

"Kill! Kill the heretics!"

His hand tightened on his sword hilt.

The shortest way to Anne Marie was down the narrow twisting alley.

He dashed across the street and into the black alleyway.

If only the full moon would provide enough light to show the way.

He started carefully along the alley, his ragged breathing loud in his ears.

Even here were occasional lighted torches and people standing in doorways, anxiously crying out to each other.

Heart racing, he hurried from torchlight to darkness to torchlight and back to darkness for what seemed like a lifetime.

There, ahead, was another torch and the alley end where it met Old Drapers Street.

Candlelight in the Derbords' first floor windows gave evidence that someone was awake.

He heard musket fire coming from the Left Bank.

He crashed his fist on the house door.

"Open up! It's Peter Denzil. Open up!"

He heard a bolt slide. The door cracked open.

He shoved it wide, nearly knocking Monsieur Derbord over. He stepped inside, slammed the door shut, and slid the bolt across.

He bounded up the stairs, Monsieur Derbord close behind, and burst into the candlelit great hall. His gaze swept past the Bossuets and the Derbord family, most only half dressed, searching for Anne Marie.

She was standing by the cold fireplace garbed in tan kirtle and shoes, copper braids hanging.

He strode over to her.

"Quickly. Fetch your belongings. You're coming with me."

She looked up at him in confusion.

"What's happening? Why are the bells ringing?"

"Orders have been given to kill Huguenots. The bells were the signal. They're already breaking into houses. You must leave here."

Even in the dim candlelight he could see the color drain from her face. She glanced at the others in the room.

"Tell them."

She rushed past him and up the stairs.

Peter turned to the Bossuets and Derbord family. He couldn't think of enough French for the ill tidings he carried. He switched to Latin, repeating what he'd told Anne Marie in English. Monsieur Bossuet's eyes bulged. A look of horror swept his face. Voice shaking, he translated Peter's message for the rest.

For a moment they stared at each other in white-faced shock. Madame Bossuet began to wail.

"Not again!"

"We will be safe at the Conciergerie," Monsieur Derbord said. "The King will protect us." He turned to Rennie. "Fetch the swords. We will go there immediately."

Rennie bounded up the stairs. Monsieur Bossuet dashed after him.

Moments later they reappeared with weapons. Anne Marie was right behind them, a bundle under her arm. Rennie handed swords to his father and brother Eduard. Monsieur Bossuet belted on his sword.

Peter heard musket fire again, this time from nearby.

Everyone froze.

"Hurry, Anne Marie," Madame Bossuet, "we must flee to the Conciergerie. The King will help us."

"I'm going with Peter."

"The King gave the order," Peter said in clumsy French.

"You are mistaken," Madame Bossuet said. "The King would never do such a thing."

There was no time to argue. He turned to Anne Marie.

"We must leave now."

With the others, they rushed down the stairs and out into the alley. The Derbord family hurried around the corner onto Old Drapers Street, Rennie and Lucet, with her slower gait, in the rear.

The Bossuets remained in the alley, Madame Bossuet clutching Anne Marie's arm.

"You must come to the Conciergerie with us."

I'll drag her away by force if necessary.

Anne Marie shook her head, quickly freed her arm, and stepped to his side. She slipped her hand into his.

His tense muscles eased fractionally.

Monsieur Bossuet pulled his wife toward the corner, hastening after the Derbords.

Anne Marie's hand clasped in his, he started back down the alley. The smell of burning pitch grew stronger. The flaming torches revealed even more half-dressed people in doorways and alley or leaning out upper windows.

He kept their pace brisk but steady. No need to give the impression they were fleeing and have someone take up the chase.

They rounded a bend in the alley. Shortly before the next bend, half a dozen men were breaking into a house. Some had white crosses on their hats. But not all. Were the others soldiers? Or had ordinary citizens joined the slaughter?

His mouth dried. Retreat was useless. Their only hope of safety was The Rose.

He tightened his grip on Anne Marie's hand and quietly drew his sword. Its hard feel brought only slight reassurance.

Well before they reached the house, the men broke down the door. They disappeared inside. Cries for mercy came from within. Then shrieks.

Even in the flickering torch light, he could read the fright on Anne Marie's face.

As they neared the house, a woman in a pale nightdress plunged headfirst out an upper story window. She landed with a thump at their feet.

Anne Marie gave a stifled scream.

He glanced down at Anne Marie. She was staring at the woman sprawled on the filthy cobblestones.

The woman lay motionless, nightdress splotched with blood, long dark hair tangling around her head, mouth agape, her slit throat forming a second gaping mouth.

The woman was past help. He must get Anne Marie to safety.

As he hurried her around the body, he heard the heavy thump of another body landing behind them.

They were nearing the alley's end when he saw several men with swords dragging a woman and two children from a house. Their frantic pleas for mercy echoed in the alley.

A priest stood nearby, urging the murderers on. The men stabbed their victims and threw them down in a pile beside the door. They reentered the house, the priest close on their heels.

He rushed Anne Marie past before they returned.

Lantern Street was just ahead. Once across it and past St. Denis, they would be nearly at The Rose.

The end of the alley had been unchained earlier. A chain now stretched across it, and three men stood there, swords in hand. The white markings on hats and arms said they were part of the militia.

The militia had orders to kill Huguenots.

He slowed their pace and quietly sheathed his sword. Best to appear harmless.

"Say nothing," he said softly. "I'll speak with them."

What to say? His mind was frozen.

As he and Anne Marie approached the chain, the men stepped forward and stopped them.

"We are English," Peter said in halting French. He pointed at himself and Anne Marie and then across at St. Denis. "We go to the church."

"English, you say," one of the men said. "Most English are Huguenot."

The three exchanged sly smiles.

"We've orders to rid Paris of Huguenots. Perhaps that includes English ones."

Peter felt sweat running between his shoulder blades. He casually rested his hand on his sword hilt.

"We go to the church."

A fourth man strode up and joined them.

Peter looked up at Demont Tricost's grim face.

"Demont," one of the men said, "They claim to be English and say they're going to mass. The English part I believe, given how bad his French is. But Englishmen are Protestant. What say you? Shall we run them through or no?"

Demont reached his hand out toward Peter. He felt calloused fingers touch the neck of his nightshirt. Demont jerked his hand away.

"What's this?"

He held up his fist before his companions. Dangling from a string between his fingers was a small silver crucifix.

"Huguenots don't wear crucifixes," he said. "They may be English but they're Catholic. I say let them pass."

He pressed the crucifix into Peter's free hand, opened the chain, and waved them through.

Anne Marie's fingers tight in his, Peter forced himself to walk at a regular pace across Lantern Street toward the passageway leading to St. Denis.

To right and left, bodies lay scattered about the street.

With Anne Marie close at his elbow, they passed between the buildings on the other side and into the dark, empty churchyard. He hurried her through it and down the path beside St. Denis. At the church corner he again halted.

The Rose was just across, two cart lengths away.

He looked toward the river, checking for danger.

A headless body dangled out the window of a dwelling on the Right Bank.

He looked right toward the chained and guarded intersection farther along. The two militiamen stationed there had their backs to him.

The torch burning in the window of a nearby dwelling added to the moonlight brightening the street. His fingers tightened on the crucifix Demont had shoved into his hand.

Anne Marie's hand firm in his and praying that the men wouldn't turn, he started toward The Rose.

They reached the door.

He knocked softly and waited. Nothing. He knocked more loudly and again waited. Still no response from within.

Dare he bang on the door and perhaps attract the attention of the militiamen?

Before he could decide, he heard the bar scrape and the latch lift.

The door cracked open; an eye peered out.

The door was suddenly wide open, and Monsieur Tricost was pulling them inside.

"Thank the saints, you are still alive." He shoved the door shut and dropped the bar across it. "And your cousin is with you."

"Demont is the one to thank," Peter said, laying the crucifix on the table next to a lighted candle.

"Quickly," Monsieur Tricost said, grabbing the candle holder, "we will hide you in the stable."

Even as he spoke, he was rushing them across the common room, through the kitchen quarters, and out a rear door. The next moment they were engulfed in the odors of horses, dirt, and manure.

"Up there," Monsieur Tricost said, pointing the candle at the loft stretching across the stable's back wall. "Hide behind the hay mounds. And remain quiet. No one must know you are here."

Peter took Anne Marie's bag and hurried her to the ladder. She caught up her skirt tails and started to climb. The moment she scrambled onto the loft edge, Monsieur Tricost and his flickering candle disappeared. Apart from the moonlight slipping through a gap above the stable door, the stable returned to darkness.

Bag in hand, he began feeling his way up the ladder toward the sound of rustling hay and Anne Marie. When his shoulders topped the loft edge, he swung the bag up onto the loft floor. It landed with a soft thud. He clambered after it.

A hand touched his shoulder, guiding him away from the edge. Then he and Anne Marie were sitting side by side in the deep darkness behind a hay pile, backs against the stable's rough wall, surrounded by the dusty scent of dry grass.

Beyond the wall, he heard screams and the sounds of gunshots.

Anne Marie clutched his arm and pressed her cheek against his shoulder. She was trembling.

He covered her hands with his free one.

Gradually, her trembling ceased. She lifted her head from his shoulder but still clung to his arm.

He sat in silence with her for an eternity, listening to the terrified screams and distant shots.

Ever so slowly predawn light began slipping in through the cracks. The haystacks and rafters were dimly visible when Peter heard a door open below. He stiffened into alertness.

"Monsieur Denzil," Monsieur Tricost called in a loud whisper. "Are you still there?"

Peter scrambled to his feet. Careful not to crack his head on a rafter, he crossed to the ladder.

Monsieur Tricost was peering up at the loft edge. In the dawn light Peter saw his worried expression relax.

"I have spoken with my wife. You will be safest here until order is re-stored. But move to the far end, away from the horse stalls. After my wife and I return from mass, I will fetch your belongings … and something to break your fast."

Monsieur Tricost disappeared. Peter heard a door shut.

He returned to Anne Marie and helped her to her feet. Her bag in his hand and his footsteps ringing hollow on the loft floor, he led the way around the mounds of hay to the far end of the loft.

Anne Marie, flinching at every burst of musket fire, began making a space for them behind the final large haystack. He tried to distract himself from the musket fire by examining the loft end.

Despite facing north, enough early morning light was coming through the cracks to reveal a ladder propped on its side against the end wall. He stepped over to take a closer look. Two short doors, now bolted together, and the ladder, said this wasn't just a wall. It was another way out of the loft.

He was about to slip the bolt and push the doors open to see what lay beyond when he heard the squeak of hinges, then footsteps on boards. They came from behind the near haystack.

Had someone discovered them?

Quietly pulling his sword, he stepped between Anne Marie and the approaching footsteps.

Hay rustled. Monsieur Tricost came around the haystack.

"Here are your belongings," he said, "and a chamber pot." He dropped Peter's traveling bag onto the loft floor and placed the pot beside it. "I will return momentarily with food, and water for washing."

Puzzled by Monsieur Tricost's sudden appearance, Peter trailed him back around the haystack. Once around, Monsieur Tricost opened a door in the side wall and stepped over the high threshold into what appeared to be the underside of a staircase. He shut the door behind him. Peter heard a key turn in the lock.

He remained waiting by the door until it opened again. Monsieur Tricost reappeared, this time carrying a tray containing a bread loaf, white cheese, jug of ale, and two mugs.

"This door from the parlor is useful," he said as he stepped into the loft.

He handed the tray to Peter then reached back into the space under the staircase to retrieve a bucket of water.

"What of the doors at the loft end?" Peter asked.

"It is simpler to transport hay from the hay boats through our back court-yard than to cart it along the street and across the stable yard."

Distant screams interrupted their conversation.

Monsieur Tricost tensed, his expression sobered.

"The citizenry have joined the slaughter," he said. "And our priests are encouraging them."

"We need to escape Paris now," Peter said. "We can take the horses we came on."

"Impossible. All the city gates are shut. You cannot leave." Then, "I will bring food for your nooning."

Monsieur Tricost stepped back through the door. Peter heard a lock turning.

With the last two city gates shut, they were trapped inside Paris. At least they were safe here. But for how long?

Blocking worries as best he could, he carried the food around the haystack to where Anne Marie sat. He set the tray down on the loft floor beside her then fetched the bucket of water.

"You heard Monsieur Tricost?" he said as they washed their hands.

She nodded, her gaze clinging to his face.

"We'll return to England," he said, with more confidence than he felt.

He squatted beside the bread and cheese, voiced a rough prayer, and poured ale into mugs.

He watched her as they ate in silence. Her thoughts were clearly elsewhere. No doubt she was fretting over the fate of Claude and the Bossuets.

By the time he'd eaten his portion, weariness was overwhelming him. Almost before he could stretch out beside the haystack, folded jerkin for a pillow, he was asleep.

He awoke sometime later to find Anne Marie asleep nearby, her arm outstretched and her hand resting on him. He carefully slid free so as not to waken her. Once on his feet, he quietly crossed to the loft doors. Full daylight was now coming through the cracks. He slipped the bolt and pushed the two doors a thumb's length apart.

There below, running between the Tricost dwelling and the boundary wall, was the narrow courtyard Monsieur Tricost had mentioned and, at the end, the gate to the quay. Looking beyond the gate, he could see the Seine and several houses on the Right Bank.

Although the four-storied Tricost home and the equally tall dwelling off to the right narrowed his view of the Right Bank, it was wide enough to see three bodies hanging out of windows there.

Anne Marie mustn't see them.

The loft doors were again bolted shut and he was sitting by the haystack when Anne Marie wakened. Not long after, Monsieur Tricost arrived with bread and pottage for their nooning. This time he brought a stool for a table and news that he'd gleaned from Demont and the few customers who had stopped by The Rose. His look was somber.

251

"Admiral Coligny has been killed along with his guards and others of his household."

Peter glanced at Anne Marie, gazing at Monsieur Tricost with a distracted look. The dead would likely include Claude. Had she comprehended that?

"There is much talk in the common room," Monsieur Tricost said, "about what was done with the corpse after his head was removed. The Huguenot nobles and officials staying in the Louvre have also been slaughtered. Only Henry of Navarre and his cousin, the Prince of Conde, were spared."

Monsieur Tricost shook his head in grave disapproval.

"The streets of Paris are littered with dead, not only men but women and their babes. The citizenry have been given a free hand. Huguenot homes are being plundered of everything of value. Even the dead are being stripped of their clothing."

"What of the Bossuets?" Anne Marie asked in a shaky voice, "and the Derbords?"

"The Derbords are the Huguenot ribbon merchants who gave Anne Marie lodging," Peter said. "Their home is on Old Drapers Street beside the alley."

Monsieur Tricost nodded.

"I will inquire."

Then he was gone.

The distressing news robbed them of appetite. Knowing they must retain their strength, Peter insisted that they finish all the food. Afterward, Anne Marie huddled in silence, arms around drawn-up knees, through the long afternoon.

He spent much of his time peering through a narrow gap in the opened loft doors or pacing the loft end. He now knew how a caged animal felt.

Monsieur Tricost brought additional news with their evening pottage.

"The King issued orders in mid-afternoon for the killing to stop," he said, sagging with relief. "Some of the militia captains are assisting with ending this massacre. Demont has joined them. The events of this day will be such a blot on Paris as nothing can remove."

"Have you news of the Bossuets and Derbords?" Anne Marie asked.

Monsieur Tricost's look of relief changed to one of sympathy.

"Demont found the shop and house. Looters had taken everything of value. As for your friends.... Only our blessed Lord knows where they are." He turned to Peter. "With the killing stopped, we may hope that the gates will open again soon. For this night, your cousin can sleep with my daughter and our serving maid."

"No," Anne Marie said, shaking her head vehemently. "I'm remaining here with Peter."

CHAPTER 23 – FLEEING PARIS

The first light of dawn was drifting into the loft when Peter awoke on Monday. Anne Marie was sleeping nearby, her arm again outstretched toward him.

The straw underfoot rustled as he rose quietly, wiped the sleep from his eyes, then crossed to the loft end. He slipped the bolt and pushed the doors open far enough to see across to the Right Bank.

The killing may have ended but one of the bodies he'd seen on Sunday was still hanging from a window there.

Hearing Anne Marie stirring, he pulled the doors closed and slid the bolt across. He turned in time to see her disappear behind one of the farther haystacks to make herself ready for the day.

She reappeared a short while later still in the same tan kirtle but with freshly braided hair. Greeting him with a quickly fading smile, she folded herself down by the haystack to sit in silence, her expression withdrawn.

This time, Joliette was the one to bring their breakfast pottage. She bustled in, slid the tray onto the stool serving as their table, then disappeared back through the door inside the staircase.

By the time they finished the bland pottage, dawn was turning into day. Joliette returned a short while later to collect the tray. She had scarcely departed when Peter, sitting against the haystack, heard a distant church bell begin to ring.

It was followed by another ... and another. Then he heard screams and musket fire.

His breathing quickened. The killing was starting again!

He looked over at Anne Marie. Her hand was covering her mouth, and her eyes were wide with fright.

Peter was chewing the end of a straw stem when Monsieur Tricost came hurrying around the haystack in mid-morning.

"It has started again," he said, wringing his thick hands. "A hawthorn was found blooming out of season in the Cemetery of the Innocents. When the priests rang the church bells to proclaim the miracle, others took it as a call to slay more Huguenots. This time, the King is making no effort to halt it. You must stay here and remain quiet."

Peter glanced over at Anne Marie. She was sitting by the loft wall, her expression blank as she fingered the ruby ring hanging from a ribbon around her neck. He tossed the straw stem away and turned to Monsieur Tricost.

"For how much longer?"

"I do not know. But the gates cannot remain shut indefinitely." Monsieur Tricost pressed his lips together. Then, "Even after the gates open, there will be guards stationed. It may still be unsafe to depart too soon."

"Then we'll go by boat. We can leave tonight."

Monsieur Tricost shook his head.

"All boats have been chained by order of the King."

"Given the right tools and someone with enough strength, surely chains can be broken."

Monsieur Tricost's dipping brow said he was considering the idea. His brow smoothed.

"I will speak with Demont."

The moon was a glowing white plate in a black, star-speckled sky when Peter helped Anne Marie onto the ladder to begin her descent from loft to back courtyard and a waiting Demont. He remained with Monsieur Tricost by the loft door and watched until she was safely down. He then dropped their bags to Demont and started down himself. Demont was again wearing the white marks of the militia on hat and sleeve. His own attire bore similar markings.

"They may provide protection should you be seen," Monsieur Tricost had said when he'd attached them a few minutes earlier.

Peter stepped from ladder rung onto hard ground. Monsieur Tricost pulled the ladder up and disappeared behind the closing loft doors.

"I have found a boat," Demont whispered as they picked up their bags. "It will be easy to free."

255

Carrying a sack of food for their journey, Demont hurried them along the courtyard, through the gate, and onto the narrow quay. The Seine flowed past before them, moonbeams shimmering on its dark surface and cool night breezes carrying its odors.

Leaving Anne Marie and the bags in the shadows, he followed Demont across the narrow quay. There, on either side of the river steps, floated a small handful of boats.

"That is the one," Demont murmured, pointing to a boat beyond the cluster on the left. "The others are chained to the steps; it is merely tied to its neighbor."

Peter looked across at the Right Bank. The bright moonlight made them easily visible to anyone who might be watching from the dwellings there.

He glanced up at the moon. A bank of clouds was drifting toward it.

"When the clouds reach the moon...." he said softly.

He stood with Demont, muscles tense, watching the slow progress of the cloud bank.

The thin cloud edge finally drifted across the moon, turning it into a fuzzy ball of light. Five heart beats later, the ball of light was gone, swallowed by heavy cloud. The world was plunged into darkness.

Demont started down the rough steps to the boats. Peter hurriedly fetched Anne Marie and the bags.

The cloud bank was still cloaking the world in ebony as they made their cautious way down the river steps. One misstep could see them both plunging into the Seine.

They reached the lapping water. Demont was a large dark figure sitting in a boat on the left.

"That one," he whispered, holding up the chain to a boat just beyond the one he occupied.

Another moment and Demont was helping them step clumsily from one rocking boat into the other.

Once there, Anne Marie moved to the bow. Peter bent onto a smooth wooden seat in the middle, their bags and the food sack at his feet, and wrapped his gloved hands around the hard oar handles. He glanced up at the black sky.

The cloud bank had nearly cleared the moon. Very soon they again would be visible.

Candlelight in windows of at least two different dwellings said that not all citizens of Paris were sleeping. Despite his wearing the marks of a militia-man, were someone to see them, they still might be stopped.

Demont tossed the clinking chain into their boat then shoved the craft toward the current.

Peter began rowing toward the high, dark shape that was Pont Notre Dame.

Even as the current caught the boat, the moon slipped free of cloud. Its light reflected off the river and touched the roofs of the houses lining the bridge.

He glanced back at the river steps. Demont was gone.

They were nearly to the bridge.

Candlelight appeared in one of the windows above it.

Praying fervently that they would go unnoticed, he rowed toward the sable opening between two of the bridge's large supporting arches.

They passed into blackness, the sound of oars slicing water echoing off the arching walls, then out again into moonlight.

They were clear of Pont Notre Dame and coming up on Pont au Change.

For the second time they entered an arch, once again trading moonlight for blackness then returning to moonlight as they cleared the archway.

He looked ahead.

Stretching before him on the right was the long quay holding numerous chained boats, rows of dwellings with a candlelit window here and there, and the Louvre with a king who had not stopped the killings.

To his left was the Conciergerie complex and the west end of the Island of the City.

Both bridges were now behind them, along with some of the island's stench. But not the danger. At any moment they might be seen. And any of the boats, now chained to the quay, could be used to give chase.

He glanced up at the moon, praying for a cloud. There was none. He could only row as quickly and quietly as possible.

257

As he passed the Conciergerie complex, his thoughts briefly turned to the Bossuets and Derbord family. Had they found shelter there? Or had they met the same end as the Huguenot nobles lodging at the Louvre?

He looked at Anne Marie, sitting in the bow, her bent face in the shadow. No doubt, she had the same question.

They reached the end of the island; the divided Seine became one again. It stretched before them, ripples shimmering in the moon's light, flowing slowly toward a curve.

Once they were past the Louvre, just ahead on the right, they'd be outside the city walls and nearly to the curve. Hopefully, after they rounded the bend, they should be safe.

For some time now, as he rowed, he'd noticed pale objects floating here and there in the river. As the curve drew nearer, the number of floating objects gradually increased.

Were they logs? With the moonlight glinting off the river's dark surface, it was hard to tell.

He continued rowing toward the curve.

Suddenly, a pale log bobbed up beside the bow and bounced off his oar. It rolled over. A man's bearded face and bare chest appeared.

He heard Anne Marie gasp.

These weren't logs. They were naked bodies!

His stomach knotted. He had to get them away.

He began to row frantically past the bodies all around them.

They rounded the first bend.

Here were still more dead: men, women and even small children. A few had washed up on the curve, one with the head missing. Others were lying on the sandy edges of small islands in the river.

His oar grazed a woman's face, becoming entangled in her long gray hair.

Anne Marie gave a strangled cry as he pulled the oar free. The woman's body brushed the hull and bobbed away.

He sent the boat racing down the river, desperate to escape the bodies.

Some distance ahead, a long hill crowned with buildings stood black against the starry sky. Between it and them, the Seine bent again, almost doubling back on itself, flowing around the hill.

They were nearing the sharp bend.

Light from the moon revealed countless naked bodies littering the inside curve's sandy shore. Many more jostled each other at the water's edge.

He swung wide, sweeping around the bodies, putting the sharp turn and its horrors behind them.

They were approaching a massive stone bridge stretching across the Seine. With five more oar strokes, they passed under it then out once more into moonlight.

Ahead of them the Seine curved again, wrapping itself around the base of the hill, dark pewter in the moonglow and, at last, empty of bodies.

Drawing a shaky breath, he lifted the oars and let the current carry them around the hill.

He glanced at Anne Marie, sitting mute in the bow, then ripped off the militia markings and threw them in the Seine. They may have escaped Paris and its foul odors; they would never escape the memories.

He slid the oars into the water and began rowing again. He could do little else.

He'd lost track of the number of curves they'd taken in this winding river when, behind them, the horizon began to slip on its dawn dress. Two more curves and the new risen sun was lighting the blue-brown river ahead.

The black, indistinct trees previously seen lining the riverbanks were now hazel, sweet chestnut, ash, oak, and field maple in their various shades of green while the breaks in the forest became fields stretching back to a village or monastery.

He glanced at Anne Marie. For the last several hours she'd been curled up asleep in the bow. Now she was beginning to waken. When she was fully awake and sitting, she undid her copper braids, pulled comb from bag and began to do her hair.

His rowing slackened. He watched, entranced, as she repeatedly drew the comb slowly down through the bright tresses draping her slender shoulders. His loins began to heat. If only he could pull her close and run his fingers through those wavy strands.

But for Catherine….

He must maintain control.

Tearing his gaze from Anne Marie, he forced himself to focus on the river stretching before them. Tightening his grip on the oar handles, he resumed rowing.

The sun was now well above the horizon. A short distance ahead a cormorant dove under the water. The black bird surfaced moments later, a flopping fish in its yellow beak. It shouldn't be long before they began encountering river traffic coming up the Seine.

Once Anne Marie had finished binding up her hair, he swung the oars into the boat. Leaving the current to carry them, he reached for the bag of food Monsieur Tricost had given them. He pulled out a bread loaf and tore off a piece.

"Here," he said, handing it to her.

Her eyes flooded with tears as she took it. When she spoke, her voice was little more than a strangled whisper.

"I saw Madame Bossuet in the river."

He was silent for a moment, searching for the right words. They escaped him.

"I'm sorry."

In all this time she'd never once mentioned Claude. Had she truly cared for him and grief was now silencing her?

The thought troubled him.

After they'd eaten and shared a mug of ale, he began rowing again. Over the morning they met several small cog boats loaded with goods bound for Paris. He didn't want to consider what those aboard would find when they docked.

They passed another cog boat in the early afternoon. By that time, with muscles aching and eyes burning, he knew he must soon rest. Shortly afterward, the Seine took them through a stretch of low wooded hills where the forest reached down to the river's edge.

There, just ahead, the branches of one large chestnut tree draped the water like a deep green cape.

He headed for the bank and rowed the boat in behind the drooping branches. Even someone purposely looking would have difficulty seeing them through its thick foliage.

After securing the boat to a convenient branch, he stepped up onto the bank and handed Anne Marie up. Together they climbed past the chestnut's massive trunk to more level ground where a dense layer of old leaves rustled quietly beneath their feet. He stood gazing with tired pleasure at the forest stretching out around them: tall, spreading old trees, slender young ones, bushes of all sizes, and grassy sunlit patches. Here and there bright scraps of sunlight slanted down through leafy branches to dot the ground about them.

A thrush, startled by their presence, took flight with a whir of wings from a nearby bush.

For a moment he remained standing, inhaling deeply, savoring the welcome scents of sunlight on dusty leaves and rich brown earth. Another moment and he was stretching out on the thick layer of leaf litter behind a field maple, head on bent arm and sword at hand.

Anne Marie settled down nearby.

He smiled wearily. They'd soon be home. He closed his eyes and let sleep take him.

Anne Marie sat with her back against the maple's light brown trunk watching Peter as he slept. The love she'd previously had for him was nothing compared to what she felt for him now. If not for him, she'd be floating in the Seine with the Bossuets and Derbords. As much as she grieved for them, her thoughts always returned to Peter.

He'd risked his very life to save her. That he'd done it out of his sense of duty changed nothing, neither in her love for him or in the crushing weight of guilt she carried. Whenever the unbidden images of the dead bodies rose, every dead body was his dead body. Had he been killed, his blood would have been on her head, for it was her shameful, impetuous actions that had brought him here.

Peter opened his eyes to find the woods around him in cool shadow and the sun well down the western sky. He looked over at Anne Marie.

She was gone!

Heart pounding, he scrambled up, his gaze darting here, darting there, searching for her. Something rustled in the tall bushes beyond a nearby clearing. Instinctively, he reached for his sword.

Anne Marie stepped around the bushes. His legs wobbled with relief even as his hand tightened on the sword hilt. She wasn't alone.

A young dark-haired couple wearing taut expressions and well-cut but soiled garments were with her. As she came toward him, the couple hung back, cautious uncertainty marking their faces.

"Peter, they're killing Huguenots around Rouen also," Anne Marie said, her eyes tearing. "Jean-Luc said it started this morning. He and Simonne barely escaped. They've been hiding in the woods since."

"You know these people?"

She nodded.

"This is Jean-Luc Guyot and his wife, Simonne. He is a dyer. They are…." her tongue stumbled, "were friends of the Bossuets."

Anne Marie had not spoken this much since he took her from the Derbord house.

He loosened his grip on his sword.

"I've told them we're going to England," she said. Then, hesitantly, "They want to come with us … provided you approve. The boat is large enough."

"To England?"

"They're willing to go anywhere to escape France."

"If they wish."

For the first time in days, her face lit.

She turned back to the Guyots and began talking in French.

After a moment he interrupted the conversation.

"How far is Rouen?"

Anne Marie had a brief exchange with Jean-Luc. Then,

"It is only a mile or so. But it could be dangerous to try passing now. We might be seen."

"Then we'll wait till nightfall."

The now waning moon was high in the black sky when Peter maneuvered the boat from its hiding place and began rowing out into the current. Anne Marie was again sitting in the bow; Jean-Luc and Simonne were in the stern. Not long after, the roofs and steeples of Rouen appeared off to the right, a jagged black line drawn across the slightly lighter black sky. While the moon's rays picked them out, they also showed him the way safely through the gap in the broken bridge and past the various vessels anchored in the Seine.

Very quickly Rouen was behind them. His tension eased, and he handed the oars to Jean-Luc. After the river made another turn, they stopped for a few hours of sleep. He then took the oars again. By the time dawn colored the sky behind them in pinks and gold, they had exchanged the leafy green forests for marshland, sand hills, and willow trees.

He began to see white herons wading along the river's reedy edges and numerous brown grebe diving for their breakfast. The breeze brushing his jaw now carried a salty ocean scent.

The sun was fully up and the tide was running high when they entered the estuary with its rim of low rolling hills. They passed the town of Honfleur off to the left, its silted harbor now only usable for small craft. Well ahead on the right, a limestone plateau rising behind it, Peter could see the walled town and harbor of Le Havre.

It didn't seem possible that, trailing Anne Marie, he'd arrived at this port scarcely over a fortnight ago.

Struggling against the incoming tide, he rowed toward Le Havre where estuary and English Channel met.

Even from this distance he could see at least two galleons and a carrack anchored there as well as numerous smaller craft coming and going about the estuary. A fifth ship, this time a caravel, was coming in their direction. Helped by the strong incoming tide and the gusting coastal winds, it soon sailed briskly past them up the Seine.

Arriving at Le Havre, he grounded the boat near other small craft on the sandy shore outside the town wall. Jean-Luc and Simonne entered the town to buy victuals for them with some of Peter's last coins while Anne Marie remained with the boat. He walked about the shoreline and dock area studying the vessels riding at anchor. Of all those he saw, none bore an English name.

When the Guyots returned with bread and ale, Jean-Luc also brought welcome news. According to the tavern owner, a Dutch merchantman with a cargo of Bordeaux wines was sailing for London once the tide turned. Having earlier seen only one Dutch ship, Peter knew where to begin his search for the vessel's captain.

They broke their fast on the sandy shore then he set off with Anne Marie, leaving Simonne with their belongings and Jean-Luc to sell the boat if possible.

Before the sun was halfway up the morning sky, he was standing with Anne Marie on the Dutch vessel's narrow deck talking with its grizzle-haired captain. Using her ruby ring as pledge for later payment, Peter gained passage for the four of them.

By the time the sun reached its zenith, Jean-Luc had sold the boat for two coins and they were settled aboard the square-rigged merchant ship. Soon the tide began to turn, flowing toward the English Channel.

Anne Marie was standing at the starboard rail when the captain's sharp order to hoist sail sent sailors scrambling up the rigging. Sails began to drop and billow in the wind. The little merchantman moved out into the ocean currents and began to pick up speed.

She looked back at the quickly receding tile roofs and stone towers of Le Havre. Her vision blurred. Soon they would reach England, and Peter would be wedding Catherine Cox.

Given what he'd risked for her, she had forfeited all right to voice objection to the match, even in her heart. Owing him her very life, she had the responsibility to do everything she could, sacrifice everything she must, to see that he had what he most desired. And that was Catherine Cox. She not only could no longer object, but she must actively support him in his decision. Only in this way could she repay the debt she owed him and, perhaps, ease her burden of guilt.

She glanced up to find Peter approaching along the narrow deck. She hurriedly blotted her tears and turned a brave face to him when he stopped at her elbow.

Peter, looking down at her, saw the tears in her eyes just as he'd seen her backward glance at Le Havre. Her wan look could only mean she was grieving. Certainly for the Bossuets, but was she also grieving for Claude? If so, she must have cared for him more than he'd realized.

It was time he said something.

"I'm sorry about Claude."

Anne Marie dropped her gaze.

"He was where he wanted to be." She turned away from the rail, and from him. "Excuse me. I promised to begin teaching English to Simonne."

He watched her walk away. It was going to be a long voyage.

CHAPTER 24 – SEPTEMBER 1572 – ENGLAND

Peter stood gripping the rail, cool breeze stroking his face, eagerly peering ahead as the Dutch merchantman made its slow way up the Thames under a bright cloudless sky. The oaks, beech, ash and elms lining the banks were still garbed in green, but now and again he spotted a field maple that was donning its yellow autumn dress. They'd already passed the Greenwich docks. Very soon now they'd be dropping anchor in London.

He breathed a prayer of thanks that the seemingly endless voyage was nearly over. Anne Marie had remained despondent during the journey, hardly speaking to him. Instead, she'd mostly spent her time with the Guyots and the handful of other Huguenot refugees who were aboard.

Coupled with his concern for her was his need to confront the Coxes about Cyril and to settle matters with Catherine. Unable to deal with these pressing issues until he was again at Wynnfield, he'd frequently paced the deck as the ship's prow sliced its way through the dark ocean swells.

Now, on this third morning of September and with London so near, his pacing was over. All around them the shimmering blue river was alive with water traffic – cargo-laden lighters, tilt boats ferrying passengers, the gilded barges of noblemen, and, now and again, a merchant ship sailing past toward the Straits of Dover.

Hopefully by this time tomorrow, they'd be on their way to Wynnfield.

Of course, he first must redeem Anne Marie's ruby ring and see his parents. She could bed at Cousin Jonathan's house until they departed. As for the Guyots, they and the other Huguenot refugees planned to seek lodging from the Strangers' Church on Broad Street.

The Thames took a wide turn. St. Katharine's hospital drifted into view ahead on the right. Just beyond it, the Tower of London's white curtain wall and keep were gleaming in the sunlight.

Footsteps sounded on the wooden deck behind him. He turned. Anne Marie was approaching. The Guyots and the handful of other refugees followed her.

His heart lifted as she joined him at the rail.

"We'll soon be home," he said with a smile.

Her answering smile was so fleeting it did nothing to brighten her dejected look.

The refugees crowded against the rail, excitedly pointing ahead at London's massive bridge and its towering wall of half-timber houses stretching across the Thames.

Not long after, the merchantman dropped anchor.

Once ashore, standing on the quayside with Anne Marie and the Huguenot refugees, he sighed with relief. They had arrived. And while London carried odors, they were not nearly as foul as those of Paris.

With traveling bag in hand and feeling like a shepherd with a flock of sheep, he led the way along bustling Billingsgate Street, past the secondhand goods shops on Birchin Lane, across Three Needle Street and up Broad Street to the pale stone church that had once belonged to the Priory of Austin Friars and now, by royal charter, housed the Strangers' Church.

After bidding farewell to the Guyots and other Huguenot refugees at the chapel door, he set out with Anne Marie for the Peterman home on St. Mary Avenue.

The servant who answered Peter's knock informed them that the family were at table. Leaving their bags in the great hall, they crossed to the dining parlor. He paused in the doorway with Anne Marie. Lettice, seated at the table's foot, must have heard them for she looked over. Her faded blue eyes widened in surprise, and her plain face lit with welcome.

"Peter, you've returned … and brought Anne Marie." She motioned to them. "Come, join us. There's still bread and some roasted chicken." She glanced at Dorcas, seated on the far side with Prudence. "Fetch tableware for them."

His growling stomach willingly accepted the invitation. While Dorcas was bringing trenchers and mugs from a nearby cabinet, he settled at the table with Anne Marie. Once the tableware was in place, Lettice turned to Anne Marie.

"Are your chests in the courtyard? I'll have a servant take them up to your chamber."

"They were left in France," she said, not looking up from her trencher. "I've only one bag."

Lettice gave her a puzzled look.

"We departed rather hurriedly," he said. He reached for a piece of bread.

Jonathan's brow dipped with concern. He set his mug down on the white tablecloth.

"Was there a problem?"

At Jonathan's question, Peter saw again a black river filled with naked bodies. He glanced at Anne Marie, holding a chicken wing. Her face had paled. Was she also seeing the same image? He swung his gaze back to Jonathan. His jaw set.

"This is not the time to talk of it," he said, his tone firm. "I'm sure you'll hear soon enough."

In the awkward silence that followed, he poured cider into his mug.

"Well," Lettice said, "Belongings can be replaced. I'm thankful that you've brought Anne Marie back to us."

"No," he snapped. "She's returning to Wynnfield with me." Realizing he'd spoken sharply, he softened his tone. "I would be grateful if she could remain here, at least for tonight. I'll be with my parents."

"Yes," Jonathan said, his look growing sober, "your parents. Before you go, there's something you should know."

Peter tensed.

"Has something happened to my mother?"

"Your mother is well. It's your father. He's been sent to Bedlam."

"To Bedlam? Why? What's happened?"

"It's best you hear it from Roger." Jonathan's expression brightened, a smile touched his lips. "Roger is much changed in these last weeks. He's turned his back on his previous life and is now studying the scriptures with me. Truly God can bring good out of even the worst situation."

Anxious to talk with Roger, Peter quickly finished the meal. Leaving Anne Marie in Jonathan's care, he hurried to Guthran Lane. The bell over the door jingled as he entered the goldsmith shop.

He strode past the shelves of gold boxes and plate to the workshop door where heat and the odors of molten metal and acid greeted him. Roger, in leather apron, was at his workbench adding blue enamel to an elaborate gold vase.

Peter paused in the doorway and spoke his brother's name.

Roger's look of intense concentration broke. He glanced up; his eyes widened momentarily.

"Well, you've returned." He wiped a sleeve across his sweaty brow. "And Anne Marie? Did she return with you?"

"She's at Cousin Jonathan's."

A look of embarrassment colored Roger's face.

"Tell her I'm sorry for my earlier behavior," he said quietly.

His apology caught Peter by surprise. "I'll do that." Then lowering his voice also. "Cousin Jonathan said I should ask you about Father."

Roger's eyes narrowed as he glanced at the apprentices. One was carving a mold, the other scooping ashes from the furnace.

He laid his tool down.

"We can talk elsewhere."

Peter followed him out of the workshop and up to the accounts room. Once inside, Roger shut the door behind them.

"You want to know about Father?" he said, perching on the edge of the accounts table. "While you were chasing off to France, he was in the drunkard's cage on Cornhill." His look tightened. "When he was released, he brought the devil home with him. He claimed Mother wanted to kill him. Later he came at me with a knife." Roger paused, rubbed his upper arm. "I've the scar to prove it." He dropped his hand, his expression grim. "The following day he tried the same with Master Nashe ... claimed he'd stolen our designs. Thankfully Master Nashe wasn't injured. The authorities could see he was demented ... and dangerous, so they locked him up in Bedlam."

Despite Jonathan's earlier warning, Roger's tale left him speechless.

Roger wandered over to the accounts cabinet, shoes whispering across the wood floor. "All these years ... imagining that someday I'd be just like him." He turned to face Peter, and his mouth thinned. "Did you know that our grandmother was demented? Mother told me." An introspective look crept over his face. "The sins of the fathers...."

Peter found his voice at last.

"What of Mother? How has she taken it?"

"With difficulty." Roger settled back on the account table edge. "I'd not realized that she'd always prided herself on being the wife of a prosperous goldsmith. Now to be known as the wife of a lunatic.... She's feeling much shamed." He paused, stared at the floor. He looked up again. "I've promised her that she'll soon be known as the mother of one of the finest goldsmiths in London. Once I've finished my masterpiece and been accepted by the guild, she'll see."

"I'm sorry I wasn't here to help."

Roger bristled.

"I don't need your help, big brother. I told you I can take care of them ... and I will." His indignant expression changed to one of resolve. "I'm not going to end as Father has."

"I should probably visit him before I leave London."

Roger shook his head.

"I wouldn't advise it. Father believes we all want him dead. I accompanied Mother there to arrange for his care shortly after he was committed. When he saw us, he became like a wild animal. We've not gone again. Now I send others to see his needs are provided for." He straightened off the edge of the accounts table. "I must get back to the shop. I've a masterpiece to finish and apprentices left on their own can fall into mischief."

Peter dropped his travelling bag in the bedchamber he used when in London, then went in search of his mother. He found her in the back garden picking herbs. At sight of him, her lined face brightened momentarily. In the short time he'd been away, she seemed to have aged considerably.

"Roger told me about Father," he said gently. "If you'd like to come to Wynnfield for a time...."

She shook her head.

"Roger needs me here to keep the accounts," she said in her harsh whisper. "And Maud must be better taught how to manage a household."

"I thought to go to Bedlam to see Father-"

"No!" She gripped his arm. "You mustn't. He's not your father anymore. He's become a devil."

After seeing his mother, Peter set off with coins borrowed from Roger to redeem Anne Marie's ring and pay the stable owner for boarding his horse in his absence. Business finished, he returned to Guthran Lane just before the evening meal.

As he followed the two apprentices into the dining parlor, he glanced at his father's place at the table head, expecting it to be empty. Instead, Roger was seated there. He himself was given a seat across from Maud. To his surprise, before they helped themselves to the stewed carp, artichokes, and turnips, his brother voiced a prayer for the food. Peter also discovered the meal conversation had changed. Rather than the previous frivolous exchanges between Roger and Maud, the meal was eaten mostly in silence. What conversation there was had a more serious tone.

He was thankful that no one questioned him about his trip to France.

At meal's end, the apprentices disappeared, and Roger departed for the Peterman home to study the scriptures with Jonathan.

Once the sound of his feet on the stairs had faded, Maud turned to Peter, a pout on her face.

"Roger's become quite boring. He burned his astrology book in the fireplace, disposed of our card games, and scolds me if I talk about gowns. Now, rather than spending his holidays with his friends, he goes to hear preaching. I don't know what's happened to him."

Despite Jonathan's claim that Roger had changed, he'd been skeptical. Now listening to Maud, his doubts faded.

"Clearly something good."

"He's told me, if he's ever to find me a husband, I'd better change my ways or no sensible man will have me. He's also complained to Mother that I don't know how to manage a household properly." Then, "At least he's promised that I'll not have to marry someone I don't like."

Early the following morning Peter bade his mother farewell, collected his horse, and rode to St. Mary's Avenue for Anne Marie. With their two bags dangling beside his knees and Anne Marie behind him, arms hugging his waist, he set out for Wynnfield.

Twilight was fading when they rode through Hensey and turned up the dark forest track to the manor house. When they rounded the red-berried hawthorn bushes, the manor dogs bounded out of the gatehouse with a noisy welcome. Leaving his horse at the stable and carrying a traveling bag in each hand, he started across the base-court with Anne Marie. While most of the windows were dark, he saw candlelight in the great hall windows.

Peter looked at the house with a detachment he'd never before felt as he thought of the plundered Huguenot homes. It was folly to base a life on fields and houses. They could so easily be lost. They could also be replaced. But not lives … especially not souls. Father had lost his soul. But not Uncle Richard. His own soul would only be safe if he let it rest with God.

They entered the house and stepped past the screen into the great hall where surprised servants, clearing evening meal remains from trestle tables, greeted them. One dashed off to fetch the house steward. Another accompanied them to the winter parlor and lit candles there.

The candlelight revealed Anne Marie's lute sitting in the corner. Peter saw tears gather in her eyes at the sight of it. Just then the house steward arrived.

"I left my horse at the stable," Peter said. "Have our chambers prepared and bring food. Anything will do."

The house steward left. Peter followed him back into the great hall.

"Send someone to Cox Hall now," he said quietly. "Ask Master Cox if I may call on him in the morning."

The house steward nodded and left. Peter rejoined Anne Marie in the winter parlor. She wandered over to gaze out the window into the dark pleasance.

He searched for something that might stir her to conversation.

"No doubt the pleasance has grown new weeds in our absence," he said. "Perhaps in the morning you could deal with them. I'm sure the cows would like the extra fodder."

She gave him a fleeting smile.

"I'll do that."

Servants arriving with cabbage pottage and bread ended their brief exchange.

Night had fully arrived by the time they finished their silent meal. Lighted candle in hand, he accompanied Anne Marie and her candle across the blue parlor and up the stairs to their bedchambers.

He paused outside her open chamber door, searching for a final comment. Before he could think of one, she bade him good night, stepped through the doorway, and shut the door.

Anne Marie pressed her ear to the door, listening to Peter's fading footsteps. She heard his chamber door shut. Although he was just across the passage room, in reality he had stepped completely out of her life.

Blinking tears away, she set her lighted candle on the mantel then picked up her bag, brought up earlier by a servant. She crossed to the bed and dumped out its contents.

When she began hanging her few garments on hooks in the wardrobe, she found her old russet kirtle already there. She'd forgotten that, deciding it unsuitable for London, she'd left it here. It would save her having to wear one of her two remaining nicer gowns when weeding the pleasance in the morning.

After dealing with her garments and toiletries, she removed the ruby ring hanging from the ribbon around her neck. It lay in her hand, the red gem a symbol of love. Peter had returned it to her before they'd left London. If only....

She lifted her chin. She must put all such thoughts away.

She added the ring to her purse of coins, collected from the Bossuets' business partner the previous afternoon, and stuck them under the feather mattress. Hopefully, she could soon find a more secure place for the coins. She'd need them to make a life for herself in Hensey and to assist Gwen and Will with their business.

Once Peter and Catherine were wed, she had no intention of accepting help from them. Not that Catherine was likely to offer. But given his sense of responsibility, Peter well might.

Perhaps she'd return to London someday. For now, Peter wanted her here, so here she'd stay.

Dawn had arrived, and Anne Marie was preparing herself for the day when a maidservant entered with bread, cheese, and cider. By the time she'd broken her fast, donned her russet kirtle, and done up her hair, the sun was beginning to brighten the base-court.

The dew was still on the roses when she went out to the pleasance with gloves and a digging tool to start weeding the asters, pinks, and cosmos.

She had finished one plot and had moved to the next when Peter, wearing his Sunday garb, came striding up the path.

She stopped her work and, forcing a smile, looked up at him.

"I've a matter to see to," he said. "I shouldn't be gone long. We can talk more when I return."

He turned and strode off.

Fighting tears, she watched him disappear through the gate. Even though he hadn't told her, she knew he was going to the Coxes to offer for Catherine.

Once through the forest and across the mown meadow, Peter galloped up the slope to Cox Hall. He dismounted beside a tree, tied his horse to a low branch, and strode across the base-court to the red brick manor house. A house servant, answering his knock, informed him that the Coxes were waiting for him in the parlor.

When he stepped from the screen into the great hall, he met Catherine, garbed in her yellow satin gown and an embroidered cap covering her blond head.

"Where have you been these last weeks?" she said, sweeping up. "Off to London on family matters according to your cousin. It's time you returned. My father is growing impatient for your answer."

"Then I mustn't delay."

Before she could say more, he started along the great hall. With Catherine at his side, he put the great hall behind him, passed the closed chapel door, and stepped through into the large paneled parlor. His gaze swept the richly furnished room with its oak cabinets, red padded benches, and colorful arras cloth to settle on Eustace Cox and his black gowned wife seated beside the fireplace.

Catherine trailed him as he approached her parents. Eustace Cox came to his feet and greeted him coolly. Mistress Cox remained seated, her expression impassive.

"If you've finally come to offer for Catherine," Eustace Cox said, "You've taken your time."

"My apologies for that. As to a match between Catherine and myself, there will be none. Not now, not ever."

Stunned silence filled the room. Catherine broke it.

"Don't tell me," she said, her tone indignant. "You've been off courting some London maid. Well, she's welcome to you … and the common way you dress."

He turned to her.

"Actually, I've just returned from Paris."

Her blue eyes widened.

"Paris? Whatever were you doing there?"

"While I was there, Catholics slaughtered hundreds of Huguenots."

Eustace Cox's face darkened.

"Is that why you're rejecting this match? Because you've decided Catholics are murderers?"

Peter shook his head.

"Catholics saved our lives."

"Our?" Catherine's blond brow raised. "Who was with you?"

"Anne Marie." His mouth softened, thinking of her. "She's currently pulling weeds in the pleasance."

Catherine's lip curled.

"You'd never find me doing a servant's work."

"I know." He turned back to Eustace Cox and his wife, "Before the slaughter, I met a young Catholic priest. He looked exactly like Cyril … even to the ear."

Mistress Cox's color drained. She threw a frightened look at her husband. Eustace Cox turned to him.

"What do you plan to do?" he asked, voice unsteady.

So, they did know that Cyril was alive.

"Do?" Peter said. "What's there to do? It's common knowledge that Cyril is dead." Then, "Someone recently told me that people shouldn't be killed merely because they hold different religious views. I've come to agree with her ... even when it applies to Catholics."

Some of their color returned.

"Of course," he said, "should they be caught actively trying to overthrow the Queen...." He let his comment hang in the air for a moment. "One final matter. When Bro. Lawrence retires, I'm giving the living to Will Weaver's brother." Then, with a nod to each, "Good day, Master Cox, Mistress Cox, Catherine."

Peter turned on his heel and strode out of the parlor, through the hall, and back out of the house to his waiting horse.

Galloping back to Wynnfield, he felt so light and burden free he could have floated the whole way. Now that he had ended all responsibility to Catherine, he no longer had to remain silent.

When he arrived at the manor, he dismounted, handed his horse to a stable hand, then headed for the pleasance.

He stepped through the gate and looked around, searching for Anne Marie. She was there, weeding a patch of thyme. He strode toward her, eager to open his heart to her and, at the same time, apprehensive as to how she might respond.

He stopped beside her, glanced down at the pile of weeds.

"More fodder for the cows, I see."

She came slowly to her feet to gaze up at him with a somber look.

"Did your business go well?"

"Yes, quite well. I had something to discuss with the Coxes."

Before he could continue, Anne Marie lifted her chin. Words began pouring out.

"I'm sure Catherine was so glad to have you back. Now that you and she will soon be wed, I want to assure you that I'll assist you both in every way I can. Of course, there's the marriage banquet to prepare. And, before that, I'll see that the manor house is thoroughly cleaned and made ready for a new mistress. Then after the wedding, I can move to Hensey. I'm sure Gwen would be happy to have me there. And Catherine-"

Peter could think of only one way to stop the flood. He leaned down and did what he'd long been aching to do. He covered her mouth with his.

The kiss, catching her in mid-sentence, was clumsy and brief. But it had the desired effect. When he raised his head, she gazed at him in wide-eyed silence, her expression dumbfounded, her complexion rosy.

"Hush, now," he said, his voice all at once thick, "and let me talk. I went to Cox Hall to tell Catherine … and her parents … that I'm not having her to wife."

Confusion replaced her dumbfounded look.

"You mean you aren't marrying Catherine Cox?"

"That's exactly what I mean. I want to wed you … if you'll have me."

"You want to wed me?" This time she was the one with the thick voice.

"Yes … if you'll have me."

Her eyes teared and she began shaking her head.

"I don't deserve you." Now she was crying, her words coming in broken sentences. "I believed Roger … didn't ask you … just believed that you were horrible. I was so sure I was right. But I was wrong. I should have asked you. Instead, I ran away to Rouen. And when you followed me … I lied about marrying Claude. I was angry … and jealous of Catherine Cox. Then I nearly got you killed in Paris. If you had been, it would have been my fault. Everything was my fault."

Of all the things she said, one thing stopped his breath.

"You weren't going to wed Claude?"

She shook her head.

"Madame Bossuet wished it. But I didn't want him. I wanted you. I planned to run away again after you left."

His every fiber singing, he pulled her into his arms. This time when his mouth found hers, the kiss was long and satisfying. When he finally straightened, he kept her wrapped close in his arms.

"I don't deserve you either," he said. "I was so focused on acquiring Cox manor … as if a few acres of land were all that mattered. I didn't even pause to consider the consequences either for my life or my soul. When I went to London to talk with my parents…. I should have told you what they said.

277

Aunt Emma was right. Uncle Richard meant for your mother to have Wynn-field ... not me."

Anne Marie moved back in his arms to look up at him. Though her eyes were wet, she was glowing.

"I'd already told you that you could have Wynnfield."

"I know. But I still couldn't bring myself to tell you the truth. If I had, you might not have left for France. That night when the killing started.... Everything suddenly became clear. These last days ... there was so much I wanted to say to you. But I couldn't ... not until I could come to you free of any commitment to Catherine." He paused and his shoulders lifted, reveling in that freedom. "I am now."

He released her, stepped back and caught her hands in his. Even before he voiced the question again, he read the answer in her face. He still wanted to ask and savor the ecstasy of hearing her reply.

"So, will you have me?"

"Oh, yes." She slipped free to throw her arms around his neck. "And I promise to always listen to you and to never run away again and to do what-ever you want for my whole life."

"The 'yes' is enough," he said with a smile. "Bro. Lawrence can start calling our banns this next Sunday. I heard him playing the organ when I rode back through Hensey. I'll go now and inform him. You'll have just over three weeks to get a wedding gown stitched. If that's too short a time, I'll take you dressed as you are. I'm not waiting longer."

After one final kiss, he left her to return to her weeding. He headed for the pleasance gate. He'd stepped through and was starting to pull it shut be-hind him when he heard singing. He halted. She was singing a Huguenot hymn. His vision blurred.

The maid who'd so unexpectedly stepped into his life five months ago, who'd challenged his thinking and helped open his eyes and his heart to life's genuine treasures, that maid had returned to him. Soon she would be his wife.

He closed the gate and headed for the stable to collect his mount. If he hurried, he might convince Bro. Lawrence to start calling the banns today.

Three and a half weeks later, clothed in a beautiful light blue gown stitched by the village's best seamstress, loosened hair a copper cloak draping her shoulders, Anne Marie stood with Peter on the porch of St. James the Less to be joined in wedlock by Bro. Lawrence. The whole village gathered for the ceremony and later tramped to Wynnfield Hall for the banquet to follow.

Anne Marie sat at the head table, her new husband at her side, and gazed at the guests filling the great hall. An indescribable joy welled up within her. From George Terrell and his wife, Gwen and her family, Emma Harvey and Bro. Lawrence, down to the lowest Hensey resident, they were all here.

She was no longer alone, not belonging anywhere or to anyone. She had a place for herself, a man with whom to share her life and, as Peter said, a job to do for God.

Together they would be good stewards of the manor and its people that God had given into their care.

The End

ADDITIONAL INFORMATION

The book you're currently holding, THIS TANGLED SKEIN – The Elizabethan Dilemma – is the final one in "The Reformation – A Family Divided" trilogy and contains spoilers for the first two books.

The first book in the trilogy – THE RUBY RING, Battle for an English Bible – won a National Indie Excellence Finalist Award. The second book – A TALE OF SOULS, The Church in Turmoil – continues the story, focusing on the first book's main characters and their children. This final book focuses on the grandchildren. All three novels can be found, both in paper and digital format, on Amazon.

Please leave a review with your honest opinion of THIS TANGLED SKEIN and help me catch the attention of prospective readers. Thank you.

Besides my trilogy, I also have a stand-alone historical suspense/romance novel set in 1868 – THE LAUGHING PLACE – on Amazon in both print and e-book.

Contact me at my Facebook page www.facebook.com/Author.KarenRees/

The following is a glossary of some unfamiliar words.

Arras cloth: colorful cloths hung on walls to both decorate a room and reduce drafts

Canons Regular: dignitaries attached to a cathedral or a collegiate church

Coif: a cap, often embroidered, covering the hair and keeping it out of a woman's face

Convocation: a gathering of English and Welsh bishops and clerics, under the supervision of the Crown, which set the religious policies (Canon Law) of the Church of England.

Footpads: robbers

Huguenots: French Protestants

Low Countries: Netherlands

Stews: houses of prostitution

Time-pleaser: one who yields to the apparent demands of the time, without principle

Voiding dish: dish where bones and other unwanted food remnants were deposited

The historical characters that appear onstage:

Gaspard de Coligny, Henry of Navarre, Princess Marguerite, Queen Mother Catherine, King Charles IX.

Historical characters that appear offstage:

Queen Elizabeth I, Mary Stuart – Queen of Scots, Thomas Cartwright, John Knox, John Field, Plumber's Hall group, Fitz's congregation, Henry – Duke of Guise, Charles – Cardinal de Bourbon, Henry – Prince of Conde and cousin of Henry of Navarre, English ambassador Sir Francis Walsingham, King Philip II of Spain, Fernando Alvarez de Toledo – Duke of Alva, William of Orange and his younger brother Louis of Nassau.

The cover picture represents the wedding of Huguenot King Henry of Navarre and Catholic Princess Marguerite of Valois at Notre Dame Cathedral on 18 August 1572. The marriage was an attempt to end the religious wars tearing France apart. After the exchange of vows on the Cathedral porch, Marguerite entered Notre Dame to hear Mass while Henry, being Huguenot, remained outside.

The picture is actually that of Marguerite's parents at their wedding. Apparently, no artist felt inspired to paint a picture of Marguerite's wedding. Artists did depict graphic scenes of the St. Bartholomew's Day massacre which began six days later, plunging France into further religious wars.

It takes a lot more than a royal wedding to end a war.

Across the English Channel, Queen Elizabeth kept Catholics and Puritans firmly in check by taking a middle ground regarding religious practices. Her government grew more repressive toward Catholics after the Pope excommunicated her and the St. Bartholomew's Day massacre happened. Her policies, coupled with astute handling of relations with King Philip II of Spain, kept England largely at peace throughout her reign.

Denzil-Horne Family Trees

Note: Jane Horne (protagonist of *The Ruby Ring*) was step-sister to Lucy Horne and half-sister to Nicholas, Richard, and Cecily Denzil. Some names of people not mentioned in *This Tangled Skein* are in gray oblique type.

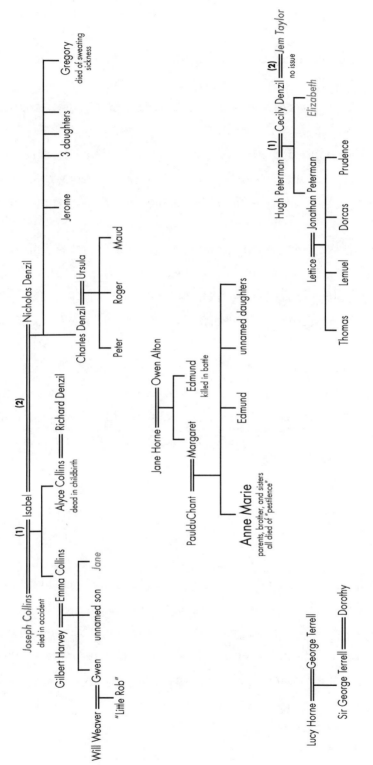

Not related to these families, Eustace Cox was a rejected suitor of Margaret Alton, before she married Paul duChant, as told in *Tale of Souls*.

BOOK CLUB DISCUSSION QUESTIONS

Which character do you most identify with? Why?

Share a favorite quote or scene from the book. Why did it stand out for you?

The culture of the 16th century was quite different from today's culture. Other than sanitation, what differences especially caught your attention? What elements of the story regarding the characters are still true of people today?

Anne Marie's longing to find a place to belong was a major motivator for her. In what ways did her personality and religious beliefs hinder her efforts but also protect her from choosing wrongly? How can we protect ourselves from making wrong choices because of this timeless need to belong?

At the beginning, Peter and Roger were opposites in their sense of responsibility. Over the course of the story, how did each brother change in this area? What caused the changes? How much responsibility toward others, and in what areas of responsibility, do you think a person has? Why do you think this?

How does Peter's attitude regarding his ownership of Wynnfield change over the course of the story? What events cause the change? Have you ever had something happen that changed your attitude toward material possessions?

When Peter proposes to Anne Marie, she confesses to him all the wrongs she'd done. In turn, he confesses his own faults to her. Do you think their confessions will help or hurt their future relationship? Why do you think this? Have you ever confessed something of a serious nature to another person? What effect did your confession have on the relationship? On you?

Made in the USA
Monee, IL
25 October 2023

45178072R10169